Outstanding praise for the urban fantasy novels of
Richelle Mead!

STORM BORN

"My kind of book—great characters, dark worlds, and just the right touch of humor. A great read."
—Patricia Briggs, *New York Times* bestselling author

"Richelle Mead has a way of cutting through the cliches to get to the heart of her story. This is urban fantasy the way it's meant to be: smart, clever, magical, meaningful, with great characters and real heart rather than empty fireworks."
—Carrie Vaughn, author of *Kitty and the Silver Bullet*

SUCCUBUS DREAMS

"Includes plenty of action, surprising mysteries and hot sex."
—*Romantic Times*

SUCCUBUS ON TOP

"Like all great heroines, Georgina Kincaid is an intriguing blend of contradictions; sexy but sweet, an immortal who remembers her humanity, and a girl who knows exactly what she wants in a man and a drink, but who can still lose herself to both. (More than once I found myself thinking, 'I'll have what she's having' . . . and I wasn't talking about the gimlet!) With sharp prose and a powerhouse voice, Richelle Mead took a death grip on my imagination and refused to let go. I, too, fell prey to the enchantments of her succubus, and couldn't stop thinking, wondering, and caring about her until I turned the final page. In short, Georgina Kincaid has been my ruin . . . now no other succubus will do!"
—Vicki Pettersson, author of *The Scent of Shadows*

"Don't take this book to bed—you'll be up all night. Richelle Mead delivers sexy action and tongue-in-cheek hellish humor—if damnation is this fun, sign me up!"
—Lilith Saintcrow, author of *The Devil's Right Hnad*

SUCCUBUS BLUES

"Mead cooks up an appetizing debut that blends romantic suspense with a fresh twist on the paranormal, accented with eroticism."
—*Booklist*

**Please turn the page for more outstanding praise for
Richelle Mead!**

More outstanding praise for *Succubus Blues*!

"An excellent paranormal."
—*Romantic Times*

"One of those books that had me engrossed from the very first page."
—*RomanceJunkies.com*

"*Succubus Blues* is great fun."
—*The Romance Readers Connection*

"An engaging read."
—Jim Butcher, *New York Times* bestselling author

"Deliciously wicked! Dysfunctional, funny, and sexy. I look forward to reading more tempting morsels about this succubus-with-a-heart-of-gold."
—Lilith Saintcrow, author of *Dead Man Rising*

"What an incredible debut novel! *Succubus Blues* is exciting, witty, sexy, intriguing and had me captivated from the first page."
—Cheyenne McCray, author of *Seduced by Magic*

"*Buffy* meets *Sex and the City*. Guilty pleasures don't get much better."
—David Sosnowski, author of *Rapture* and *Vamped*

"Sexy, scintillating and sassy! Richelle Mead is now on my must-buy list."
—Michelle Rowen, author of *Bitten and Smitten*

"Take a beautiful, sassy immortal. Mix in suspense, murder and plenty of hot sex. Pour yourself a great read and enjoy the hell out of this story."
—Mario Acevedo, author of *The Nymphos of Rocky Flats* and *X-Rated Bloodsuckers*

"Writing this good tempts me to believe in angels . . . or deals with the devil. *Succubus Blues* is original, exciting, seductive stuff, filled with characters I'd sell my soul to meet."
—Rachel Caine, author of *Firestorm* and *Glass Houses*

SUCCUBUS HEAT

Books by Richelle Mead

SUCCUBUS BLUES

SUCCUBUS ON TOP

SUCCUBUS DREAMS

SUCCUBUS HEAT

STORM BORN

THORN QUEEN

Published by Kensington Publishing Corporation

SUCCUBUS HEAT

RICHELLE MEAD

KENSINGTON BOOKS
http://www.kensingtonbooks.com

For my sister Deb, who shares my views on red hair, coconut rum, and guys named Jay

Chapter 1

Sleeping with my therapist was a bad idea.

I knew it too, but I couldn't really help it. There were only so many times I could hear "Why don't you explain that" and "Tell me how you feel." So, I finally snapped and decided to *show* the guy how I felt. I've gotta say, for a decent guy who had never cheated on his wife, he wasn't that hard to take advantage of. And by "not hard," I mean "ridiculously easy." His pseudo morals gave me a strong succubus energy fix, and when you consider that what we did was probably the most productive thing that ever took place on his couch, it was almost like I did a good deed.

Still, I knew my boss was going to be pissed, seeing as he was the one who'd ordered me to seek counseling in the first place.

"Do *not* tell Jerome," I warned my friends, tapping my cigarette against the ashtray. "I don't want to deal with that kind of fallout."

My friends and I were sitting at a booth in Cold July, an industrial club down in Seattle's Belltown district. The place was dark and loud, with crisscrossing pipes on the walls and ceiling forming the bulk of the décor. Because it was a private club, it didn't have to adhere to the city's public smoking ban, which was a perk for me. In the last few months, I'd found nicotine was one of the essential things helping me cope. Other things on the essential list: vodka, Nine Inch Nails, a steady supply of moral men, and an all-purpose bitchy attitude.

"Look, Georgina," said my friend Hugh. He was an imp, a type of hellish legal assistant who bought souls for our masters and did assorted middle-management tasks. He had dark-cropped hair and was big without being fat. "I'm no expert in mental health, but I'm going to go out on a limb here and say that probably wasn't a helpful step on the road to healing."

I shrugged and let my eyes scan the crowded room for potential victims. There were some pretty good pickings here. "Well, he wasn't that good. At therapy, I mean. Besides, I don't think I need it anymore."

Silence met me, inasmuch as silence could meet me in a place so noisy. I turned back to my friends. Hugh was making no pretense of hiding his *you're fucking crazy* look. Our vampire friends, Peter and Cody, at least had the decency to avert their eyes. I narrowed mine and put out the cigarette.

"I don't suppose," said Peter at last, "that this is anybody you'd maybe, uh, like to date long term?"

"Yeah," agreed Cody, eyes wide and hopeful. "I bet a therapist would be a great listener. And you wouldn't even have to pay for it."

"My insurance pays for it," I snapped. "And I don't really appreciate your passive-aggressive attitude about my boyfriend."

"It's not that passive," said Hugh. "You could do better, sweetie."

"The guy's corrupt and going to Hell. How is this a problem for you? And you didn't like my last boyfriend either. Maybe you should stop worrying about my love life and go back to figuring out how to get your latest secretary into bed."

In what had to be a weird twist of the universe, none of my friends liked my current boyfriend, a dark magician named Dante. Dante's morals were pretty nonexistent, and he owned stock in bitterness and cynicism. That would make you think he'd fit in perfectly with this group of damned souls, but for whatever reason, he didn't.

"You aren't meant to be with someone bad," said Cody. We were all immortal now but were considered "lesser immortals." That meant we had once been human before selling our souls into Hell's service. Cody was young compared to the rest of us in our little circle. Hugh claimed almost a century. Peter and I had millennia. As such, there was almost a naïveté about Cody, a charming idealism that rivaled the kind I used to have.

It had been shattered when my previous boyfriend, a human named Seth, had left me for a friend of mine. Seth was a good soul, quiet and infinitely kind. He'd made me believe in better things, like that maybe there was hope for a succubus like me. I'd thought I was in love—no, I *had* been in love. Even I could admit that. But as a succubus, I brought a dangerous element to any relationship. When I had sex with a guy (or a girl—it worked either way), I stole their life energy, which was the power that fueled every human soul. It kept me alive and sustained my immortal existence. The purer the guy, the more energy I took. The more energy I took, the more I shortened his life. With Dante, I had almost no effect. He had little energy to give, so our sex life was relatively "safe," and I therefore sought my fixes from meaningless guys on the side.

With Seth . . . well, that had been a different story. Sleeping with him would have had very detrimental effects—so I'd refused to do it. For a while, we'd lived on love alone, our relationship being about a lot more than a physical act. Over time, however, that had taken its toll, as had a number of simple relationship complications. Things had finally blown up when Seth had slept with my friend Maddie. I think he'd done it to encourage me to break up, hoping to spare me future pain. Whatever the initial intent, he and Maddie had actually gone on to establish a fairly serious relationship in the following months.

I hadn't taken that very well.

"There's no pleasing you guys," I growled, beckoning the waiter for another drink. He ignored me, irritating me further. "You don't like good ones. You don't like bad ones. What the fuck does it take?"

A new voice suddenly cut into our circle. "Please tell me

we're discussing your romantic hijinks, Georgie. There's nothing I enjoy more."

There he was, standing beside our table: my boss Jerome, archdemon of Seattle and its greater metropolitan area. I glared. I didn't appreciate the mocking tone—or him calling me Georgie. He sat down beside Hugh, and the waiter I'd been trying to summon dashed over immediately. We ordered a new round of drinks.

Jerome was clearly in a good mood today, which always made our lives easier. He had on a black designer suit, and his hair was styled exactly the same as John Cusack's had been in a recent TV interview I watched. That probably bears mentioning: Jerome's human body of choice was a clone of John Cusack. Succubi can change shape because that's part of what helps us with seduction. Demons can change shape simply because—like angels—they're insanely powerful beings who have been around since the beginning of time. They're "greater immortals." Because of a weird fan obsession that he adamantly denied, Jerome chose to interact in the mortal world looking like the actor. The strange thing was that when we were out like this, humans never seemed to notice the resemblance.

"You haven't been out with us in a while," I pointed out, hoping to change the subject. "I thought you've been busy with demon stuff." Rumor had it that Jerome was sparring with another demon, though none of us knew the details.

He took one of my cigarettes out of the pack without asking. A moment later, the end of the cigarette lit on its own. Show-off.

"Things have actually taken a pleasant turn," he said. He inhaled deeply and then let the smoke swirl around him. "One less thing to deal with. I'd hoped the incessant babbling about your romantic woes was also going away, but I suppose that's too much to hope for. Are you still with that charlatan?"

I threw up my hands. "Why does everyone hate Dante? You guys should be embracing him as a brother."

Jerome considered, dark eyes thoughtful. "He annoys me. You can do better."

"Jesus Christ," I said.

"Maybe she'd see that if she'd stop doing stupid shit like sleeping with her therapist," noted Hugh, in what was apparently supposed to be a helpful tone.

I turned on him, eyes wide. "Did you listen to anything I just said?"

"Plenty," he said.

Meanwhile, Jerome's lazy, pleased expression disappeared. He fixed his gaze on me, eyes burning like flame yet inexplicably making me feel cold all over. He smashed the cigarette out and shot up from his seat. Grabbing my arm, he jerked me up from my own spot and started dragging me from the table.

"Come with me," he hissed.

I stumbled with him out to the hall that led to the restrooms. Once out of the sight of others, he pushed me against a wall and leaned toward me, face filled with fury. It was a sign of his agitation that he was behaving like a human. He could have simply transported both of us to some isolated place.

"You fucked your therapist?" he exclaimed.

I gulped. "I wasn't making much progress."

"Georgie!"

"Why is this a problem? He was a good soul. I thought that was what you wanted me to do!"

"I wanted you to get this fucking chip off your shoulder that you've had ever since that boring mortal dumped you."

I flinched. It was kind of a weird thing. I'd been so depressed after the Seth breakup that Jerome had finally flipped out and told me to go seek help because he was tired of listening to me "bitch and moan." The strangeness of a demon encouraging counseling for one of his employees wasn't lost on me. But honestly, how could he understand? How could he understand what it was like to have your heart smashed? To be ripped from the person you loved most in the world? My whole existence had lost meaning, and eternity had seemed impossible to bear. For weeks, I wouldn't go out or talk much to anybody. I'd isolated myself, lost in my own grief. That was when Jerome had thrown up his hands and demanded I snap out of it.

And I had, kind of. I'd swung the other way. I'd suddenly become angry—so, so angry at the way life had treated me. Some of my misfortunes were my own fault. But Seth? I didn't know. I didn't know what had happened there, and I felt wronged by the world and the lifetimes of hurt it kept giving me. So, I'd started getting back at it. I'd stopped caring. I'd thrown myself into full succubus mode: seeking out the most moral men I could, stealing their life, and breaking their hearts with little remorse. It helped with the pain. Sometimes.

"I'm doing what I'm supposed to!" I yelled. "I'm scoring soul after soul. You have nothing to complain about."

"You have a bitchy attitude and keep picking fights with everyone—and you aren't getting better. I'm tired of it. And I'm tired of you."

I froze, my antagonism turning to pure fear. When a demon said he was tired of you, it often resulted in being recalled to Hell. Or being smote.

"Jerome . . ." I tried to assess my best strategy here. Charm? Contrition?

He stepped away and took a deep, calming breath. It didn't help much. His anger came through loud and clear.

"I'm sending you away. I'm going to outsource you to someone."

"*What?*" My anger returned, pushing my fear away momentarily. Outsourcing was a huge insult to a succubus. "You can't do that."

"I can do whatever I fucking want. You answer to me." A lanky guy turned down the hall, heading toward the restroom. Jerome fixed him with a piercing, terrifying look. The guy yelped and hastily headed back the other way. "There's an archdemon in Vancouver who wants someone to keep an eye on a cult he has an interest in up there."

"Up there . . ." My mouth dropped open. "You mean Vancouver, BC? You're sending me to *Canada*?" Fuck. I really had gone too far. There was also a Vancouver in Washington.

That wouldn't have been so bad. At least I would have stayed domestic.

"He'd wanted a succubus since he only has one and couldn't spare her. They've got their work cut out for them up there, you know. I almost considered sending them Tawny." He made a face at the mention of his recently acquired and very, very inept succubus. "But, well, she's not . . . optimal. I hadn't wanted to give up you either, but now I think it'll be worth missing my useful succubus for a while to get you out of my hair. I need some peace and quiet."

"Look, Jerome," I said, hoping I sounded penitent. "What do you want me to do? Get another therapist? I can do that. I'll get a woman. An ugly one. And I'll try to lay off the attitude and—"

"That's my decision, Georgie. You need something to occupy you, and this'll make Cedric happy. He figures a succubus is the best choice to infiltrate his little devil-worshipping cult."

"Devil wor—what, you mean like, Satanists?"

"Something like that."

I stared. "Canadian Satanists? You're sending me to a group of Canadian Satanists?"

His only answer was a shrug.

"If this were happening to anyone else, it would be hilarious," I said. "But why *are* you doing it? Since when do you help anyone—let alone another demon?" Demons tended to be insanely competitive with each other.

Again, Jerome didn't answer. He took out a cigarette—honestly, if he had his own, why'd he steal mine earlier?—and did the lighting trick again. He seemed a little less tense after taking a deep drag on it.

"Something else is going on," I said warily. "You're using me to use him. What's this really about?"

"Altruism," he said, rolling his eyes.

"Jerome . . ."

"Georgina," he returned, eyes hard. "You have no right to question this, not as much as you've pissed me off lately. Now go pack your things and brush up on the metric system."

Chapter 2

I don't really have anything against Canadians. They're nice. Really nice. But that didn't mean I wanted to go curling with them, and there was always a danger that if Jerome was in the right mood, he might decide to make this temporary assignment a permanent one.

I didn't think he would, though. Underneath all the gruffness, Jerome liked me—inasmuch as a demon could truly like anyone. Admittedly, he'd liked me a little less since Seth had turned my life upside down last fall, but when I wasn't sporting massive attitude, I think I amused Jerome. Amusing things are few in the face of eternity, so hopefully that would be enough to ensure my job security.

I left Belltown and headed over to Queen Anne, another Seattle neighborhood. I both lived and worked in Queen Anne, and if I was about to disappear for a while, my mortal employer should probably know. Unfortunately, going into work meant facing some unpleasant things that I wasn't really in the mood for tonight.

"Georgina! What are you doing here?"

Maddie Sato, the Brutus to my Caesar, came scurrying up to me as I entered Emerald City Books and Café. In Maddie's defense, she hadn't known Seth and I were dating when they'd slept together. So, it wasn't like she'd knowingly stolen him from me. That didn't really change my feelings toward either of them, though.

"I need to see Warren," I said, suspecting I probably reeked of vodka and smoke. "Is he here?"

She shook her head, making her glossy black hair sway. It was worn in a long, sleek style I'd taught her how to do. "He left about an hour ago. Didn't want to stick around for closing."

I glanced at a clock. I'd barely made it in before they locked the doors. I tapped my foot impatiently, wondering if I should call Warren at home. Finally, I asked, "You got a sec to go over some schedule stuff? I'm going to be out for a few days . . . or maybe more."

"Sure," she said, smiling and showing dimples. "You want me to grab Doug too?"

"He's here?"

Both assistant managers closing in one night. It was a stroke of luck. I headed off to my office while she went to fetch her brother Doug. My desk was organized for a change, and I found the clipboard bearing the schedule for the next couple of weeks. I skimmed it, relieved to see we had a full complement of staff for a change. My immortal friends didn't understand why I cared so much about this job. There had been days recently—days when I didn't want to get out of bed because I was so depressed—that I'd wondered the same thing. But the truth was, eternity was an extremely long time, and I'd spent most of my time always occupied with some activity. It was part of my nature; I couldn't be idle. And sometimes—*sometimes*—I could get so caught up in the day-to-day affairs of the human world that I could almost pretend for a heartbeat that I was one of them again.

"I don't think we'll need anyone to cover me," I said when I heard the office door open a few minutes later. "Someone'll just need to take over my—" I looked up.

Maddie had returned, along with Doug, but they weren't alone. Seth was with them.

All the easy confidence I'd shown in the store, all the brashness and bravado I'd shown at the club . . . it all shriveled up into a cold, hard knot as I looked at him. Walls slammed down around me. How could he affect me like this, particularly while wearing a Buck Rogers T-shirt? It had been three months. Why wasn't I over him? Why did I still want to cry or break something whenever I saw him?

"Whoa, Kincaid," said Doug, partially distracting me from my angst. He glanced at my outfit and raised an eyebrow. "We interrupting your social life?"

I wore a knee-length black trench coat over a short red dress. My makeup was done to seductive perfection, whorish dark eyeliner and lipstick to match the dress. Shape-shifting in the car would have been a snap, but I didn't feel like I needed to prove anything here. In fact, I kind of reveled in my tramp look tonight.

"Apparently this is my social life, if I'm pathetic enough to come in on a Saturday night." I forced myself to focus on Doug and Maddie only, trying hard not to look at Seth's soft, coppery brown hair or gentle eyes. Why did he have to be here of all nights? The answer: he was here *every* night. He was an author and did his best work in coffee shops. When we'd broken up, he'd tried to tactfully find another and stay away from me, but Maddie—oblivious to his reasons—had begged him to stay at the bookstore's.

"Where are you going?" asked Maddie. "Is everything okay?"

"Yeah, yeah," I said brusquely. "Long story."

I beckoned Maddie and Doug to the clipboard, explaining again how I was pretty sure the store would be fine without my labor, so long as they could cover the tasks I did as manager. We sketched out a brief list of my responsibilities, like payroll and inventory, and began divvying them up.

Doug tapped the list. "I've done all these before, at one time or another. They're no problem. I'll take the first half." He elbowed his sister. "What about you? You gonna take the rest and pull your share here?"

Maddie pursed her lips. She was immensely talented but suffered from bouts of insecurity, which I'd repeatedly told her was ridiculous. She'd improved a lot over the months—again, thanks to me—but still faltered. "I didn't realize you did so much. I hope I can learn it all."

"Stop playing coy. I'll teach you," said Doug. "You'll be as good as Kincaid in no time."

"Yeah," I said dryly. "We're practically interchangeable anyway." Out of the corner of my eye, I saw Seth shift uncomfortably.

"The whole thing seems kind of sketchy, though," remarked Doug, tilting his head so that his black hair fell away from his face. "You're going to be gone, but you're not sure when or how long? I thought you were the reliable one around here."

"It's . . . family stuff," I told them. "Just gotta be dealt with. Besides, now you can have a chance to be responsible. You should be thanking me, Doug." He stuck his tongue out at me.

"Is Warren going to be okay with it?" asked Maddie, still fretting on my behalf.

"Let me deal with Warren," I assured her.

Doug scoffed at that, but Maddie didn't catch on. Warren, the store's marginally moral owner, had been a longtime sex buddy of mine. He gave me about as much energy as Dante, but he was convenient and suited my mood lately. I'd stopped our tryst while dating Seth but had since returned to old habits. Doug had known about my affair with Warren then and now but was tactful enough to leave me to my own choices, aside from the occasional bit of eye rolling. I suspected Seth knew what was going on too, but I didn't care. Warren wasn't going to give me any grief about taking time off. I was too good at what I did, both at work and in the bedroom.

We shuffled one shift where I was supposed to have closed, and then I tossed the clipboard back on its pile, suddenly needing to get out of there as soon as possible. "Alright. Thanks, team. I'll leave you to your work."

"Off to hit the town?" asked Doug, still amused. "I can join you in about a half-hour. I know a killer party."

I shook my head. "Already hit the town. I'm heading home."

"Loser," he called after me.

Maddie wished me well with my mysterious time off, and then I left them, walking through the store and exchanging greetings with my other co-workers as they scurried around with their closing tasks. I'd nearly made it to the door when I heard someone call my name. I turned and saw Casey hurrying toward me. She was twenty or so and went to the University of Washington. She'd worked here almost the entire time she'd been in college and was one of our best employees. So, I stopped and forced a smile, my eyes straying longingly toward the door.

"Hey, what's up?"

She grinned, dark eyes sparkling. "I wanted to know if you were going to go to my party next weekend," she said. "You never answered the e-mail."

I didn't remember any e-mail, but then, I'd been pretty trigger-happy with the delete key lately. "I didn't get it," I lied. "What's going on?"

"It's my graduation party. This Sunday."

I frowned. "It's April."

"I'm graduating early. I got all my credits finished up, so I don't have to do spring quarter. Pretty cool, huh?"

"Whoa," I said, actually impressed. "That is cool. Math, right?"

"Math and Latvian."

"Why on earth—never mind." Now was not the time to pursue why someone of Filipino heritage was studying Baltic languages. "I wish I could go, but I'm leaving town tomorrow for some family stuff and don't know when I'll be back. I'm really sorry."

Casey's face fell a little, but she told me she understood. And like Maddie, she wished me well and hoped my "family" business would be taken care of easily. That made two of us. She left me and went to finish her closing tasks.

As soon as I cleared the store's door and was outdoors, I stopped and exhaled. Breezy night air washed over me. Being in Seth's presence was smothering. It stirred up too much in me. Even while talking business and numbers with Doug and Maddie, most of my attention had been on Seth—exactly how far away he stood from me, the way he smelled, the way his messy hair stuck up today. Everything else had been background noise compared to him.

Reaching into my purse with shaking hands, I pulled out my cigarettes, desperately needing one for the walk home. I'd smoked for a century or so and stopped ten years ago, something I'd been very proud of, even though I was immune to the effects. Stress had driven me to pick up the habit again. I felt a little bad about subjecting others to secondhand smoke, but honestly, smoking was the least of my problems right now.

"Fuck." I flicked the switch on my lighter and got nothing. Three more flicks produced similar results. Holding the lighter up to my ear, I shook it. Nothing. It was out of fluid. "Fuck," I repeated. I only lived a few blocks away, but somehow, that walk was now going to be agony.

Suddenly, I heard what sounded like a boot scuff around the corner of the building. Frowning, I took a few steps forward, wondering if anyone was there. This area was pretty safe, but Lower Queen Anne still had its share of vagrants. Yet, when I glanced around the corner, there was no one there.

There was, however, a pack of matches lying on the ground.

Kneeling down, I picked the book up and examined them. Mark's Mad Martini Bar. I'd been there a long time ago. It was in Upper Queen Anne, not too far away if you didn't mind trekking up the hill. It wasn't unreasonable that a pack of their matches would find their way here. What was weird was that the matches showed up right when I needed them.

Behind me, I heard the store's door open. "Georgina?"

I rose and turned sharply around. Seth.

"Hey," I said, hoping for blandness. The smothering feeling returned.

Light from inside the store lit up his features in the twilight, and I ate up every line and angle of his face. His eyes looked dark in the dimness, but in full light, they were brown infused with amber. He stuffed his hands into his pockets, and his gaze wouldn't meet mine. It was painfully reminiscent of how he'd been when we first met, too shy to look directly at me.

"I wanted to see if you were okay," he said after several awkward moments.

I turned the matches over in my hand a couple of times and then placed them in my purse's outer pocket. "I'm fine," I said, keeping my voice cool and distant.

"It's just . . ." He relaxed slightly and gave a small, rueful laugh. "When you're vague about your activities and mention 'family,' it usually means immortal business. And immortal business always means trouble."

I started to smile, then immediately squelched it. "Yeah, it does, and believe me, it's a great one this time." Even after everything that had gone down between us, there was such a comfort and familiarity with him that I immediately wanted to launch in and recap the story for him. I could already see us both laughing at the idea of Canadian Satanists. I could perfectly picture the way Seth would shake his head in exasperation. But it wasn't to be. I was too hurt and too proud to even allow him friendship, so I just shrugged and said, "But it'll work out. It always does."

"Yeah . . . but usually not without a lot of hassle. I'm just worried about you, that's all."

"You don't have to be." *Not anymore.* "I'm not in any danger. Mostly just annoyed."

He opened his mouth to speak, and I knew the gesture. He wanted to argue that there was still cause for concern—but times had changed. He swallowed and let the comment go. More silence fell. I knew I should leave, but somehow, I couldn't make myself do it. He apparently couldn't either. "You . . . you look really great tonight," he said at last, still fumbling for conversation.

There was a catch in his voice. He knew my looks tonight had to do with more than just my body and outfit. The energy I'd stolen from sleeping with the therapist wreathed me. Life and its power were irresistible to all creatures, mortal and immortal alike. Immortals could literally see that life glowing around me. To mortals, I simply looked beautiful. Unearthly. Perfect.

For the sake of politeness, I pretended he was complimenting me for normal things. "Thanks. I was out with the others when all this . . . stuff . . . went down. It's kind of put a damper on my partying, though."

He nodded by way of answer and shifted so that he actually made eye contact. I wished he hadn't. My heart melted inside me, and I felt a sob building in my chest. Desperate for something to do, I took out the serendipitous matches and lit the cigarette I'd been holding the whole time. I took a long drag and exhaled. Seth stepped back. He wasn't a fan of smoking. It was like I suddenly had armor.

"Well," I said, feeling bolder, "I should go home and pack. See you around."

I turned and had only taken a step when he called out to me. "Georgina?"

I glanced back. "Yeah?"

"Do you . . . um . . ." He faltered, and again, I was reminded of that long-ago Seth. Bittersweet feelings burned within me. "Do you need someone to feed your cat?"

I didn't know whether to laugh or cry. "No, but thanks. Cody'll do it." I spoke the next words, fully knowing they'd inflict damage. "Or Dante will."

Seth flinched, and somehow, I felt both triumphant and sad at the same time. "No problem," he said haltingly. "Just thought I'd, you know, check."

"Thanks," I said again. We held each other's gazes a few more moments, and then I turned away and walked off into the night.

Chapter 3

I neither packed nor called Dante when I got home. I was exhausted. Talking to Seth had been too depressing. I lived too close to the bookstore, I decided. What had once been convenient now felt oppressive. A few blocks simply wasn't enough distance between Seth and me. I kind of wished Emerald City had another branch somewhere that I could work. In lieu of that, maybe I was the one who needed to find a new residence. My lease here was ending soon, and until now, I'd never considered anything except renewing. Moving was a startling—and weirdly appealing—thought, and I pondered it as I drifted off to sleep that night, my cat Aubrey snuggled against my legs.

The next morning, I had to scramble to pack my things. Jerome hadn't given me any specific time to be in Vancouver, only "soon." I decided not to test the exact terms of that. Packing didn't take long, fortunately. I could shape-shift any clothing I wanted, but I had some favorites I preferred to just take with me. It was another lingering human habit. There were also cosmetics and other toiletries I wanted with me; I liked to do my own hair and makeup if I had the time.

I was pouring my third cup of coffee in the kitchen when I felt the tingle of immortal signatures appear in my living room. Only a higher immortal, like a demon or angel, could directly teleport in, and I immediately recognized these two. Grace and Mei.

They were Jerome's lieutenant demonesses. Heaven ran its

agenda in a haphazard way, but ours was carefully organized. Territory was parceled out to archdemons, who in turn
controlled a network of subordinate demons and lesser immortals like me and my friends: succubi, vampires, and imps.
Jerome handled the big issues in the area, went to meetings
with the demons who were above him, and was in charge of
discipline. Grace and Mei handled the minutiae and paperwork and also kept an eye on the far reaches of Jerome's territory, areas he was too busy for and uninterested in. His full
jurisdiction actually stretched along the coast of western Washington, though his base of operation was the Seattle metropolitan area. That was also where most of his staff was located.
He only kept an occasional eye on the outskirts and left it to
Grace and Mei to keep him apprised of what occurred there.

For whatever reason, the demonesses always wore matching clothing. Today they sported black pantsuits, tailored to
a perfect fit. Grace was blond and Mei black-haired, but their
hairstyles were also similar: bluntly cut at the chin. Both
wore brick-red lipstick.

"Good morning, Georgina," said Grace.

"We're here with last-minute instructions," said Mei.

"Oh, okay." I was relieved. I'd been afraid Jerome had
sent them to find out why I hadn't already crossed the Canadian border. "You guys want some coffee?"

I offered them something every time they were here, and
every time, they refused. So, I was a bit astonished when Grace
asked, "What kind?"

"Um . . . Starbucks. Their house blend."

"No," replied Grace and Mei in unison.

I shrugged and sat down on the couch. Aubrey had been
lying there a minute ago but was nowhere in sight now. She
hated these two. Mostly they creeped me out. "Okay," I
asked. "What's the scoop?"

They remained standing. Mei crossed her arms. "Jerome
wants you to understand the situation with Cedric. The two
of them have had a . . . disagreement over territorial lines."

This perked my interest. "Ah. It's him, then. We'd heard Jerome had something going on with another demon."

"The two of them had been eyeing each other's areas," explained Grace. "In the hopes of expanding their own boundaries into one large Pacific Northwest . . ." She paused thoughtfully.

". . . empire?" I suggested. She shrugged by way of agreement.

"Something like that," said Mei. "But eventually, they put the dispute aside and gave up, each settling for their current territories. That's why Jerome is lending you to Cedric, as a sign of good will."

I was too intrigued to retort about the degradation of Jerome "lending" me to anyone. "Jerome doesn't do things out of good will," I pointed out, recalling his snide remark about altruism last night. "There's more going on."

Grace nodded. "Indeed. Jerome suspects that Cedric actually hasn't given up the struggle and is still plotting against him. Jerome wants you to spy and report back."

Oh, I didn't like that. Not at all.

"He wants me to spy on another demon? An *arch*demon? Do you know what kind of trouble I could get in if Cedric finds out?"

Neither demoness said anything. It was no concern of theirs if I got smote. Considering Jerome's current attitude toward me, it probably wasn't much of a concern for him either, aside from having to send a requisition to Personnel for a new succubus.

"So," continued Mei, "you'll have two agendas. You need to let Jerome know what Cedric's doing. And, you need to infiltrate Cedric's problem cult and keep them in line—although, if you make things a little uncomfortable for Cedric along the way, Jerome won't mind."

"Right. The Canadian Satanists. What on earth are they doing that's such a big deal? Putting 666 on the backs of hockey jerseys?"

My joke had no effect on either demoness. Someday, I

thought, I'd get one of them to crack a smile. "They're attracting attention, enough that Cedric's superiors are embarrassed. They'd prefer this cult conduct its evil in more subtle ways."

"Last I knew, true Satanists aren't actually evil per se," I mused. The rep aside, most Satanists were more into just acknowledging chaos and humanity's wild, base nature. "Most aren't actually out conducting bloody rituals or spray-painting pentagrams on walls."

"Actually," said Mei, "this group *is* spray-painting pentagrams on walls."

"Oh," I said. "That's lame."

"They think they're evil . . ." began Grace.

". . . but they're not," finished Mei. "They need to be reined in."

"Okay, sure. No problem." Influencing wannabe Satanists was a piece of cake compared to spying on a demon. I glanced at the time. "Anything else? I should probably head out."

"Yes," said Mei. "Jerome wants you to check in on Tawny."

"Seriously?" I groaned. "He hates me."

The demonesses neither confirmed nor denied this statement.

"See you around, Georgina," said Grace.

"We'll check in," said Mei.

They vanished.

With a heavy heart, I finished my packing and told Aubrey good-bye. Then I lugged my suitcase down to my Passat, off to play Mata Hari. I just hoped my end would be better than hers.

Once you clear Everett, a naval city just north of Seattle, the drive up to Canada is pretty easy. The speed limit goes up, and the most exciting attractions along the way are casinos and outlet malls. About a half-hour from the border, I reached Bellingham, the current residence of Tawny Johnson.

Tawny was a succubus, a very new succubus. Technically, I was her mentor, but her assignment in Bellingham mercifully limited our interactions. She'd come to Seattle back in December and had gotten involved with an imp named Niphon who'd been trying to make my life more of a living hell than it already was. He'd roped her into his plans, and as angry as I'd been about it, I knew the fault was his more than hers. She hadn't really known what she was doing and had been convinced he could help fast-track her career. Nonetheless, she'd gotten in enough trouble that Jerome had sent her out of the city. It was better than being sent back to Hell, so really, the arrangement suited all of us just fine.

I gave her a call, and we met up at a café just off I-5. Tawny was easy to spot when she entered the place. Despite the fact that Tawny had been kind of a con artist when she was a mortal—a profession you'd think would lend itself well to succubus work—she was actually pretty horrible at seduction. Oh, she could still get guys to sleep with her, but it was more thanks to her availability rather than any particular wiles on her part. In particular, she was convinced that the most alluring form she could take was that of a six-foot blonde with breasts that would have given a human a back injury. Tawny also had a penchant for spandex and metallic fabrics that I found disturbing but that delighted Hugh and the vampires to no end. I made a mental note to tell them about the chartreuse hot pants she wore today.

"Georgina!" she exclaimed, dancing over to my table on gold stilettos. "I'm so happy to see you." She held out her arms, like maybe I was supposed to stand and hug her, but I remained sitting. Taking the hint, she sat down as well. "What are you doing here?"

"I'm going to Vancouver," I said, wrapping my hands around my white chocolate mocha. "Jerome wanted me to stop by and see how things were going."

Her eyes lit up. "Great! I've been spending a lot of time over at Western." She leaned forward and spoke in a sage voice. "You know, if you're ever having trouble getting someone into bed, you should go check out college guys. They're *so* easy."

"Thanks for the tip," I said dryly. "I'll keep it in mind."

She pursed her lips and eyed me. "Doesn't look like you need it, though," she added wistfully. "I could never get a glow like that."

Too bad she hadn't seen the glow in full effect yesterday. It would have blown her away. "You will," I said. "Someday." Some day far, far away. Tawny had miles to go before gaining the subtleties required to land really moral guys.

"I don't know how you do it. You aren't even blond. I mean, maybe a little, but mostly you're a brunette. I just don't see guys going for that."

My hair was long and light brown, lightly highlighted with gold. My eyes were a hazel-green that I also suspected didn't fit in with her worldview of what was sexy, at least if her baby blues were any indication. "Yeah, well, some people are into kinky stuff, I guess."

The waiter showed up and took our lunch orders. I made myself comfortable and prepared to do some mentoring.

"So," I said. "You got any questions?"

Tawny titled her head, long-lashed blue eyes filled with thought. "Yeah. There's something I've been wondering about."

"Okay, go for it."

"These colleges guys . . . they're kind of, like, fast."

"Fast?"

"Yeah. You get them into bed, and it's over before it begins."

"They're eighteen or twenty. Still pulsing with adolescent hormones. They don't really know what they're doing yet."

"Yeah, yeah, I know," she said. "Except, when you're going down on them, it takes *forever*. You know what I mean?"

I forced a straight face. "It's one of the mysteries of the universe, Tawny. You just gotta roll with it."

"But my mouth gets sore," she whined. "Makes my jaw ache the next day! Isn't there any way to speed it up?"

My immortal friends would die if they could hear this conversation. "You can try the 'don't stop' trick. Or maybe tell them you want them to come on your face. That'll get things moving."

"Ew! That's disgusting."

I shrugged. "Don't ask the question if you don't want to hear the answer."

"But how can I even say anything when my mouth is, well, you know . . ."

Thus went the rest of our lunch conversation, and blow jobs turned out to be the mildest of topics. Fortunately, no one sat within listening distance. I ate my chicken salad as fast as I could, eager to be on my way. As we were paying the bill, a thought came to me.

"Hey, Tawny. You're practically on top of Cedric's turf here. You ever see any signs of him and Jerome fighting?"

She shook her head. "No. I've never even met Cedric. But there's a vampire here in town who's mentioned them fighting before. He seems to think it's a big deal."

"Everyone seems to, and yet . . . I don't know. I have a weird feeling about all this. Like that someone's trying to cover up something."

Tawny placed some cash on the table, her clawlike nails lacquered and red. For half a moment, she looked remarkably wise. "Back when I was doing cons, the best way to pull one past people was to make a big deal about something else. Misdirection."

It was quite possibly the most intelligent thing I'd ever heard Tawny say. "Yeah, but if so, what are we being misdirected from?"

"Hell if I know. That's for smart people like you to figure out. I'm just trying to get college guys to speed up their blow jobs."

My first minute in Canada, I got pulled over.

Right after you go through customs, there's a short stretch of the freeway with an incredibly low speed limit. Every time I drive through there, I try to drive that speed. And I'm the only one who ever does it. All the locals zip through that area, already driving the speed that the freeway clicks up to about half a mile (or kilometer or whatever) later. Every time, just before I officially hit the higher speed zone, I finally crack and speed up too—and that's always when the cops get me. I've been pulled over three times.

This was my fourth.

I handed over my license and other pertinent paperwork to the cop. "American, eh?" he asked, like it wasn't perfectly obvious.

"Yes, sir," I said.

"You know you were speeding, don't you?" He mostly sounded curious, not harsh.

"Was I?" I asked blankly, looking at him with doe eyes. I saw the succubus glamour seize him. "But the sign said sixty-five."

"Sixty-five *kilometers* per hour," he corrected gently. "We use the metric system here."

I blinked. "Ohhhh. God, I forgot. I feel so stupid."

"It happens a lot," he said. He handed my stuff back without even running it. "I'll tell you what. I'll let you go this time. Just make sure you get the units right, eh? Your speedometer's got kilometers per hour underneath the miles per hour."

"Oh, that's what the little numbers are for, huh—er, eh?" I gave him a dazzling smile. "Thank you so much."

So help me, he tipped his hat. "Happy to help. Be careful now, and enjoy your stay."

I thanked him again and headed off. It's worth noting here that while I've been pulled over four times in this stretch, I've also gotten off four times.

Canadians. So nice.

I made it into downtown Vancouver without further incident and checked into my hotel. It was a boutique one over on Robson Street, and I decided maybe Jerome didn't hate me after all. Or at least, Hell's travel agency didn't hate me. Robson was a fun neighborhood, full of restaurants and shopping. I threw my stuff into my room and then headed off to meet Cedric. He would have sensed me crossing into his territory, but I wanted it officially noted for the record that I was here so that I didn't get in further trouble with Jerome.

Unlike Jerome, who was impossible to find sometimes, Cedric actually had a suite of offices over in the Financial District. I kind of liked that. The front desk was staffed by an imp named Kristin. She seemed pleasant enough, just incredibly busy. She told me I'd lucked out and that Cedric could fit me in right now. Walking into his office, I found him at his desk, reading something on Wikipedia. He glanced up.

"Oh. Jerome's succubus." He turned from the monitor and gestured to a chair opposite his desk. "Have a seat."

I sat down and immediately began assessing the office. Nothing about it screamed evil. It was neat and sleek, with an expansive window full of office buildings beyond him. Silver perpetual motion balls sat on his desk, and one of those framed motivational posters hung on the wall. It had a picture of a struggling pine sapling in front of a larger tree and read, DETERMINATION.

Cedric himself didn't look too evil either. He had an average build and pretty blue-gray eyes. He kept his hair shaved army-style, and like Kristin, the biggest vibe I got off him was busy. Inasmuch as one could be busy surfing Wikipedia, that is. I glanced at the screen, curious as to what he'd been looking at. Demonic takeovers, perhaps?

"Oh, that," he said, following my gaze. "Just a hobby of mine. It's the entry on marsupials. I just like going in sometimes and putting in incorrect information. It's always fun to see how long it takes them to notice. They're better about it than they used to be, but that just makes it more of a challenge. I just wrote about how marsupials are an integral part of the Lutheran Eucharist." He chuckled at his own ingenuity. "God, I hated the Reformation."

I smiled, not entirely sure what to say.

Cedric clasped his hands in front of him, face turning serious. "So, let's get down to business. You're here to spy on me."

My mouth opened, but nothing coherent came out right away. "Um . . ."

He waved his hand. "No, no, it's fine. You don't honestly expect me to believe Jerome would do me a favor without strings attached? Whatever. I don't have anything to hide. He can keep his territory—I'm too busy watching my own. You can tell him whatever you want so long as you do what I need you to."

"Right," I said, finding my voice at last. "Your embarrassing Satanic cult."

He grimaced. "God, those guys are such a pain in the ass. What do you know about them?"

"That they aren't Satanists like the usual groups, not like Anton LaVey's followers or the anti-Christians." I felt like a student reciting in front of a class.

"They think they're anti-Christian, but mostly, they're just ridiculous. Just some flakes in search of identity who got together and thought it'd be cool to be evil. They have meetings in robes and keep making up secret handshakes."

"And that's a problem?"

"Nah, I don't care about any of that. They can play dressup all they want. What's annoying is that they're doing all the things people *think* evil people do but don't actually do. They ripped up a bunch of bibles once and left them on this church's lawn. They also appear to have a fondness for spray paint."

"I heard about that."

"They keep writing stupid stuff like 'The Angel of Darkness is Lord' and 'What Would Satan Do?'" Cedric rolled his eyes. "Yeah, like *that's* original."

"I can see why you'd be embarrassed," I admitted.

"No kidding. The worst part is that they're attracting some media attention—*especially* among local churches. So, now those guys are doing their own sort of backlash and triggering a whole bunch of demonstrations about faith and light and all that stuff. Not what we need. Kind of defeats our purpose, really."

"What do you want me to do?"

"Kristin hangs out with them sometimes. They know her

and recognize what side she works for, but frankly, she doesn't have the people skills to manipulate them. She'll take you to them and give them some bullshit about how you're high-ranking in the ways of evil or something equally absurd. Then, I want you to hang out with them and just be part of their group. Stop them from doing more stupid things. Get them to go back to their role-playing in the basement. Hell, if you can convince them to disband, go for it." He eyed me. "You're a succubus. You've been around for a while. You should be able to talk them into anything."

I nodded. "I can."

"Good. I'm tired of them. I'm not allowed to interfere directly, and my own people are too busy." He stood up and walked toward the door. I took the hint and followed. "Do whatever you want the rest of the day. Kristin'll take you over to them tomorrow. Check them out. See what you think. I've got some appointments in the morning, but stop by anyway and give me your impressions of those fools."

"Is there anything in particular you want me to find out for you?"

"Yes," he said. "In addition to keeping them out of trouble, I want you to simply observe them. They're not just attracting media attention—they're attracting attention from my superiors." Ah, yeah. Hell could get pissy about that kind of thing. "If someone's purposely manipulating them, I want to know."

"Okay."

He gave me a narrow-eyed look. "And I hope it's not Jerome."

He still had that mild, businesslike exterior, but I heard the stern note in his voice. I shivered but gave him a smile anyway, trying not to think about misdirection.

"I hope not either."

I was a bit surprised at how short my meeting with Cedric had been. I was more surprised still that after all the grief Jerome had given me about the urgency of this trip, I now had nothing to do. Of course, if he was trying to get rid of me, this was as good a way as any. My bad attitude and I were out of Seattle.

It was dinnertime when I got back to Robson Street, so I found food at an Ethiopian restaurant a few blocks from my hotel and lingered over the remains of my meal with a novel I'd picked up a few days ago. Afterward, I wandered up and down the street, looking at various shops and designers, but eventually had to stop after passing two T-shirt stores. One sold retro stuff and had a dark purple Quiet Riot shirt in their window. Another sold Canadian souvenirs and displayed a shirt showing a map of Canada in red with a map of the U.S. below it in blue. The caption read: "Canada Likes It on Top." If I'd still been dating Seth, I would have bought him both. He would have shaken his head and given me a slight quirk of the lips as he tried to hide his smile.

The thought depressed me, and I found myself growing sadder and sadder as I walked back to my hotel. In that moment, I would have given anything to be with Seth again, to right the wrongs we'd done to each other back around Christmastime. Losing him was losing a part of me that—

Searing, white-hot anger suddenly shot through me. What the fuck was I whining about? Why should I miss him? Why should I pine for someone who'd betrayed me and hurt me with *my friend*, of all people? Seth didn't deserve my longing or my love, and as I continued walking, that dark despair within me transformed to rage and spite—just as it had done nearly every day for the past four months.

When I got back to the hotel, I was no longer sad. I was pissed. I hated everyone and everything, but especially Seth. I wanted to make him pay. Unfortunately, there was no way to do that, not here in Vancouver. Passing near the hotel's bar on my way through the lobby, I paused and surveyed the patrons. It was a veritable smorgasbord of men, most of them lone travelers making transient friends over their drinks. My succubus lust sprang up in me, and suddenly, all I wanted was to get drunk and go to bed with some guy. I wanted to lose myself in the haze of alcohol and fucking, in the hopes that it might all dull the pain that lay buried under my anger.

And as I scanned the room, one guy in particular caught my attention. The face was all wrong, but he had hair almost the same color as Seth's. It was worn messy too, though it appeared as though he'd achieved that look with gel, rather than the lack of brushing Seth employed. No, this guy wasn't a perfect match by any means, but he was close, and there was an aura of shy vulnerability about him that I liked.

Putting on a smile, I strolled across the room to introduce myself. I might not be able to actually punish Seth, but at least for tonight, I could pretend that I could.

Chapter 4

"**C**an I call you?"

The Sorta-Seth-Lookalike lay naked in bed, still worn out even though he'd come hours ago. I stood near the door, fully dressed, slipping on my shoes. It turned out he was actually here on business from Seattle, and he'd been ecstatic to learn we lived in the same city.

"Mmm." I pursed my lips as though I were giving this a lot of thought. "I don't think that's such a good idea."

"Really?" His brief, happy look faded. He'd turned out to be as vulnerable and shy as I thought. I was only the second woman he'd ever slept with. "But I felt like . . . well, I felt like we really connected."

I fixed him with a cold look. That smothering rage from last night no longer consumed me, but I was still angry at the world and needed to lash out at anyone I could. "Our bodies connected. That's about it. The truth is, I already have a boyfriend."

His eyes widened. I realized then I should have mentioned having a boyfriend before we had sex. It would have doubled his guilt and given me a stronger fix. Still, the agony he now felt over sleeping with someone else's girlfriend was undoubtedly blackening his soul even as we spoke.

"R-really?"

"Yup. Sorry. This was just a way to pass the time. And honestly, baby? You want some feedback? You've still got a lot to learn. It really wasn't that great."

I left before I could see the full effect of my words. It would hurt, I had no doubt about that. Devastating him didn't really make me feel better, but it had frozen me up enough so that I didn't have to process any real emotions. I was numb, which was about the best I could hope for.

Kristin was waiting for me at a coffee shop down the street so that she could drive me over to the cult leader's house. Her mousy brown hair was pulled up into a neat French twist, and her crisp suit reminded me of something Grace or Mei might wear, save that this was navy as opposed to their usual black or—on daring days—red. She drank what looked like a cappuccino and picked over the remains of a bagel, her eyes lost in thought as she no doubt pondered the coming day's wheeling and dealing.

I bought a white chocolate mocha and slid into the chair opposite her. "Good morning," I said.

She looked me over, noting the glamour. "And a good night?"

I shrugged. "Okay night."

"You ready to meet the Army of Darkness?"

"Sure. I—wait. What did you say?"

"The Army of Darkness. That's what the cult calls itself."

"They know that's a movie, right?"

She shook her head. "Honestly, it's hard to say. They may have named themselves after the movie, for all I know."

"This is so absurd as to be unreal," I told her. "It all sounds like a joke."

"If only," she muttered. "Believe me, I'll be glad when you get rid of them. Aside from the fact that Cedric makes *me* talk to them, I have to file a ream of paperwork each time they do something stupid. It's really stressing him out. I keep trying to get him to do relaxation exercises, but he won't."

Her tone sounded genuinely concerned, almost as though she worked for Cedric out of true loyalty, rather than the forced servitude the rest of us bowed to.

"Well, I'll see what I can do. Don't you guys have a succubus up here? Why isn't she working this group over?"

"She's busy seducing the premier. Cedric didn't want her distracted."

"Whoa," I said. It had been centuries since I'd had the initiative to go after a major politician. "I feel like a slacker."

Kristin cut me a look. "Mostly I hear that you're a trouble-maker."

"I like to think I'm just misunderstood."

She snorted. "We're *all* misunderstood. You have no idea how many times people try to use that as a reason to break their contracts."

Between mourning Seth and being the target of Jerome's annoyance lately, I'd had little time to think about much else. Kristin's words suddenly triggered a memory, one I'd tried to keep buried for some time now.

"How many times do people try to break their contracts over an error?"

When Niphon had been here last winter, he'd gone to great pains to complicate my life and get me recalled to Hell. Since he'd been the one to trick me into selling my soul so long ago, I had plenty of reason to hate him. But why he'd hate me and want to ruin me? That had been—and still was—a mystery. Hugh had speculated that when an imp went to that much trouble to mess with their acquisition, there was usually a reason—specifically, a potential problem with the original contract.

My casual air didn't fool Kristin. "You think there might be an error in yours?"

I kept my nonchalance. "Hugh—my imp—thought there could be. But he wouldn't look it up." His refusal to help me still stung.

"He's smart. Looking into others' contracts can get us in big trouble. The vaults of Hell are not a place you want to get caught snooping around in. It would take a lot to get an imp to risk that."

I had no proof, but something told me that Kristin was older and higher-ranking than Hugh and that she might have more access than he did. I smiled sweetly. "What would it take for *you* to risk that?"

"Nothing you can offer." She flashed me a wry grin and slipped on sleek Oakley sunglasses. "Come on. Let's get this over with."

We ended up at a house out in suburban Vancouver. It was a lower middle-class area, not particularly polished but not the kind of place you had to worry about getting mugged either. Kristin parked on the street and led me up the house's driveway, her heels clicking on the concrete. Along the sides of the yard, someone had recently planted marigolds and geraniums.

She rang the doorbell, and a moment later, a man in his mid-twenties answered the door. He had messy black hair, like maybe he'd just woken up, and possessed the friendly, low-key feel of someone who worked at Home Depot or Circuit City.

"Hey, Kristin," he said, voice cheerful and blasé. "Come on in."

She stepped just inside the doorway, and I followed, offering the guy a friendly smile of my own. "I can't stay," she told him crisply. "I'm just dropping her off. Evan, this is . . ."

Kristin glanced at me, apparently waiting to see if I wanted to use my own name. I usually used different identities and shapes when seducing victims, but it didn't seem worth it for this.

"Georgina," I supplied.

"Georgina," said Kristin. "This is Evan." He and I shook hands. "Georgina's one of the founders of a sister chapter in Seattle. She's here to see how things are done and possibly form some connections between the groups." She tipped her head down, looking at him over the tops of her sunglasses. "I want you to show her every courtesy and involve her in your activities. It's very important."

He nodded, still looking mild and pleasant—but a little nervous at the strictness in her voice. "Absolutely." Cedric had said Evan knew Kristin was a power player on Team Evil, and he clearly seemed to respect her. She supposedly didn't have the people skills to "deal with" this group, but from the way Evan regarded her, it didn't seem like it'd take much to get his attention.

To me, Kristin said, "Call a cab when you're done. We'll expense it."

With that, she headed back out to her car, leaving me with the alleged general of the Army of Darkness.

"You want anything to drink?" he asked, stifling a yawn. "I've got some RC in the fridge."

"No, thanks. I'm just anxious to learn how you do things up here."

He grinned. "Sure. I should probably show you the temple first."

I glanced around, taking in the flowered sofa and grand-father clock. "Temple?"

"Yeah, it's in the basement. You sure you don't want something to drink?" There was nothing I wanted to drink that was under 80 proof, so I declined once again.

He led me down some rickety steps, pulling a chain at the bottom that turned on a bare lightbulb. We stood in an un-finished basement with rough cement floors and brick walls. Fold-up chairs were arranged in a semicircle around a low bookcase about as high as my waist. On top of the case was a propped up painting with an angel's black silhouette set against a gray and purple nebula. It looked like it had come straight off a sci-fi novel's cover. Half-burned red and black candles were scattered around the painting, along with an inverted cross. Off to the side of the room, more candles sat on top of a washer and dryer. Evan walked over to a light switch and turned it on. White Christmas lights twinkled to life on the brick walls.

"Wow," I said. My astonishment was not faked.

"We aren't finished setting up here," he said modestly. "We have to change our location a lot to avoid discovery. You know how it is. So, there's still some stuff we need to un-pack." He pointed over to a cardboard box in the corner. I couldn't see all of its contents, but I did make out a black feather boa and a glow-in-the-dark plastic skull. On the side of the box, black marker succinctly declared: TEMPLE STUFF.

I counted the chairs. Fifteen. "How many members do you have?" I asked.

"About a dozen. A little less than that that are truly active." He sat down in one of the chairs and gestured for me to do the same.

"And how long have you been meeting?"

"Oh, about a year now."

I smiled, turning on the charm in an effort to not sound like an investigative reporter. "I've heard about some of the things you've done. Pretty impressive. Like the Bibles and the, um, spray paint."

He beamed at the praise. "You heard about that? Cool. We do as the Angel of Darkness directs us."

"What other things have you been directed to do?"

"Well, there was the one time this Methodist church was having an ice cream social. We broke in beforehand and left all their ice cream outside the freezer to melt."

"Uh-huh."

"Then, this other time, we went to the petting zoo and hung pentagram collars on all the goats. We also painted their horns red and black. Let me tell you, that wasn't easy. They don't like to stand still."

"Uh-huh."

"Oh, and then we made all the TVs show *Rosemary's Baby*."

"Uh—TVs?"

"Yeah, I work at Circuit City, and we have these big walls of TVs, so I synced them all up. My boss never suspected who did it."

On and on the litany went. About ten minutes later, I interrupted, unable to listen to any more. "Look, Evan, this is really amazing stuff you've been doing. I mean, this is stuff my people in Seattle would never, *ever* dream of doing in a million years."

"Really?" he asked happily.

"Really," I said flatly. "But, although it makes a big statement, wouldn't it be more in line with the, uh, Angel's purposes to work on securing souls for him?"

"Her," corrected Evan.

"Her. Right." Lucifer, Satan, the Devil, whatever. There were lots of names for what humans regarded as the supreme entity of evil, and I'd heard tons over the years. Considering the popular idea of Lucifer being a fallen angel, this "Angel of Darkness" thing didn't surprise me, but the female part did. "Sorry," I told him. "We know the Angel as male."

"It's okay," he replied. "The Angel is all things to all people."

"Right. So, anyway, I mean, the ultimate goal is to convert as many people to her as possible, right? To lead them down the left-hand path. It doesn't seem like melting ice cream would do that—not that that isn't cool," I added hastily. "I'm just wondering if you should be more focused on leading people into temptation instead."

Evan didn't seem bothered by my criticism in the least. "Maybe that's what your group is directed to do. But this is what ours is supposed to do. We all serve different purposes in the greater plan."

I was sure I had an idiotic look on my face, so I tried to shift back to the alluring, seductive mode that had landed me this job in the first place. Surely it couldn't be that difficult to sway him, particularly considering how fresh my succubus glamour was. Reaching out, I took his hand and delicately stroked it with my fingers.

"You're doing amazing things," I reiterated, moving closer. "Really amazing. But maybe it's time to move on to the next level, to truly bring darkness to the world."

His eyes studied my hand for a moment, then looked back up. His breath caught as the full effect of my glow enchanted him. He swallowed nervously. "Perhaps. But not now. This is our purpose for the time being."

"Only because you haven't tried something else. Maybe

that's why I'm here, why the Angel sent me: to expand your influence." I leaned my face close to his, lips only inches away from the side of his face. "I can teach you things. All sorts of things."

Zealous or no, I was definitely affecting him. He took another deep breath, trying to steady himself. "We're already doing what the Angel wants."

I ran my lips across his check, letting my tongue flick out. "Are you sure? Let me show you how we honor the Angel . . ."

He shot up abruptly and put his back to me. After several deep breaths—honestly, he was in danger of hyperventilating—he turned around to look at me. Warring desires danced in his eyes. He still had that crazy yes-man zealot look, but he also looked like he was already envisioning me naked. It was intriguing that his devotion to a largely fictitious entity could stand up to my charms, but religious fanatics had a history of being tenacious. "You're very . . . sweet," he said at last. "Very. But I can't—we can't. I mean, this is what we do. What the Army does. We can't change that, not without talking to the others."

Progress. I kept the smile turned on, wondering if I should keep pushing on him now or try to enthrall the whole group. I opted for the latter, largely because I could think of few things more unarousing than having sex on the black Ozzy Osbourne plush rug on the floor. Especially if Evan decided to turn on any black lights. "Of course," I purred. "When can I meet them?"

He raked a hand through his hair, still a little hot and bothered. "Well . . . you should come to our next meeting. It's Saturday at ten a.m. Over at the big Tim Hortons on Broadway."

"Okay, I'll be—" I blinked, my sultry façade faltering. "Did you say Tim Hortons?"

He recovered himself and returned to his upbeat nature. "Oh, yeah. You guys don't have them, do you? They're these donut shops and—"

"No, I know what they are. I'm just surprised, that's all." Aside from seeming like a mundane place for a Satanists' meeting, Canadians going to Tim Hortons was like the biggest stereotype ever.

"Are you kidding? Their coffee's the best."

I left after that, my head reeling. These weren't Satanists. These were frat boys doing hazing pranks. They probably smashed beer cans on their foreheads at their dark ceremonies.

Kristin wasn't at her desk when I returned to Cedric's office across town. Presumably she was off doing imp things. Or maybe she was at lunch. His door was closed, making me think he must be busy, but honestly, I didn't have time to pay much attention to that. Something else immediately caught my attention.

There was a demoness in his waiting room.

A full-fledged archdemoness, actually. I recognized her, even though we'd never formally met. Nanette, Portland's archdemoness.

"Hi," I said, too stunned for much more than that. I might backtalk Jerome, but other demons were an entirely different matter.

She glanced up from her magazine like she'd just noticed me, though I knew she'd sensed me long before this. "Hello. Georgina, right?"

I nodded, wondering if I should shake her hand or something. She didn't seem like she was keen to get up, so I simply sat in another chair. Why was Portland's archdemoness waiting to see Cedric? And why was she waiting, period? That wasn't in demonic nature at all. They were too impatient.

Nanette wore a short, peach-colored shift dress that showed off long, shapely legs. Her blond hair fell just over her shoulders, smooth and sleek from a flat iron—or, well, from demonic magic. She was beautiful, but it was edged in the cold fierceness demons so often had, like the way a cobra or a katana is beautiful.

I wasn't afraid to talk to people. Striking up conversation was part of what I did. But I wasn't entirely sure what to say to her. Demons were prickly about how they interacted with lesser immortals. Some were quite snobby about it. I didn't know too much about Nanette or how she might react. I knew she was less powerful than Jerome and that the two didn't have much contact. I'd never heard of her being particularly bitchy or trigger-happy, so I took that as a good sign.

My concerns about what to say were put to rest when she spoke first.

"Boy," she said. "I wouldn't want to be you for the world."

"I—I beg your pardon?"

"This." She gestured toward Cedric's closed door with a French manicured hand. "All of this. I presume you've been out to see his little Army of the Night?"

"Darkness," I corrected. "Army of Darkness."

"Whatever. Those nuisances. Jerome sent you here to 'help' because Cedric wanted an infiltrator?"

"Something like that." I wondered how this news had spread so fast.

Nanette shook her head in mock sympathy. "You're going to be the one to take the fall if something goes wrong. If things go bad between Jerome and Cedric or if that cult won't play ball . . . well, like I said, I wouldn't want to be you. You're being played from every angle and don't even realize it."

"What's there to play? I just got here. And I don't see how things can go wrong," I said slowly. "I mean, this group just does stupid stunts." I recalled how even a little seduction had affected Evan. If I'd started stripping on the Ozzy rug, I was certain he wouldn't have been able to hold back. "They're no real threat to Cedric, and I don't think they're going to be that hard to rein in. And as for him and Jerome . . . I mean, they patched up their differences already, right?"

"Come now. You're what, a millennium old? Millennium and a half? So young." She smiled. "Georgina, demons *never* settle their differences. Even you should know that. Do you really think things are stable around here? With the way Cedric's let this cult run wild? And after the way Jerome's barely been able to keep control in Seattle?"

I thought about Jerome booting me to Canada in less than

twenty-four hours. "Jerome seems like he's got control to me."

She uncrossed her legs and leaned forward, blue eyes gleaming. "Jerome has had *three* nephilim in his territory in the last six months. Three. Do you know how unheard of that is? I'm guessing you'd never even run into a nephilim your entire life before this. Not in all those years."

"No," I admitted.

Nephilim were the children of humans and angels—well, angels who had fallen and were now demons, seeing as having kids was a breach of Heaven's employment agreement. Considered abominations by both good and evil alike, nephilim were the scourge of the immortal world. They had a lot of power and were pissed off at the way greater immortals treated them. They were unruly, destructive, and given to killing sprees.

Jerome had actually fathered two nephilim, twins who were among the three Nanette was referring to. One of them, Roman, had been my boyfriend for a bit while he secretly wiped out immortals on the side. I'd been instrumental in his undoing—something I was certain he was still pissed off about, particularly since it had resulted in the death of his sister. We hadn't seen Roman since then. Shortly thereafter, a nephilim named Vincent had come to Seattle, following an angel he loved. Vincent was actually a very sweet nephilim, though I wasn't sure how kind he was feeling these days since Heaven had kicked out his girlfriend when she killed another angel to save him. Vincent too had disappeared.

"Three nephilim," repeated Nanette. "And two got away. Sloppy, very sloppy."

"It wasn't Jerome's fault," I said loyally, a bit unsure how you'd even assign blame in that situation. It had never occurred to me that our unexpected visitors could be seen as a sign of Jerome's weakness or his inadequacy as archdemon. "The angels could have done something. It's their territory too."

"Not in the eyes of our superiors," she said slyly.

I frowned, losing a bit of my timidity. "With all due respect, what are you doing here?"

Her smile grew. "What do you think? I have two demons in my backyard who are in an arms race. Both are getting attention from demons outside the Northwest." I didn't like the sound of that and recalled Cedric affirming as much. "You think I want to be involved in that? You think I want to be played the way everyone's playing you? My territory's small, and I'm weaker than both Jerome and Cedric. I don't want them to decide to annex Portland while they play their cosmic game of Risk. I want them to leave me alone." Her voice was hard, but I heard a bit of worry in there too, and I realized what was going on.

"You're here to . . ." I considered "suck up" or "beg" but thought better of it. ". . . negotiate with Cedric. For protection. To keep you out of it."

Nanette looked away, unwilling to acknowledge this in front of a succubus. Just then, the door opened and Cedric stepped out. He glanced around. "Kristin's still gone? I wish she'd hurry up and bring back those donuts."

"Tim Hortons?" I guessed.

He gave me an incredulous look. "Of course." He turned to Nanette. She'd stood up, and he kissed her hand in a polite, antiquated way. "Sorry. Phone call with Tech Support. You know how that is." To me he said, "We'll talk later."

I took it as a bad sign that he said "later" and not "soon." Settling into my chair, I braced myself for patience. Ten magazines later, Cedric opened the door again. Nanette was nowhere in sight, so I presumed she must have teleported back to Portland.

I took my same chair in Cedric's office, noting that his screen showed Match.com rather than Wikipedia today. When he saw what I was looking at, he hastily minimized his Web browser.

"So, what have you found out?"

I gave him a report of my morning with Evan. "They're ridiculous," I declared as my final assessment.

"I already knew that," he said. "You think you can put an end to this? Soon?" The impatient sound in his voice made me wonder if he'd expected me to cinch things up already.

I thought about it. "Yeah, pretty sure I can as soon as I meet the others. This guy looked like he might crack on his own. But I won't see them until Saturday."

Cedric tipped back in his chair, face thoughtful. "All right. They probably won't do anything before then anyway. Go to their meeting and work over the rest of them. In the meantime, you might as well head back home."

I straightened up in my chair. "Really?"

He shrugged. "No point in you sticking around unless you want to sightsee. Just come back Saturday."

"But . . ." I hesitated. "Jerome sent me here because he was mad and didn't want to deal with me. If I go back and he doesn't want me there . . ."

Cedric snapped his chair forward and sat up. "He can take it up with me. I'll tell him I didn't want you here either." There was something mischievous in his eyes, like he almost hoped Jerome might pick a fight. Uneasily, I remembered Nanette's words. *You're being played from every angle and don't even realize it.*

"Okay," I said finally. "Thanks."

Cedric glanced toward the door, his expression lightening. "Ah, Kristin's back." A few moments later, I sensed the imp's signature as well. I stood up, and he gestured me to the door with a smile. "Have a good drive. And grab a donut on your way out."

Chapter 5

Jerome was waiting for me in my apartment as soon as I stepped through the door.

"You have some nerve," he growled.

I set my suitcase down. Normally that tone of voice would have set me hiding, but I was in no mood to listen to him now after my long drive—or rather, lack of a drive. There'd been an accident that had put traffic at a standstill, and I'd sat in my car for a very long and very annoying time.

"Look, Cedric told me to," I said, crossing my arms as though they might actually shield me from him. "I didn't do anything wrong."

"You're not supposed to do what he says." Jerome sat on the arm of my couch and flicked his cigarette over a nearby ashtray, which I took as a great courtesy on his part. "You're supposed to do what I say."

"He told me to go home. He didn't have anything for me to do until the Satanists had their breakfast meeting."

Jerome's glare momentarily faltered. "What are you talking about?"

"What are *you* talking about? I'm talking about Cedric sending me home early."

"And I'm talking about your failure to notify me of his little stunt last night."

Last night? I racked my brain. Last night I'd been killing time shopping and destroying a man's self-esteem. To my knowledge, Cedric had done nothing after I left except continue his quest to destroy Wikipedia's informative empire.

"What'd he do?" I asked. "I didn't even see him."

Jerome didn't answer right away, his face thoughtful. I realized then he was reassessing his initial anger. It wasn't my early return that had upset him.

"There was a vampire brawl last night," he said finally. "Somehow, a few of them thought their hunting ground lines had been rearranged. So they started roaming into others' areas . . ."

". . . and bad things ensued." Vampires were as territorial as demons in some ways. Vampires had specific areas that they guarded to stalk victims and were very touchy about other vampires using them. The archdemon of a region usually drew up vampiric lines and enforced them through force and will.

"Unfortunately, yes. Grace and Mei are still sorting it out."

A panicked thought suddenly struck me. "Are Cody and Hugh okay?"

He shrugged. "A little bruised and battered, but nothing that won't heal on its own."

My fear was unfounded, of course. Lesser immortals, like vampires and succubi, couldn't kill each other, and we healed extremely quickly. Still, the instinct to worry about my friends was one that would never leave me. "Why were you yelling at me over this? I certainly didn't have anything to do with it."

"Because the vampires who thought they'd been reassigned got official notification that said they had: a stamped and sealed demonic missive. They thought it was from me."

"But it wasn't," I guessed, seeing where he was going with this. Jerome had the area comfortably parceled out and would have no desire to change the status quo. He was too lazy. "There was no name?"

"No, clearly. But they don't need it—not if the seal is good. It was, and only another demon could have drawn something like that up."

"And so you assumed Cedric did it," I finished.

Jerome nodded. "Yes, and I'm going to let him know exactly what I think of this. I'm not happy over that—or you slacking off in reporting his activities to me."

"You're giving my spying ability more credit than I deserve here," I warned. "It's kind of limited. He's not really sharing his inner secrets with me, and anyway, he already knows that's what you want me to do."

"Of course he does."

I sighed. "Look, if you want my opinion . . ." The look Jerome gave me suggested he really didn't put a lot of stock in my opinion. ". . . I don't think Cedric's the type to do anything like that. He's more interested in Web surfing."

"After all this time with demons, you really should know better than that, Georgie." Jerome smashed his cigarette into the ashtray and stood up.

"Yeah, yeah, I know, you sound just like Nan—" I frowned. His wording had tickled a memory. "Oh, I do have some info for you. Cedric was meeting with Nanette."

Jerome had been straightening his sleeve, but his head jerked toward me at the mention of the archdemoness's name. "Nanette?" The word was carefully enunciated, icy in its tone.

I relayed what I knew. Jerome's face grew dark as I spoke. Whatever his thoughts on the new development were, however, he didn't share them with me. "Looks like you might be doing your job after all." He paused. "But why *are* you back?"

"There's nothing to do until Saturday. Cedric sent me home." I held my breath, waiting for him to blow up, but it didn't come.

"Well, seeing as you aren't being too much of a bitch for a change, I suppose that's okay." By that wording, I was apparently still being kind of a bitch.

Jerome vanished.

Aubrey immediately came out from behind the couch, giving me the censuring look cats always give owners who have been away for a while. I knelt down and scratched her chin. She was solid white with a few black specks on her forehead, often giving the impression that she couldn't keep her head clean.

"Yeah, I know," I told her. "Believe me, I don't want to go back there either."

Glancing at the clock, I saw that it was dinnertime. Too early to see the vampires quite yet, particularly since the days were getting longer. I'd have to wait until after sunset to get their version of the bloodsucking showdown. I gave Aubrey a few more conciliatory pats and then straightened up to call Dante. He didn't answer, and I wondered if he actually had a customer for a change. When not concocting vile spells, he made his living giving fake Tarot and palm readings. I left a message, telling him I was back.

With time on my hands, I started fretting about Emerald City. I knew the bookstore really could function without me, but the motherly instinct kicked in nonetheless. And since I did have the time, I decided to go over and check on things.

As expected, all was well. It was almost seven, and people on their way home from work were stopping in to pick up things. Business was steady but not crazy.

"Georgina! You're back."

I'd been watching the registers from a distance and turned to see Maddie standing behind me, lugging a cardboard display for a new book coming out tomorrow. I smiled. No matter how hard things had been for me with her and Seth, there was something about her bright, open personality that could lighten dark moods.

"For a while. I just wanted to check on things."

She grinned back. "That's just like you. Get time off, and come back to work. How are things? Still crazy?"

I shrugged. "Yeah, a little. But it's nothing I can't manage. I'm hoping it'll improve soon."

"Is it something that might improve with a drink?" She wore a mischievous look, and I couldn't help but laugh.

"Only if I'm drinking alone. You're still here for a couple more hours."

"Nope. I had to come in early to cover someone, so Janice is going to close."

It was always nice if a manager could close, but Janice was

certainly competent enough. I hesitated. I'd been avoiding Maddie since Christmas, but before Seth, I'd always really liked her a lot. We'd had a lot of good times together, and our personalities clicked well. Seth wasn't here now, and a drink suddenly seemed like an even better way to pass the time than doing managerial things when I wasn't actually required to do them.

"Okay."

She finished up, and about fifteen minutes later, we stepped outside. I got a cigarette out automatically, then paused. "Do you mind?"

"Nah. I don't like them, but it's okay. Where do you want to go?"

"I don't know." I reached for my lighter, remembered it was out, and pulled out the matches instead. I ran my fingers over its cover and frowned. "You want to go to Mark's Mad Martini Bar?"

Mark's was at the top of Queen Anne Hill, making for a rather steep hike. Living around here, I did it fairly regularly, but Maddie was breathing hard when we reached the bar.

"Man," she said. "I need to go to the gym more."

I held the door open for her. "Do this every day, and you won't need to."

"I think I need a little more than that." Her weight was a continual source of worry for her. "I think I need to pick up some weird sport. You want to start playing squash with me?"

"Why squash?"

"I don't know. Never tried it. Figured I should."

Along with the other changes in her life, Maddie had recently adopted an attitude of getting out there and trying new things. Before my recent funk, I'd had kind of a similar view. Faced with centuries of existence, I'd found experimenting with new activities was a great distraction. There was always something new to learn in the world.

Mark's was dimly lit, done in matte black décor. I flipped through the expansive drink menu, which upheld the restaurant's name. When the waiter came around, I ordered a martini called First Blush: white chocolate liqueur, Chambord, and vodka. The menu called for Stoli, but I asked for Grey Goose.

"You ever considered dancing?" I asked Maddie. "It can be a good workout. You're less likely to get hit in the head too."

Maddie had ordered Sing the Blues: Blue Curacao, pineapple juice, and Ketel One. Her face lit up.

"I've always wanted to. Doug said you used to teach swing at the bookstore."

"Yeah, I did some group lessons last fall. My friend Cody helped me." A pleasant wave of nostalgia swept me as I recalled those days. Things had been simpler, and I'd had a lot of fun teaching my friends and co-workers while doing one of my favorite activities.

"I wish I'd been there," she said wistfully. "I'm kind of uncoordinated, but you know . . . if I don't try, how will I learn?"

"Maddie, you should be doing motivational speaking."

She laughed. "I don't know about that. But I'd do dance lessons if you ever taught again. Hint, hint."

The waiter returned with our drinks. I nearly died when I tasted mine. It was an 80 proof, raspberry dream. "I don't know. The staff pretty much learned all they could with swing."

"Then teach something else. Doug says you know every kind of dance in the world. I'd help you organize it."

"Maybe I'll do salsa or something," I told her, not sure if I meant it. "When all this drama's over."

"Is there anything I can do to help? You know that I'm here if you need something."

The earnestness and compassion on her face made a lump form in my throat. I'd spent the last few months hating her, but her friendship and faith in me had never faltered. Suddenly feeling guilty, I glanced away from her eyes.

"Nah, don't worry. I'll deal with it." Silence fell, silence that bothered me immensely. I felt a need to give something back to her for her kindness. My thoughts from a few nights ago about moving flashed into my head. I glanced back up. "Maybe you can help me find a new place, though."

As I'd hoped, her face grew eager at the proposal. "Really? You're going to move?"

"I don't know for sure. Just thought it might be time for a change."

Maddie became even more excited. "What are you looking for?"

"Not sure about that either," I admitted. "The only thing I'm sure of is that I want to try something outside of Queen Anne."

"Okay, that's a good start. How big? New construction or historic? Do you want to keep renting? The condo market's flooded, you know. Great time to buy."

I tried to keep a straight face but couldn't. "Were you a real estate agent in another life?"

"No! I just think it's exciting, that's all. I want to help."

"Okay. I could rent or buy. It would depend on the place."

"What's your price range? If you don't mind me asking?"

I hesitated, wondering if I should let on to the truth about my finances. I decided it didn't matter. "Well . . . let's put it this way. I've got a lot of savings."

"Fair enough." Despite the rapid rate she was drinking, there was a sharp, businesslike air to her. "You want a similar kind of neighborhood? Shops? Restaurants?"

"Yeah, I wouldn't mind that."

"Anything else?"

"I told you, I haven't thought much about it."

She sighed in frustration. "You've gotta help me out here. Anything you've been wanting for a long time? Something you've missed?"

Unbidden, a memory of my childhood came to me. The Cyprian town I'd lived in returned to me in startling clarity, its colors, smells, and airs.

"I grew up around beaches," I said softly. "Sun and surf." I shook myself out of the wistful memory, feeling a bit embarrassed at my dreamy state. "But I'm in the wrong place for that."

"Yeah," she agreed. "You'd have to move to California for that."

We had another round of drinks and talked about other things, and to my surprise, I had a really great time. I remembered now why I liked Maddie so much. She was so easy to talk to, so funny and smart. I didn't have a lot of female friends, and there was a big difference between her and the guys I normally hung out with. Women needed other women sometimes.

I was signing my credit card bill when Seth walked over to our table.

Maddie looked up, beaming. "Hey, sweetie." She stood up and kissed him, something that unnerved both Seth and me. All of a sudden, the warm and pleasant feeling that had been building within me shattered. Maddie glanced at me explanatorily. "I called Seth to get a ride while you were in the bathroom."

I smiled tightly. "Ah."

Maddie turned back to him. "You're missing out. This place has great drinks. You sure you don't want to break the rules? We could stay another round."

"Actually, I need to go," I said, thinking of few things more agonizing than drinking with the two of them.

"And I'm not ready to break the rules," said Seth, avoiding my eyes. "Besides, I've got work to do."

Maddie looked only moderately disappointed. "Oh, well. No problem. Let me run to the bathroom, and we'll go. We'll give you a ride, Georgina."

I should have run away then and there, but Maddie dashed off quickly, and I felt it would be rude to leave without saying good-bye to her. Seth sat down in her chair and clasped his hands in front of him. Our usual wall of awkwardness slammed down between us.

"I don't need a ride," I said abruptly.

Seth glanced up at me. "It's a long walk."

"Not really. It's only six blocks."

"Yeah, but you've been drinking."

I scoffed. "I had two drinks. I'm hardly going to walk into traffic, if that's what you're worried about."

"No, but it's no problem for me. I just want to make sure you get home okay." It was one of those rare times when his mild mood had been replaced by something more adamant. For whatever reason, that ratcheted up the anger within me.

"I'll be fine," I snapped. "It's not your job to look after me anymore."

"Georgina, please."

"Please what? You know I'm right."

"You're making this into a bigger deal than it is. It doesn't always have to be about us."

"Of course it does . . . I mean, inasmuch as there is an us. You got out. I'm not your concern."

"I can still worry about you. Still care."

I leaned forward, possibly emboldened by my martinis. "You made it perfectly clear how much you care, and that's fine. I've got a whole new life now."

His look turned wry. "Yeah, your new life seems great."

That incensed me further, largely because I wasn't really convinced my new life was all that great either. "It is. I can do whatever I want now. I don't have to worry about hurting your delicate sensibilities when I sleep with someone or having to modify our dates to boring things that don't take you out of your comfort zone or interfere with your writing schedule."

It was horrible of me. Mean, mean, mean. I would have expected him to flinch, to look hurt. Instead, he fought back.

"And *I* don't have to worry about being hypocritically judged for being both too boring and too risky. I also don't have to wonder anymore if everything I'm being told is a half-truth or an outright lie."

That made *me* flinch. It was also when Maddie showed back up. She tried to cajole me into a ride, but I firmly refused—a bit more harshly than I needed to with her. She looked a little abashed, but I was too upset over Seth's words to care too much. I left, storming down the hill so hard, it was a wonder my footsteps didn't make the ground shake.

Chapter 6

It was dark by now, so I headed straight for my car and drove over to the vampires' apartment in Capitol Hill. Well, technically it was Peter's apartment. Cody was his apprentice and lived there by Peter's good graces, so long as he adhered to Peter's neurotic cleaning standards.

"Georgina," said Cody happily, opening the door for me. The lingering yellow bruise of a black eye showed on his face.

"Wow," I said, shocked enough by his appearance to let go of the Seth-rage that had consumed me the whole drive over. "It's true. You really did get in a fight."

"Oh, yeah," he said cheerfully. "It was great. Totally *West Side Story*."

I stepped inside and glanced around. "You also finally changed the carpet." They used to have velvety plush carpet stretching throughout the living room in ivory. This new stuff was a blue-gray Berber.

Peter stepped out from the kitchen and arched an eyebrow at me. I could smell pork chops and rosemary cooking. "Yeah, well, after three months of trying to scrub off that wine you spilled, I finally gave up."

"That was an accident," I reminded him. "Kind of." My final showdown with Niphon had involved me punching him and throwing him around. Peter's china cabinet and a full wineglass had been the casualties. I looked away from the corner where our fight had taken place. My heart had been raw and bleeding that day, fresh from the break-up with Seth.

"This is Scotchgarded," continued Peter. There was a challenge in his voice, like he was daring me to spill something on it now.

I settled myself on the couch, in the same way they often made themselves comfortable at my place without asking. I started to take out my cigarettes, but one look from Peter made me put them away with a sigh. Sometimes he allowed smoking but apparently not around new carpet.

"So what happened last night?" I asked.

"Maude, Lenny, and Paul came hunting in the city," explained Peter. There was an uncharacteristic anger in his eyes, rivaled only by the time he'd found out the color he'd used to paint his kitchen had been discontinued. "And then Elsa went over to the eastside, which pissed off Aidan."

I wasn't up to date on all the vampires in Washington, but I recognized most of the names and knew their territories—they were from far-out areas like Spokane and Yakima. Seattle would be a huge step up for them—except for the fact that Peter and Cody already controlled most of the city limits. My friends were laconic and mild most of the time, but I suspected I would have seen a whole other side to them last night when they discovered others in their hunting grounds.

"Three in your turf," I mused. "I bet that was fun."

"Oh yeah," said Cody, face still aglow. "They're not going to come trolling around here anymore. We kicked their asses like you wouldn't believe. It was awesome."

I couldn't help a smile. "Your first fight?" He nodded, and I glanced at Peter. "No marks on you."

Peter looked offended. "Of course not. Do I look like an amateur?"

"Hey!" said Cody. "What are you saying about me?"

Peter shrugged and returned to the kitchen, saying, "Just telling it like it is. I've been around a lot longer than you. Been in a lot more fights than you too. And *I* wasn't the one who got a black eye last night."

Cody looked like he might start a fight then and there, so I hastily asked, "And nobody knows how the mistake was made?"

"I heard it was Cedric," called Peter. "And that you've been cozying up with him."

"Hardly. I just met him yesterday."

Cody was apparently out of the loop. "What?"

"Georgina was sent to Canadian Boot Camp for sleeping with the therapist," explained Peter.

"Seriously?" asked Cody. I could already tell he was envisioning images of pine trees and snow-capped mountains.

I shrugged. "Figure of speech. It's some stupid job I have to do for him. I was there earlier today and got sent home empty-handed because there was nothing for me to do."

"I can't believe you'd do that," said Cody.

"Work for Cedric?"

"No. Go to Canada and not bring us back Tim Hortons."

The vampires invited me to stay for dinner, as I'd known they would, and we mulled over the mystery of last night's fight and other demonic politics. For the first time in a very long while, I had something to distract me other than Seth and the woes of my love life. There was nothing going on that really indicated some large, disastrous immortal scheme at work. A misunderstanding among vampires. A troublesome cult. An old grudge between demons. Yet, I couldn't shake the feeling that there was something else going on—something just beyond my reach. I kept thinking of what Tawny had said about scams and misdirection.

I eventually gave up on trying to figure out the mystery for now, and the vampires soon started replaying every last detail of the previous night's fight—a topic they never seemed to tire of. The stories bored me after a while, and I instead found myself studying little things, like the layout of the apartment, the new appliances, the granite countertops . . .

"Do you think I should move?" I asked abruptly.

Cody stopped mid-sentence. I think he'd been describing

how he'd had Lenny the vampire in a chokehold. "What?" he asked.

"I'm thinking of getting a new place."

"Were you even listening to my story?" asked Cody, looking slightly hurt.

"You've lived over there for years," said Peter. "As long as I've known you."

"I know. Maybe it's time for a change. It's small, and it's old."

"That's because it's a historic building," argued Peter.

"And," added Cody, "it's close to where you work. You'd have to drive in if you moved—unless you're just going up the street or something."

My eyes focused on the far side of the room without really seeing it. I remembered talking to Seth the other night and how it had seemed like I couldn't get far enough away from him. I thought about our fight earlier tonight. "No," I told them quietly. "I'd move somewhere else. Somewhere farther out."

"Ah," said Peter in understanding.

Cody frowned. "I don't get it. Why would you want to move far away from your—ow!" Peter had kneed him. Cody started to demand why, but then he seemed to catch on too. He was naïve about immortal affairs, sometimes, but not human ones. His face turned sympathetic, which I hated. "Maybe change is good."

I didn't know if it was, but I didn't want them to sit and feel sorry for me, so I coaxed more fight stories from them for the next half-hour or so as a way to distract them and make amends for not paying attention earlier.

I left shortly thereafter, wondering about whether it really was time to shake things up a little and move. Seth had already shaken my life up for the worse, and part of me wanted to rid myself of all those memories. Changing everything that I'd had while we'd been together—like my apartment—could be a way to do it. A clean cut. If I was really desperate, I could even consider switching jobs or cities. I didn't know if I was ready to go that far. It all depressed me.

"Hey, succubus. You sure know how to keep a guy waiting."

I'd been walking up to my building without really paying attention, too lost in my own thoughts. Now, in the faint glow of the light above the building's entrance, I saw Dante sitting on the steps. His black hair was brushed away from his face, and he wore a light coat over his usual attire of jeans and a long-sleeved shirt. He probably had a watch on under there too but almost never wore any other ornamentation or jewelry. I mustered a smile for him.

"Sorry," I said. "I called you earlier."

"And I called you back."

"Did you?" I pulled out my cell phone and saw three missed calls from him. "Oh, shit. I had the ringer off. Sorry."

He shrugged and stood up. "It's okay, just part of the endless torment I go through for you. One mysterious message saying you're going to Vancouver indefinitely. Another saying you're back but don't know for how long. Then no answer."

I realized I hadn't even thought much about how this international travel would affect Dante. That kind of radio silence would have never happened with Seth. I wouldn't have rested until we'd made contact and would have quickly noticed the ringer problem. With Dante, I'd left the voice-mail message and promptly put him out of my mind.

I gave him a quick kiss on the lips and unlocked the door. His face was scratchy and overdue for a shave. "Sorry," I said again. "How's it been going?"

"Same as it always does. Had a couple of drunk teens come in for palm readings last night, so that was a windfall. I could have taken you out someplace nice for a change."

"It would have beat what I was doing instead."

As we went upstairs to my apartment, I briefly gave him an overview of what was going on. As someone attuned to the paranormal world, there was little about demonic affairs that surprised him. I'd met Dante back in December, during the mess with Niphon. As part of his plan, Niphon had used a chaos entity named Nyx to suck energy from me in my sleep via realistic, emotionally charged dreams. Not knowing what was happening, I'd come to Dante for dream interpretation. He'd been abrasive, sarcastic, and infuriating throughout the entire process yet had steadily grown on me—until I learned the truth about his past. He'd done horrible things—hurt people, killed people, betrayed his own principles—in the name of selfish desires and a quest for power. Those atrocities had left him with an empty soul and bitter self-loathing. I'd loathed him too and swore I was done with him.

Then, things had fallen apart with Seth and me. My world had been torn apart, and I found myself with an empty soul and bitter self-loathing of my own. Seth had inspired me to believe in better things in the world, but all that hope had disappeared with our love. Dante's bleak, cynical outlook seemed more realistic now and more in line with my own worldview. He and I had hooked up, eerily compatible in our mutual despair. I didn't love him, but I liked him.

I poured us glasses of Grey Goose once we were inside. I preferred gimlets but didn't feel like going to the trouble of finding my lime juice. We settled on my couch with our drinks and cigarettes, and I finished up the story of my Canadian misadventures.

"Wow," he said when I was done. "All that because you fucked your therapist?" Unlike Seth, who hadn't liked knowing details about my succubus sex life, Dante took it all in stride.

I shrugged. "Well, I had nothing to do with the vampire gang war last night. But yeah, the rest is on me, I guess. You think they're related?"

He swirled his vodka around. "If you don't think Cedric did it, then probably not. The vampire thing is likely a coincidence. But that Portland demon was right. You probably are being played." There was almost a growl to his words, uncharacteristically protective.

I groaned. "But how? Everyone keeps saying that, yet I only got involved twenty-four-hours ago. How am I being manipulated in some huge affair in so short a time?"

"Because you've walked into something that's been going on for a while. It's not built around you per se, but now you're in it."

I leaned back against the couch and stared bleakly at the ceiling. "I should have never slept with Dr. Davies."

"Was he good?"

"Are you jealous?"

"Nah. Just trying to figure out what turns you on."

"Scathing wit, if present company's any indication."

"Somehow, I'm not convinced that's the allure. Besides, are you saying you're turned on right now?"

I was still staring at the ceiling. There were some fine cracks in the paint I hadn't noticed before. "Do you think I should move?"

"What, closer to me?"

"No, as in out. Into a new place."

"What's wrong with this one? You have a great place. At least you don't live where you work." Dante's bedroom was attached to his store.

I leaned forward and looked at him with a smile. "I might as well live where I work. I don't know. I feel like it's time for a change."

His gray eyes were thoughtful as he regarded me. "You've told me about this—how you get an itch for change and suddenly end up transforming your identity and moving to a different country."

Reaching out, I gently brushed some of his black hair out of his face and tucked it behind his ears. "I've only been here for fifteen years. It's way too soon to leave."

"So you say. Today you talk about a new apartment, tomorrow you could disappear. For all I know, maybe you're scoping out new employment opportunities in Vancouver."

I laughed and knocked back the rest of my vodka. "No, definitely not. Although, I think Cedric would be easier to work for than Jerome. Or at least a little less annoying."

"Even in Canada?"

"Canada's not that bad. Vancouver's actually a pretty cool city. But don't tell anyone I said that."

Dante set his glass down and reached into his shirt pocket. "Maybe I can bribe you to stick around. Or at least be on time."

A flash of gold caught my eye as he lifted out a watch. It was delicate, almost looking more like a bracelet than a true watch. It had gold links for a band, and its face had a filigree pattern that glittered in the light. I often found watches boring and utilitarian, but this was beautiful. He handed it to me, and I held it up to get a better look. I could shape-shift any jewelry I wanted onto me, but something manmade— something given as a gift—always had more meaning.

"Where did you get this?" I asked. "Did you steal it?"

He scoffed. "Figures. I do something nice, and you have to question it."

"Sorry," I said, feeling a tiny bit bad. That had been pretty ungrateful of me. "But you can't tell me this is part of your normal budget, not with the business you get."

"I told you, I had a good streak last night. And since you weren't around for a night on the town, I figured I'd show you my undying affection some other way. Now, are you going to say thank you, or are you going to keep bitching me out?"

"Thank you," I said. I fastened the watch onto my wrist and admired the way it looked against my tanned skin.

"Maybe you'll be easier to find now—or at least be on time."

I grinned. "Oh, this wasn't affection. This was pragmatism."

"Nah. A little of both. I wanted to get you jewelry, but necklaces and rings are too sappy." He held up his own wrist. "Only thing that didn't make me want to throw up."

"And they say there's no romance left in this world," I laughed.

He gently reached out and touched the watch, tracing a circle around my wrist. Then, his hand trailed up my arm and along the edge of my blouse's V-neck, letting him slip his fingers underneath it. Slowly, carefully, he moved over to one of my breasts, his fingertips dancing around the edges of my nipple, which already stood up hard under the thin fabric. He circled the nipple, pressure increasing, until he finally pinched it between his fingers, squeezing it so unexpectedly hard that I gave a small gasp of surprise.

"Whoa, you don't waste any time," I said. "You give a gift, and thirty seconds later, it's a free-for-all?"

His eyes were hungry and intense now, reminding me of storm clouds. "I've missed you," he said. "I keep thinking I'll get used to you . . . that you'll stop being so sexy. But it never happens."

Impromptu or not, I felt my own lust stirring. We hadn't been together in a while, and there was a big difference between sleeping with strangers and with those you were close to. He wrapped one hand in my hair, holding it tight, not caring if it hurt me or not. Domination and power, the ability to inflict pain if he wanted, always turned him on, and I had gotten used to this game. He jerked me to him and pressed his lips against my neck as I tilted my head back. His breath was hot against my skin as his teeth grazed me. Meanwhile his hands reached out and grasped the sides of my blouse, ripping it open. A couple of buttons scattered across the floor.

Heat was building between my legs, and I moved closer as his hands closed around the cups of my black satin bra. He pushed the edges of it down so that my breasts spilled over the tip, then pinched both nipples down, nails digging in. I moaned again, and while I really wasn't into pain, I always liked the way he mingled it with pleasure. Satisfied at my reaction, he moved his hands down to his jeans and unfastened them, pulling them and his boxers down partway, revealing the erection that had been straining against the fabric.

He gripped my shoulders and shoved me down to the floor, needing no words to make his wishes apparent.

I didn't hesitate. He leaned back against the couch, and I

took him into my mouth, letting him fill it up and nearly touch the back of my throat. My lips slid back and forth on him as his hands tangled in my hair, pulling hard. I sucked more urgently, letting my tongue dance and tease as I moved. He'd been hard when I started, but he swelled even more as I brought him in and out of me.

"Harder," he grunted.

I met his eyes, which were filled with a primal desire that exalted in putting me in such a submissive role. I sucked him harder and faster, my lips hitting his body over and over as they glided along that hard length. His breathing became heavier, his moans louder. I felt him grow in my mouth until it seemed like I couldn't take anymore. He suddenly shifted forward to the edge of the couch, letting him thrust his hips forward and take control. Still holding my shoulders, he shoved himself into me, fucking my mouth as hard as he could. I gave a surprised muffled grunt that seemed to turn him on further.

Then, with a great groan, he gave one last hard thrust and abruptly pulled out so that he came half in me and half on me. It left my skin and breasts warm and sticky. Still gasping, he pulled me up and ran his hands all over my body, uncaring of the increasing mess. His fingertip traced the edges of my lips, and I kissed it.

A look of supreme satisfaction crossed his features. Still keeping me standing, he slid a hand between my thighs and up my skirt. His fingers slipped under my panties, thrusting deep within me. He exhaled with pleasure.

"God, you're wet. Kind of wish I'd fucked you now."

I kind of wished that too, but his fingers were going a long way to make up for that. I burned and ached for his touch, having grown more aroused than I'd expected to. He slid his fingers out of me, then moved them up to my clit and the center of my desire. He stroked and encircled, and I felt heat build up, ready to explode. I leaned forward, resting my hands on his shoulders where he sat. This put my breasts right in his face, and he leaned forward, sucking hard on one of them, teeth nipping at that sensitive skin. It wasn't going to take much to make me come.

He pulled his mouth and fingers back at the same time. I whimpered, wanting—needing—him to touch me again.

"You want that? You want me to get you off?" His voice was soft and menacing.

"Yes . . ."

"Beg me," he said menacingly. "Beg me to."

"Please," I begged, my body arching back, straining to get closer to him. "Please . . ."

His fingers and mouth returned, and like that, I exploded. The orgasm made my body spasm as I struggled to stay upright. My knees and legs were weak, but I knew if I collapsed, he wouldn't be able to touch me anymore, and I wanted his fingers to keep stroking me as I came, bringing me to further and further heights of ecstasy.

Finally, when I couldn't take it anymore, I gave in to my trembling muscles. I sank to the ground and rested my head against his knee. His hand found my hair, stroking it gently this time. The couch made for an uncomfortable respite, so we retired to my bedroom and collapsed onto the bed.

Sighing, Dante lay back against the covers and half-pulled the sheet over him. I hadn't taken up much energy from him, but he still wore the exhausted, blissfully lethargic look of so many men after sex. I didn't feel particularly wiped out, and upon realizing I'd left my cigarettes in the other room, I promptly climbed out of bed to retrieve them.

"I almost believed it this time," he said when I reached the doorway.

"Hmm?" I asked, pausing and glancing back.

"That you were into it," he explained. "I almost believed you were."

I narrowed my eyes. "Are you accusing me of faking?"

"No, you never fake. But that doesn't mean you're always into it either. Sometimes I get the feeling you sleep with me simply because you've got nothing else better to do."

"That's not true," I said. "There are plenty of guys better than you."

He crooked me a smile. "But none who are as convenient or who can provide the illusion of a regular partner and bed warmer."

"Man, you sure do know how to ruin the afterglow."

"Nah, I'm just being realistic, that's all. I don't mind you using me." His joking aside, I could see the underlying affection. Bitter and cynical he might be, but the look he gave me was filled with sincere caring.

I rolled my eyes. "I'm not using you." But as I walked off to the living room, I wasn't sure if I believed that myself.

Chapter 7

"**M**ore Timbits?"

I shook my head for the third time. If I'd learned anything about the Satanists—excuse me, the Army of Darkness—in my breakfast meeting with them two days later, it was that they really liked donuts. A lot. They kept trying to force food on me and seemed particularly fond of the aforementioned Timbits, which were like donut holes except with a cuter name.

"No thanks."

After the donuts, a large part of the meeting focused on me. They all wanted to know who I was, where I'd come from, how my own group operated, etc. I spun lies out as fast as I could, rapidly building up a backstory for my Seattle Satanist group. The Army listened eagerly, and I hoped I'd be able to remember everything I was saying if quizzed afterward.

"You'll just have to come visit us sometime," I said, hoping to allay the questions. "That's the only way you'll really understand. For now, I mean, Kristin wanted me to come here to talk about *you* guys."

The mention of Kristin sobered them up. Evan nodded. "Georgina thinks we maybe need to expand our activities."

There were six total gathered here, the truly "active" members. They ranged from 20s to 40s in age, and like Evan, they had that same sort of pleasant demeanor that was more suited to helping you pick out a DVD player or lawn mower than sacrifice a goat. Maybe it was just a Canadian thing. One of the members, a tiny blond college student named Allison, frowned. "But why? We're already doing what the Angel wants."

They all looked at me, and I saw conflict on their faces. I'd slept with a man far more moral than Dante last night and was in the full throes of succubus charisma. I could tell it affected them. It was part of why they were so intrigued by me, and it would give me leverage here. Yet, I also realized, no matter how powerful they thought Kristin was and no matter how much they respected her endorsement of me, I was still an outsider and not necessarily to be trusted, appealing or not. Again, I marveled at the strength of their conviction.

"Well, I don't want you guys to stop . . ." That was, of course, exactly what I wanted. "But most of what you're doing is scaring people." That wasn't exactly true, but how else could I describe it? "It seems like now that you've established yourselves, you should use that strength to start influencing people toward the Angel's will. Surely you'll best do his—*her* bidding by actually leading people into darkness." I made eye contact with each person as I spoke, smiling and putting as much coaxing charm as I could into my voice.

A guy with a shaved head, whose name I'd forgotten, popped a chocolate glazed Timbit into his mouth and chewed thoughtfully. "That makes sense."

Allison didn't agree. "If that's what the Angel wanted us to do, we would know. Right now, we need to keep doing just as we have. We *are* getting strong, and we need to make sure that strength doesn't wane in the face of our enemies."

I forced myself to keep smiling. These people didn't understand anything, let alone their so-called enemies. I turned toward Evan and looked at him through lowered lashes. "Why settle for one goal, though? Evan, I thought you of all people really wanted to make this group great. I thought you wanted to bring more souls to the Angel's side."

"That's what we're already doing," argued Allison. She didn't seem to like me using the come-hither eyes on Evan.

For his part, Evan didn't like being caught between us. He started to stammer out something but was interrupted by the shaved-head guy.

"How?" he asked Allison.

She frowned. "What do you mean, Blake? How what?"

"How are we bringing more souls to the Angel's side?"

"By striking out at those who deny her greatness."

"Yeah . . ." Blake frowned and finished eating another Timbit. "But I don't think doing that is bringing more souls to our side."

"Are you questioning what we've done?"

"No, I stand by it all. It's just . . ." Blake shrugged. "It seems like the things we're doing aren't really swaying souls toward the Angel. If anything, it's just making them take a harder stand against us." Finally! Finally someone got it. I could have kissed Blake. Maybe I would later. "I mean, I'm not really sure the Zamboni plan is really going to darken souls. It'll just make people want to defend themselves against us. Maybe it's time to do the Angel's will through more subtle means."

"Yes," I cried. "That's exactly what I—Zamboni?"

With much enthusiasm, they explained an idea they'd come up with to spray-paint a Zamboni with Satanic messages right before it came out on the ice during a hockey game. Still keeping that idiotic smile on my face, I said in a level voice, "I think maybe you should reconsider that."

Debate went on for the next hour or so. I was a bit dismayed that I hadn't swayed them all to my point of view immediately, but I'd sent enough ripples through them to make a difference. No matter what they claimed, none of them were really sure what exactly the Angel did want, of course, and while some were comfortable in their rut, others were starting to grasp my logic. I took it as a great sign of victory that when we finally got up to go, they'd decided against taking any action—say, like, the Zamboni plan—until they'd met again.

As we walked out of the restaurant, I caught up with Blake.

I'd decided Evan was a lost cause. Blake seemed to be the smartest of the group, and I thought it might be time for a leadership change. With a little help, it wouldn't take much to topple Evan.

"Hey," I said, beaming at Blake. "I really liked what you had to say. Are you busy right now? Maybe we could talk some more."

He smiled back at me, genuinely interested. I probably wouldn't have even needed any succubus glamour to convince him. "I wish I could . . . but I have to go to work. Are you free later tonight? Like after dinner?"

"Sure." We swapped numbers, and as we were about to part, I asked in a low voice, "You don't think they'll do something anyway, do you? Despite what they said about . . . you know, putting the Zamboni plan on hold?"

His grin broadened. "No, they won't do the Zamboni plan. I'm sure of it."

"How?"

"Because they're out of spray paint."

"So they'll get more."

He shook his head. "Not without me. I'm their supplier. I work at Home Depot."

I again found myself with time to kill in Vancouver. It was a beautiful day, and the temperature was unseasonably warm for April. So, I went and walked along the waterfront. The water seemed bluer than our own Puget Sound back in Seattle, but maybe that was just because the weather tended to be sunnier here. I wandered through Stanley Park afterward and then finally meandered back to my hotel. As I did, I again passed one of the T-shirt shops. They'd changed their display and now showed a shirt with a U.S. map on it that read: *Dear Canada, Please Invade.*

Back in my room, I booted up my laptop to check my e-mail. There were a few from the bookstore's mailing list that I ignored, as well as the usual spam. Along with those messages, I had one from greygoose.com's mailing list, a picture of a cat with some nonsensical caption that Cody had forwarded me, and a letter from Maddie.

It was a mass e-mail she'd sent out this morning. It read: *Hey, guys! I decided to start a blog. Check it out.* A link followed. Even though every instinct told me not to, I clicked it.

Should have listened to those instincts.

Pictures of her and Seth bombarded me. They'd gone to the Seattle Aquarium last night and taken assorted photos posing by puffins, squids, and other sea creatures. Worse, Seth's nieces were with them. That nearly killed me. Seth had five adorable blond nieces, ranging from four to fourteen. I loved them to pieces, and breaking up with him had been like breaking up with them too. The girls all looked reasonably happy, and I wondered if they even remembered me. Well, of course they did. It hadn't been *that* long. But I knew I'd keep fading from their minds until eventually, I was just some vague memory of their uncle's ex.

I shut down the laptop and decided to head down to the hotel's bar.

It wasn't quite dinnertime, so the place was fairly deserted. I took a seat at the bar near the television and promptly made friends with the bartender. Three gimlets later, I'd also made friends with an older couple visiting from San Francisco and some businessmen in town from Winnipeg. We were laughing about a recent movie when the TV suddenly changed from a curling match to static. The bartender pushed buttons on the remote ineffectually.

"What's going on?" he demanded.

A few moments later, the picture returned, but this time it was on a different channel, one showing a local news program. My smile faded, and my stomach sank.

"No," I breathed.

The camera crew was reporting from Queen Elizabeth Park, another gorgeous area in the city that I'd briefly considered going to after Stanley Park. I wondered if I might have seen this atrocity and been able to stop it if I had visited.

The Army of Darkness had staged a demonstration there

late that afternoon. I counted about ten of them, so they must have recruited some of their auxiliary members. They were clothed in robes and hoods made out of cheap black and purple velvet, but I recognized two figures that looked suspiciously like Evan and Allison. Some of them held signs with pentagrams and assorted "evil" slogans while they walked around chanting something I couldn't make out. One of them had stuck a pole in the ground with a giant rubber goat mask on top of it. The mask wasn't affixed very well and kind of hung off to the side, making it look more like a mutant goat than an emblem of Hell. The footage showed a crowd gathered around and, later, police coming to break everything up.

I quickly charged the drinks to my room and sprinted off, pulling out my cell phone as I did.

"Blake? This is Georgina."

He groaned. "I know, I know. I just found out."

"What the hell happened? They said they weren't going to do anything. *You* said they weren't going to do anything."

"I didn't think they would!" He sounded sincerely upset. "I was at work until about a half-hour ago. I had no idea—honest. They did it on their own. I guess a bunch of them got arrested. Evan, Joy, and Crystal made it out, though."

I sighed and canceled our plans for tonight. I had to do damage control before Cedric or one of his associates came after me—and I knew for a fact they would.

I drove over to Evan's house. He answered the door, still wearing the robe but not the hood. His face was radiant and excited. "Georgina! Did you see the news? Did you see what we did?"

"Yes!" I pushed him back inside, closing the door behind me before any of the neighbors could see him. "What happened? You said you wouldn't do anything else until we met again! What happened to influencing people for the greater goo—evil?"

He finally caught on that I didn't share his excitement. "You don't think we influenced people?"

"I think you influenced some people to think you were

freaks. A bunch of churches are probably going to have sermons tomorrow about staying pure and true or something like that."

Evan flounced onto his couch, speculative but still glowing with the rush of their stunt. "No, this was powerful. Its effects will be far reaching."

Far reaching enough to get me smote, no doubt. "What happened? What made you decide to do it? Had you been planning it all along?"

"No. It was just decided—a couple of hours after we met."

"But why?" I asked, frustrated.

"Because the Angel told us to."

"But you said you wouldn't!"

He looked at me like I was crazy. "But the Angel told us to. We *had* to obey her."

I started to argue the idiocy of that and then paused to reconsider something I hadn't given credence to before. "Are you saying the Angel actually spoke to you?"

"Yes, of course. How else would we know what she wants?"

An uneasy feeling came over me. This whole time, when they'd spoken of doing what the Angel "wanted," I'd assumed it was in the way so many religious zealots presumed they understood their deity's desires. Those who said their deity spoke to them were usually crazy.

"Does she, like, speak to you in dreams?"

"No," he said. "She appeared to me. Right here. Well, over there, actually. By the TV."

"The Angel appears to you," I said flatly. "In the flesh. Shows up and tells you what to do?"

"Of course. How else do you think we'd know?"

That uneasy feeling increased. "What does she look like?"

Evan sighed, a dreamy expression filling his features. "Oh, Georgina. She's beautiful. So beautiful. She glows—she's almost hard to look at. Her hair—it's like a cloak of gold, and her eyes . . ." He sighed again. "I can't describe them. Like all the colors in the rainbow."

My phone rang just then, interrupting his similes. I didn't

recognize the number, but it was a Vancouver area code. "Hello?"

It was Cedric. "If you are not in my office in ten minutes," he said. "I will come and bring you here. And you won't like it."

I shoved my phone into my purse and stood up. "Evan, I've gotta run. Look, if the Angel talks to you again, can you give me a heads up next time?"

He turned hesitant. "Um, maybe."

I paused at the door. "What's that supposed to mean?"

"Well, you see . . . Don't take this the wrong way, but she told us not to tell you. She said to keep this to the inner circle. Probably she just needs to get to know you better."

That sent my mind reeling, but Cedric's words had a greater impact at the moment. I had no time to argue against an entity that might or might not be real. "We'll talk about this later."

I sped over to the Financial District, not bothering to count the minutes for fear of what I'd find. Nothing happened to me by the time I reached Cedric's office, so I assumed I'd made it. Kristin wasn't in the reception area, but his door was open.

"Get in here," Cedric barked.

My heart pounding, I walked into his office.

His face was filled with rage, and if I'd had any thoughts that his mild manner made him seem undemonlike, that idea was immediately banished. He clenched his fists as he glared at me, and I thanked whatever luck I had that he had remained sitting and didn't throw me across the room. Meekly, I slid into my usual chair.

"What are you doing?" he demanded. "Or rather, what *aren't* you doing?" He pointed to his computer screen. It didn't have Wikipedia on it for a change. Instead, it showed pictures of the demonstration for a local paper's website. "You were supposed to stop this kind of thing! Did Jerome send you here to sabotage me *and* spy?"

"No! They did this without telling me. I'd actually convinced them this morning not to do this other thing with a Zamboni, and then they went behind my back because their Angel of Darkness allegedly spoke to them."

As quickly as I could, I recapped the day's events and conversation. When I finished, his glower hadn't changed. He still clearly didn't believe me.

"Jerome said you were good, but I had no idea you were *this* good. You manipulated this group right under my nose."

"No," I repeated. "I'll swear to you by whatever you want. I tried to stop them."

He continued as though I hadn't spoken. "I am going to get shit for this from everyone. Our own people are going to come down on me—in addition to making me a laughing-stock. And eventually, the other side is going to raise an eyebrow too. They don't like this kind of overt attack."

The other side. Heaven. The angels.

Angels . . .

"Who's your counterpart here?" I asked. "Among the angels. There must be an archangel here too, right?"

The question caught him off-guard enough that his pissed-off look momentarily lifted. "Of course. Her name's Isabelle. Why?"

"Well . . . Evan and the others keep saying they're directed by an angel. All this time you thought they were just worshipping some all-purpose Satanic ideal. But what if a *real* angel is controlling them? I mean, Jerome's given up the fight with you. If anyone had reason to give you shit, it wouldn't be our side. It'd be theirs."

Cedric was silent for several moments. "This isn't their style. It's not Isabelle's either. I've known her for a long time." When greater immortals said "a long time," they usually weren't kidding.

"Is she blond?"

"Yes, but that doesn't mean anything. We can look like anything we want. Someone appearing to this group—and I don't think anyone is—could easily make themselves blond or bald or whatever. I think you're trying to shift the blame off yourself and Jerome."

"I'm not! Look, I don't want to get mired in any of this. I just want to finish my job and go home. And if you ask me, I think someone's trying to work you over and send you looking in the wrong places." Good Lord. I sounded like everyone else now. Soon I'd be telling him he was "getting played."

"Isabelle wouldn't do it," he maintained. "We're friends . . . well, kind of."

It was funny that demons lied and betrayed each other all the time, yet he somehow stood by the character of someone who was technically his enemy. I understood it, though. Jerome maintained a similarly bizarre friendship with Seattle's archangel, Carter.

"Can you get me in touch with her?"

Cedric regarded me in amazement. "You're really going to run with this?"

"I'm not sabotaging you—but I want to find out who is."

"That's a lot of work just to take the attention off yourself."

I simply looked at him, maintaining as determined a look as I could in the hopes that he'd believed me. I also hoped the taboo demons maintained about messing with the employees of other demons would hold. Apparently it did because he said at last, "I'll show you how to contact her, as pointless as that is."

I exhaled the breath I'd been holding. "Thank you."

He shook his head. "But don't think you're in the clear. I'm still going to be watching you."

Chapter 8

Grace called me that night while I was on my way to talk to Isabelle.

"Hello, Georgina. This is Grace."

I waited patiently for Mei's complementary greeting. When it didn't come, I asked in surprise, "It's just you? Not Mei?"

Grace's voice, while as flat as usual, held the tiniest puzzled note in it. "Why would Mei be here?"

It apparently hadn't occurred to her that I had *never* received a call or a visit from either of them alone. They always functioned as a unit, kind of giving the impression that the fabric of the universe might rip open if they were ever apart. This was as weird as them nearly accepting coffee the other day.

"Never mind. What's up?"

"Jerome wanted me to tell you that he is . . . pleased."

"Over what?"

"Over you successfully embarrassing Cedric."

"But I didn't—" I bit my lip, suddenly wondering if I should be so quick to deny my involvement. Jerome hadn't been happy with me recently. While the stupid spectacle at Queen Elizabeth Park had put me on Cedric's shit list, it might very well take me off Jerome's and hasten my permanent return to Seattle. I stayed silent.

"He's glad you took his talk to heart," Grace continued. "Although, he does wish to remind you that you being sent to Cedric is supposed to be a gesture of good will. So try not to be too efficient. Jerome encourages you to keep up with these small jabs but to remember that you do ultimately want this group undone."

I sighed. "Noted."

Grace disconnected. Great. This was all I needed. Jerome thought I was guilty too—of trying to score extra credit with him.

Cedric had told me I could find Isabelle at a jazz club a few miles from my hotel. It was over on a street lined with clubs and bars, and the excitement and energy in the air as I walked toward Isabelle's hangout was palpable. It was Saturday night, after all, and the streets teemed with humans eager and excited for life and love. I couldn't see their souls or energy the way an imp like Hugh could, but I didn't need to. It was apparent in the way they moved and talked and eyed each other for potential hook-ups. Even after my recent tryst, being in this electric atmosphere made me itch for another conquest. I'd have to cruise these clubs once I'd concluded business with Isabelle.

The jazz club was small and dark, exactly the way you expected such places to be. All the tables were filled, and lots of people stood by the bar or along the wall. I didn't have any trouble finding Isabelle, though. The signature of a greater immortal filled up a place like this. Hers made me think of sunlight shining through crystals, fracturing into sparkles of color.

She sat alone at a corner table. Most obviously single women in there were being hit on—in fact, I got a number of appraising looks as I walked through—but no one other than the wait staff seemed to notice Isabelle. It reminded me of how no one ever noticed Jerome's resemblance to John Cusack. Isabelle wore a long blue dress with spaghetti straps, surprisingly risqué for an angel. Her hair was sunny blond and worn loose to her lower back—not unlike a golden cloak, I thought wryly.

She sensed me, of course, and didn't seem surprised at all when I sat down across from her. With a smile, she glanced up and crooked a finger toward the nearest waiter. He hurried over and took my gimlet order. Once he was gone, Isabelle turned her attention on me.

"So. Jerome's succubus."

Cedric had called me the same thing when we first met. I kind of resented my identity being based on my association with—or rather, possession by—someone else.

"Yeah," I said. She watched me pleasantly, neither cold nor friendly. With angels, you never knew which extreme you might get. Mostly, she looked curious, so I figured I could get right down to business. "So I—"

"Shh."

"Wh—"

She held up her hand, dark eyes focusing on something beyond me. The band was in the middle of a song, and the trumpet player had just put the instrument to his lips. A long, high note came out, kicking off what turned into a mournful solo. When he finished a minute or so later, I turned back to Isabelle and saw the waiter had brought my gimlet. The angel's face was alight with wonder—and wistfulness.

"Did you hear that?" she asked me. "Those notes weren't complicated, yet he managed to put so much into them. His heart, his emotions, his soul. A world of sorrow, exquisite agony . . . all in those few notes." She took a sip of her wine. "You can't do that. Not even I can do that—not the way he did."

Her words surprised me, but I knew exactly what she meant. Part of the reason I was always a little in awe of Seth's books was because he, as a mortal, had a talent that an immortal like me never could possess. "Only humans have the gift of creation," I murmured.

Her eyebrows rose slightly, and she smiled. "Yes, exactly. So tell me, what can I do for you, Jerome's succubus?"

I felt a little weird interrogating her now. There was something a little sad and vulnerable about her that made her appealing. Nonetheless, I pushed forward. Angels and demons came from the same stock. Both were good at making you believe what they wanted. "You . . . you know about those so-called Satanists, right? The Army of Darkness?"

Isabelle's smile twitched. "Great movie, silly cult. Did you have anything to do with their display today? I really liked the goat mask."

I shook my head. "Actually, I was wondering if you had anything to do with it."

"Me?" She laughed. "I only wish I could think up things that good—but there we are again: humans and creation. Why do you ask?"

"Because they say they're being directed by an angel." I gave her an abridged version of what the group had told me.

"And you assume they literally meant an angel?"

"I'm trying not to assume anything. But I think someone or something is directing them, and your side has as good a reason as any to stir up trouble for Cedric and make the authorities on all sides come down on him."

"And your side has just as good a reason. Demons try to oust each other all the time."

I tapped my nails along my glass's edge and eyed her warily. "And you haven't actually answered my question," I pointed out. "You haven't directly denied being involved." Angels couldn't technically lie, but oh, they were masters at not always telling the truth.

Isabelle finished off her wine and smiled at me again. "Oh, you are delightful. This is just like being on a TV cop show. No wonder Carter likes you so much."

I sighed in exasperation, realizing I was going to get nowhere. Fucking angels.

Her grin dimmed a little, but she was still clearly amused. "Look, Georgina," she said. She knew my name; no real surprise. "I like you. You're clever and endearing, but here's how it is: I don't want to see Cedric leave Vancouver. I like him. And anyway, that saying about keeping your enemies close is true. I know him, I understand him. And when you're playing a game like ours, the better you know the pieces on the board, the better you'll do. I don't want to have to live with an archdemon I don't know, one who's a lot more unpleasant than he is." A new glass of wine had been delivered, and she paused to take a sip. "And that's the truth."

I didn't know what to say. I wanted to believe her but had no idea if I could. I simply sighed again.

"What are you thinking?" she asked.

"I wish I could believe you when you say you aren't involved. Even with the whole not-lying thing, I don't know that I can. I don't think that I can trust anyone."

"That," she said firmly, "is absolutely something I agree with: you can't trust anyone. On any side. Everyone's got their own agenda, and there's something in the air right now—it's like a building storm, to use a cliché. Be careful." Her face looked momentarily troubled, and then she relaxed again as her attention returned to the stage. "Ah, the soloist is back."

I slid my empty glass to the center of the table. I started to take out some cash too, but she waved it away. "Thanks for talking," I told her, rising from my chair. Suddenly, I hesitated. "You mentioned Carter. I don't suppose . . . I don't suppose you know where he's been lately?"

I'd never thought I would utter those words. Carter had tormented me for years with his unsolicited, cryptic advice. He'd particularly loved to comment about Seth and me, as though he had some special interest in our relationship. Since it had ended, I'd hardly seen Carter at all. He used to come hang out with my friends and me but had only surfaced a couple of times in the last few months.

Isabelle smiled. "He's closer than you think."

"Typical angel answer," I groaned. I turned around to leave and then yelped.

Carter stood by the club's entrance.

Abandoning Isabelle, I hurried across the crowded room. Oblivious to the dress code, Carter wore his typical grungy clothing, ratty jeans and a plain gray T-shirt. A flannel shirt was tied around his waist, and his blond hair could have handled a good washing and brushing. He smiled expectantly at my approach and stepped outside to the crowded street. I followed.

"What are you doing here?" I asked, taking out my cigarettes. I grabbed one for myself and then offered him the pack. He took one too.

"What are *you* doing here?" he returned pleasantly.

"You know what I'm doing here. Everyone knows what I'm doing here." I fumbled in my purse for my new lighter and found a matchbook instead. I pulled it out. Mark's Mad Martini Bar. I'd forgotten them.

"What's wrong?" asked Carter, noting my frown.

I shook my head. "Nothing." I traded the matches for my lighter, and we lit up. "You were lurking with your signature hidden," I continued. "Why?"

"Element of surprise," he said. "It was worth it to see your face."

We walked past the club lines and drunken groups, no clear destination in mind—at least none that I knew of. "You haven't been around in a while," I accused.

"Why, Daughter of Lilith, have you missed me?"

"No! But I was starting to feel like you were only interested in me while I was dating Seth."

"Of course not." There was a long, overly nonchalant pause. "So . . . have you talked to him lately?"

I rolled my eyes. "You *are* only interested in Seth! You're going to have to let it go, Carter. Seth and I are finished. Why can't you obsess on me and my new boyfriend instead?"

"Because you can do better."

"Everyone keeps saying that. But I'm a succubus. How much better can I do?"

"The fact that people keep telling you that should be answer enough."

"Seth broke up with *me*," I said through gritted teeth. "He doesn't want me anymore, end of story."

"Oh, come now. Do you really believe that?"

"Seeing as I was there at the break-up? Yes."

Carter tsked. "Georgina, Georgina. You're letting your

anger and other emotions cloud your reason, which is unfortunate since you're a lot smarter than people give you credit for. Go back and think. Why did Seth break up with you?"

I stared off at the far side of the street, refusing to look at him. "Because he thought if we stayed together, we'd both get hurt. That it would be better if we split, no matter how painful at the time."

"And you think that makes him a bad person?"

"Yes." I turned back toward Carter. "Because I didn't agree. I was willing to take the risk. He gave up."

"Sometimes it takes more courage to know when to retreat than to keep fighting."

"I don't think it could have taken that much courage. He ended up with Maddie pretty quickly." No matter how hard I tried, I couldn't keep the bitterness from my voice.

"That takes courage too, forcing yourself to start over with someone new, to keep moving on with your life."

"Seems more like a rebound to me."

Carter took a long drag on his cigarette. "Seth didn't leave and go to Maddie because he stopped loving you. If there were no complications in the world, you would be the one he chose. You are his ideal, his first choice."

"That's not flattering to Maddie."

"It doesn't make her less. It just means he loves her differently. And when you decide you have to move on, that's how it is. Just because things don't work out, it doesn't mean there aren't other people you can't love. Love is too big a thing for you to go without it in life."

"Oh yes," I said. "I have *so* missed these cryptic conversations."

Carter crooked me a grin. "I'm glad to see you're back to your old self."

"I've missed the sarcasm too."

"No, I'm serious. You weren't a lot of fun these last few months. You were kind of . . ."

". . . bitchy?"

He shrugged. "I don't know. You were angry and depressed and frustrated. You stopped caring about the people around you. You weren't . . . well, you."

"You don't know me or what I am."

"I know you better than you think. I know you're still hurting and think the universe has given up on you. It hasn't. I also know that as far as all this demon business is concerned, your curiosity is going to tangle you up further in something you shouldn't be involved with in the first place. Jerome," he declared, "is a fool."

"Do you know what's going on?" I asked eagerly, coming to a stop. "Who's leading that cult? Who's supposedly running this huge game that's going on that I can't see?"

"No," said Carter, expression dark. "I don't know any of that. But if I were you, I'd get back to Seattle soon. Stay close to Jerome."

"He hates me right now."

"No, he doesn't. Stay close to him. He'll protect you. If he can't . . . well, I will. If I can."

There was nothing romantic in his offer of protection. It wasn't spoken with chivalrous fierceness. His manner was uneasy, like he was dealing with a last resort. I also couldn't help but replay his last words: *if I can*. Angels—or demons—didn't use the word "if" very often.

"What do you mean if—"

"Go back home, Daughter of Lilith." He tipped his head back to stare at the night sky, blew smoke into the air, and then looked down at me with his silvery gray eyes. "We'll talk soon."

He dropped the cigarette to the sidewalk and vanished.

I glanced around, worried someone had seen us, but we'd walked far from the partiers. I stamped out the cigarette, turned, and headed back in the direction of all the nightlife to go find some guys I'd noticed checking me out. A night with drunken men might still leave me feeling hollow, but at least their motives were easier to understand than angels'.

Chapter 9

I was starting to envy the teleportation that higher immortals used. I'd always complained about it in the past (it tended to be a bit disorienting), but suddenly, a spot of dizziness seemed trivial compared to doing the Vancouver-Seattle drive yet again. Annoying or not, I was anxious to talk to Jerome, so as soon as Cedric gave me leave to go home the next day, I hit the road back to the States.

Isabelle had seemed convincing enough in denying her role in the Army's shenanigans, and both Carter and Cedric seemed certain she wasn't involved either. I couldn't dismiss any leads here, however, not when my permanent return to Seattle was on the line and certainly not when someone was actually messing with Seattle itself. Isabelle might truly be innocent, but I wasn't going to shut the door on this until I'd run it by Jerome.

"It seems like you're here more than you are there," noted Hugh when I called to tell him I was back in town. "Doesn't really seem like you're being punished all that much."

"Punishment's subjective. Do you know where Jerome's at?"

"Last I knew, he was meeting someone."

"The Cellar?"

"Mmm, no . . . that new bar in Capitol Hill. Clement's."

"Is he going to be mad if I show up while he's at a lunch meeting?"

"If he doesn't want to be interrupted, you won't be able to find him."

Fair point. Without going home, I drove straight to Capitol Hill, finding street parking that wasn't actually too far from Cody and Peter's apartment. Clement's was a new place that had gone in recently, a bit sleeker and trendier than the Cellar, which was a divey haunt in Pioneer Square we immortals often frequented. Clement's had the same upscale feel and designer drink menu that Mark's had had, and I had a hard time convincing myself that a drink probably wasn't the best idea while I was here in the midst of demonic business.

I spotted Jerome right away. He was at a back table, facing the doorway. His eyes met mine as I approached, my signature declaring my presence, just as his came through to me. Only, his wasn't the only immortal aura there. I recognized the bearer's identity before the woman seated across from him even turned around.

Nanette.

I came to a stop by their table, speechless more from surprise than fear. Jerome and Nanette together? When had this come about? There was a sly smile on her face, like she was in on some joke the rest of us weren't. She had on another cute sundress, lavender silk that looked great with her blond hair, though the spring weather didn't quite seem warm enough for it yet. Of course, when you were a demon, I supposed the fires of Hell kept you warm.

"Georgie," said Jerome, not unpleasantly, "it seems like you're here more than you are in Vancouver."

"Cedric sent me home. He doesn't seem to want me around if I'm not doing something specific."

Nanette chuckled and paused to take a drink of what looked like a Lemon Drop martini. "I imagine so, after that spectacle yesterday. Brilliant work, I might add."

I grimaced, deciding to out myself and risk losing Jerome's regard. "I actually didn't have anything to do with that. They did it without telling me."

Jerome didn't seem to mind. "That footage is all over YouTube. I've watched it a hundred times."

This whole thing was so confusing. Jerome ostensibly wanted me to help Cedric unravel the cult, yet my boss clearly took great pleasure in seeing the progress stall out. Again I felt like I was missing a piece of the picture here, making me even less secure about my position.

"Look," I said. "I don't want to interrupt your drinks. I'd just been hoping to chat with Jerome, but I can find you later."

Nanette downed her martini and stood up. "No, no. We're finished here. Have my seat."

I was hesitant, but she was insistent, and Jerome didn't appear to be too put out at her departure. She walked out of the bar like a normal human, not bothering with any elaborate teleportation—at least not while others could see her. He gestured toward her chair, and I sat down.

"So, what can I do for you, Georgie?" Jerome was drinking brandy, something more suited to a night by the fire than a Sunday afternoon.

"You were hanging out with Nanette?" I asked, momentarily putting Isabelle on hold.

"As you saw."

"I told you about her meeting with Cedric."

"And?"

"And, doesn't it seem weird that she's meeting with each of you behind the other's back?"

"It's not behind anyone's back," he countered. "I know she met with Cedric, and she knows I know."

Isabelle was moving farther and farther to the back burner of my mind. Suddenly, it all seemed perfectly obvious. Isabelle had denied being the angel because she didn't want her situation to change. Nanette, however, did want change. She wanted to stop feeling like Cedric and Jerome were eyeing her territory and squeezing her between them. She'd claimed her meeting with Cedric was defensive on her part, yet I couldn't help but wonder if she might be more on the offensive than any of us realized.

"Georgie," said Jerome dryly. "I can see those wheels in your head spinning. What are you thinking?"

Starting with the meeting at Tim Hortons, I gave Jerome a full report of my experiences with the Army and the theories I'd put together about the Angel of Darkness being a literal angel—Isabelle.

"Ridiculous," said Jerome. "It's not her."

"You sound just as certain as Cedric did."

He shrugged, almost looking embarrassed to have agreed with his rival. "Because she's not running any cult. I've met her. She's not the type."

"Well, I'm actually starting to agree." I took a deep breath and pushed forward. "I don't suppose it's occurred to either of you that Nanette could be the one behind this?"

Jerome's face grew even more incredulous. "Nanette? Georgie, this is out there, even for you."

"What, demons eyeing each other's territories? Come on, Jerome. That's not out there at all! It's what you and Cedric were—maybe still are—doing for each other. If something blows up, Nanette's in a far better position to benefit from it than Isabelle would. Nanette's running to both of you, claiming she's worried about the other when really, she's playing you both off each other."

Jerome rolled the brandy in his glass. "And let me guess: she's blond too, like this alleged golden-haired angel."

"Well . . ."

He sighed, took a last swig of the brandy, and set the glass down hard. "Not that I have any reason to explain our goings-on to you, but here it is. Nanette doesn't have the balls to try something like that. Oh, sure, some of your points are correct. This wouldn't be unreasonable demon behavior, particularly one feeling threatened. But not her. She might want to do something like this, but she won't. She's a lot of talk but not much on action."

I didn't usually get answers that detailed from Jerome and was a bit taken aback. "You're certain?"

"I am," he said firmly. A waiter delivered a new glass of

brandy. "Leave her and Isabelle behind. Find some other reason for what this absurd group's doing. Barring that, disband them like you're supposed to. And barring *that*, do give me some credit that I can take care of my affairs without a succubus' help."

I left not long after that, leaving Jerome to drink alone. As I pushed the door open, I glanced back and studied him. His face was momentarily unguarded, troubled as he stared into the depths of his glass. He seemed very alone, literally and figuratively, despite his bold words. I felt a strange pang in my chest, a bit of sorrow over what was undoubtedly an eternity of torment made worse when complications like our current ones ensued. But then, maybe these bursts of demonic drama helped break up the monotony.

I considered errands after that but decided heading straight home sounded best. My phone rang just I stepped into my apartment. I kicked the door closed with my foot while my free hand dug through the depths of my purse. Doug's number showed on the caller ID.

"Is everything okay?" I asked as soon as I answered.

"You know what's sad here, Kincaid? You aren't asking if *I'm* okay. You saw my number, assumed there was some crisis at work, and want to know if the store's okay."

"Your point?"

"The store's fine. I wanted to know if you're in town. Maddie made it sound like you can cross time and space now and be everywhere all the time."

"I wish I could, but yeah, I'm at home. What's up?"

"You going to Casey's party?"

"Casey's what?" Even as I spoke the words, I remembered Casey pulling me aside in the store and asking if I'd attend her graduation party. "Ugh. That's today, isn't it?"

"Yup. You want me to pick you up?"

"Doug, I don't think I can go. In fact, I even told her I couldn't."

"Right. Tell me right now, immediately, what you have to do instead."

"Well, I, uh—"

"Too slow. You have nothing going on."

"I'm just not in a party mood."

"The beauty of that is that when people aren't in party moods, that's actually when they need a party the most."

"Doug—"

"Come on! How can you not acknowledge the achievements of some brainiac math major who's graduating early, for fuck's sake?"

"Latvian."

"What?"

"Math and Latvian. Dual majors."

"You're making my point for me. It would be sad and wrong if we didn't help her celebrate. She overcame a life of adversity, coming to this country in the hopes of making a better life for herself and her family."

"Doug, she's, like, fourth generation. Her dad's a neurosurgeon."

"Come on! Maddie's gotta stay and close, so I have no one to go with. That, and it's kind of creepy how I've been going to social events with my sister lately. I need you to make me look like a man again."

"Doug—"

"See you in five minutes, Kincaid."

I knew how Doug could be in these moods. He wasn't kidding about showing up in five minutes, and he was also right that I had nothing else to do. With so little time, I simply shapeshifted into a plain gray skirt and black blouse that seemed appropriate for a graduation party. While rustling around for a blank card that I could stick a check into, I dialed Dante to let him know I was in town and to see if he wanted to come with us. Like usual lately, I went to his voice mail. What was it with me and unreliable men? I'd had trouble getting a hold of Seth when we dated because he was always caught up writing. Now I had trouble getting a hold of Dante because . . . well, because he was unreliable. I left Casey's address with the message and hurried to get ready. I'd wanted to wear

Dante's watch but couldn't find it before Doug showed up—honestly, it had been more like four minutes—so I ended up just running out the door without accessories.

Casey's family lived over in Clyde Hill, a beautiful lakeside suburb befitting a neurosurgeon's family. The party had been going on for about an hour when we arrived, and we found their expansive backyard filled with music, food, and people. Dusk was falling, and the soft glow of lanterns strung along trees and the fence line gave everything a sort of elfin mystique. We paused at the yard's entry, assessing our surroundings and looking for others we knew.

"This is kind of wholesome for me," Doug noted. "There are kids here."

"Of course there are. This is a graduation party, not one of your after-show keggers."

"Oh, hey," he said brightly. "There's a bartender. Looks like this'll be tolerably wholesome."

Casey found us getting drinks and threw her arms around both of us in a massive double hug. "Oh! You guys came! Thanks so much." She was aglow with excitement and energy and could barely stay still. She accepted my card with another hug, told us to let her know if we needed anything, and then dashed off when she saw her great aunt from Idaho arrive.

"Wow. All this kind of makes me wish I'd stayed in college," Doug mused. A few of our coworkers waved at us from the far side of the yard, and we began winding our way toward them.

"Yup. You could have had all this fun waiting for you after school."

He grimaced. "The problem is, I was having all this fun *during* school."

The other bookstore staff were happy to see us, and we all fell into comfortable conversation that varied from the party itself to shop talk from work. Casey's family had spared no expense, and waiters came around with various types of finger food. None of us had eaten dinner, so we practically devoured the trays and probably looked like savages in our corner.

I was contemplating a second drink when Beth suddenly said, "Oh, hey. Seth and Maddie are here."

I stiffened. One of the reasons I'd answered the door when Doug came to pick me up was that he'd said Maddie was closing. Knowing I'd get a reprieve from her and Seth had made this prospect bearable, but apparently, there'd been some sort of incorrect intel afoot.

I did an immediate 180, hoping I had misheard Beth. Nope. There they were: Seth and Maddie. Worse, Seth's little niece Kayla was with them. She was the youngest of his brother's girls, four years old with blue eyes and a mop of blond curls. I'd recently discovered that Kayla had the makings of a psychic and was able to sense the unseen world, much as Dante or my friend Erik could. She was a long way from having their skills or having any idea what they meant yet. For now, she was just a happy little girl—albeit a very quiet one—and seeing her with Seth and Maddie jerked painfully at my heartstrings.

"I thought you said she was closing," I hissed to Doug.

He didn't notice the upset tone in my voice and read it as surprise. "I thought so. Maybe she got Janice to do it. I know she's been giving her more and more responsibility. Makes me wonder about my own job security."

The bookstore gang greeted the newcomers with cheering. Kayla broke from her guides and, to my astonishment, ran over to me. "Georgina!"

I scooped her up, and that dark, angry serpent within me settled down a little. Not only had Kayla sought me out, she'd also spoken—a rarity. I hugged her to me, and with her in my arms, it suddenly seemed as though all had to be right in the world.

"You've got a fan, Kincaid," laughed Doug. He winked at her. She gave him a shy smile in return and then turned back to me and rested her head on my shoulder.

"She spoke," said Maddie in wonder. Maddie knew I'd

been friends with the Mortensens and thought nothing of me knowing the girls.

"An entire soliloquy," I laughed.

"We're watching her while the others are at a school play," explained Seth.

"This party's unreal," said Maddie, gazing around at all the fanfare. "Does anyone know why she dual-majored in Latvian?"

"Blow-off major?" suggested Beth.

"Anthropology and Women's Studies are blow-off majors," said Doug. "Not Latvian."

"Hey!" said Maddie, elbowing her brother. She often wrote freelance articles for feminist magazines.

"Hey, don't take it out on me. I'll never forget you taking that class called Evolution of the Dress."

"It was harder than you think!"

The rest of us watched the Sato siblings with amusement, and to my dismay, so did Seth. I guess I'd kind of hoped he'd be shooting furtive, longing glances at me. Instead, he watched Maddie almost . . . fondly. Like he found her smart and funny—which she was, of course. He was watching her the way any guy would watch his girlfriend.

"Hey," I said to Doug. "Why don't you stop annoying your sister and go get us a refill?"

"You're a bad role model for the kid," he warned. But he took my cup anyway and headed for the bar.

If anything, it seemed me holding Kayla gave Seth and Maddie a chance to be more affectionate. They held hands. So, I paid more attention to Kayla, snagging novel appetizers as they went by and explaining to her what quiche and brie were. Once Doug returned with my drink, I took it down pretty rapidly, still conscious of the fact that I held a child. When I'd finished my third, I knew enough to hand her off. Maddie took her by the hand and led her to look at a koi pond on the far side of the yard.

This left me alone with the others, and whether it was alcohol or succubus charisma or just a desire to show up Maddie,

I found myself coming to life. I joked and talked to everyone, making sure each person was included in the conversation. I saw them all light up, caught up in the aura of comfort and good cheer I created. Maybe I had ulterior motives, but despite that, I actually enjoyed myself. It had been awhile since I'd been able to just have a fun, effortless social encounter.

When Maddie returned, however, I decided it was time for my fourth drink. I headed across the yard, graceful in spite of the alcohol. While waiting in line, the guy behind me struck up conversation.

"I've seen you somewhere."

I glanced up at him. He was tall, late thirties, and had bronzed hair. I gave him a winning smile. "That's a very bad pick-up line."

"No, I'm serious." He frowned. "In the paper . . . were you in some sort of date auction?"

"Oh my God. You *do* recognize me." Through Hugh's machinations, I'd participated in a charity date auction last December. I'd ended up going for an obscene amount of money and had made the paper.

"If I remember, you did a lot for that charity."

"What can I say? I love kids."

Our turns came, and we each got new drinks. Stepping off to the side, we continued our conversation. "I don't suppose," he said, "that I'd have to pay that much for a date?"

"You're asking me out?"

"Seeing you in person? Yeah. I kind of understand the price now."

"Wow, you don't waste time on formalities."

He shrugged. "I don't have time to. Too busy with work."

Ah. One of those guys. I didn't have Hugh's ability to see souls, but something told me I wouldn't get an enormous energy fix from this guy. Of course, just then, it didn't matter. I was drunk and distressed and a sleazy guy seemed just like what I needed right then, no matter how inappropriate the setting. In fact, the inappropriateness kind of added to it.

"No, not that much. Though to tell you the truth, I'm kind

of busy myself. I don't like to waste time on something that's going to fizzle out. I'm sort of a try-before-you-buy girl."

He studied me very carefully, face serious. "What exactly do you have in mind?"

I inclined my head toward the house. "They must have a bathroom in there."

As expected, he didn't take much coaxing. The house was wide open to anyone who needed to get in there, and we passed wait staff moving in and out as we sought one of the house's many bathrooms. We finally ended up at a small one on the second floor that was adjacent to a guest room. It didn't look like it saw much use, and as soon as we shut the door, we were all over each other.

He'd told me along the way that his name was Wes and that he had some sort of corporate position in a bank down-town. I'm not sure why he was trying to impress me, seeing as I'd made this painfully easy for him, but I appreciated the weak effort anyway. My biggest concern was his relationship to the family, but it turned out he was a friend of a friend of a business associate, so I had little worry about this getting back to Casey.

My skirt came off almost immediately, followed by a rapid unbuttoning of my blouse that pulled off a button. It skit-tered across the floor, lost forever. He left the blouse itself on, simply hanging open, and ran his hands over my body, taking in the black lace bra and matching panties.

"Good God," he breathed. "You might be worth more than that auction price."

"I'm not a call girl," I snapped, irritated for some reason I couldn't entirely understand. "And make this fast. My friends are going to be waiting for me."

Wes seemed a little surprised that I wasn't fawning all over him, but he didn't argue. His pants and briefs came off next, and he grabbed a hold of my hips, tilting me so that I sat on the edge of the counter, with my body at an angle and my head and shoulders against the mirror. The counter and his height lined up perfectly, and a moment later, he was in me, neither rough nor gentle, just somewhere in the middle. It was a little boring, actually, like he couldn't quite make up his mind and take a stand.

But as he gripped my ankles and held my legs up, the pace steadily increased, and I saw sweat break out along his brow. The life energy seeping into me was moderate, just like everything else about this tryst, but compared to Dante, it was fairly significant. That energy made up for the rest of it, and when he came with a primal sort of grunt, that burst of life coursed into me in its entirety. Like fine tendrils of light, it raced through my body, reinvigorating me and making me strong.

He staggered back, and I hopped down off the counter to quickly put my clothes back on. "Wow," he gasped. "That was—"

"Do *not* say worth the money," I warned. "Particularly since you didn't pay."

He shut up, and I smiled. With a quick kiss on the cheek, I moved over to the door. "Thanks," I said. "It was fun."

He fumbled for his underwear. "You want to go out sometime?"

"Nope."

I left him to get dressed, discreetly closing the door behind me and remembering to take my drink with me. No one was upstairs, so our encounter had gone unnoticed—or so I thought. When I reached the bottom of the stairs, I nearly walked right into Seth.

"Oh my God," he said, giving me a once over. "You really did it?"

"Did what?" I asked in a saccharine voice.

"You know what. You've got that—that glow. That, and you're missing a button."

I glanced down at the guilty gap in the blouse and shapeshifted it to its former state. "There. Good as new."

He shook his head, keeping his voice low so we wouldn't be overheard. "I didn't really believe you'd do it. I saw you walk off with him and thought, 'No, she wouldn't. Not here.' So I came over and—"

"You what? Came to stop me?" I couldn't help an incredulous laugh. "Seth, what I do or don't do is none of your business."

"What about Dante? You just cheated on him."

"I cheat on *all* my boyfriends. Did you forget? It's what I do."

"You didn't need the energy fix. I could tell."

"Yeah, but I wanted the energy fix. What are you, jealous?"

"What happened to you?" he demanded, evading my question. "How did you change so much? You're better than this."

"I've always been like this. You were just too starstruck to notice."

I turned and left him, heading back out to our friends, making sure I neatened up my appearance in tiny increments as I walked. The alcohol was really kicking in at this point, but I was pretty sure I still managed to walk without looking obviously drunk. When I reached the group, Kayla gestured to be picked up again. I was a little hesitant, but she seemed so insistent that I handed my drink to Doug and lifted her into my arms again. Mercifully, I didn't fall over.

She studied me with those big blue eyes, and I wondered what she sensed. Something about her gaze affected me in a way that Seth's chastising hadn't. I felt bad for what I'd done. Dirty. Cheap.

"She sure does like you," said Maddie. "And you're great with her too. You should have kids of your own."

I ran a hand over Kayla's fine hair, recalling the dreams Nyx had sent me while she'd stolen my energy. They'd all shown an impossible future, me with a daughter and husband. "Can't," I said. "Doug would be lousy at child support."

"Oh, be quiet," he snapped back good-naturedly. I think he'd been drinking as much as me by now.

Seth returned just then and touched Maddie's arm, his expression grim. "We should head off. Terry and the others will be back, and Kayla's probably getting tired."

Maddie's face fell a little. "Already?" It was the first time in their idyllic relationship that I'd ever seen signs of clouds.

"We need to get her back," Seth reiterated mildly. "And I've got a chapter to write."

She rolled her eyes. "Ah. Now the truth comes out."

Interesting. Maddie had to put up with the same stuff I had.

"Stay," Doug told her. "I'll give you a ride."

"Yeah, like I'd trust you behind a wheel right now."

"Then you drive me and Kincaid home, and Mortensen can go now."

They all finally decided that was a good idea. As Seth and Kayla were about to go, Maddie suddenly did a double-take. "Oh! Wait. You have to give Georgina her present."

I blinked. "Present?"

Seth's face turned almost—*almost*—mischievous, though he was still clearly bothered by what had taken place in the house. "Uh, yeah. I just got a box of advanced copies of the next Cady and O'Neill book and wondered if you wanted one."

"I . . ." I stopped, unsure what to say. Maddie laughed.

"You've been the belle of the ball all night, and this is what makes you speechless?"

"Hey, it's not that easy. I mean . . . this is Cady and O'Neill. You know how I feel about them. I've sort of accepted that I wouldn't get to read their next installment until October. If I get it now, my whole universe will be thrown out of whack."

"So you don't want it?" asked Seth.

"Oh, I want it. Just seems . . . I don't know. It feels like cheating."

"They're in the car right now," teased Maddie in a sing-song voice. "Sure you don't want one?"

I looked at Seth's smile, and something weird passed between us. I could hardly believe that minutes ago, we'd been fight-

ing in the house. The looks we exchanged, the way I felt . . .
it was almost like it used to be. I hastily turned away.

"Yes," I groaned. "Of course I do."

Seth said good-bye to the rest of the bookstore gang and
tried to find Casey, but she was surrounded by a throng of
relatives. Giving up, he led me out of the yard to where he'd
parked a block or so away. Kayla was still in my arms. None
of us spoke, and it was just as well because my feelings were
all tangled up. Every post-breakup interaction between us
had been angry or painfully tense lately. Yet, in these last few
moments, things had become almost comfortable again. Was
it possible we'd ever move past this phase? Could the pain I'd
gone through with him really ease up so quickly?

He unlocked the car and got the book for me. I hoped I
didn't gape like a schoolgirl when I saw it. *All Fools Night*.
The cover showed the skyline of Washington, DC, blurred like
a Renoir painting and overlaid with dark indigo. All sorts of
warnings about it being an advanced copy and not for sale
were on it, but I paid those no heed. I didn't want to sell it. I
wanted to read it. Now.

When I dragged my eyes up from the cover, Seth regarded
me with happy amusement. "I can't believe you're really that
excited."

"Why wouldn't I be? And why are you surprised? Lots of
people love your books."

He shook his head. "Yeah . . . but it's still surreal to think
that I can write something—create something—that affects
people so strongly that they get an emotional involvement
with what I've pulled from my head. And to realize that
someone I know personally . . . knowing it affects you like
that . . . well, like I said, surreal."

The sweet, earnest look in his eyes was making butterflies
dance in my stomach, so I hastily looked back at the cover. I
almost wished we'd start fighting again. "Seth . . . why . . .
why are you doing this?"

"Giving you the book?" He was puzzled.

"No, I mean . . . being nice. And worrying about me back there."

"You don't think I'm normally nice?"

I looked back up and sighed. "You know what I mean. We've been avoiding each other since New Year's, and when we have been together, it's been disastrous. Yet, here you are bringing me this . . . I just don't understand it. Was it Maddie's idea?"

He stared at me for a long time, or at least it felt like it. A chill ran down my spine, and for a second, I felt disoriented, like I was in this time and another, reliving the same moment over again.

"No. I did it because hate shouldn't last forever," he said finally, voice soft. "Because eventually, you have to forgive. You can't just stop caring or . . ." He didn't finish the phrase. "I think we'll always have a connection, no matter where we go or what we do. And if so, I'd like us to be friends."

For the second time that night, I was speechless. There were a hundred things that would have made good responses. Telling him I agreed. Telling him I forgave him. Telling him I wanted us to be friends too. Yet, I couldn't muster those words, and I never had a chance to ponder exactly why because Kayla suddenly jerked in my arms, coming awake with wide-eyed alacrity.

"Hey," a voice called to us. We turned.

Dante was about half a block away and walking toward us. With each step, Kayla recoiled further and further from his approach. Dante's lifetime of power-seeking and wicked deeds had left a taint on him, one that Kayla could sense the way she could sense my aura. I didn't entirely know what it felt like for her, but it couldn't be good.

"Here," I said to Seth. "Trade me."

Kayla went to him eagerly, and he handed over the book just as Dante reached us. He put an arm around me and kissed my cheek. "Got your message and thought I'd come by. Hey," he said, by way of greeting to Seth.

Seth nodded back, and whatever fragile companionship he

and I had been rebuilding disappeared. Eager to distract, I employed the conversational gift I allegedly had.

"Seth was leaving and just had to get this book for me." I held it up as explanation. "How was work?"

Dante kept his arm around me in a way that was almost proprietary. He'd always regarded my past with Seth nonchalantly, but I think me being so deeply involved with someone bothered him sometimes. His eyes lighted on Kayla for a moment. She was trying so hard to keep away from him that she was practically crawling off Seth. Mortal magic and abilities varied considerably, but I imagined Dante must be able to sense her too. A ghost of a smile crossed his lips, and then he turned his attention back to me.

"Slow, as usual. I did get a couple of high teens wanting Tarot."

"Oh, lord. Your favorite kind of teens."

"Yup. Never questioned the price. I don't even know if they comprehended the fortune, to be honest."

"You didn't tell them about tree frogs, did you?"

"Tree frogs?" asked Seth.

"Yeah, Dante had these kids on acid come in once, and as part of their reading, he told them to beware of tree frogs."

Grinning, Dante shook his head at the memory. "Shit, that freaked them out. You should have seen them when they left the store. They were practically crouching on the ground, looking up everywhere, peering at every window and telephone wire. That would have almost been compensation enough."

The image always made me laugh. "But not this time?"

"Nah, this group was just sluggish and out of it. On the bright side, they paid me ten dollars for a bag of Doritos I had sitting around. Gotta love kids spending their allowance."

Dante and I were both amused by his clients' antics, but glancing over, I saw that Seth was not. Something cold clenched inside me, and I could suddenly see us through his eyes. He didn't really find taking advantage of teens under the influence of drugs funny, whether it was monetarily or psychologically. When I'd first met Dante, I'd actually been appalled by the charlatan side of his business. When had I come to accept it? When had I come to enjoy it?

I felt ashamed all of a sudden and hated what Seth must think of me. Then, I became angry for feeling that way, for letting myself feel judged. He had no power over me anymore. It didn't matter what he thought. The last of the coziness between us shattered, and I felt my icy exterior slip into place. I moved closer to Dante, and Seth's body language told me he'd seen the transformation I'd just undergone.

"Well, you guys probably need to go," I said abruptly.

"Yeah," Seth said uncomfortably. "I guess we'll see you later."

"Thanks for the book."

He merely nodded and then turned to put Kayla into her car seat. Her eyes met mine and I waved a good-bye, but the look of horror on her face never faltered. I knew it was for Dante, not me, but it hurt nonetheless.

Dante wanted to head home and had mostly come to give me a ride. By that point, I felt weary and emotionally disoriented. Home sounded good. We went back inside to drop off my glass and tell Doug I was leaving. Doug looked about as thrilled to see Dante as Seth had, but he said nothing that wasn't in his usual jovial style.

On the drive home, I stared vacantly out the window and ran my hands over the book's cover.

"You were kind of chummy back there," noted Dante.

"Huh?"

"With Mortensen. I felt like I was interrupting something."

"Oh. No. I just got kind of giddy over the book. You know how much I like them."

We came to a red light, and he glanced down at the cover. "Advanced copy? We could make a lot of money on eBay."

"Dante!"

"Just a joke, succubus. Well, kind of. If you ever wanted to work your wiles on him and get more books, you could start a little side business."

"I don't need any extra cash. And my wiles are no good. Things are done. He and Maddie are happy."

"That doesn't mean anything. You don't think he still wants you? You don't think he'd sleep with you if he could?"

"Why do you assume the worst about everyone?"

"Because it's always true. I'm trying to break you of seeing the world through rose-colored glasses." He paused while we merged onto the freeway and headed back toward the city. "And he can want you all he wants. I don't care, as long as you don't want him back."

"There you go again, acting jealous." I tried to keep my voice teasing in order to deflect how close he'd hit to home. "I thought you didn't care who else I slept with."

"I don't. Just so long as you don't like them better than me."

I laughed and left that as my response, indicating how foolish a notion I thought it was. And yet, as we rode back in silence, I found myself hugging the book closer and closer.

Chapter 10

Dante promptly passed out after sex later that night, but I stayed awake for a while. Rolling over at last, I turned my back to him and stared at my bedside table. I'd set Seth's book there, and now its spine stared out at me, like we were having a showdown to see who would look away first. Seth had given it to me as a gift, possibly a peace offering, yet I was afraid of it, afraid of how I might feel if I opened it.

After ten minutes of staring, I finally reached for the book and scooted closer to the bed's edge so that I could get more light from my tiny reading lamp. Curling onto my side, I took a deep breath and opened up *All Fools Night*.

First came the title page, then the dedication: *For my niece Brandy, who dreams of great things and will achieve greater ones still*. It was embarrassing, but I had almost for a moment speculated whether he might have dedicated the book to me. He'd finished it right around the time we first started dating, but he'd been editing and making small changes right up until the time we broke up. It was vanity, I supposed, to think there might be some sign of my time with Seth in the book.

Yet, when I turned the page, I wondered. Before the first chapter, Seth always had a quote, something from a speech or possibly a verse from a poem that was relevant to the book. This was from a song:

> And if I only could
> I'd make a deal with God

And I'd get Him to swap our places
—*"Running Up That Hill," by Kate Bush*

I read the lyrics a couple of times, wondering if there was more to them or if I just wanted there to be more to them. I'd heard the song a long time ago, and it had had that poppy synth feel so common to music in the 1980s. I didn't recall this particular part. Finally, dragging my eyes away, I moved onto the heart of the book.

Before meeting Seth, I'd rationed myself while reading his novels. I would only read five pages a day because I'd wanted to prolong the sweetness of that first reading. When something was really good, it was easy to dive into it, and before you knew it, the moment was gone. You'd burned through it. I experienced that too frequently in my long existence, and a strict reading schedule was a weak attempt to slow things down. When I settled into this book, though, I didn't really have a plan, and before long, I knew stopping at five pages was impossible.

It was exquisite. While he had a few self-standing novels, this series—Cady and O'Neill—was his flagship one. At its basic level, this was just a mystery book, yet there was a wonderful, lyrical quality to Seth's writing that elevated him above the genre ghetto. Sure, there was action and a trail of clues, but his characters were also evolving, always growing in ways both wonderful and heartbreaking. Seth had a way of describing their feelings and their reactions in a style that was so real, it resonated with my own life and left an ache in my chest. Whether that was for his art or for the man himself, I couldn't say.

It was only when Dante rolled over that I'd realized I'd been sniffling.

"Are you crying, succubus?"

"It's this book," I said.

I had just read a section where Cady and O'Neill were having a profound talk about life, and O'Neill had commented that all people were seeking both damnation and forgiveness, needing each to make sense of their existence. I was crying because it was true and because Seth had known it was true.

"There are a lot of things to cry about in this world," Dante said through a yawn. "Not sure a book should be one of them."

The clock read 4 a.m. by that point, and my eyes were bleary from tears and a need to sleep. I put down Seth's book—which I was now more than half-way through—and turned off the light. Dante shifted and threw an arm around me, resting his chin on my shoulder. His breathing grew heavy and regular, and before long, I joined him in sleep.

The phone woke me up at an ungodly hour later in the morning. Dante was gone already. I found that surprising, but seeing as he hadn't gotten three hours of sleep, it might not have been that much of a leap.

"Hello?" Finding the phone had been feat enough, let alone checking the caller ID. A frantic voice answered me.

"Georgina? This is Blake."

"Blake?" I didn't think I knew any Blake.

"Don't tell me you forgot about us?"

He pronounced "about" as "aboot," and it came back to me through my sleep-addled brain. "Oh, God. I'm sorry. Blake. From the Army." Him calling me couldn't be a good sign. I sat up straighter in bed. "What's going on?"

"They're doing something today . . . I'm not supposed to tell anyone, but I'm worried. I don't know much, except that it's big."

I was up and moving now, clothes and hair shape-shifting as I walked. "Do you have anything else? A time or place?"

"Not yet. Evan's being really secretive about what he's telling us. He says the Angel wants it to be a need-to-know-thing and that we won't find out the details until the absolute last minute."

"Fuck." I suspected the Angel was also trying to limit my knowledge as well. Flattering, but frustrating. "Okay, well, listen, I'm in Seattle, but I'm getting on the road right now. I should be there in two hours."

"You can't get up here in two hours," he said incredulously.

"I can if I don't drive the speed limit."

There was a bit of congestion within the city itself, but once I got a little north of it, the traffic cleared up. It was the morning commute; everyone wanted to get into Seattle. Once I had clear highway ahead of me, I dialed Cedric. I knew he wasn't going to like my lack of information, but considering how angry he'd been after last time, I had to at least make the attempt here to keep myself out of trouble. It was Kristin who answered.

"He's having breakfast right now," she told me. "It's kind of a special time for him. He doesn't like to be disturbed." There was an anxious tone to her voice, and I could almost picture her arranging a breakfast tray just-so for him.

"Yeah, well, he might be disturbed whether he likes it or not." I told her what Blake had said, and her response was similar to mine.

"That's all you've got?"

"Their Angel's working on a need-to-know basis now," I said bitterly. "I'll let you know more when I learn more. I just figured Cedric should know."

She sighed. "You're right. Thanks. Man, this is going to piss him off. He'll have no appetite at all."

I made the drive in the two hours I'd quoted Blake and miraculously didn't get pulled over. I hadn't heard from him the entire time, so I dialed him once I was over the border and buying coffee. I'd found a Starbucks and took a secret thrill in defying the Tim Hortons domination. Except . . . once I had the coffee in hand, I decided a donut would be really good with it, so I walked over and got one from the Tim's across the street.

Blake didn't answer, so I tried Evan next and also got no answer. Frustrated, I drove over to Evan's house and knocked on the door for a while. I was nearly on the verge of climbing in through a back window when my phone rang again—and ironically, it was Evan himself.

"Georgina!" he exclaimed, sounding ecstatic. "Where are you? We need you here."

"Where are *you*?" I demanded.

"On the observation deck," he said.

"Observation deck of what?"

"The Space Needle. You live close by, don't you?"

I nearly dropped the phone. "You're in *Seattle*?"

"Yeah!" I could perfectly picture that eager, zealous look of his. "Cool, huh? The Angel wanted us to expand our message. So, we're all up here with these banners that we're going to unfurl at the same time, and then we've got a few more surprises to—"

"Evan," I begged, sprinting toward my car. "Don't do it. You're stirring up more trouble than you realize."

"That's the point!" he chuckled. "How long until you can be here?"

Once I told him I wasn't in the city, he lost interest, and my pleas became meaningless. As soon as we disconnected, I dialed Cedric, expecting to get Kristin. Instead, I got his voice mail. Somehow, that made me angry.

"Cedric, this is Georgina. The Army isn't doing their thing here—they're down in Seattle right now. I hope you finally believe I didn't have anything to do with their stupid plans now! When Jerome finds out, it's going to be *my* ass on the line, and knowing my luck, he'll think you and I are working together."

Yes, this was one of those situations in which there was no way I could win. I was going to get in trouble no matter what I did, but again, I had to attempt damage control. Jerome had a cell phone that he never answered and didn't even have voice mail for. Hugh was the best way to get a hold of him—but he didn't pick up either.

"Damn it!" I cried into his phone. "Doesn't anyone answer their fucking phones anymore?" I gave him a hasty recap of what was happening and told him to let Jerome or one of the demonesses know about the cult's plans, or else Jerome was going to get the same scrutiny from the higher-ups that Cedric had been getting.

After that, there was nothing left for me to do except hit the road to Seattle again—something I was *not* happy about. Fortunately, I was fully outside the commuting times now and again could enjoy easy driving as I zipped down I-5 at 75. *Pretty Hate Machine* blared on my speakers and was oddly soothing to my agitated mood. I eventually fell into that trance-like state drivers often get, with one part of my brain watching the road and the other frantically wondering if my warning had reached any of the Seattle demons in time to intercept the Army.

I had just cleared Everett, about a half-hour outside of Seattle, when *it* hit me.

A jolt of electricity shot through my body, making the world spin and my vision blur. I felt hot all over. My hands slipped on the wheel, nearly causing me to swerve into the neighboring lane. I had just enough bearings to slam on my hazard lights and pull off on the shoulder before I hit someone. A wave of nausea rolled through my stomach, then settled down, then swept through me again. Shifting the car into park, I put my head down on the steering wheel, hoping for some clarity. There was a buzzing in my ears, and my whole body shook.

What the hell? I didn't get sick. Ever. The only thing that could really affect me like this was drinking too much or indulging in other substances. I'd had food poisoning a couple of times, but it had been short-lived, and somehow I doubted that donut I'd had was doing this to me.

I lifted my head up a little, but the world kept rocking. Closing my eyes, I rested my cheek against the steering wheel and took a few deep breaths, hoping I wouldn't throw up. I had no idea what was going on here, but it would pass. It *had* to pass.

And it did—a little. I don't know how long I sat like that, maybe about fifteen minutes, but the next time I dared a peek up, the dizziness had lessened. The nausea was still there, but it too had dropped to a lower level. Deciding to risk it, I turned back onto I-5, anxious to finish my drive to the city and figure out what was wrong with me.

I made it back to town without causing an accident and nearly fell over trying to make it up my building's stairs. I didn't even bother with my suitcase and simply left it in the car. Once in my apartment, I headed straight for my room and crashed on the bed. Aubrey joined me and peered curiously at my face. I gave her a few pets, then let my hand slip down as I fell asleep, too weak to hold it up any longer.

I woke up almost two hours later, shaken out of sleep by knocking at my door. I sat up, relieved to find my stomach had settled. The light-headedness had also gone away. Maybe the donut had been defective after all . . . and yet, I had this weird feeling—this tiny, nagging suspicion—that something wasn't right. Only, I had no clue or evidence as to what it was. Ignoring it for now, I stumbled out to the living room and opened my door, not even bothering to look out the peephole.

Cody and Peter stood there, both of them grinning from ear to ear. "What do you want?" I asked, stepping aside for them when the door opened. "I was sleeping."

"I can tell by your hair," said Peter, flouncing on my couch. "And what are you doing asleep? It's the middle of the day."

Still groggy, I squinted at my clock. It was a little after three. "Yeah, I know. I didn't feel good. It's weird. I just suddenly felt wiped out and dizzy."

That smile had never left Cody's face. He sat beside Peter. "How do you feel now?"

I shrugged and settled onto my loveseat. "Fine, I guess. A little tired, but the worst is over." That nondescript *something isn't right here* feeling was still with me, though.

"You shouldn't be cooped up inside," said Peter. "It's a great day."

"Look at all the sun," agreed Cody. "It's like summer came early."

I followed his gaze to the window. Warm golden light spilled in onto my floor, much to Aubrey's delight, and beyond the neighboring building, I could see blue sky. Still, I wasn't impressed. "We're barely into spring. This is a fluke. It'll probably be cold tomorrow."

Peter shook his head. "You sure are grumpy when you wake up." They both seemed so absurdly pleased with themselves, and I couldn't figure out why.

"Maybe you should get outside," said Cody, exchanging smirks with Peter. "We were going to go for a walk after this. It might cheer you up."

"Yup. Nothing like a bright, sunny afternoon to perk up the old spirits." Peter's grin grew even bigger.

I leaned my head back against the loveseat. "Okay, okay. What's the joke I'm missing here?"

"No joke," said Peter. "We just think it's a great day."

"A beautiful, sunny day," Cody concurred.

"Will you two stop already? I get it. It's a nice day. The sun is out the, the birds are singing—"

I stopped. I felt my eyes go wide.

I looked at the smirking vampires, then looked at the sun-filled world outside, and then looked back at them. I swallowed.

"How," I asked quietly, "are you guys out in the middle of the day?"

Their pent-up mirth exploded, and they both dissolved into laughter.

I felt wide awake now. "I'm serious! What's going on? You can't be out in daylight, and how—wait. I didn't sense you guys at the door. I *still* can't sense you."

"I know," said Cody. "Isn't it crazy?"

"No! Well, I mean, yes. But it's not . . . it's not supposed to happen," I argued. I didn't understand how they could find this so entertaining. Something was wrong. Very wrong. All the drama with the Army was gone from my mind. That niggling worry that I'd woken up with turned into a hard knot of fear. My heart was pounding in my chest, and I'd gone cold all over. "How is this possible? The sun should fry you."

"Hell if we know," said Peter. "We were in our coffins and then just suddenly . . . woke up. We got out, and there we were. Out and about in the middle of the day. You know what else? I don't want blood. No desire whatsoever. Not even a drop."

"And so what, you guys just decide to go stroll around and enjoy the day? You didn't contact Jerome? You didn't question the fact that something has seriously altered your immortal existence?"

A mischievous look crossed Peter's face. "Not just us, Georgina."

They both watched me expectantly.

"Don't look at me like that," I told them. "I've always been able to go out in the sun."

"You don't have a signature either. We can't sense you," said Cody.

I stared at them for several heavy seconds, trying to parse the meaning here. An uneasy feeling began building in my stomach as I recognized their implication—except what they were implying was impossible. Unthinkable.

"You're wrong," I said.

Slowly, carefully, I touched my face. It was exactly the same as it had been this morning. My build was the same. My height was the same. I was still me.

I exhaled with relief. "I'm the same."

Peter's eyes danced. "Fix your hair. It's a mess."

Shape-shifting is an instinct for a succubus or incubus, practically subconscious. It's like tightening a muscle or taking a deep breath. You barely think about it, send the message from your brain, and it happens. So, I thought about my hair, willing it to smooth out and tidy itself into a ponytail. There was usually a slight tingle when that happened, resulting from the burn of using up a piece of my stored energy. And of course, there was always the tangible evidence—the actual change of my appearance.

This time, there was nothing. No tingle. No hair movement.

Peter leaned forward. "Ooh, it did happen to you! You're the same. None of us are working."

"No," I said frantically. "That's not possible."

I tried again, willing my hair to change—to turn a different color, grow short, restyle itself . . . but there was nothing. I tried to shift my clothes, urging my jeans and Henley to become a slip dress. Or maybe a track suit. I even attempted to make my clothes disappear altogether.

Nothing happened.

Nothing.

In pure desperation, I did the unthinkable: I tried to give up the unconscious hold I always maintained in order to keep a form that wasn't my natural one. I let go of all control, allowing my body to shift back to the one I was born with, the one my essence always wanted to return to—the one I fought very, very hard to hide from the world.

Nothing happened. I stayed the same.

I couldn't shape-shift.

It was like having my arm cut off. Until that moment, I didn't realize how much of my self was tied into shape-shifting. As a mortal, the power had been unimaginable. After having it for a millennium and a half, it had become part of me, and its absence was now unbearable. I didn't have to see my face to know I wore pure panic. Peter and Cody were still laughing.

I shot up, incredulous. "This isn't funny," I cried. "We have to talk to Jerome. *Now.* There's something seriously wrong with us!"

"Or right," suggested Cody.

"Why do you think this is a joke?"

"We don't," said Peter calmly. Underneath his mirth, I saw the tiniest bit of concern in his eyes, concern he was clearly trying to ignore for now. "We just think it's cool. You don't think Jerome already knows about this? Whatever it is, they'll fix it soon enough. Nothing we can change."

The tirade I was about to unleash on them was interrupted by more knocking. Just like with the vampires, I sensed no immortal signature. Anyone could have been at my door. Yet, peering out the peephole, I saw Hugh. I let him in, feeling relieved. Hugh would sort this out. He always knew what was going on since he and Jerome maintained such constant communication. Hugh's confidence and typical know-it-all air would fix everything.

Instead, he looked miserable. Dejected. He trudged in and dropped onto where I'd just been sitting. He put his elbows on his knees and rested his chin in his hands.

"Hey, Hugh," said Cody. "Isn't it a great day?"

I knelt down on the floor in front of Hugh, so I could look straight into his eyes.

"Hugh, what's going on?"

He simply stared at me, dark eyes mournful and bleak. I'd seen Hugh angry, elated, and exasperated over the years, but I'd never seen him depressed. It would have bothered me, if not for the fact we had a few other things to worry about than his hurt feelings just now.

"Hugh! We've all lost our . . ." I frowned, not sure what to call it. Powers? That sounded too Justice League. ". . . abilities."

"I know," he said at last. "So have I."

"What powers did you even have?" asked Cody, apparently not minding the superhero comparison.

"Multitasking?" teased Peter. "The ability to balance books and collate?"

I shot him a quick glare over my shoulder and then glanced at Cody to explain. "Imps see souls—everyone's life energy. They can tell whose soul is good and whose is bad."

"I know that," said Cody. "I just thought there was . . . more."

Hugh sighed. "You can't imagine it, Georgina. Not having that ability now. It's like losing one of my senses. Or going colorblind."

"I know exactly what you mean," I told him.

"Not likely. When you can't see energy and souls around living beings, the world is so . . . empty. It's dull."

"Why did it happen?" I asked gently, trying my best to squelch my own escalating fear. Internally, I was still reeling.

My shape-shifting was gone. My immortal signature was gone. The marks that defined *me* as Georgina Kincaid, succubus, were gone. "What's going on?"

Hugh's eyes were still sad and unfocused, but finally, he looked at me and studied my face, like he'd just noticed me in front of him. "We get our various gifts and immortality for selling our souls," he began slowly. "Those unique abilities— and their side effects—come from our contract with Hell and are filtered through our archdemons. It's what lets them keep track of us. We're . . . connected . . ." He frowned, grasping at how to best explain the system through which Hell managed its employees.

"I know what you're talking about," I said. Cedric would know if I crossed into his territory simply because he could sense me when I was close enough. Jerome, so long as he was my supervisor, knew where I was at all times and if I was hurt. He was always aware of me, always tied to me. "Our . . . powers . . . are transmitted from Hell, through Jerome, to us."

"Right," Hugh said. I waited for more, but that seemed to be all he had to say.

"Right what? Why are our abilities gone?"

A bit of the normal Hugh exasperation glinted in his eyes. "Because *Jerome* is gone."

"Jerome's gone all the time," Peter said. "We can never get a hold of him. We can't get a hold of him now."

Hugh shook his head. "You aren't getting it. When I say gone, I don't mean hiding from us at a bar. I mean *gone*. Vanished. Disappeared. Might as well not exist for all intents and purposes. No one knows where he is. Not our side, not the other side. He. Is. Gone."

Dead silence hung around us for what felt like an eternity. And that was saying something.

Peter's voice was hard to hear when he finally spoke. "And as long as he's gone . . ."

". . . then so are our abilities," I finished.

Chapter 11

Cody asked the obvious question.

"So . . . if he's *gone* . . . how did that happen?"

Hugh rubbed his eyes. "He was summoned."

"Oh, shit," said Peter. His fun-in-the-sun joy disappeared. He looked as grim as Hugh and me. "That changes everything."

I glanced between him and Hugh, feeling as naïve as Cody. "What's that mean exactly? I've heard of summoning, but that's about it. I don't know any specifics. I don't know anyone it's happened to."

Peter nodded. "Me either, but I know what it is. Basically, a powerful human calls and binds a demon to his or her will. That human can then imprison and control the demon."

"Like Marlowe's *Dr. Faustus*."

We all turned to stare at Cody. Citing highbrow literary references was usually my thing, not his.

"What?" he asked, looking uncomfortable under our scrutiny. "I had to read it in high school."

I looked back at Peter. "Okay, we're immortal, and we could never even scratch a demon. How could a human control one?"

"Humans who use magic wield a different kind of power than immortals. Besides, from what I've heard, those who summon demons often have help," explained Peter. He glanced at Hugh for confirmation.

"From another demon," the imp said.

"Whoa. Let's go back to the part about controlling demons. What exactly is this human making Jerome do?" asked Cody.

"Probably nothing," said Hugh. "Or else someone would have found him by now. My guess is he's just being hidden."

Cody frowned. "Why? If you've got a pet demon, why not use him? Otherwise, what's the point?"

It all came together now. "To get him out of the picture," I said slowly. "That's it. The final piece in all this weird demon intrigue. That's what all the misdirection was building toward."

"Right. Cedric gets rid of Jerome, and suddenly there's an opening in Seattle for a new archdemon. And if Jerome doesn't return soon, they *will* get a new archdemon and reestablish the hierarchy here." Hugh gestured to all of us. "The status quo will resume."

"Let's stick to 'when' he returns and not 'if,'" I said. "And I don't think Cedric's behind it."

"Of course Cedric's behind it," said Hugh. "They've been fighting over territory, right? You of all people should know that."

I shook my head, recalling Cedric's exasperation and Nanette's smug look. "No . . . I think Cedric's being set up here. If you ask me, it's Nanette who's behind it." I gave them a quick recap of my observations of her with both Cedric and Jerome.

Hugh arched an eyebrow. "Portland Nanette? She's hot, I'll give you that, but she's not that strong."

"All the more reason for her to mess with Jerome and Cedric. She's been worried about them dragging her into their turf war. Besides, if she combined her power with a human capable of a summoning . . ."

"Yeah," he admitted. "She could maybe do it . . . but that doesn't mean she did. My money's still on Cedric."

"Wouldn't she get in trouble for that?" asked Cody.

"Only if she's caught," said Peter.

I sighed. "And in the meantime, this is bad for Jerome."

"Glad to see your powers of stating the obvious didn't disappear with your shape-shifting," remarked Hugh.

I shot him a glare. "I mean reputation-wise. Nanette told me lots of people have been keeping an eye on Jerome because of all the stuff that's gone down here—particularly with letting nephilim escape. They think he can't keep control. Even if he surfaces tomorrow, I've got to imagine that getting summoned in the first place won't look good."

"It won't," agreed Hugh. "In fact, that's the other reason I stopped by. A bunch of demons are having a meeting tonight to talk about replacing him. Back room of the Cellar at seven."

"Wow, they move fast," said Cody.

"It's nothing official. Once word got out that Jerome was gone, every demon maneuvering for power moved in like that." Hugh snapped his fingers. I refrained from pointing out that *all* demons were maneuvering for power as a general rule. "They're mostly just here to assert themselves—show how tough they are, cozy up to Grace and Mei. They might try to schmooze us a little, actually."

"Why? We don't have any say in this," said Peter. He glanced between us all. "Do we?"

"No, but eventually someone from Management will come here to size up the situation and will talk to us in their assessment. Everything plays a part. Those wanting the position will strut around, show how they could keep this place in line, and put their bids in."

"Is Nanette going to be at this meeting?" I asked suspiciously.

"Yes," said Hugh, eyeing me. "And so will Cedric."

I eyed him right back. "I'm telling you, it's not Cedric. I'm certain of it."

"What, you have donuts with him for a week, and now you guys are BFF?"

"No, but I know him better than you do. And I think I understand Nanette better than you too," I shot back.

"So, you guys . . ." began Cody, a questioning note in his voice.

"Are you sleeping with Cedric?" Hugh demanded. "Are you playing both sides now?"

"No!"

"It kind of sounds like it."

"You guys," repeated Cody.

"Look," I said, "you just want to believe Nanette's innocent because you think she's hot."

"She *is* hot. For a demon."

"You guys!" yelled Cody. We turned to him. "What about us?"

"What about us?" I asked.

"What *are* we?" Cody's face was pinched and worried. Like Peter, he no longer seemed that excited about his newfound freedom. "Are we human?"

I opened my mouth to answer and then fell silent. I honestly didn't know. Hugh glanced at me and shrugged.

"Not exactly," said Peter. "I think we're kind of . . . in stasis. We're neither mortal nor immortal."

"We have to be one or the other," argued Hugh. "There's no purgatory equivalent to mortality."

Peter shrugged. "Hell's still got the lease on our souls. That's not going to change, no matter who our archdemon is. Removing him from the equation cuts us off from the abilities we get with immortality, but that's temporary."

"But does it cut us off from immortality itself?" asked Cody. "Can we die?"

Silence fell.

"Shit," said Hugh.

"I think . . ." Peter bit his lip. I had a feeling he was at the end of his knowledge on this subject. "I think they'd bring us back if we did."

"You *think*?" asked Cody incredulously.

Peter threw up his hands. "I don't know! This has never happened to me before, okay? Maybe we are human. Maybe we can get sick. Maybe we can lose in a fight. Maybe Georgina'll get her period. I don't know, okay?"

"Whoa," I said, straightening up. "What do you mean—"

"Just stop it, all of you," exclaimed Hugh. "We're not going to figure any of this out right now. Just go to the meeting and find out there. Grace and Mei are trying to manage things for now, and they'll know what's up. No point in panicking now."

We sat there, and I knew that despite his words, we were all indeed panicking. My stomach was rolling, but this time, it wasn't a reaction to the severing of my bond with Hell. This was born of pure terror. When things were bad in my life—particularly after Seth and I had broken up—there had been times when I'd hated immortality. Death had sounded appealing. I honestly hadn't been able to fathom how I could endure the centuries to come and had envied the finite life spans of humans. But now? Faced with the idea that I could actually die? Suddenly, desperately, I wanted to cling to my immortality with every scrap of my strength. Death was bleak, dark, and frightening. All the world's dangers descended on me at once, all the things I'd hitherto been able to ignore. Car accidents. Electrocution. Bird flu. The world was no longer safe.

If the vampires felt any such fears, they apparently decided it wasn't going to get in the way of their last few days as free men. They rose as one and made motions to leave.

"Well, if Jerome's going to get replaced with or without us, then there's no point sitting and moping," said Peter.

"We got cut off without warning," I told him. "We could get reconnected to Hell's circuit board just as suddenly, you know. Aren't you a little nervous about getting caught out in the sun?"

"They're not going to make any decisions in the next five hours," said Peter brashly—too brashly, I thought.

He paused a moment, his gaze drifting to my window and the blue sky beyond it. There, in his dark eyes, I saw the tiniest, *tiniest* bit of longing. It occurred to me then just how much he must have missed the sun these last thousand years or so. Like the rest of us, he'd willingly sold his soul for immortality. Along with that, he'd gotten superhuman strength and speed in exchange for a dependency on blood, a denial of sunlight, and a job as a dispenser of fear and nightmares. I certainly had regrets about my hellish deal some days; no doubt he did too. And maybe, despite his lax, overconfident attitude about the sun, he truly was aware of the risk of getting fried—and thought it was worth it after all this time.

He and Cody left, leaving me and a still bleak-looking Hugh. I gently touched the imp's shoulder. "I'm sure this'll work out."

He cut me a wry look. "Really?"

I laughed softly. "No, not really. I'm just trying to make you feel better. I never realized before how much you liked your . . . what would you call it? Imp vision?"

This finally got him to smile. "You always thought of me as a paper pusher?"

"Nah, no one uses paper anymore. It's all electronic."

"Not in Hell," he said, standing up. "They kind of like cutting down forests."

I followed him to the door. "Well, hang in there, and I'll see you tonight."

"What are you going to do with *your* newfound freedom?" he asked, hand on the doorknob.

I frowned. "What do you mean? This whole thing isn't quite the same for you and me as it is for the vampires."

The look Hugh gave me then was genuinely amused and almost pitying. "Georgina. Your shape-shifting and other abilities are fueled by human life. If you can't do those things, then you don't need the energy—just like Cody and Hugh don't need blood. Can't you feel it? The whole system's probably shut off."

I froze and almost stopped breathing for a moment—which might not have been so wise in my current state. "*What?*"

He laughed again. "How could you have not considered that?"

"Well . . . because I was more focused on the entire fabric of Seattle's demonic hierarchy being unraveled. That and the possibility that we could all die." Inside, my mind was replaying his words over and over, like a record that kept skipping: *You don't need the energy, you don't need the energy . . .* I shook my head. "I can't believe that. It isn't possible." I'd wanted it for too long, the ability to be with someone without the dire side effects. It was one of those things you always longed for but knew, deep down inside, could never happen. Like winning the lottery. Or, um, living forever.

"Neither is a vampire going into the sun," said Hugh. "Yet here we are." He leaned down and kissed my cheek. "Think about it. This is a once in a lifetime—er, eternity—chance."

He started to leave, and then something I'd nearly forgotten about popped back into the forefront of my mind. "Hugh? Did you get my message earlier? About the Canadian Satanists?" After everything else, a few signs on the Space Needle suddenly seemed absurdly unimportant.

"Yeah," he said, with a grimace. "They had a huge spectacle there, freaked people out. They made the news and got arrested. Not sure what'll happen now. The international thing makes it all interesting."

"Were you able to tell Jerome?"

"No, couldn't get a hold of him—not surprising if that was near the time of the summoning. I ended up getting a hold of Mei, and I think she did something to minimize how much the media found out. She was hoping that nobody in Management would notice."

"Yeah, well, they're all noticing us now."

Hugh's face was hard as he nodded his agreement. "That's an understatement. Have fun, sweetie."

He departed, leaving me standing there and staring at the door.

I was still breathing heavily, my heart thudding in my chest. I needed to calm down and think this through. After all, who knew what could happen if I had a panic attack? Would I go into cardiac arrest or something? All bets were off now. Anything was possible.

I sank down to the floor, wrapping my arms around myself, and focused on slowing my breathing. This was all too surreal. I couldn't process it. It wasn't possible that I could be mortal. It wasn't possible that I could die. It wasn't possible that I could actually touch a man without harming him. Over and over I told myself those things. Meanwhile, Aubrey strolled over to me and rubbed her head against my leg. Reaching out, I stroked her back, barely aware of my actions.

What was I going to do? We had five hours until the meeting, which couldn't come soon enough as far as I was concerned. I needed answers *now*. I couldn't live with this uncertainty. My heart started racing again. Fuck. I really was going to have a heart attack. Hugh was a doctor in his day job; maybe I should call him about my blood pressure.

Call . . .

An idea hit me then, and I stood up to go find my purse. Producing my cell phone, I dialed Dante. If anyone might know about this, it would be him. He probably wouldn't know the intricacies of how this affected my infernal standing, but he had to know something about demon summoning. Dark magic was his specialty. Besides, I wanted more than just his expertise. I suddenly just wanted . . . well, comfort. I wanted to see him. I wanted him to hold me and reassure me. I needed him to tell me everything was going to be okay.

But the phone rang and rang without answer, sending me to his voice mail's friendly message: "Talk."

So much for that plan. I disconnected and leaned against my counter. Slowly, steadily, I felt my brain waking up, trying to find a scrap of reason through my fear. It wasn't in my nature to be passive. I had to do something about this. I couldn't wait until tonight for answers.

"Let's research this ourselves, Aubrey," I said. The average human knew nothing about the true nature of Heaven and Hell and how we operated. Yet, every once in a while, if you looked hard enough into arcane writings, you could stumble across a piece of truth that some adept mortal had uncovered. Ninety-nine percent of what I'd find would be inaccurate, but an Internet search could uncover some grain of truth about demon summoning. It was a total long shot, but it was the best I could do for now.

Only, when I went to get my laptop, I discovered an unfortunate fact: I'd left it at the bookstore. I groaned. Now what? Another plan shot down.

You idiot, a voice inside me chastised. *You're a few blocks away. Get off your ass and get it.*

That logic made perfect sense, of course. Until I looked out the window.

The same fear I'd had earlier returned. The cars moving along Queen Anne Avenue seemed too fast, the wind stirring the trees too strong, the people on the sidewalk too dangerous. How could I go out there? How could I put myself at risk? Better to stay in here where it was safe.

And yet . . . how could I wait around? I was going to go crazy if I sat here. Glancing down at Aubrey, I saw her watching me with her green eyes. She had that infinitely wise look cats had sometimes. It wasn't exactly encouraging, but it soothed me a little.

Okay. I could do this.

I found my coat and started to shape-shift my messy hair into a neat arrangement—except, of course, I immediately realized I *couldn't* shape-shift it. Not a problem, I assured myself. I did my hair all the time when I wasn't in a rush. This was no different. With a quick dash to the restroom, I brushed my hair into a sleek ponytail and prepared to face the world.

Stepping outdoors, I was blasted with stimuli. I stood on the steps to my building, shell-shocked and unable to move. This had never happened to me. Never, never had I been afraid of the world. I'd always rejoiced in it and been eager to see what it had to offer. Slipping my hand into my purse, I reached for my cigarettes, seeking them like a safety blanket. When I took them out, I realized something else. I wasn't necessarily immune to them anymore. This stasis probably wouldn't last long . . . but how could I risk it? How could I expose myself to carcinogens when I had no idea how vulnerable I truly was?

Putting the cigarettes back, I took a deep breath and plunged forward.

The distance to the store was barely three blocks, but it felt like miles. I walked as far away as I could from traffic and flinched each time someone passed me. When I finally reached the intersection to cross over to Emerald City, I was sweating. Queen Anne Avenue is *not* an overly crazy road. This particular spot had three lanes and steady traffic, with a moderate speed of 30 (which meant people could usually be found going 35–40).

Nonetheless, standing there, I might as well have been trying to cross I-5 itself, with five lanes racing in each direction. The crosswalk was red, giving me time to build up courage and remind myself that I'd crossed here hundreds of times—jaywalking more often than not. I was being irrational, freaking out at things I had no business worrying about. The light dinged and gave me the go-ahead.

I set out, each step agony. I'd almost reached the far curb when a Honda turning on red from the cross street suddenly pulled into the intersection, having only checked for cars and not pedestrians. Seeing me, the driver slammed on her brakes a bit more harshly than she probably needed. They squealed, and the car came to a stop about two feet from me. While moderately alarming, this wasn't anything that probably would have scared me too much under ordinary circumstances. The car had stopped, after all, and I was almost across anyway. Yet, I was so on edge already that when I heard the brakes and saw how close she was, I simply froze. I stood there, caught—literally—in the headlights.

I couldn't think or move. It was so stupid. Seven more steps, and I would have been safe. The woman's panic over avoiding me turned to annoyance when she realized I was blocking her way. She pressed down on her horn, which was a particularly loud and obnoxious one. Unfortunately for her, it was ineffectual. If anything, the noise simply froze me up more.

Suddenly, someone grabbed a hold of my arm and started tugging me to the curb. The bitch in the Honda kept honking, and I think I was nearly as startled by it as I was when Seth yelled to her, "Oh, shut *up* already!"

His steady hands guided me to the sidewalk where I promptly froze up again, oblivious to the curious cars and pedestrians. Cupping my face, he forced me to look up at him. His eyes were like warm molasses, and something about them spread comfort through me and brought me back to myself.

"Georgina, are you okay?"

My whole body trembled, and it took me a moment to gather myself and speak. "I . . . I think so . . ."

His voice was so, so gentle when he spoke. "What happened there?"

I blinked back tears. "Nothing . . . that is . . ." I couldn't finish. I was going to break down, then and there, right on Queen Anne Avenue. I hated myself for being so weak and scared.

"Never mind," said Seth, taking hold of my arm again. "It doesn't matter. You're safe. Let's go inside."

If any of my co-workers saw Seth leading me through like an invalid, I didn't notice. In fact, I was barely aware of the trek at all until we were inside my office. Seth sat me down and then shut the door. He leaned down toward me.

"Do you need anything? Water? Something to eat?"

Slowly, almost robot-like, I shook my head. "N-no. I . . . I just came for my laptop."

The normal look of timidity he'd worn around me lately had vanished, replaced by something stern and concerned—something that wouldn't rest until he knew I was okay. He was no longer the shy author who feared looking at me and always gave me a wide berth. He was once again the man I'd dated, the man who'd always been able to read my moods and step up to help.

"Georgina, please. Please tell me what happened."

It looked as though my tears were going to stay away, and now that I was indoors, in familiar territory, I allowed myself to feel a little braver. "Why are you being so nice to me again?"

He frowned. "Why wouldn't I be nice to you?"

"Because . . . because . . . I wasn't very nice to you the last time we talked. Even after you gave me the book."

He made a noise in his throat, almost like a laugh, but not quite. "You weren't yourself, not after all those drinks. It's fine."

"I don't know," I said contrarily, "maybe I was myself."

He shook his head. "It wouldn't matter. Now tell me, what happened out there?"

The warmth in his voice, the concern . . . it was tearing me apart. There was something so familiar and safe about him that I longed for right now, and I couldn't evade him.

"It's . . . complicated," I said at last.

"Immortal intrigue?"

I nodded, feeling tears well in my eyes again. Fuck. I think half of my emotion now was from the way he was looking at me and had nothing to do with the rest of my life's madness. I stood up and looked away, hoping he wouldn't see my face, but it was no use.

"Georgina, what's happened? You're scaring me."

I dared a glance back. "You . . . you wouldn't believe me if I told you."

His face was still filled with worry, but the hint of a smile turned up the edges of his lips. "Can you seriously believe that after half the stuff I've seen you go through? Try me."

"Fair enough," I admitted. "But I don't want to get you involved."

"I want to help," he said, moving closer. His voice was like velvet, wrapping me up in softness and security. "Please. Tell me what's going on."

I wanted to tell him there was nothing he could do, but suddenly, words spilled from my lips.

"Jerome got summoned—which means he's trapped somewhere and—"

"Whoa, wait. Summoned? Like in *Dr. Faustus*?"

"Um, yeah. And so long as he's gone, we're all in this weird state. Peter calls it 'stasis.' None of us have our pow—abilities anymore. I can't shape-shift. Hugh can't see souls.

The only ones who are happy about this are the vampires because they can go in the sun again, which'll probably end up killing them. And if we don't find Jerome soon, someone else is going to take over here, and I really don't want that. And yet . . . I really don't want to go another second like this either, being in this limbo. I want everything to go back to how it was."

Seth's face was unreadable as he regarded me for several heavy seconds. Finally, he said, "Is it . . . is it so bad going without shape-shifting?"

I shook my head and began to ramble further. "It's not that. It's the fact that I may not be immortal anymore. I can't . . . I can't handle that. Coming here was horrible. The walk from my apartment. I'm afraid of everything. It's stupid. I mean, you guys—humans—get by all the time and don't think about it. But I'm scared to leave the house. Scared of what could happen to me. And when that car didn't see me right away—fuck. I just froze. I was paralyzed. God, I feel like an idiot. I must sound crazy."

At long last, a tear leaked out of the corner of one eye, the final stamp on my weakness. Seth reached out and gently wiped it away. He didn't withdraw his hand when finished, though. He slid it to my shoulder and pulled me to him. I rested my head on his chest, swallowing back more tears as I sank into the protection he offered.

"Georgina, Georgina," he murmured, running his hand over my back. "It's going to be okay. Everything's going to be okay."

Those words . . . there was something so wonderful about them, simple as they were. When people are distressed, others have an instinct to want to actually do something tangible to help—men in particular. And there's nothing wrong with that—often, it's very much desired. But what a lot of people don't get is that sometimes, all that's needed is to hear those words: *Everything's going to be okay*. It's enough to know that someone's there, that someone cares about you. It isn't always about the next logical course of action.

My next words, spoken into his Hong Kong Phooey shirt, came out muffled. "I don't know what's going to happen. With any of this. I'm so scared. I don't think I've been this afraid since I thought Roman was going to kill me."

"Nothing will happen to you. You said yourself this won't last more than a few days. Just wait it out."

"I don't wait very well."

He laughed and leaned his cheek against my forehead. "I know you don't. Don't worry. Most of us do far more dangerous things than walk two blocks, and we survive just fine. Yeah, that car kind of sucked, but even still, nothing happened."

"It's two and a half blocks," I corrected. "Not two."

"Right. I forgot that extra half one where the sharks and land mines are."

I pulled away slightly so that I could look into his face. His arms stayed around me. "I have to find Jerome, Seth."

His smile faded. The worry returned. "Georgina . . . if you want to stay safe, going after him probably isn't the way to do it. You don't always have to take this stuff on yourself, you know. Let someone else look for him. Stay home."

"That's the thing . . . I'm not sure anyone will be looking for him. Why would the other demons want him back? They want his territory. They aren't going to be happy if he's found."

Seth sighed. "Great. Now I'm the one worried about you leaving the house."

"Hey, I thought you said everything was going to be okay?"

"Gotta be careful what I say." Eyes thoughtful, he reached up and smoothed some hair on the side of my head. "Why are you so brave?"

I scoffed. "Are you insane? Didn't you just witness my near breakdown?"

"No," he said gently. "That's the thing. You are scared. You don't know what's going on or what could happen to you. Yet, in spite of that fear and uncertainty, you're going to throw yourself out there to hunt him down. No one else would do that, and you do that kind of thing all the time."

Inexplicably, I flushed under his praise. "I was only going to do a Web search."

"You know what I mean. I think you've got more courage than anyone I know—and what's truly amazing is that it's so subtle, hardly anyone ever notices. You do so much, and it goes unseen. I wish I was that brave sometimes."

"You are," I said, growing increasingly unsettled by our proximity. I also noticed then that he was still smoothing my hair back. "What are you doing to my hair? Does it look bad or something?"

"Your hair never looks bad." He dropped his hand sheepishly. "It's just . . . a little messier than usual."

"I brushed it fifteen minutes ago!"

Seth shrugged. "I don't know. It's just kind of frizzy, but that's probably normal. There's a little humidity out."

"Frizzy? My hair's never frizzy."

"Georgina," he said wearily. "Considering everything else going on, I don't think you need to worry about your hair being frizzy."

"Yeah, yeah. You're right." I made a face. "I just feel like I got a raw deal here. The vampires are having a non-stop party. Me? I somehow get bad hair. Not sure the energy break is really worth it."

Seth tilted his head, face puzzled once more. "Energy break?"

"Yeah. Along with everything else, I lost the need for life energy, so I'm not—"

I stopped. The world stopped.

I met Seth's eyes, those beautiful golden-brown eyes that were filled with utter and complete shock as we both realized the full weight of what I had been about to say. His hold on me stiffened. The casual embrace suddenly became so much more. I was acutely aware of every place we were touching and exactly how much distance was between the places we weren't touching. He felt warm, so wonderfully warm, and every place he touched me tingled—not necessarily in a sexual way but in a *Oh my God, it's Seth* way. My entire body was on full alert, waiting and watching—and hoping—for him to touch me more.

He swallowed, eyes still wide. "So you aren't . . . I mean you can . . ."

"Yeah," I said, my own voice husky. "That's the theory, at least. I haven't really tested it . . ."

My words faded off because they didn't matter. My relationship with Seth had been plagued with a hundred small problems, everything from communication to trust and the myriad details in between. And always, always underneath that had been the knowledge that we could never be physically close. Oh, we'd been able to hug and do some kissing—there was even a fair amount of tongue we could get away with before my succubus hunger started stealing his life. But ultimate intimacy? Sex? Making love? It was totally off-limits, and that denial had tortured both of us, no matter how much we talked about love being the most important part in a relationship.

And now . . . here we were. Those barriers were removed. I hadn't tested if my succubus stealing really was gone, but I didn't need to. I could feel it, as Hugh had said. The perpetual craving that always lurked within me was completely dormant. I could touch and kiss anyone without restraint. I could touch and kiss Seth. There was nothing standing between us now.

Well, except for one thing.

A knock sounded on my door. "Georgina? Are you in there?" Maddie called.

It was like cold water in the face. Seth and I sprang apart. He backed toward the door, and I promptly sat down at my desk. My heart was pounding again. Damn it. I was going to have to talk to Hugh and get an anti-anxiety drug. "Yeah, come in," I called.

Maddie stuck her head in, surprised to see both of us. "There you are," she said to Seth. "I just got here and couldn't find you."

Seth was still in shock. "I . . . yeah . . . I saw Georgina was here and stopped by . . ."

Maddie peered at me. "You okay? You look a little worn out." Her eyes flicked to my hair and then back to my face. "Did you just wake up?"

Apparently, I no longer looked like I was on the verge of a nervous breakdown, which was something. I hadn't liked the way she eyed my hair. "Well, not exactly. It's, uh, been a long day." I stumbled over my words. I was so flustered, I could barely string a coherent response together. Seth's presence was like the sun, blinding me and warming me all over, and Maddie was making me feel guilty and dirty for enjoying that sun.

"Is everything okay with your family?" she asked.

"My—oh, yeah, they're okay. Still just a little crazy, but it'll, um, pass." I stood and picked up the laptop, hoping I sounded casual and calm. I needed to get out before I said something stupid. As it was, I couldn't even make eye contact with Seth now. "I really just came by for this."

Maddie studied me a few seconds longer and must have decided I was more or less telling the truth. She relaxed and seemed oblivious to me trying frantically to get to the door.

"Hey," she said, "I was thinking you might not need to go to California for beaches."

"For . . . what?"

"Remember our conversation at Mark's?"

"Er, yeah." Miraculously, I did. The condo thing, when I told her I had a beach itch.

"I have the perfect solution: Alki."

"Alki?" asked Seth, confused.

"It's a secret." She winked at me. "I thought that might be a good place to start looking. What do you think?"

"Sure. Sounds great." Alki Beach was a region of West Seattle that stuck out into Puget Sound. While it was a far cry from a Cyprian beach, it was, well, a beach. And if agreeing that it was a good idea would get me to the door . . .

"Cool! And what about dancing?"

"Huh? What about it?" I probably looked like a deer in

the headlights again. This agitated state of mine didn't make for good topic-jumping.

"Teaching salsa. I mentioned it to Beth and Casey, and they were pretty excited."

"Oh. Yeah. Sure. I can do that." I was seriously about to agree to anything to escape.

Her face lit up. "Oh, thank you! Is this week too soon? I bet we could get everyone together on, oh, Thursday."

"Sure, sure, that's fine." I was almost at the door.

"Oh, thank you! This'll be fun. I'll double-check the day with everyone and e-mail you. If something comes up . . . I mean, I know you're under a lot of stress . . ."

I waved it off. "It's fine, really. Have a good night, okay?"

I put on a winning smile and quickly walked past both of them. As I stepped out the door, though, I glanced back and met Seth's eyes. My smile faltered. A thousand messages passed between us, just as they used to when we were dating. Only this time, I wasn't sure what any of them were saying.

I kept walking, suddenly realizing I had a lot more than mortality to worry about.

Chapter 12

Searching the Internet didn't turn up much, just as I'd feared. Still, I took some satisfaction in at least *doing* something. It kept my mind off my possibly impending death. It kept my mind off demons descending on Seattle. Most importantly, it kept my mind off Seth.

Because if I thought about him, I was going to think about touching him and kissing him and . . . well, a lot of other things. My feelings for him were starting to consume me, almost to the extent that my other problems seemed trivial. So, I lost myself in Google searches, hoping for any scrap of information about demon summoning. As expected, most of my hits sent me to sites on role-playing games and Dr. Faustus. Still, I felt better than if I'd just sat around.

Driving to the meeting at the Cellar was about as agonizing as walking to the bookstore had been. I took slow back roads, unwilling to face the congestion and speed of the freeways. The Cellar was a pub a lot of Seattle immortals liked to frequent. Whoever had organized this event had apparently reserved the restaurant's back room, which was normally used for banquets and wedding receptions. I didn't have to sense demonic magic to know they'd sealed off the space from prying ears.

The dimly lit room was crowded when I entered. I recognized some of the local lesser immortals, but most were demons I didn't know. Few sat at the long table, which was covered with appetizer plates and bottles of wine. Most people stood around the edges, deep in conversation, or had pulled chairs up in tight, furtive clusters. Grace and Mei were both working the room, looking as businesslike and efficient as ever—albeit edged in an uncharacteristically frazzled air. For the first time ever, they were dressed differently, and I wondered if stress had prevented them from coordinating their wardrobes. Mei wore a red skirt and blazer with a necklace made of tiny alternating gold and silver rings. Grace wore a linen pantsuit with a chunky stone choker with a crescent moon pendant.

Peter, Cody, and Hugh stood in the corner and waved me over.

"Hey," I said, "what's going on?"

"Not much," said Hugh. "This seems to be more of a meet and greet. Not a lot of organization."

We fell silent, all of us watching the interactions. In the opposite corner, I saw Cedric gesturing dramatically as he spoke. His face was dark and intent, and Kristin stood nearby with a clipboard and rapt expression, taking notes. Not far away, Nanette stood with her lovely, unreadable face while listening to another demoness talk.

"So, you must be Jerome's staff."

The four of us turned. None of us had noticed the demon approaching, thanks to losing our ability to sense immortal signatures. This whole experience, I decided, really was like being bereft of sight or smell. This particular demon was no one I knew. He had a big toothy smile and skin that looked like it had had a tanning job go bad. His spiky white-blond hair wasn't doing him any favors either.

He extended a hand. "I'm Tom. Pleasure to meet you all."

We each shook his hand in return, introducing ourselves. He held our hands with great vigor, like a politician on the campaign trail. If we'd had a baby, I had no doubts he would have kissed it.

"I imagine this must be pretty strange for you," he commented. "But I want you to know that we're all here for you. There's nothing to worry about—things'll be back to normal before long."

"Thank you," I said politely, giving as good a succubus smile as I could in a non-succubus state. Snark around a demon was never a good idea. Snark when you didn't have your normal powers? *Horrible* idea. "We're just anxious to get Jerome back."

His smile faltered a little but quickly resumed. "Yes, yes. Of course. We're all doing everything we can. But, of course, you know there's a chance Jerome might not be found . . ."

"So we've heard," said Hugh, speaking as politely as I had.

Tom nodded. "But don't worry. In the tragic event that happens, we'll make sure you guys are taken care of. You can rest assured that Seattle's next archdemon will rule with control and competence, making sure you're able to perform your duties in an efficient and effective manner."

I had a feeling he was on the verge of telling us how, if elected, he'd cut taxes and increase jobs, but we were interrupted by a high-pitched voice.

"Georg-*gee*-na!"

A seven-foot woman was heading toward us. She had ebony-black skin that looked horrible with her orange hair. The combination made Tom's features look supermodel gorgeous. Gold eye shadow shot all the way to her eyebrows, its glitter rivaled only by the multicolored sequins of her dress. A black feather boa flared around her as she walked. Several demons in the room froze and watched her, which was remarkable. Demons are not easily fazed.

"Who's that?" asked Cody. Just like with Tom, Cody could sense neither the identity nor even the type of this immortal. But I needed no such clues.

"Tawny," Peter and I said in unison.

"How do you guys know?" asked Cody.

"The clothes," said Peter.

"The whine," I said.

Tom was standing there, mouth half-open. A moment later, he recovered himself. "Well, it was nice meeting you all. I hope you'll come talk to me if you have any questions or concerns. I'm very eager to get to know you all better." He scurried off just as Tawny reached us. We stared.

"What the hell happened to you?" exclaimed Hugh.

Tawny pouted. "Well, there was this really nice guy that I wanted. Really pure and—"

"Tawny," I interrupted. "I've told you a hundred times. Stop worrying about the good ones."

She shook her head. "No, no. He was into me. Well, he was into this." She gestured to her body. "I figured out that he had these weird fantasies his wife didn't know about. So, I put on this shape, and we did *it*. And the energy . . . it was amazing."

I couldn't hide my astonishment. Tawny had managed to score a decent guy. She'd used a strategy that, while basic, was also highly effective: exploiting secret desires. It could shake the unshakable soul. "Wow," I said at last. "That's great. I . . . well, I can't believe I'm saying this, but I'm proud of you."

She sighed. "But I didn't get to enjoy the rush. Like, ten minutes after it happened, it went away. Everything went away. I started feeling sick and—"

"Yeah, we know the rest," said Cody, not unkindly.

"And I was wearing this body, and now . . . now I'm stuck with it."

Under normal conditions, this would have provided hours of hilarity. For now, I actually felt bad for her. "Well, hang in there. They say this won't last for long."

Tawny nodded unhappily. "Yeah. Here's hoping." Then, unexpectedly, she brightened a little. "Oh, but hey, you were totally right about the blow-job thing."

Hugh's head whipped around to stare at me. "What?"

Before I could say anything, Mei thankfully shouted for everyone's attention. And when I say shouted, I mean it. She used her power to amplify her voice, so it rang painfully through the whole room, making a lot of us wince and cover our ears. Several people backed away, giving us a clear view of her and Grace.

"We want to thank everyone for coming," Mei said, returning to her usual flat, emotionless voice.

"And we appreciate everyone's help as we try to keep things running around here. Mei and I have everything under control right now, but the concern everyone's shown is certainly . . . admirable." There was the slightest wry note in Grace's voice as she glanced around at the assembled demons. Many of them straightened up and smiled, acting as though they truly were here out of concern for us.

"We know you're as anxious to find Jerome as we are," said Mei. "And we'll be doing everything we can to locate him." Some of those smiles tightened a little, and the crowd shifted uncomfortably. As I'd told Seth, not everyone was so eager for Jerome's return.

"Yes, of course," a booming voice said. Tom had joined Grace and Mei in the spotlight. "Jerome is our top priority, of course. And if—I mean, when—he's found, I'm sure Management will be most eager to talk to him about how this happened in the first place. No doubt he will need a little . . . rehabilitation, and should he be unable to fulfill his duties, I for one am ready right now to step up and run infernal affairs in Seattle."

"Well, Tom." A dark-haired demoness from across the room straightened up from where she leaned against the wall. "If memory serves, your leadership in Tuscaloosa didn't end so well."

Tom glowered. "That was *not* my fault."

So it began. The meeting slowly degenerated into chaos and mostly became about each demon talking about why he or she was the best choice—and why all of the others were completely unfit. It was like a year of presidential campaigning condensed into an hour.

"Look at Grace and Mei," noted Hugh. "They look like they want to smite this entire room."

"Well," I said. "That's the thing. All these demons are talking about keeping hellish affairs in order here, but those two are the ones who are actually doing it right now."

"Hell should just let them take over if Jerome doesn't come back," said Cody. I gave him a sharp look. "Er, I mean, not that there's any question of that. He'll be back."

"Let's hope so," a new voice said. Cedric had strolled over and joined our circle, Kristin in tow.

"Whatever," I said, unable to hide a smile. "You can't tell me you want him back. This is your perfect chance to create your great Northwest empire."

He shook his head. "No, believe me, I want nothing to do with any of this. Compared to some of these losers, Jerome suddenly seems like an ideal neighbor." It was very much like what Isabelle had said. "I don't suppose," Cedric added, "that you're going to be coming back up to Vancouver?"

I hesitated. Was I? Who did I answer to now? Did Jerome's orders still stand? "I . . . I don't know," I admitted. "I don't know what I'm supposed to. If I should leave."

"Well," he said. "It wasn't like you were doing that great a job."

"I was too! I'd gotten them to back down before their so-called angel spoke to them. She told them not to trust me." I frowned, wondering if I should go on. I didn't know who to trust without Jerome around, and as Hugh had said, Cedric was still a very likely candidate for Jerome's summoning, in spite of my gut instinct. "And you know . . . I think I have an idea about who did this and who that angel is . . ."

Cedric groaned. "Will you give up on Isabelle already?"

I shook my head and lowered my voice. "I don't think it was her. I think it was Nanette."

The incredulous look on his face didn't change. "That's as ridiculous as Isabelle. You were there. You saw Nanette come to me because she was simply worried about managing her own territory."

"Funny, she had a similar meeting with Jerome not long after that."

Cedric's face kept that cool, skeptical expression that demons excelled it. But, I was pretty sure I could see a spark of inter-est in his blue-gray eyes. "That doesn't mean anything." Another gut feeling told me he was lying. He started to turn, but then Cody spoke, voice hesitant.

"Excuse me . . . do you know . . . are we mortal?"

Cedric hesitated a moment and then laughed. When none of us said anything, he glanced between all our faces. "Oh. You're serious?"

"Why is that such a crazy question?" I demanded. "We've lost everything else that makes us immortal."

"You've lost it to keep you out of trouble," said Cedric. "Nobody wants you guys running around unsupervised with your normal abilities. So when you lose an archdemon, you get cut off. But you're still immortal. You think you can get out of your contract with something as easy as death?"

"So we could get hit by a car and still be okay?" asked Cody.

"Of course. Sure, it'd take awhile to recover. You'd heal like a human, but you'd eventually heal."

"What if we got decapitated?" asked Peter.

"Yeah," agreed Cody. "Like in *Highlander*?"

Cedric rolled his eyes. "Don't get decapitated, and we'll never have to find out." He focused on me. "Look, stay here for a while. Something tells me that the Angel of Darkness isn't going to be making any appearances anytime soon. I suspect the distraction is over."

"I agree. Thanks."

He gave me a curt nod and started to turn. Then, he glanced back at Tawny and did a double-take. "What's your name?"

"Tawny," she replied.

He eyed her from head to foot and then turned to Kristin. "Get her number and set up a date."

I saw a spark of something in Kristin's eyes, and it took me a moment to identify it. Jealousy. Reflecting back on the way she doted on his affairs, I shouldn't have been surprised that she had a crush on him. She flipped through a few pages in her clipboard, her lips tight and disapproving.

"You've got a lot of appointments this week. You hate it

when you've got back-to-back events." She spoke levelly, but I could tell that while part of her warning came from true concern, another part of her welcomed the chance to throw a kink into his dating life. Cedric didn't appear to notice.

He waved a dismissive hand. "Cancel something unimportant. You'll know what to do."

He wandered off while Kristin took down Tawny's number. "We'll be in touch," Kristin said flatly.

"Huh," said Tawny, once Kristin was gone. "He's kind of cute. Maybe this body isn't so bad after all."

I exchanged glances with Hugh and Peter. They looked a lot like I felt: weary and frustrated, with the secret suspicion that this was all almost funny.

"Well," I said, watching Tawny smile with delight. "At least someone's happy with all this."

Chapter 13

Hearing Cedric assure me I couldn't die lifted a huge weight off my shoulders. I left the Cellar with much less anxiety, though I still had no intention of doing anything that might test how exactly we'd heal from decapitation. So, while I still operated with caution, I no longer felt suffocated or threatened by every aspect of the world.

Rather than go home, I drove down to Dante's shop. His store/apartment was in Rainier Valley, on the southeast side of Seattle. He had no regularly posted hours for his assorted "psychic" services, but he would usually hang around there at night if he had nothing else to do. It tended to be the time drunk people or couples out on dates (or high teens) would wander in looking for fun and novelty. Daytime business hours didn't generally bring out that many who were seeking help from the divine unless, perhaps, it was someone seeking advice on stock trading.

Dante had no customers tonight, however. The shop and its flickering neon sign seemed sad and lonely. I pushed through the unlocked door and found him leaning against the check-out counter, leafing through a copy of *Maxim*.

"What gives?" I asked. "Your subscription to *Frauds and Scams Weekly* run out?"

He glanced up at me with a smile, flipping black hair out of his face. "Just needed something pretty to look at since I didn't know when I'd be seeing you again."

I planted a kiss on his cheek. "Holy shit. That's the sweetest thing you've ever said to me."

"Yeah, well, I can make some filthy sexual suggestions to you if you'd prefer."

"What, and ruin foreplay for next time?"

This made his grin grow, and he shut the magazine. "To what do I owe the pleasure? Shouldn't you be visiting our neighbors to the north? Or is that done? I honestly can't keep track."

"Well. About that." God, how I was going to explain what had happened? Had all of this seriously happened in just one day? It felt like a year had gone by since I got woozy in the car. "Something strange happened today."

"Strange like you sold out of Jane Austen books at the store or strange like the rules of time and space as we know them are about to be ripped apart?"

"Mmm . . . more like that last one."

"Shit."

I took a deep breath, figuring I should just get the big stuff out of the way. "There's no easy way to put this, but . . . I'm not a succubus anymore."

"I never believed you were a succubus."

I groaned. That had been an old joke between us when we'd first met. Oh, the irony. "I'm serious," I said. "No more succubus. And Jerome's disappeared too, possibly opening up Seattle to a new demonic reign."

Dante stared at me, eyes speculative as he assessed me for the truth. He was speechless for the first time I'd known him. Not waiting for more witty commentary, I plunged forward. I explained about the summoning, what it had done to all of us lesser immortals, how demons everywhere were now sizing up Seattle, and why I needed to find Jerome as soon as possible.

When I finally finished, it took Dante several moments to gather his thoughts. "So . . . you've seriously lost your succubus powers?"

"Abilities," I corrected. "And yes, I have. Are you saying that after all that other stuff I just told you about the balance of power in Seattle, my succubus status is what caught your attention the most?"

He shrugged. "You gotta admit it's weird. Besides, that other stuff doesn't affect me. You do." His eyes narrowed. "Am I going to have to use a condom now?"

"What? No. Of course not."

"You sure?"

"You've never batted an eye over me stealing pieces of your soul these last few months, but the nonexistent threat of child support suddenly scares you?"

"Well, yeah, seeing as my bank account's got more in it than my soul."

I glanced around the shabby room. "Debatable."

"Cute," he conceded. "But I'd be asking a few more questions about all of this if I were you. Like, can you die?"

"I already asked that one," I said smugly. "And the answer is no. Our immortal bodies are still essentially the same. We're just cut off from all the perks." I hoped he didn't ask about decapitation because I honestly wasn't in the mood to debate that.

"Okay, so what do you want from me?" he asked.

"What makes you think I want anything?"

He looked at me.

"Okay, maybe I do want something. But come on, who else would know more about this stuff than you?"

"Who knows more about demons? Hmm, let me think. I know. How about *the demons you work for*, the ones who are all-powerful and have been around since the beginning of time?"

"They're not all-powerful. Otherwise they wouldn't need a human for the summoning—or end up getting summoned in the first place. And that's what I need you for. There can't be that many humans in the area capable of doing this, are there? You have to know who they are."

Dante opened his mouth, no doubt with a snappy reply

ready, and then abruptly closed it. "I don't know," he said slowly. "I don't keep track of those things."

I leaned toward him, incredulous. "Of course you do! Do you not want to tell me? Why?"

He sighed, his hesitant expression turning typically annoyed. "Because those kinds of people get pissed off if you start advertising their names."

"What, you're afraid they're going to come beat you up?"

"No. Not exactly. But there's sort of . . . a professional courtesy in these circles."

"I'll be discreet. I won't tell them where I got the information."

"Most of them already know we're together. They'd figure it out. They keep an eye on those kinds of things." He turned considering. "Of course, in that same vein, a lot of them know you as a succubus and might just think you knew through your own connections."

He still seemed hesitant, so I played a mean card. "Well, I can always go ask Erik if you're too nervous about it."

Erik was another mortal in town who dealt with the occult and paranormal. Unlike Dante, who was a practitioner, Erik simply studied and built up knowledge of the magical undercurrents in the city. He had a psychic's gifts and was attuned to what most human eyes didn't see. Sometimes he could even see what immortals couldn't. He and Dante had an old, old grudge and didn't enjoy being around each other, to put it mildly.

My attempt to bait Dante didn't work, though. "Don't even try it, succubus. Making me jealous of the old man won't make me help you."

I looked up at him pleadingly. "What will make you help me?"

He traced the outline of my lips with his fingertip, gray eyes wicked and thoughtful. "Not sure it's anything you can do while cut off from your super-secret powers. You're not a sex goddess anymore."

"Hey, I don't need super-secret powers to be a sex goddess."

Just then, three twentysomethings stumbled in, staring wide-eyed at the shop as they tried to stifle nervous giggles. They undoubtedly had the same kind of potential that high teens did. I gave Dante one last frantic plea. "Please? Just give me the names. You don't have to do anything else. And I won't say anything. I swear it."

Dante scowled, glanced at me, at the potential customers, and then back at me. He told them he'd be with them in a minute and then hastily jotted four names down on a scrap of paper. Two of them I recognized.

"Thank you," I said. I beamed, and to my surprise, something in his cynical expression softened a little.

"God, that smile," he muttered. "You might just be right."

"About what?"

"You really don't need any powers to be a sex goddess. Your hair's a little messy, though." He walked around the counter and gave me a quick half-hug. "Be safe, succubus. Don't test the limits of that not-dying thing."

"And buy some condoms?" I teased.

He shrugged. "You're the one who was having prophetic dreams about having kids a little while ago." Turning away from me, he put on his jovial con-man persona and beckoned the group over with pitches about palms and Tarot.

He'd spoken the words in a light, off-hand kind of way, but as I slowly walked back to my car, they slapped me in the face.

Prophetic dreams . . .

Nyx's dreams.

The things she'd shown me during that time had been so vivid that they seemed almost more real than my own life. The thing is, by almost all accounts, Nyx had a grasp on the future and could show people things that would happen to them. That was how she spread chaos in the world, by showing people these visions and making them think they knew how their futures would unfold. Unfortunately, while the visions came true, they never came true the way their victims thought they would. She'd led a lot of people to their deaths that way.

Nonetheless, it seemed fairly clear that the dreams she'd sent to me had been distractions, not destructive images of what would come. In my visions, she'd shown me—over and over—with a daughter, waiting for a man I loved to come home. The dreams had consumed me, almost making me want to sleep and have my energy taken each night. As I'd noted while holding Kayla, there was no way any piece of the vision could ever happen to me. I couldn't have any sort of relationship like that. And I certainly couldn't have a daughter, not of my own blood. Immortals didn't reproduce. When I'd sold my soul for immortality and shape-shifting, I'd given up certain aspects of my humanity. There could be no child for me. Not ever.

And yet . . .

I came to a stop on the sidewalk, still about a block away from my car. What if Dante had inadvertently stumbled onto something? What if being in this stasis had altered that piece of me that had lost the ability to conceive? Cedric had said I was still technically immortal, but he'd also said my body would respond and heal like a human's. What all did that entail? Would unprotected sex lead to conception? Is that what Nyx's visions had been pointing to? She'd sworn she'd shown me the truth. Had she?

I was breathing fast again, though at least this time, I knew I didn't have to worry about giving myself a heart attack. Okay. I needed to calm down. This pregnancy possibility was as distracting as the hooking-up-with-Seth possibility. I'd never get anything accomplished if I lost myself in fantasies.

With a sigh, I glanced down at Dante's piece of paper, now crumpled in my hand. I'd clenched it into a ball without even realizing it as I walked. I'd been too preoccupied to even notice . . .

Babies and Seth. The things I wanted most.

I forced myself to keep moving toward my car. But as I unlocked the door, I had to wonder ruefully if maybe I shouldn't be so quick to get Jerome back after all.

I started following up on Dante's leads the next morning. Leaving my place was a little harder than I'd expected, though. Despite the fact I got ready plenty of mornings without shape-shifting, my closet seemed terribly small. And while my hair seemed fine when I finished it, I had a feeling it'd be frizzy the next time I checked the mirror. The only bright part was when I found Dante's watch under the bed. I thought I'd lost it yes-terday, so at least my accessories collection was still respectable. Nonetheless, I had a feeling I was soon going to discover just how much I'd come to rely on my abilities.

Locating addresses from Dante's list of names required a little sleuthing here and there, but for the most part, I didn't have much difficulty finding them. Unfortunately, once found, these magicians weren't exactly helpful.

One of the ones I visited knew me. She was familiar with Hell's local servants, and while she gave me a small degree of respect, she was as hesitant to answer questions as Dante had insinuated. Two of the other names were people who didn't know me, and that immediately created a problem. With my succubus powers shut off, I had no immortal signature, and both of these people were the types who could sense that. Me coming in and claiming to be a succubus was met with scorn and disbelief. I managed to glean some information from them but nothing of any use.

Equally difficult was that not only could they not sense me, I couldn't sense them. Admittedly, a succubus didn't have the same ability to gauge human power the way a full-fledged demon could, but I could occasionally sense magic around a person or object. Today, I was completely blind. I had to rely on my strength to read people, but these dark magicians were as good at cons as Dante. They were well-versed in the art of concealing the truth.

It was almost noon by the time I visited the last name, a

guy named Greg. I felt pretty discouraged by this point and even cracked and had a cigarette along the way. Greg had no storefront like Dante and mostly worked his spells out of his house, a small bungalow in Wallingford. When he answered the door, his disheveled state told me I'd woken him up. On the bright side, he recognized me, which meant I wouldn't have to convince him I was a succubus.

"What do you want?" he asked suspiciously. He was built big and could have had an impressive physique if he'd ever gone to the gym. It was obvious he hadn't.

"I wanted to talk to you about demon summoning."

"I don't know anything about it."

He started to shut the door. I stuck my foot out to block it. "Wait. Do you know anyone who would?"

"No. And even if I did, what makes you think I'd tell you?" He tried to close the door again, then paused. He narrowed his already too-small eyes at me. "There's something weird about you. No aura."

I didn't answer right away. "Maybe you're losing your touch."

This actually brought a small smile. "Not likely. What happened? Who got summoned?"

"No one. And even if they did, what makes you think I'd tell you?" I mimicked.

He laughed, a guttural sound that came from low in his throat. When the laughter faded, he studied me for several long seconds, face cunning and speculative. "Okay. I'll talk to you." He pushed the door open. "Come on in."

I gingerly stepped into his living room. The place was a disaster. Dirty dishes were piled on the coffee table, the remains of food hardened and crusty. Dust coated every piece of furniture, and the wood floor looked like it hadn't been swept since the last century. Uneasily, I wondered if my new human-like body was susceptible to germs.

Several books were piled on the couch, their covers meant to look sinister in shades of black and red with drawings of pentagrams. It put me in mind of Evan's faux Satanic accoutrements, though as hard as it was to believe, Evan had a thousand times more class than this guy.

Greg offered me neither a chair nor refreshments, which was fine by me. He stood in front of me, arms crossed. "Well? What do you want to know?"

"I want to know if you've done any demon summoning lately."

"Not that any demons have been summoned, of course."

"This is speculative," I replied with a simpering smile. I studied as much of his home as I could while I spoke. Beyond him, I could see an equally messy kitchen with a gas stove and magnet-covered refrigerator.

"You think if I'd summoned a demon, I'd be living like this? Fuck, I'd have plasma-screen TVs and concubines."

I recalled the discussion with my friends, noting that any human who'd summoned Jerome would simply keep the demon hidden and not use it for personal gain and errands. Still, if Greg had summoned Jerome on behalf of another demon, there would have been some reward involved. Maybe it wouldn't entail TVs or concubines, but it seemed like there'd be some sign of a windfall here. Maybe he'd gotten a Swiss bank account.

"Okay. You know anyone who recently acquired concubines?"

"Nope. But I can give you some names of people who'd be more likely." He listed two of the magicians I'd already visited.

"I've talked to them."

"Sorry. Not my problem." My eyes returned to the books on the couch. I stepped toward them. "May I?"

"Knock yourself out."

I picked up one of the books, skimming through it in hopes of finding information about summoning. Nope. It was fluffy "evil" stuff, exactly like the Army of Darkness' propaganda. The second book proved the same. The third, however, was a legitimate spell book, filled with the kind of dark rites Dante practiced. Hopeful, I flipped through the pages one by one. It had some vile contents, but there was nothing about summoning. Greg's willingness to let me browse the books should have been a tip-off that they contained nothing of use.

"All done?"

I jerked around. Greg's voice was close to me—too close. I'd had my back to him while checking out the books, but now he was right behind me. I took a few steps back and bumped the couch.

"Yeah," I said nervously. "Thanks for the help. I should leave now."

"Not yet," he said, moving closer. "You just got here."

I tried to wriggle off to the side, but his hands suddenly reached out and grabbed a hold of my arms, pinning me into place.

"What are you doing?" I demanded. There went my heart rate again.

"I don't know what's going on with all this summoning stuff, but I do know there's a succubus here who doesn't feel like a succubus anymore, which probably means you can't fight like one."

I tried to break from his grasp, but his hands were like steel. "You're crazy. Of course I'm a succubus. You know I am."

"Yeah? Then shape-shift away from me. Turn into a bird. Turn into a bodybuilder."

I clenched my teeth and tried to shake his hold again. "Let me go, you son of a bitch. You hurt me, and a whole host of demons are going to show up and rip you limb from limb."

"Not so sure about that," he chuckled. "This is a once-in-a-lifetime chance. You think any succubus would fuck someone like me?"

He shoved me down onto the couch, one strong arm pinning me in place while the other hand fumbled awkwardly under my shirt and grabbed a hold of my breast. Moving his head close, he tried to press his lips against mine, but I turned my head just in time.

"Let me go!" I screamed. I managed to wriggle a leg free and knee him in the gut. It wasn't enough to free me, but it made him scowl.

I'd worried about getting hit by cars, meteors, and structurally unsound overpasses. Never, never had I thought about being raped. It hadn't been a fear of mine for centuries, not since I realized I could shape-shift into someone larger and stronger, someone capable of throwing off any assailant.

Maybe it shouldn't have bothered me so much. I'd had sex with plenty of people I didn't like over the years. I'd always grimaced and waited it out. But there was something about this that was different. It wasn't my choice, and compounding it all was the feeling of helplessness I had. I hated not having options. I hated not being able to think my way out of something. There was nothing to be done, though. Not this time.

The most I could do was keep struggling and flailing. I did have some self-defense training, after all. I'd learned to use weapons and punch over the years. I'd nailed Niphon pretty good at Christmas. Unfortunately, what I could do now was limited with Greg on me like this. He simply outweighed me. Still, my efforts must have proven annoying because Greg growled and grabbed both my arms in an attempt to flip me over. I yelled profanities at him and got another knee-jab in, close to his groin but not close enough.

And that's when it happened.

The smell hit me first. An overwhelming and suffocating odor of natural gas. I stopped struggling for half a second. I didn't need to be human to know that meant trouble.

Before I could process that further, the kitchen exploded into flames.

Fire expanded out into the living room. It didn't quite reach us, but I think Greg must have still gotten burned because he screamed in pain and released his hold on me. His body had shielded the worst from me, and mostly all I felt was a rolling wave of heat and air.

I didn't bother to think or question anything. Greg had released me in his confusion, and I bolted. I scrambled from the couch and ran out the front door, away from the fire. Away from Greg.

I drove off as fast as I could, my Passat's tires squealing on the pavement. Sweat poured off me, and my hands could barely grip the steering wheel through their shaking. About a mile away, I heard the singing of sirens, but I couldn't spare a thought for what had happened. I couldn't think about whether Greg had made it out or not. I couldn't think about how a gas leak had miraculously saved me.

The only thing I could think about now was getting away and getting to safety.

Chapter 14

Instinct made me drive back to Queen Anne. I operated on autopilot, my mind blank. It was only when I'd parked and gotten out of the car that my senses slowly began to return to me. Still, I tried my best to stay numb, to not think about anything right away. My stomach was growling, so I decided to focus on basic needs. I walked over to a Thai restaurant between my apartment and the bookstore, seeking the comfort of a corner table and green curry. Once I was settled, there was no avoiding it.

What had happened back there? Part of me could still feel Greg's hands on me, still feel the sickening sensation of being utterly and completely helpless. But the rest of me was slowly starting to analyze the stove exploding.

I'd noticed the gas stove upon my initial inspection, but I'd noticed no smell until right before it caught on fire. With gas leaks, didn't a place usually fill up over time? This had been sudden. An out-of-the-blue surge of gas, and BAM! No warning, no anything. I supposed it could have been coincidence. Lucky timing. But in my world, coincidences didn't happen. They were usually guided by a stronger power. The question was: who or what was responsible? I had too much to worry about now without some unseen arsonist on the scene.

"Why so pensive, Daughter of Lilith?"

I looked up from my half-eaten food. "Carter!"

I was pretty sure I'd never been so happy to see the angel

in my life, except for maybe when he'd rescued me from Helena the crazy nephilim last fall. He wore the same clothes he'd had on in Vancouver. They appeared to stay in a perpetually consistent state of dishevelment—never getting worse, never getting better.

He slid into the chair opposite me. "You gonna finish that?" he asked, pointing at my plate.

I shook my head and slid the curry over to him. He immediately dug in, practically inhaling it. "What's going on?" he asked between mouthfuls of rice.

"You know what's going on. Seattle's gone to hell. Literally."

"Yeah, I've noticed. How's it feel to be footloose and fancy free?"

"It sucks. For some reason, my hair's always frizzy. I used to style it myself before this happened, and it never did that."

Carter grinned. "I doubt you were doing it all yourself. You may have still done all the labor, but some subconscious part of you was probably tweaking it just a little bit to keep it perfect."

I pulled a face. "Well, even if that's true, I've got a few bigger problems."

I gave him a brief recap of my adventures this morning and what had happened with Greg. Even speaking about it still sent a chill down my spine. I expected Carter to laugh and make some quip at my expense, but his face stayed serious.

"You need to be careful," he said gravely. "Everything's different now. It'll only be for a short time, true, but even if you can't die, you're still locked in a dangerous game."

"We have to find Jerome. Do you know where he's at?"

Carter shook his head. "Nope. He disappeared off our radars too. I don't know anything more than you do."

"You probably know more about demon summoning than I do," I pointed out.

"Depends," he said. "What do you know?"

"Pretty much what I already told you. Dante didn't have much more to offer than who he thought could do it. And those other losers didn't give up anything at all—except attitude."

Carter flagged down a waitress and ordered a plate of panang curry and Thai iced coffee. Afterward, he tapped the table lightly with his finger, face drawn and thoughtful. "I can tell you how it's done," he said at last. "But I can't do much more. This is your side's business, not ours. We're not supposed to interfere."

"Dispensing information isn't the same as interfering," I said.

He smiled. "Depends on your definitions. And your people are great at finding loopholes and technicalities."

"Yeah, but ... Carter ..." I sighed. "I don't really have anyone else."

Even if I'd had full succubus charisma going, I don't think it would have worked on him. But I still had some sort of Georgina charisma that he was susceptible to. He liked me and was concerned about my life, even if he had a funny way of showing it sometimes.

The Thai iced coffee appeared, and he paused to take a drink. "Okay. Here's how it works. Basically, a demon gets summoned into an object, and with enough magic, the demon becomes bound to that and is trapped. You've heard stories about genies, right? Well, they're kind of variations on this principle. Humans who summon demons into objects can then occasionally release the demon and make them run errands."

"But this one's keeping Jerome locked up."

"Right. Which makes it harder. What makes it harder still is that if this human has any sense at all, they've got the object hidden in a place of power." He took another sip and waited for me to process this.

I knew what he was talking about. The earth was covered in places of power—sacred sites, ley lines, magic-infused spots. Anyone sifting through mythology would come across countless references to them and the roles they'd played in human history. There was just one problem with it.

"There are dozens of those in Seattle," I said slowly.

Carter nodded. "Yup. And even if you find the right one, the power in that place is going to help mask the power coming from the bound demon. For you? Gonna be nearly impossible without your usual senses. You need another immortal to help, the stronger the better. Or possibly a human psychic."

I groaned. "But you can't help, and none of the demons will." The panang curry arrived, and Carter devoured it with enthusiasm. "Putting that aside, let's suppose I find this object, whatever it is. Then what?"

"Mmm, that's hard too," he said. "A greater immortal could just break it open."

"But not me." I was beginning to see how this worked, and it wasn't encouraging.

"No, not even if you were in your normal state. The summoner probably put a lock on it—a seal. That'll keep a lesser immortal out. The seal's used in the binding, then it's broken into two pieces that are kept separated for safekeeping. The practitioner most certainly keeps one. If he or she had a demon's help, I'm guessing the demon has the other. Or else the practitioner would hide it."

"Do you think another demon was involved?"

He swallowed. "Most definitely. If you can recover the pieces of the seal, though, then you could unlock the object and set Jerome free."

When I'd first seen Carter standing over my table, I'd been filled with hope, convinced this miserable situation was going to resolve soon and we'd get Jerome back. Now? I was more pessimistic than before.

"So, let me get this straight. All I have to do is find this mystical object that Jerome's locked in, an object I have no way of even sensing. Once I have it, I then simply have to force the pieces of the lock away from the summoner and *a demon*."

"Yup," said Carter, licking his fork. "That pretty much sums it up."

"Fuck."

"Yup."

"Well, the info's good, but I can't do anything. I have no leads on any part of this, nowhere to start."

His gray eyes twinkled. "The seal has to be made of quartz."

"Okay . . ."

"Hand-carved by human hands."

I raised an eyebrow, curious as to where this was going.

"By someone familiar with magic and runes." He looked at me expectantly.

"So?"

"How many people do you think that describes in the Seattle area?" He didn't wait for me to finish. "Not many."

Carter and his riddles. "You're saying I should find who made the seal, in the hopes they can tell me who commissioned it."

"Right. And they can also tell you what the seal's specifics are. It's almost always a disc about this big." He used the fingers of one hand to make a circle about the size of a quarter. "But the color and designs will be different and provide clues as to what kind of place it's been hidden in."

"God, this is complicated."

"You're trying to find a demon that's been captured and bound as part of a larger political power play, Georgina," Carter said. "What do you expect?"

"Fair point," I murmured. "I have one more question, though. It has nothing to do with the seal, though."

"Shoot."

"Why'd the stove at Greg's blow up?"

"Because of a gas leak."

"One that came on out of nowhere?"

He shrugged. "Compared to what we see every day? A lot stranger things happen."

I eyed him for a moment, wondering if I should press him with my real question. He'd said he couldn't directly interfere in this, but Carter had saved my life once before. His showing up here now was awfully coincidental . . . Was it possible he'd been following me all day? Had he helped expedite the stove's incineration to save me? One might argue that touching Greg would have been direct interference . . . but harming the stove wouldn't be, if you wanted to use demon-worthy technicalities. And, in a typically angelic way, Carter hadn't actually denied his involvement.

I decided to let the matter go. If Carter was keeping his

help a secret, there was a good reason. With a sigh, I glanced at the clock to my right. "Well, I'm still technically on leave, so I should probably take advantage of that and hunt down this seal maker."

"Good luck," said Carter. "But joking aside, I meant what I said earlier. You've got to be careful. At the very least, don't do this stuff alone."

"You sure you can't break the rules and come with me, then?" I asked a bit wistfully.

"Nope, but why do you need me when there are plenty of other candidates?" With a grin, he nodded at something beyond me.

I glanced back and saw Seth standing at the take-out counter. I jerked my head back toward Carter.

"Hey! How'd—"

Carter was gone.

Just then, the waitress set down the bill, which included Carter's meal. "Fucking angels," I muttered, fumbling for my credit card.

Turning back around, I studied Seth, feeling my stomach twist in that usual way. As though sensing me, he suddenly turned and made eye contact. Surprise registered on his face, and then he held up his hand in a *hang on a second* kind of way.

A few agonizing minutes later, he walked over to my table holding a take-out bag.

"Hey," I said.

"Hey."

"Is that lunch?" I was suddenly embarrassed by the fact that I had two plates in front of me.

"Yeah, I'm actually heading home to work. The café at the store's too crowded and noisy."

"I thought you could work through anything."

He shook his head. "These days I'm more . . . distractible than usual." His eyes studied me for a moment, and then he looked away. But in that moment, I'd felt a tingle run through my skin. Seth cleared his throat. "So . . . what about you?" He forced himself to look back at me. "You look . . . I don't know. Uneasy. Not as bad as yesterday but still troubled. More immortal intrigue?"

A good portion of my present uneasiness was simply due to his proximity. "Yeah, afraid so."

"So, you haven't found Jerome yet, and you're still . . ."

Now it was my turn to look away. "Yeah. I followed some leads on Jerome this morning, and it was kind of . . . um, well, it's not important. Let's just say it wasn't a pleasant experience, and I didn't find out anything anyway." I glanced back in his direction, making sure I kept my eyes on his Blondie T-shirt and not his face. "I've got one more thing to check into, then I guess I can call it a day."

"Well, that's good, I guess." He shifted uncomfortably, and that awkward tension that was so characteristic for us multiplied. I tried to think of something to say, but nothing came. "So . . ." he began at last. "I know what you said before . . . but I still have to ask. Is there anything . . . anything I can do?"

The retort was on my lips, to tell him I didn't need him, not anymore. But an image of Greg flashed into my mind, and I hated myself for the fear it invoked. I didn't want to be a damsel in distress. I didn't want to live in fear and need a man to watch over me. Greg's weight and element of surprise had shown that self-defense wouldn't always work. Sometimes it was hard to face danger alone. Carter's words repeated in my head: *Why do you need me when there are plenty of other candidates?*

I blurted out my question before I had time to reconsider. "Would you go with me?"

It was hard to say which of us was more surprised by this. "On . . . your errand?" he asked.

I nodded. "Yeah. But I mean, if you've got stuff to do . . ."

"I'll go," he said quickly. He held up his take-out bag. "Can I eat in your car?"

"You can eat right now," I said. "Seeing as I don't know where we're going yet."

Leaving Seth to eat at the table, I stepped outside to make

a couple of phone calls. The first was to Dante. He answered, fortunately, but had no clue about what I needed.

"Someone who carves crystal?" he asked incredulously. "I don't do fluffy New Age stuff."

"Yeah. I found out more about demon summoning. Apparently there's some kind of seal involved that only a master artisan can make."

"I don't know anyone like that," he said. "As much as it pains me to admit a lack of knowledge about anything."

"Well, I guess even you have limits."

"You are *so* in trouble for that the next time I see you, succubus."

After we hung up, I tried Erik. He too answered, and in his usual way, he never bothered to ask why I needed the information. "There is someone," he mused. "I've acquired crystal jewelry from her before, carved into assorted sacred symbols—ankhs and crosses. I don't know if she works with the arcane or spellcraft, but she's the only one I know in the area who comes close."

I took down her name and address and went back inside. Seth had nearly finished his meal, rivaling Carter for speed. "Do we have a mission objective yet?"

I nodded. "Yup. Out to the hinterlands, even."

Okay, Carnation wasn't exactly the hinterlands, but it was well outside the Seattle urban and even suburban sprawl. It was one of several small rural communities that clung to western Washington's edge before giving way to the wilderness of the Cascade Mountains and the desert on the other side.

I made a Starbucks stop along the way so that I could acquire some caffeine. It seemed requisite to get through this. When Seth asked me to order him a mocha Frappuccino, I nearly crashed into the drive-thru window.

"That's got caffeine in it," I said.

"I know. But they're really good. Maddie got me hooked on them."

We drove in utter silence for ten minutes after that. If not for Jerome's summoning, I would have said this was the most astonishing thing to happen to me in the last twenty-four hours. Seth was drinking caffeine. It was unheard of. He'd abstained from it for years, and despite my clear addiction and coaxing throughout our relationship, he'd never shown any interest of cracking. Yet, Maddie—*Maddie!*—had somehow gotten him to change?

I don't know why I took such offense at that. Honestly, it was an inconsequential thing in the greater scheme of the universe. Still . . . I couldn't help feeling hurt. Well, maybe hurt wasn't the right word. Inadequate, perhaps. She'd gotten him to do something I couldn't. Why? Why her and not me? Was she more inspiring? Did he care about her more?

"Is something wrong?" Seth finally asked. My silence and death grip on the steering wheel had probably tipped him off.

"Nope," I lied. "Just worried about all of this."

"You are not."

"I'm not worried about all this?"

"Okay, you are. But that's not why you're upset right now. You're upset about this." Out of the corner of my eye, I saw him wave the Frappuccino. After all this time, he still knew me.

"That's stupid. Why would I care about that?"

He sighed. "Because I know you. You're irritated that I did something I never said I'd do."

"Why should I care?" I replied stiffly. "I'm happy you're expanding your horizons." The look he shot me told me he knew better.

We reached the address Erik had given me without further argument, largely because we didn't talk. The house was an older rambler set on a huge yard that would have held an entire subdivision back in Seattle. Lawn ornaments—a deer and a gnome, to name a few—cluttered the grass, and wind chimes dangled on the porch.

We knocked on the door, and several moments later, a woman in her late forties or early fifties answered. She had hair dyed an unnatural shade of red that put me in mind of Tawny's current hue. Her tight-fitting top pressed a lot of cleavage into her scoop neckline and was also not that far off from something Tawny might wear, albeit a little less tacky. The look the woman gave us wasn't unfriendly so much as curious.

"Yes?"

"Hi," I said. "Are you Mary Wilt—"

"*Oh my God!*" she squealed. She had just done a double-take on Seth. "You're Seth Mortensen!"

Seth stiffened and exchanged looks with me. "Well, yeah . . ."

Her blue-shadowed eyes bugged as she practically drooled over him. "I can't believe it. I can't believe it! Seth Mortensen's on my porch! I recognize you from your website. I look at it every day. *Every day*. Oh my God. *Oh my God*! I'm your biggest fan. Come in!"

Seth looked like he wanted to bolt then and there, but I nudged him forward. This turn of events was a bit unexpected—and creepy—but could possibly work to our advantage.

We stepped through the doorway. There was nothing particularly extraordinary about the inside of her house. The décor was more modern than the outside suggested, all done in neutral shades. There was a bit of normal lived-in clutter and far more figurines than I found tasteful, but overall, it was a nice place. Some of the figurines were carved out of crystal, which I took as a good sign.

"Come in, come in," Mary gushed, beckoning toward the living room. "Sit, sit! Can I get you anything? Iced tea? Coffee? Tequila?"

"Er, no. I'm fine," said Seth, who was clearly becoming more and more uncomfortable with all of this. "Thank you."

He and I sat down on the couch, and Mary sat in an armchair across from us, leaning forward in a way that afforded an ample view of her breasts. "What can I do for you?" she asked. "Are you here to buy something? I'd do anything for you. *Anything*." She grinned at Seth, making her "anything" intentions obvious. "You're so much cuter than I expected. Will you sign my books while you're here? I own all of them."

She gestured toward a set of shelves on the wall, and sure enough, Seth's books stood out prominently. I had been a longtime fan girl of Seth's before we started going out, and I wondered uneasily if I'd sounded this crazed and desperate way back when. She probably would have passed out if she'd known about the advanced copy Seth gave me.

"Sure," said Seth. "I'd, um, be happy to." He elbowed me, no doubt in an effort to get me to state our business and save him. Still a little irritated from our car argument, I almost enjoyed watching him in her clutches.

"We're actually not here to buy anything," I told her. "We wanted to find out about a piece you might have recently made for someone."

Mary turned toward me, seeming to notice me for the first time. Her gleeful, ravenous expression dimmed and even turned a little suspicious. "Who are you again?"

"Georgina. We're wondering if you recently made a piece for a client. A carved disc about this big with some sort of arcane symbol on it." I approximated the size Carter had shown me.

Her face grew more wary and pinched. "I can't say."

I frowned. "You don't remember?"

She shook her head. "I keep records of all my pieces. But that's confidential. I can't give that kind of information away."

"This is really important," I said. "We think . . . there may be a crime involved."

"Sorry, Giselle. I can't tell you about that. Not unless you're with the police or something."

"Georgina," I corrected. Her adherence to client confidentiality was perfectly understandable—but well, I wasn't really concerned with what was morally correct right now. Giving Seth an elbow poke of my own, I hoped he'd jump in and use his author god power. It took him a few moments, but he did.

"It would help us so much, Mary. We'd—*I'd*—really appreciate it." He stumbled over the words a little, but from the way her face lit up, you'd think he'd just murmured the sexiest thing in her ear.

"Oh, Seth," she sighed. "I really would do anything for you . . . but, well, I do try to respect my clients' privacy. Surely a man like you understands that."

"Well, yeah, of course I—" I elbowed him again. He shot me a quick glare and then returned his gaze to her. "That is, I do understand, but like I said, this is really important."

Indecision warred on her face, and I kind of admired her principles. She actually looked uncrackable, and I had a feeling Seth wasn't going to be too much more assertive. Glancing beyond her, I noticed a hallway leading off to another part of the house. *I keep records of all my pieces.*

"You're right," I said abruptly. "We can't expect her to give out that kind of information. Right, Seth?"

He turned to me again, giving me a curious glance. "Right?" It was more of a question than an agreement.

Mary nearly melted in relief, her eyes all over Seth. "Oh, I knew you'd understand. I could tell right away that we think just alike. Kindred spirits and all that, you know? Just from the way you write I—"

"Hey, Mary?" I interrupted.

She looked over at me, again seeming astonished that I was still there.

"Do you have a bathroom I could use?"

"Bathroom?" she repeated, like it was a crazy concept.

"It was a long drive," I explained sweetly. "Besides, that'll give you and Seth a chance to get to know each other while he signs your books."

Her face brightened again, and she turned to Seth without another glance for me. "Oh, sure! That's a great idea, Georgia. It's down the hall."

I stood up. "Thanks."

Seth and I made brief eye contact. There was a look of both panic and wariness. He didn't want to be left alone. And he also knew I wouldn't give up the fight so easily. He suspected that I was up to something.

He was right. I was about to go break into Mary's records.

Chapter 15

Mary's excited blathering rang through the house as I hurried down the hallway. I could see the bathroom at the end and three closed doors along the way. Great. Did they have to be shut? With my luck, they'd probably squeak. I could only hope that Mary would remain too loud and too distracted to notice.

The first door opened—with no squeaking—into a bedroom. The bed was unmade, and clothes had been pushed into piles against the wall. An old dresser sat against one wall, and a nightstand with some papers stood near the other. There was also a mirror on the ceiling.

Shuddering, I considered going in to investigate the nightstand papers but decided to hold out and see if I might find an office behind one of the other two doors. Shutting this one silently, I continued down the hallway.

The second door did squeak, and I froze, waiting for Mary to come tearing down after me in an effort to bludgeon me with one of Seth's books. I wasn't entirely sure how far his star power would go to save me if caught snooping. She didn't look like the violent type, but one never knew. Fortunately, she kept talking without pause, and I stuck my head inside the new room. It was just another bedroom, a guest one by the looks of the dust and lack of personal items. I closed the door, grimacing at another squeak. One more room to go.

Jackpot.

The third wasn't an office, but it did appear to be a workspace. Wide tables lay along the walls, covered in chunks of crystal—clear quartz, smoky quartz, etc.—in various states. Some were raw and jagged; others were polished and carved. Tools like blades and picks lay nearby, along with a more sophisticated and modern-looking device I couldn't identify. Maybe some type of laser cutter.

Best of all, there was a two-drawer filing cabinet against the wall. I hurried to it, still mindful of Mary's chatter, and opened the top drawer. Over a hundred file folders with names met me. I pulled one at random and saw that it did indeed have a job order. There was a description of the item, client information, job status, and a picture of the finished product. Unfortunately, having all this information meant little to me. I had no idea what name had been used for the seal—or if Mary was even the one who had made it.

Frustrated, I opened the next drawer and found financial records, like bills and bank statements. I also located folders labeled "work logs" categorized by month. I eagerly pulled out this month's and discovered a simple list of dates, client names, and brief descriptions of products. All—except for the three most recent ones—had check marks beside them. Finished products, presumably.

I scanned the dates before Jerome's disappearance, cross-checking against the descriptions. *Green Tara statue. Bracelet. Athame.* Three invoices in the last two weeks caught my attention: *round pendant, talisman, medallion.* I recognized none of the client names, but the culprit could no doubt have used an alias.

Returning to the second drawer, I found each client's file. The pendant was the right size and shape, but it had a hole drilled in it for a chain or string. I couldn't say why, but something told me the seal's original form would be whole. The talisman turned out to be the wrong shape. It was thick and oblong, more like a stone someone would keep in their pocket for good luck.

I was starting to panic now. This was taking too long, and I couldn't hear Mary anymore. God, espionage had been so much easier when I could turn invisible. With shaking hands, I pulled out the last file—the medallion. The client was Sam Markowitz, and he'd picked it up four days ago. The photo depicted a flat, quarter-sized disc made of smoky quartz with symbols I didn't recognize etched onto it. Was that it? It was the closest I had to a match of Carter's description. There could be other matches—items ordered months ago—but I didn't have time to go through any more files. I shoved the medallion photo into my purse, closed the drawer, and hurried back out to the hall, half expecting to find Mary blocking my path.

I had no need to worry, though. She had never left Seth's side—literally. She now sat in my spot, pressing Seth between her and the couch's arm. Two stacks of books were on the coffee table, and an open one was on his lap. He finished signing it and glanced up at my entrance with a relieved look.

"But you see," Mary was saying, "until O'Neill is able to confront the darkness within himself, he'll never be able to open himself to Cady. He's had his moments of vulnerability, of course—like the cave scene in *Dominant Eclipse*—but he's still keeping his armor up—just like on the veranda in *Memories of Man*—and so it's no wonder—"

"Hey," I said cheerfully. "We should probably get going."

Seth shot up from his seat, looking rather like a trapped animal who had just gnawed its own leg off and was about to run free. "Yes. We don't want to detain Mary any further."

Mary stood up too. "No, no! It's okay. Really. And you have to finish signing my books."

With a grimace, Seth grabbed the last three books and hastily scrawled his signature in them. "Thanks for talking to us," he said. "It's been great meeting you."

"Are you sure you have to go?" she pleaded. "I was going to make some dinner soon." She shot me an accusing look. "And if it's Ginger who needs to leave, I can give you a ride home later in my van—"

"No, really," said Seth, backing up to stand by me. "I appreciate it, but I have to, you know, get back to writing."

Extricating ourselves was painful. Mary begged and kept

offering everything from discount jewelry to thinly veiled sexual suggestions.

"Step on the gas and do *not* look back," Seth told me when we got in the car.

I complied, peeling out of her driveway as fast as I could and kicking up dirt and gravel in the process.

"That right there," I mused, "is the kind of fan who keeps authors in their crawlspace."

Seth leaned his head back against the seat. "Do not ever do that to me again. Ever."

"I wasn't that far away. I would have heard you screaming."

"Not if she used ether first. God, Georgina. She had her hand on my leg."

"That's Ginger to you."

"Please tell me you got something useful out of that. I know you didn't go to the bathroom."

"Nope. I broke into her workroom and ransacked her files."

He groaned. "Breaking and entering."

"Hey, I'm a creature of Hell. And she technically let us in."

"What'd you find?"

Eyes on the road, I reached into my purse and fumbled until I found the picture. I handed it to Seth.

"This is it?" he asked.

"I'm not certain. It's close to the description, but I don't know enough about this to really say."

"Hmm."

Seth studied it and then slipped it back into my purse. We rode for a few more minutes in silence until I finally asked, "I was never that bad of a fan, was I? That crazy?"

"Oh, God, no," he said. "Absolutely not. You were charming and cute and—" He abruptly cut himself off, but those words hung in the air between us. "You—you weren't like that. Nothing like that," he managed at last. There was a husky tone to his voice, hinting of some emotion but refusing to reveal which one it was.

I'd meant my comment to be light, just a way to keep the conversation going. However, like everything else lately, the words had ended up triggering far more meaning than I'd intended. I had a flashback to when Seth and I had first met, when I hadn't even known who he was. I'd rattled off my feelings for my favorite author, little knowing I was actually talking to him. Unlike Mary, I hadn't stalked him on the Internet and known what he looked like.

Seth cleared his throat. "So . . . what will you do with the picture now?"

I ran with his change in subject. "Get someone to identify it, I guess. Erik, maybe. Or Dante."

More silence fell, and I felt the tension ratchet up. *Dante.* Once again, harmless words had triggered big consequences between us. I expected Seth to try again to shift the subject, but instead, he actually addressed it.

"It's weird . . . seeing you with Dante."

"Don't you mean it's weird seeing me with anyone?"

"Well . . ."

Even with my eyes on the road, I knew he had that thoughtful, slightly distracted look in his eyes that meant he was pondering how best to phrase his next words. I used to love that look. Now I was on high alert.

"Yeah, to a certain extent, of course," he finally admitted. "It'll always be weird. But every time I talk to him, I just think . . ."

"If you say that I can do better, then I'm pulling this car over right now."

"Um, no. I was just going to say he doesn't seem like your type."

"That's nearly the same thing," I pointed out. "You sound just like Hugh and the others. I'm getting so sick of this! Honestly, it doesn't matter who I date. You're never going to be happy."

"That's not true," said Seth. "It's just . . . when you're around him, you're darker and more cynical. You're not like you used to be. This sounds stupid, considering what you are, but you're . . . well, you're a force for good in the world."

"Oh, come *on*," I said.

"No, I mean it. Maybe you are a creature of Hell, but people feel better when they're around you. You have this way of talking and smiling that affects everyone. You're nice, you're good-hearted, you worry about others . . ." He sighed. "But when you're with Dante, it's like all that light that normally shines out from you gets sucked away."

"That light got sucked away a long time ago," I said bitterly. "Long before he came along."

"No, it didn't. It's there, and if you're going to be involved with someone, you need someone who sees it, someone who loves you for it and wants to help bring it out."

I had someone like that, I thought. *You.*

"Dante and I work well together, no matter what any of you think. He understands me."

"No," said Seth flatly. His voice was low, but I could hear the anger in it. "He doesn't."

"What other options do I have? You're throwing me into an impossible situation. You know I can't date anyone who's good. I can't risk hurting them, but I don't want to be alone. This is my only option."

"No. It can't be. Before we were together, it wasn't like this. You weren't drinking all the time and having sex with anonymous guys in bathrooms!"

And that's when I did it, just like a dad on a road trip. I pulled the car over to the side of the road. It was a long, country highway, and there wasn't much traffic. Seth stared incredulously.

"What are you doing?"

"Saving us from an accident," I growled, turning so I could meet him straight in the eye. "And you'll be lucky if I don't make you get out and walk the rest of the way. Look, you want to know why I wasn't dating loser guys when we met? Because I wasn't dating *anyone.* I took my hits and went home alone. Why is it so wrong for me to want to be with someone now?"

"It shouldn't matter if you're dating someone or not. You still shouldn't be acting like this!"

"You're telling me what I should and shouldn't be doing? It's my business. You have no right!" I yelled back.

"Friends have every right to tell friends when they're on a bad path," he snapped back.

"Bullshit! I've never seen you interfere with anyone else's life, no matter how badly they were screwing it up. I'm the only one you seem to want to mess with. Why do you care so much about what I do?" Seth and I had raised our voices only rarely while dating, and it had never even come close to this. It was a wonder we didn't shatter the windows.

"Because I care about you! I told you that at the party. Breaking up doesn't mean you stop caring about someone."

"Yes, but it means you have to let them go." I was so upset that I was on the verge of tears. "You can't have it both ways. You can't get rid of me and then try to pull me back . . ."

"I never wanted to get rid of you."

I stared at him for several heavy moments and felt those traitorous tears brimming heavier and heavier in my eyes. "Then why did you do it?"

After all that yelling, his voice sounded barely like a whisper.

"Because . . . I wanted to save you."

"You can't," I murmured, swallowing the tears back with great effort. "You can't keep saving me, can't keep trying to. It's too late."

"No," he said. His heart was in his eyes, and it was ripping mine apart. "Not for you. Never."

I don't know how it happened exactly, but suddenly we were kissing. His lips were just as I remembered, soft and powerful and wonderful. It wasn't a chaste kiss, nor was it a ripping-off-each-other's-clothes kiss. It was hungry and desperate, like we'd been struggling through a desert and only just now found the water we needed to survive. Best of all, it was just kissing. Just me and Seth. There was no life energy or succubus schemes involved. There was no need to back off for fear of what might happen. We could drink from each other without pulling back.

Except, well, we did.

We jerked apart, and I knew the shock on his face mirrored my own. What had we just done? Had we . . . had we really done it? It was a kiss. A real kiss. The kind of kiss we'd always wanted. The kiss we weren't supposed to be having.

I turned abruptly away, staring at the road ahead. I was frozen and numb . . . and yet, alive and filled with warmth. The world had been in that kiss. But I didn't know how to react to it, didn't know what I was supposed to do now. So, I did the most inane thing possible. I started the car.

"We should get back," I said.

"Yeah," he agreed, sounding as stunned as I felt.

I dared a look out of my peripheral vision. His eyes were fixed straight ahead, his wonderful lips tightened in a line that somehow made them look strong and vulnerable at the same time. I wanted to lean over and kiss them again, to melt as I had moments ago and forget all about reason. I wanted that perfect feeling to last forever.

Instead of dealing with what had just happened, however, I did the cowardly thing and stepped on the gas. We drove back to the city in miserable silence, neither of us mentioning the kiss but both of us thinking about it. I dropped him off at the bookstore and offered a polite thank-you for his help. He returned it equally politely—giving me one last pensive look—and then walked off toward his car. I watched him go, memorizing every line of his body and how he moved. Every emotion possible warred within me, and I had no idea which deserved to win.

I was exhausted by the time I stepped into my apartment building. The day had been mentally and physically wearying, what with would-be rapists, larceny, and the kiss heard 'round the world. Later, I'd find someone to identify the photograph for me. For now, I just wanted to sprawl on the couch and watch TV, preferably TV that had nothing to do with the magical or paranormal—or any romantic tension.

Unfortunately, the magical and paranormal was waiting for me.

What's Nanette doing here?

That was my last coherent thought before I was thrown against the far side of my living room.

I hit hard, my head cracking against the wall. I fell to the ground, my legs just barely possessing the reflexes to keep me from falling as black spots sparkled across my vision. Nanette faced me, terrible and beautiful in all her golden glory. She hadn't laid a hand on me, but she didn't need to, not with the power she wielded.

"How dare you," she hissed, eyes narrowed. "How dare you spread those kinds of rumors."

"What are you—ah!"

I was shoved back to the wall again. The distance wasn't nearly so far as before, but the force was so hard that the impact hurt just as much. More pain shot through my skull as I tried to make sense of all this.

"I don't know what you're talking about!" I cried.

Nanette stalked toward me, putting her face inches from mine. "Of course you do. You told Cedric that I was the one who'd summoned Jerome, that I was the one causing chaos in his territory."

"I didn't," I whimpered. "Not exactly. I just told him you'd met with Jerome."

She snarled and grabbed me by the front of my shirt, jerking me forward. "That was nothing. Nothing! But now others are suspicious."

"I just thought he should know and—"

"Do you know what you may have done?" she screamed. "I was a candidate for this city! You may have ruined everything."

She threw me again, this time toward the corner my TV was in. Its sharp angles bit into me when I hit, and I crumpled to the floor. I tried to pull myself up but never made it. Nanette was right there beside me. I had a full view of her black stiletto pumps just before she kicked me in the ribs. Pain blasted me, and my body instinctively tried to curl over and protect itself. But she was too fast and too powerful. Greg had had a lot of brute strength at his disposal, brute strength I'd been able to counteract a little. But against Nanette?

Against a demon? Her strength was beyond that of a human, nearly beyond human comprehension.

"Do. Not. Fuck. With. Me," she said, punctuating each hit with a kick to my stomach or ribs. "Do you understand? You are nothing. *Nothing.*"

"I'm sorry," I said. My eyes burned, and every part of my body was screaming, begging for this to end.

The kicking stopped, and I rolled to my side, only to have a wave of power slam down on me and roll me to my stomach, pinning me down on the floor like an invisible ton of bricks. I tried to move but couldn't even budge.

"I don't care if you're Jerome's favorite or Cedric's new darling," she said. Her voice was all ice and malice. Again, she didn't touch me with her hands, but the back of my shirt suddenly ripped open. "I could destroy you right now, blast you from the face of the earth, and no one would say anything. Instead—you're lucky I'm in a good mood today."

Her "good mood" felt like a thousand whips hitting my back. Tiny lashes of power, sharp as razors and burning like flames, slammed into me. I screamed as they slashed at my skin, ripping it open. Some part of me thought that if I screamed loud enough, maybe a neighbor would hear me. It was a useless sentiment, though. She would have soundproofed this room much as the demons had at the Cellar. Besides, what could any mortal do against this?

Again and again those invisible whips tore into me. Obviously, I couldn't see what was happening, but in my mind's eye, I imagined my flesh torn to ribbons, my entire back a horrible, bloody mess. I don't know how many times those lashings repeated. They blurred together. I was fast approaching a point where the pain was so intense, so overwhelming that I almost couldn't feel it. My vision was going black, my brain barely able to hold consciousness.

When the beating finally stopped, I wondered if I was dead. The room was still and silent. Then, the invisible force lifted off my back. I tried to roll over but couldn't. Nanette knelt down, her lips right against my ear.

"Do not fuck with me," she whispered. "You interfere again, and I *will* kill you."

She vanished. I was left alone, sobbing and bleeding. I tried to move again but still was unable to. What was I going to do? I couldn't even call for help. Of course, it probably didn't matter. The pain was so great that I was either going to die or pass out any minute now. Human devices might not kill me, but demonic ones could, regardless if I was in stasis.

Suddenly, out of nowhere, I felt strong arms slide underneath me, gently lifting me in a way that kept my back up. I stifled a small cry. Even without my back being touched, the movement hit every other muscle and place on my body that Nanette had hurt. I opened my eyes, trying to see who was there, but my vision was swimming and rapidly darkening.

"What . . ." was all I managed to get out.

"Shh, love. It's going to be okay. You're going to be okay."

Those arms gently eased me onto my bed. I moaned again as fire shot through my ribs. Cool hands smoothed back my hair, but I still couldn't see anything.

"I can't heal you," the voice said. "But I'll get someone who can help. Just don't move. It's going to be okay."

There was something familiar about the voice, but I couldn't identify it through the haze and confusion in my head. I could barely breathe, let alone think. Silence fell after that, as though my mysterious benefactor had left. Yet a few moments later, I blearily saw hands set Aubrey on the bed beside me. She leaned forward, sniffing my face. One of the friendly hands petted her head and back, in that way that could so often coax cats into lying down. It worked, and after turning in a couple of circles, she settled down beside me.

Then, the hand stroked my hair one last time. "Everything's going to be okay."

That was the last thing I remembered hearing. My savior might have stayed or left. I didn't know because a few moments later, that blackness finally won, and I sank into a dreamless sleep that was mercifully free of pain.

Chapter 16

"Georgina."

My name came to me from far away, from far down a tunnel without an end. It echoed off the walls of my mind, loud at first and eventually fading to nothing.

"Georgina. Look at me, sweetie."

"Let her sleep, Hugh."

"No, I need to talk to her and make sure she doesn't have a concussion. Georgina, come on. Open your eyes for me."

Through a mist of black fog, my brain parsed the words and slowly found meaning in them. Some basic response in me wanted to comply, but my eyelids felt like they were stuck together. Thinking—let alone answering—was too hard, but more words came to encourage me.

"There you go, sweetie. Try it again. You almost had it."

With much effort, I finally managed to open my eyes. It was excruciating. My lids felt like they were made of lead. At first, I could only perceive one thing: light. I winced, wanting to sink back into that oblivion I'd been pulled from. And with this slight stirring of consciousness, all the pain I'd escaped from before suddenly returned. My head throbbed. My back burned. The cliché about breaking every bone in the body seemed like a very real possibility all of a sudden, and I was pretty sure I'd broken a few that weren't in my body. Sure, that didn't make sense, but with as bad as I felt, little did.

"Oh God." At least, that's what I tried to say. It came out as more of an indistinct moan.

"Easy there. You don't have to say anything."

I opened my eyes again, this time making out a figure leaning over me. I knew his voice so well that I didn't need to see his face, which was a blur anyway.

"Hugh," I croaked.

"Hey, ask her what—"

"Shut up," Hugh snapped. The jerky movement of his head made me think he'd glanced behind him, but I couldn't be certain.

He moved his face closer to mine, bringing his features into sharper relief. He was paler than I'd ever seen him, his face filled with lines of worry and fear I'd never thought him capable of. He looked even more upset than when he'd come to tell us about Jerome's summoning. Reaching out, Hugh held the lids of one of my eyes open and shone a small light into it. I squirmed at the brightness—or at least I tried—but he was fast and did it to the other eye before it caused too much discomfort. When he finished, he moved his finger around in the air and studied my eyes as I followed it.

"What's your name?" he asked.

The voice behind him piped up. "You already said her name."

Hugh sighed and jerked a thumb over his shoulder. "What's *his* name?"   ♦

"Cody," I said. It was getting easier to speak, but the pain was going up the more conscious I became. Cody's voice was as familiar to me as Hugh's, and I felt certain Peter was here too.

Hugh asked me a few other factual questions, like the current year and the location, and also if I was nauseous.

"It all hurts," I said, voice still slurred. I couldn't even move, let alone distinguish nausea from the rest of my pain.

"Yeah, but do you feel like you're going to throw up? Right here? Right now?"

I thought about it. My stomach hurt, but it was less of a queasy discomfort and more of a someone-just-kicked-me-with-stilettos discomfort. "No," I said.

Hugh sat back, and I heard him sigh in relief.

"It all hurts," I repeated. "Can you . . . make it stop?"

He hesitated, and a moment later, Cody appeared beside him. "What's the matter? You've gotta give her something. Look at her. She's suffering."

"Understatement," I mumbled.

Hugh's face was still drawn. "I'm not gonna knock her out if she's got a concussion."

"She passed your tests."

"Those are field tests. They're not one hundred percent accurate."

"Please," I said, feeling tears well in my eyes. "Anything."

"We know it won't kill her," I heard Peter say. I'd been right about him being here.

Hugh hesitated only a little longer. "Go get some water."

Cody disappeared, and Peter replaced him by Hugh's side. Hugh's expression was still grim. "Sweetie, I've got to clean up your back, and it's going to hurt."

"Worse?"

"A different kind of hurt. But this has to be cleaned up so you don't get an infection, and then I need to shift you to check out the rest of you. The drugs'll help, but it's all going to hurt at first."

"Go for it," I said, steeling myself. At this point, I couldn't really imagine worse pain. Besides, Hugh was a doctor. Everything was going to be okay now.

Cody returned with a glass of water. Hugh made me drink some first, just to make sure I could keep it down. When I did, he gave me two pills to take with the rest of the water. I nearly choked on them—my throat felt raw and swollen, maybe from screaming—but I got them down.

I wanted to ask what I'd just taken, but it seemed like too much work. "Should kick in in about twenty minutes," Hugh said.

I could see him fumbling with something in his lap. Standing up, he leaned over my back. Something wet touched my skin.

"Son of a bitch!" Again, my words were slightly incoherent, but I think he caught my meaning.

Stinging pain—a "different" pain, indeed—raced across my skin where he'd touched it. It was electric, sharp where the rest of my body throbbed. My desire to get away from that horrible stinging was so strong that I actually managed to move a little, but all that did was trigger the hurt in the rest of my body. The world blurred once more.

"You're making it worse," he warned. "Stay still."

Easy for him to say. I bit my lip as he continued. He was using antiseptic to clean the places Nanette had cut me. Necessary, as he'd said, but God, did it hurt.

"Talk to her," Hugh said to no one in particular. "Distract her."

"What happened?" asked Peter. "Who did this to you?"

"Nice distraction," said Hugh.

"Nanette," I said. Saying her name made my stomach turn, and I hoped I wouldn't have to go back on what I'd said to Hugh about throwing up. "She was . . . mad."

"I guess," said Peter.

"Mad I told Cedric about her . . ."

"Doesn't this kind of confirm your suspicions, then?" asked Cody.

Yeah, if beating up the person who'd ratted out your secret plans didn't sound suspicious, I didn't know what did. But if Nanette really was behind Jerome's summoning, why not just kill me outright and leave no witnesses?

Explaining that would take too many words and too much effort, so I just said, "I don't know."

"There," said Hugh, straightening. "That wasn't so bad, was it?"

I tried to glare, but I don't think he noticed. He rummaged in his kit once more and then leaned back over to start bandaging up the wounds. With as much as he was piling on me, I had the feeling I was going to look like a mummy.

"Why didn't Dante stick around?" asked Cody.

"Huh? Dante?" The bandage pressure wasn't as bad as the

cleaning, but it was still uncomfortable. I wondered when those goddamned drugs were going to kick in.

"He was here," said Cody. "He called Hugh and told him to come over."

Some of the exact details of what had happened with Nanette were foggy, but I felt pretty confident, head trauma or no, that I would have remembered Dante being around.

"Dante wasn't here," I said.

Hugh paused and looked me in the eye. "Then who called me? It was a guy, from your cell phone. Said to get over here and bring medical supplies—that you'd been hurt."

I frowned, and it came back to me, a shadow in the pain-filled haze of my memory. The strong arms and gentle voice.

"There was someone here . . ." I began slowly. "Not Dante. Someone else. He put me to bed."

Silence fell. A slight fuzziness was starting to tingle the edges of my senses, which I took as a good sign. It was more of a pleasant, dreamlike fuzziness—not the I-can't-handle-this-pain-anymore kind. There was still a fair amount of that, though.

The guys exchanged puzzled looks. "Are you sure it wasn't him?" asked Cody.

"Why would Dante leave her, though?" asked Peter.

Hugh snorted. "No telling with him."

"Stop," I mumbled. "It wasn't him."

"You can't remember a face or anything?" Peter asked. "Was it even someone you knew?"

I thought again, desperately trying to dig out the memory. There was nothing, though. Only that he'd been someone familiar.

"I knew him . . ." That pleasant drowsiness was growing stronger. I wished it would hurry up.

"There," said Hugh. "All bandaged up. Help me move her so I can look at her ribs."

That was *not* fun, and the discomfort of the three of them turning me over—no matter how gentle they tried to be—was enough to momentarily break me out of the drug's soothing embrace. They managed to flip me over, putting moderate pressure on my back when I rested back against the bed, but allowing Hugh to examine the rest of me. He poked and prodded and had me take deep breaths. His final analysis was that I had a couple of broken ribs and a lot of bruising and pain that would just go away with time.

"Great," I said. I was so loopy by that point that I didn't even know if I was being sarcastic or not.

Cody was still unable to give up my benefactor. "But who was here?"

"The man . . ." I said.

"You aren't going to get anything else out of her," said Hugh wearily. "Not for a while. She's going to be in Dreamland any minute now."

"Dreamland. The man . . ." I repeated. Suddenly, I giggled. "The man in the dream . . ."

I saw them exchange pitying looks, just before my eyelids drooped closed. They thought I was talking nonsense. None of them knew about the story of the man in the dream, of that alluring and improbable alternate life that Nyx had shown me.

But as I drifted off to Dreamland, it wasn't Nyx's vision I saw. It was more of that same, painless black . . . at least, it was until I got jolted by a million volts of electricity.

I let out a small cry of surprise, my eyes popping open. It felt like hundreds of icy needles were dancing along my body, piercing every nerve. The room's details, as well as my friends, came to me in sharp, crystalline detail. No more fuzziness. Turning my head slightly, I saw a fourth person.

Mei.

She stood beside my bed, face blank and emotionless, arms crossed across her black silk blouse. "What happened?" I asked. My words were still thick, but my speech capabilities had improved by leaps and bounds.

"I healed you," she said flatly. "Inasmuch as I can. You're still going to hurt."

Demons, though once angels, didn't possess that power to heal that their heavenly counterparts had. They could do it in small bursts, however, and in expanding my senses to assess my body, I could feel how she'd gotten rid of the worst of my pain. I still ached in some places, and even bandaged, my back still stung. I no longer wanted to die, however, so that was definitely an improvement.

"Thank you," I said.

Mei didn't look particularly compassionate or benevolent. Her expression darkened. "They say Nanette did this?"

I hesitated. I'd already gotten in enough trouble with the archdemoness for telling on her. Of course, my friends had undoubtedly already told Mei the truth, and anyway, she was the closest I currently had to a boss. I wasn't entirely sure if I could trust her, but if I had to place my money on the demon most likely to have my back right now (no pun intended), it was her.

"Yeah," I admitted. "I told Cedric that Nanette had met with Jerome. She'd met with Cedric too, so it seemed kind of like she was manipulating both of them."

Mei's face grew harder still. Whether she agreed with me or not, she didn't reveal. "Nanette won't bother you again."

And with no more than that, the demoness vanished.

"Girl fight," said Hugh, looking the happiest I'd seen him today.

"I don't think it's going to be in creamed corn or anything like that," I remarked dryly.

"Her sense of humor returns," said Peter. "Definitely on the road to recovery."

I tried to sit up and winced. "Or not."

"Don't push it," warned Hugh. "Mei can only do so much—"

"What the hell's going on?"

We all turned. Dante stood in the doorway to my bedroom. His face was a mixture of incredulity and utter confusion. Without waiting for an answer, he hurried over to the bed and knelt down so that he was at my level.

"Are you okay? What happened?"

His expression was so tender, so full of concern that I was

momentarily taken aback. Dante was indeed selfish and arro-gant, but he did care about me, no matter what my friends thought. And in dire situations—like now—that bitter façade of his fell, revealing someone whose soul hadn't turned com-pletely black yet. He tried hard to hide this side of himself, but I knew it was there.

"I had a run-in with a demon," I said. I gave him a brief explanation of what had happened.

He grew more and more incredulous as I spoke. When I finished, he glanced around the room, studying everyone ac-cusatorily. "How does something like this happen? I thought demons couldn't go around roughing people up. Aren't you under some kind of protection?"

"Technically Jerome's," I said. "But he's kind of busy right now."

"Maybe you're under Grace and Mei's protection now," mused Cody. "Mei looked pissed."

"She always looks pissed," said Hugh.

"I should hope so," snapped Dante. "Are they going to go kick this other demon's ass?"

"She's not likely to smite her, if that's what you mean," said Hugh. "Grace and Mei are under the same scrutiny as everyone else, but I bet Mei'll bitch Nanette out."

"Great," said Dante. "A stern talking-to. That'll show her."

"It's unlikely Nanette'll do anything else. If she was going to kill Georgina, she would have already." There was an al-most gentle tone in Peter's voice. I think Dante's outrage and concern had convinced the vampire that Dante might not be the complete and total bastard he'd always believed.

My immortal (or not so immortal) friends finally decided I was in reasonable enough condition to leave me in Dante's care. Hugh promised to check on me tomorrow, and I thanked him again for his help. He and the others looked like they wanted to hug me, but with my back, they knew better.

When they were gone, Dante went out to the kitchen and came back with a bowl of ice cream. "Good for what ails you," he said.

I was surprised to discover I had a considerable appetite. Judging from the time, I'd been out quite awhile before Mei had shown up. It had only felt like a few seconds.

"Careful," I teased. "People are going to think you're a nice guy."

"Well, I'll have to go rob some orphans to save my reputation."

He lay in bed beside me, curled on his side so that he could gently keep his hand on my arm and talk to me. As the evening passed, our conversation mostly touched on inconsequential things, topics to distract me from Seattle's increasingly dangerous situation. Finally, when it came time for both of us to sleep, Dante brought up the attack again.

"Succubus . . . who was here earlier?"

I knew he didn't mean Hugh and the vampires. I frowned. Even with Mei's healing, my memories were sketchy. "I don't know. But I think . . . I think it might have been Carter."

"Really? I still can't believe that angel hangs out with you guys. But if it was him, why didn't he heal you? He could have fixed everything."

Through the fog of that ordeal, I recalled my rescuer's words. *I can't heal you.*

"Because he's not supposed to interfere," I said slowly, remembering my earlier rumination on whether blowing up a stove was interference. "Heaven's supposed to stay out of this. He probably shouldn't have even carried me to bed— which is why he would have then gotten out of here and left it to Hugh to patch me up."

"An angel breaking the rules and a demon healing the sick," Dante said. "You and your associates just get more and more fucked up."

I shifted slightly, cautious of my back, and rested my head against him. "That's for damned sure."

Chapter 17

The sweet scent of a white chocolate mocha woke me from a heavy sleep the following morning. For a few moments, as I stirred to consciousness, it was like waking up any other day. Then, as I opened my eyes and shifted position, my body's nerves came to life, reminding me what had happened yesterday. It wasn't the horrible torturous pain I'd experienced before, but I had enough aches and soreness to dissuade me from too much movement. Still, I managed to more or less sit up when Dante entered my bedroom.

He held the mocha in one hand and what looked like a bakery bag tucked under his arm. In the other hand, he carried an enormous vase of blue and white hydrangeas, interspersed with orchids. I never would have pictured those particular flowers going together, but the arrangement worked.

"Did you rob a florist?" I asked.

Dante gave me a withering look as he handed me the mocha. "Why are you assuming the worst again?"

"Because orchids aren't cheap," I said.

"They were out of crab grass, so I had to settle." He gently placed the vase on my dresser and then freed the bakery bag. "And I beat up some kids for these."

After a long, delicious sip, I set the mocha on my bedside table and took the bag from him. Inside were chocolate croissants—my favorite kind of breakfast pastry.

"All this because I got beat up?" I asked.

He sat on the side of the bed. "I'm worried about you."

"I should get in fights with demons more often," I teased, my last few words getting muffled as I bit into a croissant. Tiny flakes and crumbs fell onto my sheets, but I didn't care.

"Not funny, succubus," he said. And to my surprise, I could see that he meant it. None of his usual sardonic humor showed on his face. There was no bitter twist to his lips. "That's never happening again. And I'm going to make sure you get better, immortal healing or not."

"Never took you for a nursemaid."

"Be quiet," he snapped. "And keep eating. Your body needs calories to heal."

Happy to oblige, I started to take another bite and then froze. "Do you think I might start putting on weight?" Calories were nothing I'd ever had to count before. I'd feared neither weight gain nor health effects from the things I ate.

"I think that's the least of your worries."

I supposed he was right. I kept eating—but with a little less enthusiasm. He still looked so serious and worried that I couldn't shake my warm and fuzzy feelings. "Thank you for all of this. It's really great."

He smiled at me, and his gray eyes were lovely in the morning light. "Not many people in this world I feel deserve my help. You're in an exclusive club."

I started to make a comment about how the rest of the club members must be imaginary, but there had already been too much snark this morning. Nanette's attack had seriously shaken Dante up.

"Thank you," I said again. A thought struck me. "I might have some other way for you to help. Will you grab my purse?"

He retrieved it from the living room and handed it over. Reaching inside, I was relieved to see the photo that I'd swiped from Mary was still there. I studied it for a moment, willing the medallion to yield some sort of revelation. All I saw was a translucent brown disc and runes or symbols that could easily be mistaken for a child's scribbles. With a sigh, I handed it to him.

"Does this mean anything to you?"

His brows knit thoughtfully as he looked it over. "No. Should it?"

"I think it might be part of Jerome's summoning. Remember when I asked you about an artist who carved quartz? This is what I turned up. Supposedly, the stone and marks are clues, but I don't know what they are. I guess that's where I need people like you or Erik."

He gazed at the picture for several more moments, and to my surprise, I saw anger building in his features. Abruptly, he stood up and tossed the picture on the floor.

"Son of a bitch," he growled.

"What's the matter?" I exclaimed.

"This," he said, gesturing at me and the fallen picture. "This is the matter. What good am I, succubus? I'm ten times more powerful than those people I sent you to go see. Aside from Lancaster, there's probably no one else in this fucking town who knows as much about the arcane as I do. And what good is it?" He paced around my room and ran his hand angrily through his hair. "Nothing. That's what it's good for. I can't seem to help you. I can't do a goddamned thing. I couldn't save you from that demoness. And I don't know anything about this medallion thing."

I was stunned by his reaction. "Hey, whoa. It's okay. Sit down. Don't beat yourself up."

"It's not okay." He came to a halt. "I feel . . . powerless." For someone who'd spent his life doing horrible things in the quest for power, I could recognize what a hard admission that was.

"You're not obligated to do anything here," I said gently. "You help me more than you realize. But this isn't your fight. This isn't your responsibility."

"*You're* my responsibility," he said. "If I can't look out for you, then why do you need me?"

"I'm not with you for what you can do for me."

"Yeah? You're with me for my winning personality?"

The truth was, I still wasn't sure at times why I was with him. I couldn't help but recall his comments about me keeping him as a bed warmer, but true or not, now wasn't the time to bring that up. Plus, he'd been sweet lately—something I'd never expected when I'd turned to him in my post-Seth rage.

"Dante, I'm serious. Don't worry about any of this. I'll take care of it and talk to my friends."

I saw from the look on his face that that wasn't quite what he'd wanted to hear. Knowing I had other people to go to seemed to make him feel more inadequate.

"You shouldn't be involved in this at all," he said.

"What, in finding Jerome? Of course I have to be."

"There are others, people who are more powerful. I don't want you getting hurt again! Why can't you just lie low and keep yourself safe?" he demanded.

"Because it's not what I do! And no one else is going to do it anyway. They're just letting this go. Letting Jerome go."

"Why don't you let it go?" he asked. "Would it be so bad to work under another demon? You've worked for others."

I turned and gazed out the window. The sky was blue, but something told me it was cold out. It was a quirk of Seattle weather. We often had warmer temperatures when it was cloudy out, colder ones when it was sunny. Dragging my eyes back to Dante, I said, "Yeah, I have. But this is different. This isn't right—it shouldn't have happened. I have to find Jerome."

"Yes. You do. It's written all over you. Why do you have to make everything so difficult and create these problems?"

"If you're unhappy, no one's making you stick around," I said quietly.

"Of course I'm sticking around. And if there's nothing to be done for your impulsivity, I might as well help." He snatched up the photo and glared at it. "Let me take this and ask some questions. I might not know what it is—yet—but there are resources I can tap."

There was a hard set to his face. He was a man with a mission, which I preferred to him being down on himself or ranting at me. I was about to send him off with my blessings, but something held me back. I couldn't let the picture go.

"I want to keep the photo," I told him.

He stared. "You don't think I'll bring it back?"

"No, I'm not worried about that. But I did a lot to get it, and besides, I want to show it to some people too. We'll make a copy of it. You can take that."

"Yeah? You got a copy machine in the bathroom?"

"Can't you just draw it or something?"

"Succubus."

"Well, I don't know! But if you want to do sleuthing, you're going to have to find a workaround. Until I feel like traipsing around the city with you, I want the picture to stay with me."

He glowered, looking very much like his usual bitter self. Finally, realizing I wasn't going to yield, he did a hasty trace of the medallion onto another sheet of paper. He added a few notes off to the side and did his best approximation of the symbols. He seemed miserable the entire time.

"Sorry," I said.

"It's fine," he said.

"You're going now?"

"If you think you'll be okay."

I assured him I would be. My phone was nearby, and I had a feeling if he stayed, he'd just grow more and more upset about how he'd let me down and about how I was putting myself at risk for reasons he didn't understand. At least this gave him a feeling of purpose. I promised to call if something happened and breathed a sigh of relief when he finally left.

I stayed in bed for a while after that, consuming my calorie-laden breakfast and thinking about his extreme reaction. I hoped he'd find something out for me, and in the meantime, I needed to do some investigating of my own. First things first, though. I needed to shower.

It turned out to be harder than I expected—but not impossible. I just had to move slowly when I walked to the bathroom, careful not to get too ambitious. Hugh's bandages still covered my back, and it took a fair bit of dexterity to remove them. They were soaked with blood, but underneath, the cuts showed signs of Mei's healing. They were still there, still uncomfortable, but had all scabbed over and were much smaller. I kept the water lukewarm as I showered and was careful when I toweled off to not break any of the scabs open.

By the time I was sitting on my couch in the living room, I felt like I'd run a marathon. I'd never wanted shape-shifting so badly in my life. I wore loose clothes—drawstring pants and a T-shirt without a bra—but it had taken some effort to put them on. My hair I'd given up on completely, figuring combing it out would have to do. I didn't have the patience to dry it and didn't want to think about the frizziness I was inviting.

Aubrey joined me on the couch as I rested from my morning labors and flipped through the channels. After cycling through twice, I gave up and left the TV on some sort of nature show about Siberian tigers. Aubrey watched it with wide eyes, but I wasn't interested.

"This is your equivalent of reality television," I observed.

"The talk shows don't come on until later," a voice suddenly said. "That's when things get good."

I sighed. "Carter. What a pleasant surprise."

The angel strolled into my line of sight and sat down on the armchair opposite me. Aubrey immediately left me and hopped onto his lap.

"Traitor," I said.

He grinned and scratched her head. "Word on the street is that you had a bad day yesterday."

"I've had worse," I said. "Marginally. You should have seen me before Mei healed me."

"Bah, demons can't heal. Not really. They lose the finesse it takes when they cross over."

"Hey, I'll take what help I can get." I brightened. "And speaking of help, I think I've got a picture of the seal—"

"No."

"No what?"

"I know what you're going to ask, and the answer is no."

"You have no idea what I'm going to ask!"

"You're going to ask me to help identify the seal so you can figure out where Jerome is."

I stayed silent. Damn.

He rolled his eyes. "And the answer is no."

"But you could make this so much easier," I argued. "Dante's out trying to figure out what the seal means. You could tell me right now."

"Georgina, I told you before. I can't interfere."

"Then why are you here?"

"To see how you're feeling. Believe me, I wish I could interfere. I'd do a better healing job than Mei."

I fell silent, mind spinning. "Were you here yesterday?"

"Doing what?"

"Look, I won't consider it interfering, but just tell me if it was you."

Carter didn't look confused very often. If anything, he was usually the one messing with other people's minds. I think under normal circumstances, when the immortal state of affairs in Seattle wasn't in limbo, he would have faked it and hidden his confusion. Now, he just shook his head in exasperation.

"What are you talking about?"

"Someone was here after Nanette beat me up. A guy. He put me to bed and called Hugh."

"It wasn't me."

"Technically, it wouldn't even be interfering."

"Georgina," he said sternly. "Listen. It wasn't me."

I held his gaze and shivered at the intensity in his eyes. His were gray, but whereas Dante's were like leaden clouds on a winter day, Carter's were like gleaming silver.

"It wasn't you," I said at last. He'd answered directly, with none of the half-truths and subterfuge angels normally employed. He'd answered directly, and angels couldn't lie. "I suppose you didn't blow up the stove either?"

"No."

"Who did, then? You said in Vancouver you'd try to protect me. I figured this was you."

"It's possible the stove blew up because of a gas leak."

"Maybe," I grumbled.

He smiled, instantly transforming him to the mocking angel I usually knew. "Believe me, Daughter of Lilith, I wish I could take credit for these things. And if it comes down to it, and I have the means and ability, I *will* try to protect you. For now, I've still got to stay out of this."

"House calls aside."

"Just a visit between friends." He winked and stood up. "I really do wish I could help more, but you're going to have to find another way. Be careful, whatever you end up doing."

"You're not warning me away from all this?"

He arched an eyebrow. "Should I be?"

"No," I mused. "But everyone else is. They say it's dangerous."

"It is dangerous. But these are dangerous times, and honestly? You're the only one that I think has the means or desire to get us out of this mess. Good luck, Georgina. And don't leave the house without checking your hair." He vanished.

"Fucking angels."

I realized then that I was starving for real food, not sugar-filled sweets. My kitchen was sparse as usual, so I decided to risk the world and go pick up something. I was tired and certainly incapable of running a marathon, but Mei's healing really had gone a long way. I could manage the one block walk to a nearby take-out Chinese restaurant. I placed the order, and by the time I was out of my robe and out the door, the food was ready. I stopped at a convenience store as well to pick up some pop, and the whole endeavor only ended up taking about thirty minutes. From the look on Aubrey's face, you would have thought I'd been gone a whole day, but then, she just wanted my orange chicken.

I changed back to my robe and relaxed with the food, pondering how to spend my day. As I'd told Dante, I didn't want to go traipsing about town, but I wanted some leads on the medallion. Erik was probably my best bet at this point, and I hoped he'd be able to ID my symbols from phone descriptions. Before I could do that, I heard a knock at my door. I expected it to be Hugh making a house call, but to my astonishment, it was Seth.

"Hey," I said, stepping aside so that he could come in.

"Hey," he returned.

I stuffed my hands into the ratty robe's pockets, wishing I hadn't been so hasty to change back to casual mode. My hair was undoubtedly a lost cause, so there was no point stressing over that. "How's it going?"

"Okay." He met my eyes frankly, something he hadn't done in a while. It sent a tingle down my back. "I was just nearby and wanted to . . . well, that is . . ." He sighed. "I just wanted to apologize for what happened yesterday. . . ."

Yesterday. The kiss. Something that only a demon attack could have dwarfed.

I shook my head, trying not to recall how I'd felt that kiss all the way to my toes. "You have nothing to apologize for. I think . . . I think I was as much to blame. Besides, it was nothing."

"Nothing?" he asked, looking both surprised and hurt.

"I mean, not *nothing*," I amended hastily. "But we were both kind of worked up, and things got crazy, and well, like I said . . . nothing to apologize for."

"Okay . . . I'm glad you're not upset. I don't want there to be anything . . . well, anything bad between us."

I thought about all the fights and arguments. "Well, I'm not sure we've reached that state. I mean, come on, do you think things will ever be normal and friendly between us?"

"Yes," he said bluntly. "No matter what has or hasn't happened romantically, I still feel like . . . like there's something between us . . . like, a connection, I mean. I feel like we're always destined to be important in each other's lives."

You are my life, I thought and promptly looked away, as though he might have heard me. "Do you regret it?" I asked before I realized I had.

"Regret?"

"Ending things."

I looked back at him, fearing his answer, no matter what it was. "I regret . . . well, I don't regret saving you from future hurt. I do regret the hurt I've caused you . . . if I'd known you'd react and spiral the way you have . . ."

"You can't take that into consideration," I said hastily. "That's not your fault." I was surprised to be saying that, but it was true. My bad behavior these last months had been my doing.

"I can't help it. I'll always worry about you. Like I said, I feel like no matter what, we're always going to be connected . . . like there's something bigger than us at work. As it is . . ."

"What?"

"Never mind."

I stepped forward, never taking my eyes off him. "Tell me."

"As it is . . ." He shrugged. "Life is easier not dating you. But sometimes . . . it feels incomplete. Like there's a piece of me missing."

"And that's easier?"

"Think of it as winning the lottery and having people waiting on all your needs, but it's at the cost of, I don't know, getting your leg amputated."

"Wow. You should be a writer with that imagery."

He smiled. "Yeah, yeah. But you know what I mean."

Except, I was missing a part of my life *and* things were harder, not easier. "You at least have Maddie."

"You have Dante."

"Dante's not Maddie, believe me."

"Fair enough. She's great . . . I care about her . . . love her . . . I don't know. It's all just different."

Silence fell, but it was comfortable. "Good lord. I can't believe we're discussing this rationally."

"See? Not so hard to be friends."

I had my doubts about that. "I guess."

"Don't worry. We'll keep trying. Before long, we'll be on a bowling league or something." He spoke his words lightly, but there was a catch that belied the truth of his words. Being friends wasn't easy for Seth either. He still cared about me and was suffering just as much as me with this separation. Seeing that made something in me soften.

"Hey, it's okay. We'll make this work."

I reached out to hug him, and he automatically returned it. I felt warm and safe and right in his embrace—until he casually squeezed my back. I cried out, jerking away at the pain that shot through me. We sprang apart, and he looked at me in alarm. "What's wrong? Are you okay?"

"It's . . . complicated." My standard answer to uncomfortable questions.

"Georgina!"

"It's nothing. Don't worry about it."

He strode toward me, reached a hand out, then pulled back. Intensity filled his face. "Are you hurt?"

I tried to keep out of his reach. "Look, I got in a fight last night, and I'm sporting some, uh, residual effects. It's mostly gone, though, so there's nothing to worry about."

"You? Got in a fight? With who?"

"Whom. And it was with Nanette. I told you, it's nothing."

"Who's Nanette?"

"She's . . . a demon."

He gave me a level look. "A demon. A full-fledged demon."

"Something like that."

"Let me see your back."

"Seth—"

"Georgina! Let me see your back."

There was anger in his words, not at me, but at the thought of someone hurting me. It reminded me a little of Dante's reaction, except that Dante always had a bit of anger in him. It was normal. To see it woken up in Seth . . . to see him so passionate and fierce . . .

Slowly, slowly, I turned around and undid the front of my robe, letting it slip halfway down my back. I heard Seth gasp at what he saw, and then a few moments later, he stepped forward and pushed my hair off my back so that he could get a better view. I shivered when his fingers touched my skin.

"Georgina . . . this is horrible . . ."

"It was worse before." I spoke flippantly, hoping to deflect his worry and realizing I'd only increased it now.

"Worse?"

I tugged the robe up and turned back around. "Mei healed it. I'm fine."

"Yeah, it seems that way."

"Look, it's nothing you have to worry about."

"Not worry about?" His eyes were filled with incredulity. "Even when you're . . . normal . . . a demon could still kill you, right?"

"Yeah."

Seth put his hand to his forehead and sighed. "This is what it's like, isn't it?"

"What?"

"What you went through with me. Living with the fear that I could die. Having it tear you apart."

I didn't answer right away. "You don't have to worry about me. This'll work out."

"Did this . . . did Nanette do this because of your investigating?"

I nodded, then crooked him a wry smile. "Still like how brave I am?"

He stepped closer to me and looked me up and down in a way that was so serious, my smile faded. "Even after this, you aren't going to stop, are you? You're going to keep pushing to find Jerome?"

"Do you want me to stop?" This was almost like my earlier conversation with Dante, when he'd made it clear he thought I was a fool for continuing with my quest.

Seth's answer was a long time in coming. "I don't want you to get hurt. But I understand you, and I know why you have to do this . . . and it's still part of that strange, brave nature of yours that's so . . ."

He didn't finish, but I saw the anguish in his eyes, the worry and heartache over something happening to me. It was mingled with something else, though. Pride. Affection. I put my arms around him again, wanting to comfort him now. "Hey, hey. It's going to be okay. I'll be okay."

His hands rested on my hips, careful of my back, but honestly, I barely noticed. My attention was on his lips, pressed against my cheek. "Georgina, Georgina," he breathed against my skin. "You are . . . incredible."

And like in the car, I don't know who exactly was to blame, but our lips met and were kissing again. Unlike before, we didn't break apart out of shock. We kept kissing. And kissing. His lips were intoxicating and felt like they'd been designed especially for mine. Our bodies pressed against one another, though his embrace was still gentle. As the kiss continued, that same sensation came back to me: this was purely a kiss. Just an expression of love between two people with no dire side effects, no soul stealing. The longer it went on, the more amazed I was. By now, as a succubus, I would have begun to taste his energy and feel his thoughts. But not now. I was alone in my own head, savoring his body and not his soul.

We pulled back slightly, and he moved his hands up to the side of my face, smoothing my hair away and touching my cheek. "Georgina. You are . . . beautiful."

We kissed again, and it was so sweet, so pure, that it didn't seem possible. I hadn't had a physical experience that could really be called sweet or pure since . . . well, since my mortal days. But this was. And by pure, I didn't mean non-sexual . . . because my body was definitely awake and yearning for his. But, it was pure in the sense that there were no ulterior machinations here, just our feelings. My love for him was the turn-on, and as his hands ran down my arms and back to my hips, it was the knowledge that it was *Seth* that made it all so powerful.

His hands carefully moved down to the robe's tie and undid the knot. He broke the kiss and studied my face as he hesitantly, almost reverently, slipped the robe off me. It hit the floor, and I stepped away from it. Seth moved with me, running his fingers along my arms, leaning down to kiss my neck. I tilted my head back as my own hands began pushing up his

T-shirt. When I had it half-way, he paused to push it up the rest of the way.

Then his hands were on my waist once more, sliding down and feeling the curve of my hips. I had on plain cotton panties—sexily cut, at least—and his fingertips traced the edges down along my thighs, every touch soft yet quivering with pent-up energy. I don't think I was being quite as gentle. I was hungry to touch him, eager as I ran my hands along his chest and the lean muscles of his stomach. I wanted to kiss it and taste it and lose myself in all things Seth.

I began backing up toward my bedroom, and he followed, turning hesitant once we reached the bed and I started to sit. "You can't . . ." he began.

"I can lie down," I said, doing exactly that. "I just can't slam my back down or anything."

After watching me for a moment, making sure I spoke the truth, Seth took off his jeans and lay down next to me. I rolled slightly to my side, pressing back to him. We resumed kissing, doing no more than that, just letting our nearly bare bodies wrap around each other. Having all this skin touching between us was heady. Never, never had I imagined it could really happen. Our hands explored each other, feeling every line and curve we'd always been denied. Every gesture between us was exquisite. Every caress was a prayer. We regarded each other's bodies with wonder and joy.

When my hands slipped to the edges of his boxers, I found his own fingers were tugging at my panties. We hardly needed any communication, and once completely naked, I wrapped my arms around him, pulling him toward me and seeking the completion with him I'd so long dreamed of.

To my surprise, he pulled from my arms and scooted down the bed. "What are you doing?" I asked.

"This," he said.

He smoothly pushed my legs apart, and I felt him shower my inner thighs with light, delicate kisses. Up and up his warm mouth moved until he made contact with my clit. I gasped softly at the fire that coursed through me from that light flick of the tongue. It was so light . . . yet so powerful. I'd been so intoxicated with the simple fact that we could touch that I hadn't been consciously aware of just how aroused I had grown. I ached and was wet and nearly melted at his touch.

He lifted his mouth up slightly. "Do you know how long I've dreamed about this? To be able to touch you? To taste you?"

I had little chance to ponder his rhetorical question because his lips returned to me, sucking and licking, somehow infinitely gentle and blazingly hot at the same time. I closed my eyes and lost myself in the pleasure of it, of Seth bringing me closer and closer to orgasm. As my muscles tightened and my cries grew more frequent, he intensified his movements, his tongue dancing and teasing harder and more rapidly.

I wanted to hold off, to prolong this as I did his books, but I couldn't help it. My climax hit me hard and fast, and I moaned long and low as I came. All the while, Seth kept his mouth down there, refusing to let up as my body arched and trembled from the sparks of ecstasy that flowed through me. When my body finally quieted, he lifted himself up again and returned to my side, showering my chest with more of those tiny kisses.

I brought my face to his, trading in the little kisses for one big one. His mouth tasted like me, and I opened my lips farther and farther as our tongues stroked each other. I might have come already, but I still burned between my legs and still needed him. I pressed myself against him, wrapping my legs around him so that there was almost no space between our hips.

"Georgina . . ." he said warningly.

It was another sign of how well we knew each other that I realized he wasn't worried about asking permission about what came next. He was worried about my back again. So, shifting over, I rolled him to his back and straddled him, looking down at him with a small smile. He gave me an answering one, amused by my ready solution. As we held gazes, I was again overwhelmed with the emotion of the experience, of how indescribable it was to finally touch someone I loved. I had been terrified at the thought of dying, but I realized then that I was only afraid of dying uselessly. For Seth, to save him, I would have gladly laid down my life. He was right. We were connected in something bigger than both of us.

Empowered by that realization, I lowered my hips, joining us at last. I felt him enter me, felt him fill me up. We both paused then, neither breathing or moving, half-expecting something to happen or end this. Nothing did, and after that, I didn't hesitate any further. I slowly moved my hips up and down, savoring the feel of him in me and underneath me as he glided in and out. My hands were on his chest and his were on my hips. Our eyes were on each other, never wavering, never breaking contact.

How to describe sex with Seth? It's difficult. It was unlike anything I'd had in my existence as a succubus. Somewhere, in the back of my head, it resonated with memories of my marriage, when my husband and I had still been happy. Every other instance after that had been lacking . . . until now. Each movement and touch with Seth was a dream, a wonder.

The intensity of our lovemaking steadily increased. My need for him grew stronger and stronger, and I rode him with a ferocity that was still tender and full of the love that burned between us. I loved the feel of him, loved how I could thrust him into me, hard and deep. And yet . . .

"It's not enough," I murmured. "We're still not close enough." It might have been a foolish sentiment, considering we were as physically close as two people could be. But Seth understood.

"I know," he gasped. "I know. We'll never be close enough."

Joy lit his face then, and when he came, his body arched up toward mine. I leaned down and increased my rhythm and hardness, wanting so badly to be even closer and have as much of him in me as I could. His mouth parted in a soft moan that mirrored my earlier one, and when he started to instinctively close his eyes, he quickly opened them again to stay locked with my gaze. There was no looking away between us, no avoiding what we felt. As I stared into his eyes and felt his body's trembling fade, energy seemed to crackle between our souls in a way that had nothing to do with succubus soul-stealing.

Carefully, I eased myself off him and lay down on my side again, draping my body over his. I was drowning in feeling and emotion.

"Georgina," he murmured, pulling me closer. "You are the world."

I'd heard that somewhere before, but I was too overwhelmed to parse it much. I was too lost in Seth. Instead, what I said was unoriginal but absolutely true: "I love you."

Chapter 18

When it was over, I rested my cheek against his chest while still staying mostly on my side. His heart beat heavy beneath my hands, and the smell of his skin and sweat nearly overpowered me. I lay there, perfectly still, scarcely daring to breathe. I was afraid that if I moved too much, I'd break this spell, this dream that I'd somehow stumbled into.

Slowly, carefully, Seth ran his fingers through my hair, idly twining the strands into loops. He let his hand drop and shifted slightly, just enough to press a kiss to my forehead. I exhaled and snuggled closer, realizing that I really wasn't going to wake from this dream.

At least, that's what I thought until his cell phone rang.

The ring was "Where the Streets Have No Name" by U2, not a particularly hard or jarring song but one that made me flinch anyway. For a moment, we each held our breath, both of us frozen. I wanted the phone to disappear off the face of the earth, to get smote the way I kept fearing some demon would smite me. I needed it to go away because if it kept ringing, it meant none of this was real. That we were going to have to face reality.

But it was already too late. The spell was broken. The phone was reality.

"You should answer that," I said.

He hesitated for the space of two heartbeats, sighed, and then slowly disentangled himself from me, still careful of my back. Sitting on the side of the bed, he reached down and pulled the cell phone from his jeans pocket. I shifted over, staying propped up on one elbow, admiring the shape of his body, even as a strange, bittersweet feeling began spilling through my heart. I knew, without knowing how I knew, that it was Maddie.

"Hey. Yeah . . . I got caught up with . . . um . . ." Seth paused, and I sensed something monumental about to take place. "I got an idea for this latest chapter."

I closed my eyes. In all the time I'd known him, I'd never heard Seth outright lie.

"Right. Yeah. Okay. Um, if I leave now, I can probably make it in . . . oh, twenty minutes. Mmm-hmm. You want me to pick you up, or . . . ? Okay. See you there."

He disconnected and continued sitting with his back to me, clasping the phone in his hands. Although he sat up straight, he had the air of someone hunched over, weary with defeat.

"You have to go?" I asked.

He looked back at me, anguish on his face. "Georgina . . ."

I managed a weak smile. "It's okay. I wasn't tricked here. I understand the situation."

"I know, but I want you to realize that it wasn't . . . that I didn't . . ."

He didn't need to finish. One of the things I'd always loved about Seth was his open, honest nature. Occasionally he'd been able to hide his feelings from me, but more often than not, they shone through on his features. This was one of those times. With a single look, I saw what was in his heart, that he hadn't had sex with me because I was easy or available. He'd done it because of how he felt about me, because he loved— still loved—me. It made all of this that much worse.

"I know," I said softly.

After one more kiss to my forehead, he put on his clothes. I watched each move hungrily, uncertain if I'd ever see anything like it again. When he was dressed and ready to go, he sat beside me on the bed, playing with my hair again. Again, those golden brown eyes spilled over with emotion. He was overcome and confused. I was too, but for his sake, I tried to appear strong and articulate.

"It's okay," I said. "It was great. Amazing . . . but I understand that we shouldn't have and that we can't ever . . ." So much for articulation.

"Yeah," he agreed.

"It was just this once. And it was perfect."

"Just this once," he repeated.

I couldn't read his voice, but something told me he wasn't entirely happy about that. Neither was I, but honestly, what could we do? We'd succumbed to passion, and now he had to go back to his girlfriend. End of story.

He tipped my head back, and our lips met in a soft, warm kiss. It was brief, only a few moments, but I felt that same, soul-deep connection that had consumed me during sex. He stood up and studied me for a few moments more, as though he might not ever see me again. I felt a little silly lying there naked, but his expression told me he thought I was beautiful.

He left after that, and I stayed in bed, drunk on my own feelings. Aubrey joined me, curling up against my leg.

"Was that how it was supposed to be, Aubrey?" I couldn't decide. Certainly the sex had been everything I'd ever imagined with Seth. But this afterglow? It was a bit lacking. Nothing about the situation was normal. I had no prior experience to fall back on.

After almost a half hour of staring at nothing and reaching no conclusions, I got out of bed. I was still reeling from what had happened, and my body burned with what Seth and I had done. I usually liked to shower after sex, but not today. I could smell Seth on me, his sweat and even a faint trace of the leather-and-apple cologne he used sometimes. I couldn't stand to wash him off yet, so I put the old cotton robe back on. Ratty or not, its fabric was soft against my bruised skin.

As I was about to leave my room, I noticed the photo of the medallion on the floor. I picked it up, intending to set it on my nightstand, and froze. There was writing on it.

Inked with a black Sharpie, neat handwriting read: *Smoky quartz indicates earth or a oneness with the earth.* The symbols on the medallion were circled, with lines drawn out from each one, leading to brief notes: *this indicates an affinity for water, a harmonious, blending state; this is similar to the water one, except it's for the earth; this is a masking symbol, meant to shield the object it protects and keep the seal strong; this one's strange, indicates blankness or whiteness—maybe white sand or stones?; this is the symbol for tears—combined with the water sign, probably indicates salt water.*

I reread the notes three times. Where had they come from? When had this happened? I retraced my steps, trying to figure out when I'd abandoned the picture. There'd been no writing when I showed it to Dante. The most likely time would have been while I was out for food. Someone could have also theoretically broken into my home and done it while I was with Carter in the living room, but sneaking past the angel seemed pretty out there.

Unless . . . was it possible Carter had helped me after all? He kept saying he couldn't; he'd even directly denied involvement with my assorted rescues. But the timing here was awfully coincidental. I kept staring at the symbols, at the notes, and the pictures of the seal. Whoever had written this was irrelevant for now. If their notes were correct, then I needed to use them to find Jerome.

Carter had said the seal served two purposes. One was to infuse the vessel with power. The other was to serve as a "lock" that could open the vessel and release Jerome. The parts of the seal itself were with the demon and the summoner, but the symbols should give some clues to the vessel's location. Supposedly, these symbols would have been used in hiding Jerome, infusing the vessel with a type of energy specific to the location that would help blend and mask Jerome's presence.

An affinity with the earth, as well as markings for water—salt water, specifically. A lot of places that were infused with power tended to be wild, natural places, though some had become centers of civilization and activity. Pike Place Market in downtown Seattle, for example, was one such ancient place of power that had been completely built upon by humanity.

But these . . . what did they indicate? Some place near salt water, apparently. The vessel was probably close enough to the water that the symbols would resonate and camouflage its location. And the earth location? Buried in the dirt maybe? Was Jerome buried on some beach near the ocean? Jerome's kidnappers wouldn't want to keep him too far away from them, but nonetheless, the Pacific flanked the entire western half of Washington. That was a lot of beach, and I knew there were a lot of places of power along there. I didn't know of any white sand beaches anywhere in the area; only further investigation could say for sure.

Groaning, I lay back on my bed, still holding the picture. The notes had only narrowed down the locations, but that was still a lot of area to cover. Yet what could I do? I had to find the vessel, sooner rather than later, or else Seattle was going to have a new archdemon. Studying the photo further, I willed it to give me some more info. Nothing. Just the medallion, the mystery notes, and Mary's cataloging info at the top which told me little—

I frowned, rereading her header. It was brief, just the materials, name, and date the medallion had been created and then picked up. But the date it had been finished . . . the date stuck in my head. Why? It was from a week ago. Something about that date was important, but I couldn't figure out why. It felt likes years had passed in this last week, but I nonetheless counted backward, reassessing my recent activities.

There. The seal had been made the day after I'd first gone to Vancouver . . . the day the vampire turf war had gone down. Would the seal's creation have triggered anyone's immortal radar? I didn't know, but if it had, Jerome, Grace, and Mei would have all been busy sorting out the ensuing vampire mess. Misdirection.

From there, other things began to arrange themselves in my head. I thought back to the Army of Darkness, wondering what events their activities might line up against. The event in Queen Elizabeth Park matched the date the seal had been picked up. And the Army's impromptu visit to Seattle . . . ? That had preceded Jerome's summoning, though no one would have wanted to direct attention to that, would they?

The answer was here. I just couldn't quite make the pieces fit yet. The Army had staged their show. Jerome, Grace, and Mei had given it their full attention. Jerome had been summoned. Where had this game's other players been?

I left the bed and its aching, alluring memories. Finding my cell phone, I dialed Kristin's number.

"Hi, Georgina," she said, pleasant but busy like always.

"Hey," I said. "How's it going?"

"Crazy." I could imagine the grimace on her face. "Cedric's stressed to hell—no pun intended—with all these demons in the area. At least that . . . that succubus is distracting him."

"Tawny?"

"Whatever her name is. Cedric's actually out with her right now." Bitterness and the tiniest hint of jealousy came through in Kristin's voice. I remembered her perpetual devotion to him—and the look on her face when he'd asked Tawny out. I felt for her but had too many romantic hijinks of my own to deal with.

"Huh." I didn't really know what else to say. "Look, I have a question for you. Do you know, did Cedric come to see Jerome the day the Army was down here?"

"Yeah. Cedric came down after you left the message. I thought you knew."

"No . . . I only heard about it after the fact, and then, the whole summoning kind of took precedence."

"Why do you want to know?"

I hesitated. I liked Kristin, but she was clearly loyal to Cedric. I didn't think it'd be wise to share my theories with her, like that the Army being in Seattle had provided a convenient reason for Jerome and Cedric to be together when Jerome got summoned. It occurred to me that I might very well owe

Hugh an apology for my adamant denial of Cedric's involvement. Something else also occurred to me.

"Um, it's a long story," I said hastily. "Do you know if he's
been hanging out with Nanette a lot?"

"Why?" Her tone was quickly turning suspicious. She didn't
like me interrogating her about her boss.

"Well . . . I told him the other day that I thought Nanette
might be involved with Jerome's disappearance. He didn't
think so, but he told her . . . and she got really pissed off. She,
um. . . . well, let's just say she got physical, and I have the
scars to prove it."

My immortal friends had pointed out that Nanette's attack
made her look guilty. If Cedric had done enough goading to
make her angry when he told her, it could have very well sent
her to me in a rage—and successfully shifted attention from
him. Fuck. I didn't want another suspect in all of this. I didn't
want it to be Cedric. Nanette had hitherto been a convenient
explanation.

Kristin was silent for several seconds. "I didn't know that,"
she said quietly. "Are you okay?"

"Mostly. Mei healed the worst of it, but I'm still a little
sore."

"I can't imagine . . . Cedric would never have told her if he
thought that was going to happen. He likes you. He wouldn't
condone that. He couldn't have known. I'm sorry."

She was sincerely contrite, hurt at the thought that her
boss—even if he was a demon and a servant of evil—could
have been involved with something that had turned out so
terrible.

"It's okay," I said. "I've gotta run, but thanks for the info.
Things are kind of crazy here too, as you can imagine."

We said our good-byes and disconnected. I flipped the cell
phone around in my hand, feeling overwhelmed. Nanette
wasn't off the table yet, but Cedric was right alongside her
now as a culprit—maybe more so. If I had enough evidence, I
could possibly take it to Grace and Mei . . . but I didn't have

that yet. Besides, knowing who the culprit was wouldn't solve the immediate issue: finding Jerome.

I glanced back at the photo, resting on my nightstand. Sore back or no, it looked like I had to do a little beachcombing.

I nearly knocked Dante over when he came home that night.

"Succubus," he said, letting me wrap my arms around him. He was careful only to rest his hands on my hips. "Happy to see you too."

My eagerness was twofold. I was excited to see him because I wanted to pick his brain about the medallion and places of power. But also . . . well, while hanging around today, I'd had a lot of time to think about Seth and what had happened between us. The memory of his body still made mine burn, and I grew breathless recalling that amazing connection and sense of rightness between us.

And yet . . . whatever rightness had been between us, it had still been wrong. He was with Maddie—my friend. I'd been upset when she and Seth had first slept together. I was no different. In fact, I'd knowingly done it, which made it worse. Now there was Dante to consider. Dante, who despite that dark, scowling nature really did love me and wanted to win my regard as more than just someone I had sex with. This was where my future lay, not with Seth.

I kissed Dante on the lips, lingering several seconds. "I missed you."

His smile turned wry. "Don't look at me like that, or I'm going to have a hard time remembering that you're injured and that I should keep my hands off you."

Those words triggered a pang of guilt. My injuries certainly hadn't been enough to keep Seth off me. I could have told Dante that I was better, that it didn't matter, yet for whatever reason . . . I didn't.

We broke apart, and I found the medallion picture for him. He stared incredulously as I showed him the phantom notes and explained my story.

"What, you have no idea how they got there or who did it?"

"Nope, but at this point, I'm not going to question it."

He shook his head, face still shocked. "Well. I wish I'd known this before I left. Would have been a lot easier to just wait and have invisible helpers come leave clues."

I recalled how he'd gone out to see what he could find about the medallion. "What'd you turn up?"

He gestured at the picture. "Same thing."

I rested my hand over his. "Sorry. I really appreciate your help. And if your research found the same thing, it means I can probably trust this."

"Maybe," he said, still not sounding happy about the wasted time. "What are you going to do? Something crazy?"

"Look for saltwater beaches, I guess."

Dante let out a low whistle. "There are a lot of those around here. Not to mention you have no way of identifying this vessel anyway."

"I know. But I've got to start somewhere. Can you help me make a list?"

We got an atlas of the Pacific Northwest area from my car and laid it flat on the kitchen table. Scrutinizing every detail, we each marked as many places as we knew. Dante knew a lot more than me, which didn't particularly surprise me. I'd once noted to Erik Lancaster that those who study religion tend to know more about it than those who practice it. Sometimes, I felt the same way about immortal affairs.

We found twelve in all that were easy day trips—and many more beyond that. "Looks like you've got your work cut out for you," Dante mused. "When are you going to look? Too dark now."

I stared at the map with dismay. "Tomorrow, I guess. Can you go with me?" A psychic like him might able to sense something, as Carter had pointed out.

He grimaced. "Not tomorrow. I've actually got a few appointments people have scheduled. Crazy, huh? I probably can go the next day or the day after, if you can wait. I'd feel better if you didn't go alone."

I was glad for his business but sad at the delay. "I don't think I can wait. Don't worry, though. I'll find somebody."

"On the bright side," he said, trying to cheer me. "I'll have money tomorrow. We can go out somewhere nice."

I mustered a smile. "Yeah, that'll be—oh, shit. I can't."

"What's going on?"

"Fuck. I promised the people at the store I'd teach salsa after work."

"Cancel," he said dismissively. My dance lessons didn't hold much importance, as far as he was concerned. "Tell them you're sick."

That wouldn't entirely be a lie . . . and yet, I hated to go back on my word. Furthermore, I could still see Maddie's radiant face, so excited and happy when I'd agreed. How could I deny her that after what I'd done to her today?

"No . . . I've got to do it. Let's go eat out now. My treat."

He drove us over to Belltown for some of Seattle's best seafood. Wine and conversation flowed, and I discovered I was healing by leaps and bounds. When we got back to my place later and went to bed, Dante snuggled up to me and kissed my neck.

"Looks like you're on the mend," he noted, moving his lips up to my earlobe. "We could do it . . . I could be careful . . ."

All around us were the sheets and blankets where Seth and I had made love earlier. The thought nearly smothered me. God. I really should have washed the bedding. I swallowed and shifted position so that I didn't meet Dante's eyes. "Maybe . . . but I'd rather wait, so we can *not* be careful." I hoped there was enough of a seductive growl in my voice to make it believable.

Dante sighed, fortunately unwilling to push me. "Fair enough."

He rolled over and left me to sleep, but it was a long time in coming.

Chapter 19

The next day, Dante was off to work, and I called Cody right after breakfast. "Hey," I said. "Are you guys still being beach bunnies?"

"You bet," he said brightly. "One of our neighbors has a sailboat and offered to let us go with him and—"

"That's not quite what I had in mind," I interrupted.

An hour and a half later, Peter echoed my thoughts. "This wasn't what I had in mind."

I'd convinced them to come out with me on my beach hunt. Unfortunately, the day was cold and threatened rain. As we walked along the water at Dash Point, icy wind ripped off the waves and cut across our faces. I snuggled into my jacket, thinking of how many times I'd taken the ability to shape-shift warmer coats for granted.

"Look, I know you guys think you're on spring break, but eventually, we *will* get another archdemon, and I'd rather it be Jerome."

"Yes, but it's not like this is exactly an airtight plan," Peter argued. "We're pretty much going to beaches at random, in the hopes of finding white sand. Look at this stuff. It's beige . . . is that close enough to white?"

I cut him a sidelong glance. "You once got in an argument with Carter about the difference between 'Denim Days Blue' and 'Summer Cobalt.' You tell me. Is there a difference between white and beige?"

Peter kicked sand up with the toe of his boot. "It was

'*Winter* Cobalt,' and Carter was wrong. There's a huge difference between those two."

Cody and I hid our grins as we continued our trek. Dash Point State Park was near Federal Way, down on the south side of Puget Sound. It had seemed reasonable to start there and work our way around the coast, back up toward Seattle. This was our second park of the day, and so far, we'd seen nothing to match the seal's cryptic clues.

On our drive to the third place, Peter was still pessimistic. "You know, this would be a lot easier if we had your deadbeat boyfriend along. We can only go off visual clues at this point. We need someone who can actually sense the power around the vessel."

"Dante's busy at work," I explained.

"Huh," Cody mused. "I never expected to hear 'busy' and 'at work' used together when it came to Dante."

"Be quiet," I said. "Leave the snark to Hugh and Peter."

"What about Erik?" asked Peter. "He's psychic."

"Yeah, I considered that, but he's getting old and his back's been bothering him. I hate to ask him to walk around and around with me . . . but well, I haven't ruled it out."

"And you don't know any more psychics?"

"Nope. Not that I trust, at least."

"Me either," admitted Peter. "But I bet Hugh does."

"Yeah, you're probably—" I stopped mid-sentence. "I might know one more . . ." It was crazy idea, one I wasn't sure I should put any real effort toward.

"Who?" asked Cody.

I shook my head and drove through the entrance of our next state park. "It's a long story, one I'm going to have to work on."

Our third stop yielded nothing either, save an inability for Peter to get sand out of his boots. It had started raining by that point, and even my mood was down by then. Sunset was still a couple of hours away, but the overcast sky was effectively killing our light. Glancing at my watch, I saw that the dance lesson was looming, so we turned north and headed back to Seattle. I dropped the vampires off at their apartment and then drove home to get ready.

My closet's dress selection seemed old and tired, but I had no new fashions to magically summon. So, I opted for a sleeveless minidress with a bright pattern of orange, green, and black flowers that had been blurred together like a watercolor painting. It was a bit shorter than it should have been for a dance with this much movement, but the colors seemed suitable and cheerful on a day like this.

It also seemed cold, though, and on impulse, I added black thigh-high stockings to keep my legs warm. Between that, black heels, and dark lipstick, I seemed to be channeling my succubus self more than my mild-mannered bookstore manager self. Of course, considering the whore wear I'd shown up in a week or so ago, this was kind of tame.

Doug naturally still teased me about it, though deep down inside, I knew he thought I looked hot. I took a smug satisfaction in knowing I'd done it without any shape-shifting. Plus, I'd practically burned my hair off trying to flat iron it tonight. I dared anyone to accuse me of frizziness.

Maddie was ecstatic, and her enthusiasm spread to those among the staff who'd decided to stay after closing for the lesson. A few of their friends had shown up as well, giving us around a dozen. It was a good, manageable size. We cleared space upstairs, and I set up my portable CD player. Cody had helped me teach swing before, but I hadn't thought to enlist his assistance this time. Instead, I used Doug as my demo. Maybe it was part of being a musician, but he had a solid sense of rhythm and could pick up moves really quickly.

A half-hour in, I trusted him enough to start assisting others, and we split up to work with some of our students. Despite my hesitation in agreeing to the lesson, I had fun, and most people were so nervous about touching their manager that I didn't have to worry about anyone hurting my back. Maddie, enthusiastic or not, was having a bit of trouble and complained loudly when her brother came in to help her. He swept her away, leaving me with her former dance partner: Seth.

I'd known he was here, of course, but I'd been trying to avoid eye contact. There was no good way around it now, and we stood there awkwardly, eyeing each other, neither of us certain what to do. Autopilot kicked in, and I held my hands out to him. I was the teacher here, and since he was one of the worst dancers on the floor, it was only natural that he'd need my help more than others.

Seth held up his hands in return, and as I took a step forward, my heel snagged on the carpet. I knelt down to check, thinking it would be pretty embarrassing to trip and fall when I was the alleged model of grace and balance here. Glancing up, I met Seth's eyes. He was looking down at me, and his face was no longer shy or confused. His expression was considering and . . . well, hungry. Looking down, I suddenly realized the view I was offering up. He was able to see right into the heart of my cleavage, which was already considerably exposed by the dress's low neckline. From kneeling, my skirt had ridden up, showing off the black lace top of one of my thigh-highs.

I don't know what in particular he found the most alluring, but his gaze raked across my body, and everywhere it touched, heat swept me. I rose, suddenly feeling like the shy and awkward one. Desire was written all over him, and it was a wonder the entire room didn't notice. He extended his hands again, and when we touched, electricity shot through my body.

Finding the beat, I led him into the steps. He was every bit as bad as I remembered, yet as I worked to guide him in the right moves, our bodies brushing together out of necessity, I couldn't help but think that while his dance rhythm might be lacking, there'd been nothing uncoordinated about the way he made love.

Neither of us spoke for a minute or so, and I was sure he was caught up in the same physical spell as me, probably reliving our encounter from yesterday as well. My arousal was growing too, and wrong as I knew it was, I actually went out of my way to make sure we occasionally touched as I guided his body. Finally, sexually charged or not, I couldn't help but laugh.

"I think this is the worst I've ever seen you dance," I told him. "And believe me, that's saying something."

He smiled ruefully, but I suspected dancing was the last thing on his mind right now. "I'm out of practice."

"Well, I'm glad you're actually here this time, instead of sitting on the sidelines."

"Things change, I guess."

I held his eyes for a few moments. "Yes. Yes, they do."

A few more moments of silence passed before he asked, "How's your immortal, um, situation going?"

"Hmm?" Seth's hand had come within millimeters of brushing against my breast when we turned. Sternly, I chastised myself to forget about the way his body had felt—and looked and smelled and tasted—yesterday and remember my other problems. "Oh, well. Not so great, actually. I got some more info, except it's hard to—"

When I fell silent, Seth tilted his head and gave me a puzzled look. "What?"

I'd forgotten the idea that I'd briefly hinted at to the vampires. "Seth . . . I have a strange question to ask you . . . and you can feel free to say no."

The look on his face still seemed to say he wanted to rip my clothes off, but there was something else . . . something serious and concerned that made sweet, sentimental feelings mingle with my own lust.

"If there's anything I can do to help, I will."

"I know," I said. "Except this isn't exactly your help . . . it's Kayla's."

If Seth had been doing any semblance of dancing now, he might have stumbled and missed a beat. As it was, it was kind of hard to tell the difference.

"Kayla?" His four-year-old niece's name was clearly not what he'd been expecting to hear.

"Do you remember when I said she had psychic powers?"

"Yeah . . . but I didn't really think much of it."

"Well, I told you the logistics of summoning, right? Now I've got a lead on where Jerome is but not how to find him once we're in the right spot. I could do it if I was back to normal, or a psychic might be able to do it. Unfortunately, my usual ones aren't easily accessible."

Worry was rapidly dominating over desire now. I was sad to see the arousal leave him, but this was a serious topic.

"I'm not sure I like the idea of Kayla getting mixed up in any of this. In fact, I know I don't like it."

I nodded. "I know. I figured you'd feel that way—believe me, I don't like it either." I loved all of Seth's nieces, but Kayla in particular always tugged at my heartstrings. "Just something that crossed my mind earlier."

"Well, I—ah!"

Another couple slammed into my back, shoving me forward into his arms. My hands reached out to catch myself, but it didn't stop our bodies from pressing together. Every part of me tingled at that contact, and if I'd had any remaining delusions that I could forget about what we'd done yesterday, they shattered for good now.

"Sorry," said Andy. He was dancing with Casey, and like her, he was a longtime staff member.

Casey groaned. "Georgina, please take him. Even Seth can't be that bad."

"Debatable," I murmured. I didn't want to move, didn't want to break my hold with Seth. I wanted to stay there and keep touching him, and because of that very impulse, I stepped back. My breathing was heavy, and it took me a moment to gather myself. I drew in one more deep breath and grinned at Andy. "Okay. Let's see what we can do with you."

Casey led Seth away, and I managed to avoid him for the rest of the dance lesson. When it wrapped up, everyone clapped in my honor and demanded I teach a follow-up. I assured them I would, but I was too flustered and preoccupied to settle on a date right now. I promised to get back to them later.

Several of them immediately jumped in to put the room back together, and seeing no further reason to stay, I hurried off to my office. My plan was to check up on some of the paperwork and hide out until everyone was gone so that I wouldn't have to see Seth again. I was half-way down the hall when I heard someone call my name.

"Georgina?"

I halted. It was Maddie. I turned, hoping the smile on my face looked neither fake nor panicked. Fuck. She was here to bust me for cozying up with her boyfriend on the dance floor. And honestly, it was no more than I deserved.

But her face was all smiles and good cheer as she handed me a stack of papers. "I went kind of crazy," she said sheepishly, "but these are some condo listings I printed for you. I've been searching online the last couple of days and kind of looked at everything since you still weren't one hundred percent sure of what you wanted. Got a lot of good hits by the beach."

I took the stack from her, stunned. This was the last thing I'd expected.

"It's probably overkill, but it should give you a lot to look at. Then, if you get some ideas, we can go on from there."

I glanced down at the top sheet, displaying a three-bedroom condo out on Alki. "I . . . wow. Thank you, Maddie. You shouldn't have."

She beamed at my thanks. "Happy to. Let me know what you think—and thanks again for the lesson. It was so much fun! Hopefully I'll be less horrible next time. Maybe I can get Seth to practice at home."

She gave me a quick hug and then hurried off to catch a ride with Doug. I trudged to my office, papers in hand, and set them on my desk. I collapsed into the chair, feeling horrible. While I'd been out doing bad, wicked things with her boyfriend, she'd been working diligently to find me a new home.

I tried hard after that to browse some spreadsheets, but my heart wasn't in it. I mostly stared at numbers without really comprehending them, and when a knock came at the door, I welcomed the distraction. I jumped up from my chair.

"Come in." I wondered if Maddie had forgotten to give me another ream. But it wasn't her.

Seth stood in the doorway.

I stared, hoping my mouth hadn't dropped open or anything embarrassing like that. "What . . . what are you doing here? I thought you left."

He looked as though he wanted to step inside but was afraid to. "Doug took Maddie home, and I came back to . . . to get . . ." He stopped and shook his head, unable to continue with a lie about having forgotten something. "I came back to see you."

I remembered the way his eyes had watched my body, the smoke in them when the skirt had ridden up my leg. That same smokiness was there now, and I felt my own body's desire flare up in response. Really, though, after the way we'd touched while dancing, the desire had never really left me. Nonetheless, I tried to be reasonable.

"Seth, we can't . . . not again . . . it's . . ."

"I know," he said. At last, he crossed the threshold. "And I told myself . . . told myself I'd let it go . . . but I haven't stopped thinking about you since yesterday. And after tonight." Hesitantly, as though afraid someone might be lurking, he shut the door behind him. "Just the way you looked out there. It was . . . amazing. Believe me, I didn't screw up dancing because I'm bad at it—which I am. It's because I wasn't thinking about it at all. I was thinking about you. God, I couldn't stop. And it's not just how sexy you are tonight. It was more. It was the way you lit up the room, the way you charmed everyone and made them happy. You don't need any special powers to do that, Georgina. It's just in you, part of who you are. How funny you are, how smart. It's what made me fall in love you back then, and it's what . . ."

He didn't finish, and I was glad. If he had said ". . . makes me love you now," I wouldn't have been able to handle it.

I noticed that he'd moved a lot closer. I took a deep breath. "It would have been easier on me if you said you just thought I was sexy." Shallowness I could handle. Not this emotional depth.

He gave a rueful smile and stepped even closer so that we were only a couple feet apart. "Oh, believe me, I do. And it would be a lot easier on me if you weren't."

I could scarcely breathe. We were so close now, and every atom in the room felt charged. I felt charged. There was no mistaking the look on his face. He wanted me too—badly. Lust and desire spilled off him, and I knew my own face mirrored those feelings. He was careful, though, standing as close as he dared, waiting for my signal. There was a tension to him, like it would only take one small sign from me for him to explode.

Desperately, I tried to grasp a hold of everything reasonable that I knew. I remembered how miserable I'd felt when he left to go see Maddie yesterday. Hell, I tried to think of Maddie herself—that cheerful, guileless face that trusted me so much. I tried to think of Dante. None of that worked, though, because all that was in my head was Seth, how perfect it had felt being with him. How perfect it felt being with him even now.

Reaching out, I took his hand and brought it up to my collarbone. It was all he needed. He stepped closer and traced the lines of my neck, then moved down to my shoulder. He pushed the dress's strap so that it slid down my arm. His fingers followed it, pulling it farther so that the top of my dress fell forward, revealing most of my breast. My nipple was already hard and ready when his hand moved over and pulled the rest of that side of the dress down, completely exposing my breast. He cupped it, squeezing its fullness and running his fingers along the curve.

His other hand moved to my other side, cupping that

breast and teasing its nipple underneath the dress's silk. My body pressed closer to his, and our mouths met, hot and intense. Yesterday had been sweet and full of emotion. There was emotion here today, but it was intermingled with raw passion, with an animal instinct that made me wish he'd ravage my body right now.

And honestly, that wasn't too far from what happened. I stumbled from the press of our bodies and found my back pressed—gently—against the wall as he continued caressing my breasts. My hands wrapped around his neck, moving up to half-tangle and half-pull his hair. He finally released my breasts and ran his hands over the length of my body, down my hips and thighs, across the sheer, silky fabric covering my legs. Sliding his hands back up, he pushed my skirt up and slipped one hand under my thigh, so that it wrapped around his waist and kept the dress up. His other hand moved down under my black lace thong panties, probing to see if I was ready.

I was. I was warm and wet and slick, and the finger he slipped into me went in so easily that he then tried two, then three. I groaned and arched my back as he moved his fingers in and out of me and his mouth left hard, bruising kisses on my neck. My own hands fumbled down, trying to unfasten his pants. When I'd tugged them and his boxers down, he gripped my hips and turned me around so that I faced the wall. He shoved my skirt back up and tugged my panties halfway down my thighs. I bent over and extended my arms, using my hands to brace myself against the wall.

He entered me, forceful and deep, with no buildup or teasing. He was just as hard and long as I remembered, just as wonderful. Steadying his hands on my hips, he thrust roughly into me, desperately trying to sate the need I'd seen in him earlier, the need I shared. I cried out each time he shoved into me, knowing I should be quiet in case someone else had come back to the store. But I couldn't be. I was too caught up in the out-of-control passion of this moment, in the sinuous, primal lust that had consumed us both. And underscoring all of it was the realization that it was Seth. Seth, Seth, Seth . . . whom I loved more than anyone else. *You are the world.*

He moved his hands up from my hips to cup my breasts, forcing me to readjust my position. All the time, he never broke his rhythm, staying fast and urgent. His fingers pinched my nipples hard, and I cried out louder. I think that turned him on even more, spurring him to thrust harder into me. Hoping to excite him further, I completely gave myself over and let go of any restraint with my voice. The louder I moaned, the more his body pounded into mine. It was all I could do to keep myself from getting pressed against the wall, and as I moaned over and over, it had nothing to do with arousing him and everything to do with the ecstatic and exquisite force of what we were doing.

And when I finally came, the heat between my thighs building to an unbearable high, it was his name I screamed. A surge of new wetness came with my orgasm, and then I heard him groan and give a thrust so hard that it did shove me against the wall. His hands still clenched my breasts, his nails digging into my tender flesh, as he shuddered and took his release. He came for a long time, his low cry slowly fading.

When he pulled out, the loss of him in my body made me feel incomplete. Nonetheless, I straightened up and leaned against the wall, gasping to catch my breath. My voice was hoarse.

"Jesus," I said. "That was bad."

Seth looked startled—and then hurt. "Bad?"

"No, not performance bad—more like dirty, wicked bad. The kind of stuff that gets an R rating."

"What, we can't do that?" He stepped forward and wrapped his arms around my waist, nuzzling my neck.

"Well, yeah . . . er, well, damn it. We're not supposed to be. Not at all. It's just that last time, it was like . . . I don't know. It was making love. This time it was . . ."

"Fucking?" he supplied.

"Oh God," I groaned. "Seth Mortensen just said 'fucking' out loud. The end times are near."

He laughed and placed tiny kisses over my cheek. "I'm not some innocent. You should know that from my books."

"Yeah, but still. You aren't O'Neill. Unless you're getting into fistfights that I don't know about."

"Mmm . . . not lately."

We stood there in each other's arms, both warm in the after-glow of what we'd done. Then, just like last time, a strange awkwardness began to grow. We didn't even need Maddie calling now. I carefully pulled away.

"You should probably go, huh?" I didn't say it, but I was certain he'd be seeing her later.

"Yeah, but . . ." He sighed and rubbed his forehead. "This is a lot harder than I thought it would be."

"What, having an illicit and cheap affair?"

He grimaced. "No. But I mean, I've spent ages imagining what it'd be like to be with you and wishing you weren't a succubus. I was always down on myself . . . I felt so shallow to be consumed by sex like that. And now that it's finally happened—now that you aren't a succubus—it's not superfi-cial or shallow at all. It's so . . . I don't know. It's powerful. I wish this was an illicit, cheap affair. I wish I didn't feel this so deeply. Otherwise, when we said yesterday was it, it really would have been it."

I wished then, more than anything, that he'd say he was going to leave Maddie and we could be together again. He didn't, though, and I certainly wasn't going to bring it up. Be-sides, what good would it do? In only a few more days, I'd be back to normal, and our relationship would be as dysfunc-tional as before. What I wanted was pointless.

"Can I . . ." He took a deep breath. "Can I see you again? I know we said no more . . ."

I knew that by "see you again" he meant "have sex with you again." And somehow, I realized we were on a precipice here. The first time had been . . . well, not accidental . . . but certainly unexpected. This time had been an out-of-control animal lust. But now? An open declaration of this affair—premeditated sex—it took things to a whole new level. There was no going back. I studied those eyes I loved, the warm and gentle lips. I assessed my body, how it ached yet still burned with pleasure. Then I glanced over at Maddie's painstakingly researched real estate packet.

That should have been my mood killer, my warning. It was a reminder of who we were both betraying here. Seth had given in, but though I was on the verge, I could still pull back and save us from this. I had the power to say no.

"Yes," I said at last. "You can see me again."

Chapter 20

Dante was waiting for me when I got home. I normally liked having the company, but after being with Seth, Dante's presence now made me feel uncomfortable and confused. He didn't seem to notice right away, though, and instead was immediately caught up by Maddie's condo packet.

"What's this?" he asked, leafing through some pages.

"Maddie's been playing real estate agent for me."

"Wow. I didn't think you were serious about that."

I leaned back on the couch, weary from dancing, sex, and the emotional miasma I seemed to be swimming through lately. Bringing up Maddie didn't make me feel so great. "I didn't think I was either. I mentioned it offhand, and she kind of went crazy."

"Alki Beach, huh? Some of these are pretty nice." He held up one print-out. "Brand-new condo, still being built. You can weigh in on the colors and trim."

I shrugged. "I don't know. I don't have time to go shopping right now."

"One of the power spots on your list is near Alki. You could swing by."

I gave him a puzzled look. "Since when are you interested in me moving?"

He sat down opposite me, still looking through the listings. "Well, if you buy locally, I can rest easy that you're sticking around. Besides, get a bigger place, and we could try some cohabitation."

That caught me off-guard. "Oh?"

"You gave me a key. I might as well live here anyway."

"You're going to freeload off me for some more space, huh?" I teased.

He sighed, looking pained. "Man, you really do think the worst. I'd pay you rent."

"With what?" I asked incredulously.

"Business has been good. I think things are on the upswing."

"No offense, baby, but your business doesn't seem like the type that can maintain that kind of momentum. I think this has been a fluke." I spoke too soon and felt bad when I realized I'd hurt him. "But we can play it by ear if you want to move in. Maybe your reputation's spreading, and business will keep booming."

He seemed a little mollified after that, yet as I spoke the words, I found I wasn't overly thrilled at the prospect of us living together. I still had Seth on the brain. Obsessing on him was foolish, I knew. This fling of ours could only last a few more days at most. I shouldn't be mooning over him when I'd just be going back to Dante anyway.

Dante wanted to know how my beach investigation had gone, and I welcomed the change in subject. I gave him a brief rundown of my non-progress.

"You want me to look with you?" he asked. "I've finally got some time tomorrow."

I hesitated. The truth was, just before we'd parted, Seth had said he'd look with me and that he'd bring Kayla. The afterglow could be very persuasive. Still, I'd had to do a lot of convincing that she'd be safe, and honestly, I hoped I was right.

"I roped some other people into it," I said. "We should be fine."

I feared he'd question me further, particularly about whether I had a psychic to go with me or not. Mercifully, he let it go. I honestly didn't think he wanted to wander beaches and was grateful for the reprieve.

When we went to bed later, there was no way I could put

his arduous advances off any longer, not without raising suspicion. I'd made a good recovery and no longer had my back excuse. Yet . . . something was nagging at me. Dante himself had been the one to first joke about whether I could get pregnant in my pseudo-human state. I still didn't know if that was possible, and even if it was, would it matter if I returned to my immortal state in a few days? I had no clue how any of this would work, but Seth and I hadn't used protection. And suddenly, I realized that if there were any chance in the world that I could get pregnant—if Nyx's vision might really come true—I didn't want to chance a paternity dispute.

So, I turned on the charm for Dante and went down on him again, something he didn't really seem to mind. He tried to get me off in return, but it was to no avail. After being with Seth, I had zero desire of my own and found I couldn't come. And so, for the first time with Dante, I faked it. I was a pretty good faker. He never suspected.

He slept late the next morning, so I slipped out early without waking him. Seth and I were meeting over at a restaurant in Bellevue, hopefully far enough away from anyone we knew to see us. While walking to my car, I felt someone fall into step beside me.

"So, I hear you're spreading stories about me," Cedric said amiably.

Startled, I glanced over at him, unease spreading through me. Cedric was my suspect du jour, and I'd already seen one demon's reaction to my theories. Of course, he didn't look particularly destructive at the moment, and there was also the fact that I had yet to tell anyone my latest theories about him implicating Nanette.

"What do you mean?" I asked.

"Kristin said you said that I told Nanette how you thought she might have summoned Jerome." He paused as though trying to make sense of that. "For the record, I didn't."

I nearly stopped walking. "Then who did?"

"Hell if I know. Just figured you should know I wasn't responsible for what happened to you." He offered no more, no condolences or queries to my health. I honestly couldn't expect that from a demon. The fact that he'd bothered to come talk to me was a rarity enough—and naturally, he could be lying.

"Well, I don't know who else could have told her, then. Or why. I only told a handful of people." The more I thought about it, the more I realized he had to be lying. I'd only told my friends.

He maintained his perfectly bland face. "Like I said, I don't know."

We reached my car, and I paused, leaning against it. "You came all the way here to tell me this?" Not that it would have been an arduous journey for him.

"Don't flatter yourself," he said with a smile. "I'm here to chat with your demonesses. Hell's pretty much ruled out Jerome coming back. There'll be someone official here in days to settle the matter."

I tried to ignore the chill that sent down my spine and parse the rest of his words. Cedric was cozying up to Grace and Mei. Not a surprise. Whoever came here to assign a new archdemon would question those two the most. "Well, thank you," I said. I didn't really know what else to say in that matter, so I switched to something else that had been on my mind. "Hey, I haven't heard much about your cult lately."

"Yeah, they've been pretty quiet. Maybe you helped after all."

"Well, I don't think I did much." I was also starting to suspect the cult had nothing left to do. Now that their "Angel" had used them as an effective distraction during Jerome's summoning, they were no longer needed. I clicked my door open, and another curious thought struck me. "How's it going with Tawny?"

Cedric grimaced. "Well . . . we went out a couple of times."

"And?"

"My private life is no concern of yours."

"Fair enough." I started to get in.

"But if you must know . . ."

I paused and arched an eyebrow. "Yes?"

"Her conversation is . . . lacking a little," he admitted.

I couldn't help it. I laughed. "Are you seriously surprised by that?"

"Beauty's skin deep, I know . . . I guess I'd just hoped for a *little* more depth."

I chose not to comment on what he considered beautiful. "Don't take this the wrong way, but I figured you wouldn't really want more than cheap sex."

He cut me a look. "Because I'm a demon?"

"Don't look at me like that. Being romantic isn't really in your job description."

"True, true. But at the very least, I'd like to have a little understanding with my cheap sex. Someone who had *some* vague inkling of what I endure on a daily basis." He was still being gruff and demonlike, but there was a faint whisper of something surprisingly human under there.

I started to tell him that I didn't think that was very likely. Then, I thought of Kristin, Kristin who watched him with doe eyes and fretted over his well-being. "Someone who sort of gets your job and has an appreciation for its absurdity? Someone who's interested in helping you when you're stressed, in connecting with you and understanding things to an extent where you don't even have to say them anymore? Is that what you're looking for?"

He snorted. "Yeah, like that'll happen."

"I don't know. Maybe there's someone out there like that."

"You may not have been human for a long time, but you still cling to their delusions. That's fairy-tale stuff. You can't have that. I can't have that. See you later." He vanished, uncaring of any mortals who might see him.

I stared vacantly at where he'd been, wondering if what he said was true. Was he missing a good match right in front of him? Or was Kristin deluding herself with her crush on him? And was *I* deluding myself with my feelings for Seth? Was I really feeling connected to him or was it all just lust?

There was no use fretting about any of it now. Cedric didn't seem to want to kill me at the moment, so that was the best I could get.

I drove over to Bellevue, just in time for the morning commute out of the city to be winding down. Bellevue was a suburb, a city in its own right, and the restaurant we'd chosen was in Bellevue's old downtown, one that had eventually been supplanted when a mall rearranged the city's trendy areas. The place was a quiet little bistro, tucked between a jewelry store and a bakery. Seth and Kayla were already there. She sat in a booster seat beside him, examining a stuffed unicorn while he leafed through a menu. Seeing both of them sent ripples of warmth and happiness through me.

"Hey guys," I said, sliding in across from them. Kayla gave me a shy smile, and Seth positively lit up. His hair was as messy as usual, and his T-shirt today advertised Trix, a cereal I'd forgotten even existed.

"Thanks for doing this," I said. "I really appreciate it."

Seth's smile grew, though I saw the tiniest bit of apprehension in his eyes. "Just so long as you're sure it's . . . you know . . ." He glanced over at Kayla, who was groping for her glass. Seth hastily intervened to help her before she could knock it over.

"It'll be easy," I said. "Maybe even boring. We'll just walk around and look for something resembling white stone or rock."

"And Kayla can help?"

I turned toward the little girl. She glanced between both of us, her blue eyes wide and eerily knowing.

"I think so. Again, at this point, she just senses stuff without really understanding why. If we get anywhere near Jerome, I think she'll show some sort of reaction, even if she doesn't know what it is." At least I hoped so.

After that, we didn't mention our mission for the rest of the meal. We made small talk instead and fawned over Kayla, but it was almost something we did on autopilot, something we weren't even paying attention to. Really, Seth and I were consumed by each other. It was more than just lust too, though I certainly hoped he'd noticed my low-cut top today. I found myself just aglow from his presence. I loved being close to him, feeling the joy that spread within me. It was like falling in love again. It was that connection and understanding that Cedric had said was a fairy tale.

And even when we finished up and went and scoped out our first beach, that electricity and warmth continued flowing between us. Kayla walked between us for a while, with each of us holding one of her hands. She struggled a little with the sand but seemed infinitely fascinated by the sights around her: the waves, the seagulls, other children. The rain had faded away today, and we had sunshine taunting us with the hope that spring had truly arrived.

We found no white rocks, however, and Kayla had no out-of-the-ordinary reactions like she'd had with me in the past, or even with Dante. When we got to our second beach, she began slowing down, and I realized this wasn't going to be the aggressive day of hunting I'd hoped for. After a while, Seth picked her up and carried her. She managed to stay awake until we finished our search but promptly fell asleep in the car.

I knew we'd have to call it a day, but we stopped off at a little café on the way home that served great desserts. We settled into a corner booth, Seth and me sitting side by side while I held Kayla on my lap. We decided to simply split a piece of cheesecake, and naturally, I required coffee. Kayla still leaned drowsily against me, but she'd valiantly woken up as though sensing the approach of sugar.

I brushed her hair back from her face. "Hey," I said gently. "Did you see anything magic today?" That was how she'd referred to me in the past.

She shook her head and reached up to touch my cheek in a mirror of my own gesture. "When will you be magic again?" she asked.

"I don't know," I told her. "Soon."

Seth's leg against mine was starting to stir up some illicit feelings, something I felt a little ashamed of with Kayla there. I was further startled when I glanced up at him and saw not lust in his eyes, but rather, something soft and tender.

"What?" I asked. "Why are you looking at me like that?"

"Because of you," he said. "Just the way you interact with her . . . it's remarkable."

"Because I can get her to talk?"

He shook his head. "Nah. More than that. I've seen it with the other girls. You have a knack with kids. You'd make a great mother."

Maddie had made the same offhand comment. I don't think Seth had ever really and truly grasped how much I'd pined for children. His words filled me with both elation and sorrow. For an instant, I considered telling him about Nyx's dream and the bizarre pregnancy theory. Those things were too fragile and too precious to me, however, and the cheesecake's serendipitous arrival saved me from further deliberation.

The cheesecake was lemon raspberry, a bit adventurous for Kayla, perhaps, but she ate it without hesitation. Seth gave up on his share before us, and she and I finished it down to the last bite.

"Perfect," he mused. "I'll return her to Terry and Andrea, just in time for her the sugar rush to kick in. They'll never let her go out again." He frowned. "Will you need her again? I think she has some kind of play-date thing tomorrow."

I sighed, and reality dimmed my golden moment. "I don't know. I'm running out of close places. I'll have to head up north next, up around Edmonds, though Dante pointed out that Jerome could be farther out—out on the Olympic Peninsula or something. The summoners would want to keep him close, but 'close' could mean ten miles or a hundred."

"You're not going to be able to go out to the coast in an easy day trip," observed Seth. Under the table, his hand rested on mine out of sympathy. "I'm sorry."

I squeezed his hand in return. "It'll be as it'll be, I guess."

"I still want to help if I can."

I offered him a rueful smile. "You want to help me get back to being a succubus?"

His return smile was equally bittersweet. "There's no way any of this can end well, Georgina. Sometimes . . . sometimes we have to choose the lesser of evils and simply enjoy our sweet moments while we can."

Like this one. And through some shared instinct, we both fell silent, savoring this brief interlude, this dream we'd gotten ourselves ensnared in. For now, it was enough to just sit together like this. His hand moved idly on my leg, offering comfort and love . . . at least for a little while. Before long, the sweet affection turned into something with a bit more desire. I met his eyes, and while it wasn't the same animal intensity that had thrown me against the wall last night, there was still a longing in his eyes that told me how much he wanted me, to be closer to me. My body responded to it, and then we both glanced over at Kayla, who had fallen asleep again. We laughed, realizing the absurdity of our current situation.

"I should get her back," said Seth.

"Yeah," I said, sad at the thought of parting but certainly not aroused enough to make out while his niece was around.

He drove me back to my car in Bellevue. Our parting kiss was gentle and light, almost hesitant. It seemed typical of this entire affair, like it was hardly real and would blow away at any moment.

"Anything you need, Thetis," he breathed into my ear. "Anything you need, I'll do it. You know I will."

A flower of agony and euphoria burst open in my chest. He hadn't called me Thetis, his old pet name for me, since the day we broke up. "I know," I murmured into his shirt. "I know."

I returned to Queen Anne not long after that, getting a nice spot right in front of my building. My head was swimming with Seth and Kayla and Jerome and a hundred other things. I was so distracted that when I stepped into my apartment, I nearly walked right past Grace sitting on my couch. Of course, considering she was the first demon all week who hadn't attacked me the instant I cleared the door, my reaction to her subtlety was understandable.

"Grace?" I asked curiously, as though maybe it wasn't her.

She was leafing through a copy of *Seattle Metropolitan* magazine, their issue on Seattle's best brunches. When she glanced up at me, there was a tiredness in her eyes that even demonic perfection couldn't hide. Seeing her alone was almost as strange as her being here at all. I'd grown so used to her and Mei being a unit that their forced separation lately seemed almost as tragic as Jerome's summoning.

"There you are," she said. "I almost left."

"Sorry," I said. I meant it. I seemed to be on her and Mei's good side lately and wanted to keep it that way. Demons didn't like waiting, and without that innate connection of an archdemon, she couldn't instantly find me across time and space.

Grace gave a half-hearted shrug. "I don't mind. It's rather pleasant having a few moments' respite from all the politics and bickering."

"I can imagine." I frowned. "No, wait. I don't think I can."

I swear, I thought for a second she might laugh, but she kept that same stone face she excelled at.

"It'll all be over soon, which is why I came to see you. Mei and I have been talking to all of the other lesser immortals today. The day after tomorrow, a corporate demon named Ephraim will be making his final decision on who will replace Jerome."

A cold lump settled into my stomach. "So soon?"

"Hell doesn't like to waste time and resources."

"I guess not."

"Ephraim's already in the area and may come speak to you as he attempts to assess the situation. He'll want to know about your job, how things ran under Jerome, etc."

With each word, my spirits sank further and further. My window to find Jerome was shriveling up. We were going to get a new archdemon anytime now.

"Don't be afraid to speak the truth," she advised. "I know

that's often a concern among lesser immortals, for fear of causing offense."

"Something like that," I muttered, thinking of Nanette.

"Clearly, you don't want to actively anger Ephraim, but he has no affiliations with anyone currently involved in the dispute here. He won't punish you for stating your opinion."

"I'm guessing he might not listen to it either."

There it was. A tiny quirky of her lips, gone so quickly that I wasn't even sure I saw it. She rose from the sofa and absentmindedly tugged on her blazer. It was deep, deep red, paired with sleek black trousers and patent leather heels. Underneath the collar of her coat, I caught a glimpse of that same chunky necklace she'd worn at the meeting. I recalled Mei's sleeker one and couldn't resist my next words.

"This may sound weird . . . but I can't help but notice you and Mei are dressing differently lately." As soon as I said that, I hoped she wouldn't get mad at me essentially calling her and Mei copycats. Fortunately, she remained as blasé as usual.

"In these times, it's wise to distinguish yourself. None of our jobs are secure right now."

I did a double-take. In all of this madness, it had never occurred to me that Grace and Mei might have something to fear. But of course they did. When Hell did re-orgs, they tended to tweak the larger structure. They could very well decide to transfer Grace and Mei and institute a whole new set of demonic leaders here. I didn't like that idea any better than losing Jerome. I wanted things to stay the same. And studying that fatigue I'd seen on Grace's face, I realized I wasn't the only one with a lot to worry about.

"Well . . . for what it's worth, I think you're doing a great job. You've had to do so much clean-up and damage control, and then with all these demons . . ." I shook my head. "I don't know. They'd be stupid not to recognize that."

The strangest look came over Grace's face. I would have almost called it surprise, but her careful, icy composure made it hard to say for sure. "Thank you, Georgina." Her voice was stiff, like dealing with compliments made her uncomfortable. "I hope you'll share your feelings with Ephraim, should he speak with you."

"Sure," I said. "No problem."

After a quick glance at my kitchen clock, she turned back to me and gave a smart nod. "I have to meet with the others. I'll speak with you again soon." She vanished, but I could offer no farewell in return.

I had just seen something. Something that changed everything.

I stood frozen. This whole time, for the last week, something had been percolating in my head. I'd noted Grace and Mei's dedication to their job, how they were always there to help when chaos broke out. I'd noted also how they'd been forced to split up a lot lately with the new workload, and as Grace had said, they would now probably be scrutinized individually. And why wouldn't they be? If someone was going to scout for a new demon to run Seattle, why not look at the ones who were *already* running it?

"Oh my God," I breathed.

But there was more to it than that. It wasn't just that Grace or Mei had the perfect motive to get Jerome summoned. I had more than motive before me. I had proof.

Sprinting to my bedroom, I searched frantically for the photo of Mary's medallion, certain it would be gone. Nope. It was still there, knocked off my nightstand to the floor. I picked it up.

"Oh my *God*."

There it was. When Grace had turned her head, I'd caught a fuller glimpse of the chunky necklace and its network of brown and black stones. The answer had been right in front of me. At the Cellar meeting, I'd noticed a piece of the necklace's stonework shaped like a crescent moon. I hadn't recognized it as anything more than ornamentation, but now, comparing the photo to what I'd just seen on Grace, the truth was obvious.

Grace had part of the seal. It was the left side of the medallion, separated in an irregular way to give it that fanciful crescent shape. But I'd seen the fine etchings of the symbols when she tilted her head. They were the same. It was the seal.

The picture fell from my hands, and I ran back to the living room, grappling for my cell phone. My hands shook, and I could barely dial. Of course, for a second, I wasn't sure who I was dialing. Hugh, I decided. I had to tell him and the rest of my friends that—

"Drop it."

A strong hand covered my mouth and jerked me backward. My back hit somebody, a tall man with a rock-solid chest. His other hand reached out and wrapped around my wrist, making the links of my watch dig in painfully.

"Drop it," he said. "I know what you saw. I saw it too. But you can't tell anyone. Not yet."

I could barely hear through the pounding of my heart in my ears, but it didn't matter. I knew this voice, knew it intimately. It had haunted my dreams—or rather, my nightmares—for the last six months. It was a sign of how truly out of it I'd been after Nanette attacked me that I hadn't recognized his voice that day.

I dropped the phone.

He released his grip on my wrist, and a moment later, the hand on my mouth moved away as well. Miraculously, I didn't start screaming. Slowly, slowly, I turned around, knowing exactly what I'd find. Blue-green eyes, just like the sea I'd grown up around.

"Roman."

Chapter 21

There was really only one thing I could say.

"You're here to kill me."

That would have been a great cue for him to say something like, "No, of course not" or "Why would you think that?" Any of those responses, or a variation, would have been immensely reassuring.

Instead he said: "Not yet."

"Shit."

I took a couple steps back, knowing it wouldn't do any good. Even if I'd been in full succubus mode, there was no way I could fight against him. Roman was a nephilim, Jerome's half-human bastard son. Nephilim were a kind of odd mix between lesser and greater immortals. Nephilim hadn't been around since the universe's creation, but they had been born immortal and could potentially possess the same range of powers as a greater immortal. Roman was every bit as strong as Jerome, but unlike my boss or his equals, Roman didn't answer to any higher power. He was rogue, which made him dangerous when he was pissed off.

And he had every right to be pissed off at me. Angry at the way Heaven and Hell hunted their kind down, Roman and his twin sister Helena had gone on a vigilante hunting spree to get back at other immortals. I hadn't known that when he and I were dating, and eventually, I'd been instrumental in stopping them—and getting his sister killed.

"What are you doing here then?" I asked at last.

Roman's posture was casual as he crossed his arms and leaned against the wall. He looked exactly as I remembered, enormously tall compared to me, with soft black hair and those gorgeous eyes. "You sound disappointed," he said. "Do you want me to kill you?"

"No! Of course not. But I can't really think of any other reason you'd be here. Somehow I doubt you're here for a social call." Despite my fear, my sarcasm still managed to function. Carter had told me it was unlikely Roman would ever return to Seattle, knowing that he and Jerome would be on the lookout. Except, I realized uneasily, Jerome was no longer here to keep watch.

"I'm here to help find my illustrious sire." Roman's voice was smug as he spoke, and I was sure he was taking a great amount of pleasure in watching my reaction. I hoped he was satisfied because while my jaw didn't exactly hit the floor, it came pretty close.

"Bullshit."

"Why don't you believe me?"

"Because you have no reason to!" My fear was being overridden again, this time by incredulity. "You hate Jerome."

"Yeah, that's true."

"Stop playing with me then. You're not here to help."

"No? Then how come I helped you with the seal's notes?"

"You didn't—" I froze for a moment. "Oh lord. That was you."

"Really," said Roman amiably. "You should be a lot nicer, considering all the things I've done for you."

"Yeah? I don't recall you wasting your time wandering aimlessly along beaches."

"Nah. I've been too busy blowing up stoves and carrying injured damsels to bed."

I sank into a chair and closed my eyes. "It really wasn't Carter." The angel had been telling the truth about noninterference. I opened my eyes again. "And you gave me the matches, didn't you? That's exactly the kind of fucked-up thing you'd do."

He put on an offended air. "That was pretty nice of me, considering how you looked like you were ready to have a withdrawal seizure then and there."

"This doesn't make sense. You can't be here to help find Jerome. What's really going on?"

"Does the reason matter if I help find him?"

"Yes! It matters if you want to find him, only so you can promptly destroy him."

"I don't want to destroy him."

"I have no reason to trust you."

His eyes narrowed a bit. "And I have no reason to trust you, if memory serves."

I shrugged, almost too weary to be afraid anymore. "Well, then, we're even, huh? Except, of course, that you can channel your mistrust into blowing me off the face of the earth."

"And you could tell the demon horde out there that there's a nephilim in the city." Roman laughed. "Oh, they'd love that, wouldn't they? If one of them could hunt down and kill a nephilim, that'd pretty much cinch their position here."

"Yeah, like I'd get a chance to tell anyone." I sighed. "Roman, if you're not going to destroy me, then what exactly do you want with me? Why did you save me all those times?"

"Because you're the only one in this fucking town with any chance of finding Jerome. And you can move around a lot more freely than I can."

"Um, last time I checked, you're the one in the Junior Smiting League, not me. I don't have any pow—abilities right now to defend myself."

"Yeah, but if you're caught poking around, people aren't going to declare open season on you . . . I mean, aside from that bitch demoness."

I grimaced at the memory, and Roman pushed forward.

"Look, Georgina, we can sit and argue whether I'm going to kill you or not, or we can try to figure this out and get your boss back. Then we can explore me killing you in more depth."

"God," I groaned, standing up. I needed my cigarettes. Roman watched me light up.

"New habit since I was last around."

"Old one, actually. And I'm not in the mood for lecturing." I sat back down, feeling much more settled with my nicotine. Aubrey wandered out shortly thereafter, apparently not afraid of a sociopathic—yet still eerily sexy—immortal hanging out with us. "So, what's there to figure out? It was Grace. You said you saw the seal around her neck."

Roman eased himself into a chair from my kitchen table and scooted up. "I did. Makes sense that she'd keep it as close to her as possible, though that takes some balls to have it out in the open that much."

"So why won't you let me tell anyone, then?"

He tsked. "Think, Georgina. Who are you going to tell? Which demon in this whole mess do you think you can trust? None of them like Jerome. None of them want him back."

"I was going to tell Hugh."

"You can't tell *anybody*. I was walking along with you today when Cedric popped in." It figured. There was no telling how long Roman had been following me invisibly. "If he was telling the truth about not telling Nanette about your theories, then that means one of your friends tipped her off."

"No," I said stubbornly. "It's more likely that Cedric was lying. None of them would have betrayed me."

To my complete and utter astonishment, Aubrey jumped on Roman's lap. He scratched her head absentmindedly. "Well, believe what you want, but I don't think it's safe to tell anyone yet. Except me, of course."

"Right. The guy who wants me dead."

"Eh, we can talk about that later. For now, let's go over what we know."

I wasn't really keen on the casual way we were tossing around my impending doom, nor did I like that I still didn't know why he was here. Keeping my mind on Jerome did help, though, and it was nice to finally have someone to truly brainstorm this stuff with.

"We know Grace was the demon who helped with the summoning," I said.

"There could be more, you know."

"Yeah, but there's only one archdemon position."

"True. Just don't rule other possibilities out. She and that other demoness here are pretty tight."

I thought about Mei, whose poker face was as good as Grace's. "Yeah . . . although, they seem to be operating pretty independently now. But, for the sake of argument, we'll stick with Grace. So, we know she was part of the summoning and has half of the seal. What we don't know: where the other half of the seal is, who helped her, and where Jerome actually is."

"Kind of daunting," he mused.

A thought suddenly came to me. "Wait a minute . . . you might make this simpler. A greater immortal can break up Jerome's prison. With you, we don't need to actually find the whole seal to free him—or get the half we know about from Grace."

Roman turned sheepish. "Well . . . I don't know for sure that I can do that."

"Why not? You've got the same powers as Jerome."

"My strength is the same as his when it comes to fighting and whatnot, but I don't have exactly the same powers. I'm not truly a greater immortal. I don't know if I could break him out without the seal."

"Lovely. We're back to where we started."

"I don't know. We should just take this one step at a time. Let's keep trying to find him and figure out where the other half of the seal is."

"We're running out of time," I murmured, stubbing out the cigarette.

"So, why *are* you smoking again?"

"That's not really important right now," I snapped.

"I don't know. If I had a mortal body, I'd be kind of worried about that."

"I'm not mortal. And I'll be back to my normal self in a few days at most. Probably much sooner."

"Is it because of Mortensen?"

"We are *not* talking about that right now."

"Never thought you'd be one to take a break-up so hard, seeing how easily you deal them out. In fact . . . has anyone ever even broken up with you before?"

I fixed him with a glare, so annoyed that I didn't care if he wanted to try to kill me. "We are *not* talking about that right now."

"Fine, fine. What other info do we have, then?"

I racked my brain. "The cult . . . the Army of Darkness. I think there's a connection with Jerome's summoning and their activities. Whoever's controlling them—well, Grace, I guess—times their stunts to take attention away from other things." I recapped what I knew of their stunts and what they lined up with. "Not all of their activities correspond exactly to some part of the summoning, though. At least not that I know about."

Roman was thoughtful. "Hmm . . . well, it's possible some may not line up with anything. A few may be red herrings, sort of to establish their presence. I didn't always follow you to Canada, so I don't know exactly what they're like."

"Wow. Your stalkerdom has limitations."

"Seemed like a big pain," he said. "Aside from maybe going to Tim Hortons."

Nephilim couldn't teleport like greater immortals, so he was limited with normal transportation when following me around. Uneasily, thinking of my activities with Seth, I wondered just how much Roman had spied on me. It wouldn't have been the first time he'd taken a front-row seat to my intimate activities. If he wasn't going to mention it, I wasn't going to.

"They've been quiet ever since the day of the summoning, when they were down here. I guess Grace has nothing left for them to do," I said.

"Likely . . ." His mind was still apparently spinning with suspicion. "But if I were you, I'd talk to them again."

I cringed. "No . . . I want to be done with them. You don't know these guys like I do. It's ridiculous."

"All I know is that you've got to turn over every rock you can find—no pun intended—if you're going to rescue Jerome."

"Oh, I've got to, huh?" I asked. I didn't really like the presumption in his voice. "I thought you were going to help find him too?"

"I will. Tomorrow. When are you going to search again?"

I thought about it. "Noon. After work."

There was a knock at the door, and I moved over to the eye hole. "It's Dante," I murmured. To his credit, he usually knocked first before using his key. I rested my hand on the knob and gave Roman a questioning look.

"I'll find you at noon," he said. "Hold the door open a sec after you let him in."

Roman turned invisible, and I pulled the door open. Dante came in, and I stood there a few more moments until I felt the sweep of someone moving past me. Everything had happened so quickly today that I barely had time to realize that not only I had just made contact with the guy who wanted to kill me, but I'd also just made arrangements to spend time with him. Man. This was going to keep me up when I tried to sleep later.

I shut the door and gave Dante a quick kiss on the cheek. He was carrying a bag, and I had to do a double-take.

"Did you buy something from Macy's?" I exclaimed. "I somehow imagined you stepping into a department store would be like a vampire stepping into the sunlight—I mean, current situation aside."

Dante rolled his eyes and set the bag down. Crossings his arms, he leaned against the wall. "Well, maybe I'm in stasis too. Forget about this for a sec and tell me if you've gotten yourself on any demon's shit list today." There it was again, the sweet concern in spite of his best efforts.

"Not that I know of, but hey, the day's not over yet."

I glossed over the specifics of who I'd gone searching with, mainly emphasizing that my time at the beach hadn't turned up anything. I also mentioned Cedric's visit and his claims that he hadn't told Nanette about my suspicions. Dante seemed skeptical of that. Finally, I wrapped up with Grace's appearance, and at that point I faltered. I wanted to tell Dante about my amazing discovery, about how Grace had the seal. Yet Roman had urged me to keep it all to myself. Why? Was he really that mistrustful of everyone? Did he have his own ulterior motives? Against my better judgment, I bit my lip on telling Dante about my discovery. It killed me to do it, particularly since I had a feeling Dante could have some insight. Roman's warning was too strong, however, as was my fear that he might actually still be around invisibly. And of course, I could hardly tell Dante about Roman.

Fortunately, Dante didn't pick up on any omission of information. "You had kind of a full day, succubus. Did the corporate demon ever come talk to you?"

"Not yet. I haven't had a chance to talk with the gang to see if he's been making the rounds." I eyed the Macy's bag, dying to know what was in it.

Dante kicked it behind him. "What are you going to tell him?"

I shrugged. "I don't know. I'll tell him what I know about Seattle, and as far as recommendations . . . well, I don't know." I could no longer trust Grace, and Mei's role was still a mystery. Dante noted my change of feelings but not the reasons.

"From what you'd said before, I thought you were a fan of Grace and that other demoness."

"Mei," I supplied. "I don't know. It's all just wearying." Eager to shift away from the subject, I pointed at the bag. "Are you going to tell me what's in that?"

He gave me one of his mocking grins. "Why do you think it has anything to do with you?"

"Because there's no way you'd shop at Macy's for yourself. You dress only marginally better than Carter."

Dante shook his head, wearing a long-suffering look. "Fine, fine. I'll keep it for myself." He picked up the bag and headed off down the hall. After a few moments, I followed and tackled him in the doorway to my bedroom.

"Come on! Give it up." I snatched the bag away, but my victory was small since he didn't put up a fight. I opened it up and gasped at what I found. Folds and folds of shimmering purple fabric, silk the color of new spring crocuses. Hesitantly, I lifted it out of the bag, revealing a long, ankle-length robe. I looked up at him in astonishment. "What's this?"

"You're the one with years and years of higher learning," he pointed out, looking extremely pleased with himself. "You tell me."

I held it up, gauging its height. It looked just about perfect. "It's gorgeous. What's the occasion?"

"I was tired of hearing you bitch about that ratty one you've got. And tired of seeing it, to be honest." He ignored my glare. "Besides, you've had a, uh, difficult time lately. Even for you."

I thought back to other things, like the flowers and breakfast. All the attempts at dinners. "Dante—"

He pressed a finger to my lips. "Look, be quiet a second. I'm not blind. I can tell how much all of this is stressing you out. And fuck, if I could get my hands on that bitch demon . . ." Anger glinted in his eyes, and he took a moment to shake it off. "Anyway, you can keep making your jokes or whatever and keep doggedly doing your best to sleuth away and find Jerome, but you're running yourself into the ground. You're depressed. You're distracted. When we talk, it's like your mind's somewhere else. Same with our sex life."

I opened my mouth to argue, but I wasn't sure what to say. He was right. I had been distracted, but a good part of that—particularly during intimate activities—hadn't had anything to do with Jerome. It had been Seth on my mind. Dante kept speaking before I could get a word out.

"See, now, you're going to apologize. Because that's what you do—but there's no need, succubus. If anyone gets some selfish time right now, it's you. In another week or so, things'll be back to normal, and I'll be the selfish one."

Something in my heart twisted. Everyone said he was scum, but in the end, it turned out I was the untrustworthy one. I averted my eyes.

"So where's the robe fit in?"

"Something to cheer you up. Since your wardrobe's been trimmed."

"Dante, you've been getting me a lot of stuff lately. You don't have to throw money at me—money you don't have— to make me feel better."

"If I didn't have it, I wouldn't 'throw' it," he remarked dryly. "And anyway . . . I'm not really the kind of guy who does, like . . . the candles or the moonlit beaches or recites poetry."

I grimaced. "I don't mind staying away from beaches for a while."

"But," he continued, "I know you well enough to know that mochas and silk make you smile, and that, at least, is something I can do."

My heart twisted further, and I reached out to catch hold of his hand. I understood what he was saying. It wasn't in his nature to do over-the-top romantic gestures, but material purchases were something he could handle, and it was the only way to show me he cared. My guilt redoubled because no matter what he said, I knew he was tight on cash. Yet, my actions and fixation with Seth were worrying Dante enough that he felt he had to do something. I was driving him to it.

"You're sweet," I said. "But don't worry. It'll be our secret."

He brushed his fingers through my hair. "Not that sweet. Look in the bag."

I did. Underneath the robe, unnoticed by me, was a bottle of bubble bath. I held it up questioningly.

"I thought we could take a bath together."

I laughed. "That's almost romantic. You might be closer to moonlit beaches than you think. Although, my bathtub's kind of small."

"I know," he said. "That's what I meant about it not being very sweet. Mostly I want to see what kind of interesting positions we can cram ourselves into while naked and in a small space."

"Well, thank God that in a world gone mad, some people never change."

It turned into a wet, soapy mess, but it was more fun than I expected. No matter what he claimed, the whole feat was semi-romantic. Conversation was easy and light, and we laughed and joked a lot. I almost forgot about Seth—almost. But when things started to get a little hot and heavy, I pulled back. No matter how sexy it was to be wet and naked with someone, it just didn't feel right if that person wasn't Seth.

What made me feel worse was that Dante was accommo-dating about my mood. He figured my lack of desire was part of my stress, and so we eventually left the tub as chastely as we'd entered. We toweled each other off and then curled up on the couch and watched TV together while I tried not to feel too guilty about the purple robe wrapped around me.

I decided the next day to finally add myself back to the bookstore's work schedule. I only put me down for part-time shifts until the demon business was settled, but at this point, it seemed unlikely I'd be recalled to Canada again. My limbo status couldn't last forever if I wanted to keep my job; War-ren's leniency would only last so long.

Roman and I had our plans to go to Edmonds at noon, so for my first official day back, I only worked a morning shift. Part of that shift involved coming in before the store was even open, and I welcomed the solitude. The store always soothed me, and if ever there was a time I needed soothing, it was right now. It was short-lived, however, since my other co-workers began trickling in not long after my arrival. Maddie was among them.

"Hey," she said brightly, popping into my office. "Is this another check-in or are you back for good?"

"For good, I think. Not that it matters. It looks like every-thing's been fine without me."

She grinned and shut the door behind her. "Oh, we've missed you, believe me. No one's been here to referee my fights with Doug."

I laughed and watched her sit down. "Well then, I guess I got back just in time. Nice shoes."

Maddie extended her legs and admired her candy apple red pumps. "Thanks. Nordstrom's having a sale."

The brown leather Mia heels I currently wore were among my favorites, but after a week now with no shape-shifting, my wardrobe was starting to make me stir-crazy. It was kind of like my hair, I realized. I hadn't realized how dependent I was on shape-shifting to enhance my appearance. I'd lauded myself for living like a human when in truth, I'd been cheating the whole time.

Seeing my wistful look, Maddie asked, "You want to go downtown for lunch and check it out?"

I shook my head with regret. Looking at shoes sounded a lot better than looking at rocks. "Can't. I've got to meet someone."

"Ah, well, let me know when you get some time. You know I'm game." Silence fell, and Maddie shifted uncomfortably. She bit her lip, like she wanted to say something. I started to prompt her, but she spoke first. "So, what did you think of the condo listings?"

"Oh, they were . . ." Fuck. I'd never even read through them. Roman and Dante had spent more time looking at them than I had. Which one had Dante mentioned? "They were great. I really liked that new one—the one where you can still get in on the choices and stuff."

Her eyes lit up. "Ooh, yeah. I loved that one too. I actually looked them up on the builder's website. It doesn't look like there are many left, but there has to be at least one, or they wouldn't be listed. We should go down there and talk to them in person."

I smiled, feeling horrible about the lie. "Sure . . . but it may be awhile before I can get a break. We'll have to do it and the shoe trip at the same time."

Maddie nodded, face kind and sympathetic. "No problem. I understand."

More silence fell, and I realized it wasn't the condos that she wanted to talk to me about. That had been a distraction to build up her own courage.

"Maddie, what's going on?"

Her cheery look disintegrated into something much more glum. It was startling. I was so used to her always being in a good mood that the thought of something upsetting her was on par with the laws of physics breaking down.

She met my eyes and immediately looked away. "Oh God. I can't believe I'm about to bring this up."

I was seriously worried now. "You can tell me. It's okay. What's up?"

She sighed. "It's Seth."

Oh, fuck.

Chapter 22

"What about Seth?" I asked stiffly. I waited then for the shouts, for the accusations. Any of them would have been understandable. What I didn't expect were tears building up in her eyes.

"I think . . . I think something's wrong. I think he's trying to let me down easy or something."

"Why would you think that?" I channeled Grace and Mei, keeping my face as still and expressionless as theirs.

"He's just . . . I don't know. He's been so distracted lately."

"Seth's always distracted. You know how he is with his books."

"Yeah, I know. And it drives me crazy sometimes." I remembered her disappointment at Casey's party. "But this is something different, I can feel it. Only, I don't know what it is. He's not around much, and when he is, it's like he's with me but not *with* me. He always says nothing's wrong, but it doesn't feel right. And we haven't . . ."

"Haven't what?" I asked, guessing the answer.

A deep pink blush blossomed on her cheeks. "We haven't been having sex. Each time I even kind of suggest it, he's just not . . . well, he doesn't really seem into it."

Talking about their sex life was one of the most painful conversation topics I could imagine, short of her realizing I was to blame for its problems. So, I kept up with my poker-faced therapist mode.

"How long has it been going on?"

"About a week."

Yup, that made sense. That was right around the time my stasis had begun. Here I'd been expecting Maddie to come after me, to pick up on one of the covert looks Seth and I had shared. But she hadn't. It had never even crossed her mind to suspect me of anything duplicitous. In fact, she'd come to me for help because I was one of the few people she trusted with something like this.

And that made it all the worse when I had to lie to her. In any other situation, I would have advised a friend to take control of her relationship, to corner her man and not be used. And maybe . . . maybe I should have. If I advised her to break up with Seth, that would clear the way for us. Did I want that again? I didn't know. I still wasn't thinking past the day I would turn into a succubus again. I was living irresponsibly, focusing on the now, and continued that here with Maddie.

My next words were spoken so winningly, so convincingly that there was no way she could ever think I didn't have her best interests at heart. I might have been relying on my succubus abilities to smooth my hair all this time, but charming and persuading people was a core part of my personality. She never stood a chance.

"A week?" I gave her a gentle smile. "That's not very long. You can't really base a major crisis on that yet—especially when you consider who you're dealing with. I mean, like you said, you've seen him get so busy with work that he cancels or even forgets things, right?"

"Yeah," she said, sniffling in a continued attempt to keep back her tears. "It's just never been like this. I don't know. I've never had a serious relationship. I don't know how it's supposed to work."

"You guys have only been going out for, like, four months. It takes longer than that to really get to know someone's patterns." With a pang, I realized she and Seth had dated longer than he and I had. "This may be one you've got to get used to. He's probably stressed, and sex is the last thing on his mind—as hard as that is to believe. Give him some time. If it keeps happening, then it might be time to worry. But it's too soon now."

I could tell by her face that my words had given her hope. "Yeah . . . you're probably right. But . . . do you think . . . do you think I'm doing something wrong? Should I do something different? Act differently? Dress sexier?"

Oh God. I so did not want to be advising Maddie on how to seduce Seth. "Well . . . I wouldn't worry about any of that quite yet. Overthinking it'll just stress you out more. Just wait a little bit. If something's on his mind, it may take him some time to work through it."

She'd defeated her tears and now adopted a resolute look. "Sometimes I don't know if I'm fooling myself, like that I'm just caught up in my first big romance. But, seriously, some days, I feel like I've found the one. Like if he wanted to run off right now, I'd do it." The love on her face was like a bullet through my heart. "If something's wrong, I want to help him through it."

"I know, I know, but you still don't know what 'it' is. If it's a writing thing, he's got to work it out. If it's something else . . . well, I'm sure he'll come talk about it when he's ready."

Her dark eyes were contemplative, looking at me without seeing me while she processed all of this. "You're probably right," she said at last. She gave me a small, rueful smile and shook her head. "God, I feel kind of stupid. Look at me. Some kind of champion for strong women, huh? Did I mess up my makeup? And oh God, did I really just ask that?"

"No, it's fine. And you're not stupid. Your feelings are normal." I stood up, needing to get out of here. The room was making me claustrophobic. I had to get away from her, away from her trust. "I'm going to go do a sweep. They should be opening any minute."

She rose as well and ran a hand over her eyes one last time. "Yeah, I've got things to do too. Thanks for listening to me." Before I could open the door, she gave me a small, fierce hug. "I'm glad you're my friend."

With that, she left to tend to her work. Meanwhile, I wished a hole would open on the floor and swallow me up. I almost wished Nanette would show up and end my misery. Thankfully, I only had two hours until I was meeting Roman. Then I'd be free of this misery and self-loathing that Maddie was unknowingly stirring up in me. But if I'd hoped store business would prove a distraction, I was wrong. A half-hour later, an errand to the café brought me face-to-face with Seth.

He sat at a table with his laptop and looked up as though he could sense that I was nearby. He smiled, and my heart raced. I smiled back before I could stop myself. He looked like he wanted me to come over, yet I worried about attracting attention or tipping others off. Of course, it might actually look more suspicious if I didn't talk to him, I realized. Long ago, it was perfectly common for me to stop by and chat with him. No one had ever perceived it as anything more than friendly banter.

So, after dropping off some books, I strolled over and sat across from him. "Hey," I said, feeling warm under his gaze.

"Hey," he replied. "You look beautiful today."

I glanced down and laughed. Along with my limited wardrobe, I was also discovering that not doing laundry decreased my clothing options even further. I was in jeans and a plain black T-shirt today, and my hair had been lucky to get a quick brushing, let alone any real styling. I'd overslept and figured beachcombing didn't require much primping anyway.

"Liar," I said. "I practically rolled out of bed this morning."

"You forget that I've seen you in just about every state imaginable. You don't have to have every detail primped and perfect. You're beautiful even when you're disheveled. Sometimes more so."

"Hey! Are you saying I'm disheveled now?"

"No, you're somewhere in the middle of primped and disheveled. And you still look beautiful."

I received compliments all the time, but from him, they were golden and wonderful. Even the smallest ones. "And you," I said, "seem to try to be disheveled."

He ran a hand over his slightly messy hair. I think his intent was to smooth it, but he only mussed it further. "People spend fortunes on hair gel to get this look, you know."

"And fortunes on shirts like that," I said, gesturing to his vintage Ovaltine T-shirt. "There are collectors who'd pay a lot of money for that on eBay."

"I am one of those people."

I laughed. "There's a treasure trove of T-shirts waiting for you in Vancouver, you know. I kept seeing them and thinking of you."

With each moment that passed, I fell further and further into that electric, consuming connection between us. Love for him filled me, made me feel complete. Leaving him would have been agonizing just then, and I saw a similar sentiment for me on his face. I'd sat down, feeling guilty and conflicted over Maddie, but once I was with him . . . well, it was selfish and horrible, but I couldn't help but stay. And honestly, it became hard for me to fret too much over her feelings because I was too caught up in my own for him. I wanted him. I wanted him to be mine. I wanted him to love me. And yet, I knew as soon as I left the table, I'd feel bad about her again. There was no way this could end well.

"Do you have any more trips scheduled up there?" He lowered his voice, the flirty look now gone and replaced by concern.

"No, I think I'm done with my international travel. I've just got to figure out things here now . . . or, well, they'll be figured out for me in another day or so. Things are going to return to normal with or without Jerome soon."

His expression grew troubled, and he glanced away from me to stare out the window. We'd both known the inevitable was coming from the beginning, yet neither of us had been able to talk about it then. It looked like we still couldn't talk about it now. There were a million things we should be discussing, but all we could think about was each other. All we wanted was each other. We'd spent so much of our time with boundaries between us that now that there were none, we just wanted to childishly lose ourselves in our longings and not think about the consequences—even though the consequences would be catching up with us any day now.

"Well," Seth said finally. "I just hope you stay safe. Are you any closer to finding him?"

I hesitated. Roman had told me not to trust anyone. I was pretty sure that Seth wasn't going to go run off to any demons in the area and report what I said. I also suspected, however, that Seth wouldn't be happy to find out Roman was in my life again, no matter how altruistic Roman claimed to be right now. Seth wouldn't trust him. Hell, I didn't trust him.

"I've got a few promising leads," I said finally. I thought about Grace. "Some more promising than others . . . I'm just not sure if I can do anything with them."

"Still traipsing beaches? Do you need me and Kayla again?"

"I thought she had something going on . . ."

The look on his face said he would do anything for me. "Yeah, but if you really needed her, I could try to pull some strings. If you wanted."

Oh, did I. A pleasant, aching yearning gathered in my chest. There was nothing I'd love more than to spend another afternoon with the two of them, even if it was searching for rocks. It had let me indulge in the illusion of being a family.

"No, I'm fine." Reluctantly, I let the image go. As much as I wanted to be with them again, Roman was the better partner on my hunts now. I would rather put him at risk than Kayla, and anyway, he was more likely to be able to know what to do if we actually found what we were looking for. I glanced at the clock. "In fact, I need to finish up my work here. My shift's over soon, and I can't be late."

Seth's face was a mixture of worry and disappointment. "No lunch, huh?"

I couldn't be certain, but I suspected lunch with him would have involved both food and sex in some surreptitious location. Damn. I wanted both.

Sadly, I shook my head. "I wish I could . . . but this comes first. I'm sorry." For half a second, I remembered Maddie in the office, so sad and heartbroken. I even thought about Dante and his compulsive spending. If I had any scrap of morality left in my damned soul, I'd tell Seth that we needed to end this, right now. But like every other time I'd told myself that, I never listened. "Maybe . . . maybe tonight, though . . ."

Roman and I would be done searching. Dante might be around, but well . . . I'd deal with that later. I felt confident I could dodge any plans he might want to make. Details like that didn't matter. Only being alone with Seth again did. How could being around him affect me like this?

He nodded, as eager as me. "Call me when you're free."

I started to joke that I'd never be free, but that wasn't what he'd meant. Standing up, I hoped I looked like I was leaving a platonic conversation and that I wasn't actually struggling with the temptation to kiss him good-bye. We stared at each other for a few heavy moments, and with his eyes, Seth said a million things, both sweet and indecent. Walking away, I was certain that anyone who'd seen us would instantly realize what was going on—but no one seemed to be paying attention to us.

My shift wound down rapidly after that, and as I walked home afterward, I heard invisible footsteps walking along with me. "I know you're there," I said under my breath. I didn't want anyone thinking I was crazy. "Glad to see your voyeur ways haven't changed."

My car was parked behind my building today, and as I rounded the corner onto a quiet block, Roman materialized beside me. He looked gorgeous, smug, and dangerous. The usual.

"I hope you had an entertaining time following me around." I took my keys out.

"You should be a reality show," he said. "It's that good. And you know, I might be a totally unstable former assassin, but man. You manage to shock even me."

"Oh, be quiet," I snapped. I unlocked the car doors and slid into the driver's side. "Your snarky commentary is neither wanted nor appreciated."

"It's not commentary. It's me thinking aloud. It has nothing to do with you, really, nor does it require any response on your part."

"This is it, isn't it?" I asked, pulling out of the parking spot. "This is why you aren't going to kill me. You're going to just torture me for the rest of eternity. Long suffering, right?"

He grinned, flashing perfect white teeth against his tanned skin. It triggered a memory in me, how I'd once found that so attractive. Now, though, my fear and unease blocked any sort of desire.

"I suppose that's one way of looking at it. And besides, don't act like there isn't some part of you that secretly enjoys playing this eternally woeful, tormented role. If you were happy, you wouldn't know what to do with yourself."

"That's not true." I was surprised to feel myself blushing. "Stop trying to fuck with me."

"I'm just intrigued, that's all. You wear this mask of moral superiority. So does Mortensen. Yet, here you two are, sneaking around."

"You don't understand. We're in love." The wry look Roman gave me immediately made me regret my words.

"Oh, I understand. Believe me, I do." I kept my eyes on the road. He had once told me he loved me, and I'd thrown it back in his face. "If you guys were so in love, why'd you break up in the first place? You were fawning all over each other the last time I saw you."

"For a lot of reasons," I mused. "It's complicated."

"It always is."

I sighed. Edmonds was about twenty five minutes away. This was going to be a long drive.

"Well, not that it's any of your business, but I mean, there were a lot of things going on. We were having communication problems, for one thing."

"How terribly mundane."

"And I was starting to freak out—you know, about how he could die. I didn't think I could handle that." I waited for

Roman's snide response to that, but there was none. "And, of course . . . I mean, there was always sex. I wouldn't do it. I couldn't stand the thought of stealing part of his life away. Our love wasn't dependent on sex . . . but well, it still muddled things up."

"And now you have no problem with sex."

"Because I can't hurt him now! Look, I can't help the timing—or the fact that we still care about each other."

"Or the fact that each of you have significant others." Now I stayed silent. Roman tipped his head back against the seat thoughtfully. "In all my observations this week, I've got to admit, I like Maddie."

"I like her too," I said quietly.

"But that guy you're dating? Well, I think you can do better."

"I'm almost starting to wish you'd kill me."

"Oh, I've thought about it," he said. To my dismay, the joking was gone from his voice.

Again, I refused to look at him. "I'm sorry . . . about Helena. I never meant for that to happen."

Roman gave a laugh that sounded like it choked him. "Oh? What did you think would happen, then? A slap on the wrist? I survived it, and I was still in pretty bad shape."

"You said you were going to kill Carter. And I didn't know who else you'd go after," I said quietly. "I didn't know what else to do. There was no easy option for me."

"There would have been if you'd really loved me like you said you did," he replied bitterly. "And I told you I'd leave the rest of them alone."

"It was too late when you told me that. By then, I'd already called for help." I didn't add that in a way, I really had loved him. It had been different from the way I loved Seth, but it had been love nonetheless.

"Well, whatever. It's not relevant now. Finding Jerome is what's important." Out of the side of my eye, I saw him study my profile. "Of course, I'm surprised you've been so eager . . . it's going to put an end to your little affair."

"It's going to come to an end anyway. I'd rather have Jerome in my life afterward than some other demon." In my mind, I could see Seth's kind eyes and gentle smile. I could almost feel the way his hands touched my body. "I'll have the memories, at least. They'll stay with me."

"Memories." Roman shook his head. "How the hell can someone who fucks random men for a living be such a romantic idiot?"

I didn't answer that, and the rest of our drive contained little conversation. The place we were going to in Edmonds was another park. Funny, I thought, that humans kept sectioning off these magical places and preserving them. I wondered if they sensed that power on some inherent level. I'd read up a little on this park and how it had some significance to Native Americans in the area. Surely that was promising. It was a small beach flanked by a woodsy area with picnic tables. Children ran around while their mothers watched.

"This place isn't very strong," said Roman, once we were out of the car. "There's a little magic in the earth but not much. I can't imagine they'd hide Jerome here—they'd want a lot more to mask it."

I refused to let that drag me down. "We have to look. We don't know anything for sure."

The park wasn't huge. I suspected it would take us less time to search it than it would to drive back. Just as we'd stepped out of the parking lot, my cell phone rang. I didn't recognize the number. "Go on without me," I told Roman. When I answered, the voice was no one I recognized.

"Is this Letha, also known as Georgina Kincaid?"

I grimaced. Only high-up hellish employees called me by my original name. "Yes."

"This is Ephraim, from Internal Affairs." The demon's voice was clipped and hurried, giving the impression that I was the one who'd called him and interrupted something. I found it amusing that he'd called me rather than speak in person. More efficient, I guessed.

I sat down at a picnic table. "What can I do for you?"

"Nothing, I'm sure. But I've been instructed to interview all lesser immortals in the area about The Jerome Situation." I could hear the capitalized letters in his voice, kind of like The Manhattan Project. "First, I'd like to know where you were when Jerome disappeared."

"On my way to Canada. Jerome had been lending me out to help Cedric."

There was a moment's pause. "My records say that Cedric was in Seattle when Jerome disappeared."

"Well, when I left, Cedric was still up there, yeah. But then when the Army of Darkness did their thing on the Space Needle, I called Cedric because I figured he'd want to know. I thought that was when he came down here."

"Did you say Army of Darkness?"

"Um, yeah. It's this cult in Vancouver that was doing embarrassing things."

"Ah. The ones with the spray paint."

"Yup. I'd been helping Cedric with them, and when he heard they were down here, I guess he came to talk to Jerome and do some damage control so Jerome wouldn't think he'd sent them."

"Your information's incorrect. Cedric never met with Jerome."

"What?" I frowned, thinking back to my conversation with Kristin. I'd asked if Cedric had come to talk to Jerome, and while she'd confirmed that he'd been down here, she hadn't mentioned them actually speaking.

"When Cedric came, Jerome was already missing. He and Mei attempted to find him, and when the lesser immortals began showing the effects of the summoning, we knew what had happened." Ephraim's words were still brisk. Clearly, he had no interest in discussing what he already knew.

I was close to something here—so, so close. Had Jerome been summoned before Cedric arrived? That would rule him out as the summoner. Of course, if Ephraim had received his information from Cedric, then it could have been a lie. Maybe Cedric was being framed. Maybe he'd actually been here the exact moment Jerome was summoned. Mentioning Mei meant that she had probably corroborated Cedric's story. Which meant what, exactly? Was she in on this too? I knew Grace was involved already. It was possible Mei and Cedric were working with her, but that meant three demons were in the conspiracy now. There was only one reward in Seattle, and I couldn't see how they'd all benefit. Getting a large group of demons to organize was hard. Getting them to do it when it offered no advantage for all of them? Impossible.

Ephraim was eager to get back on track. He asked me a few more questions about Jerome's disappearance and a bit about my day-to-day affairs. He never asked for my opinion about who should replace Jerome or what I thought of other demons. That wasn't particularly surprising, however. As my friends and I had discussed, our input probably wouldn't play a large role here.

I hung up and went to find Roman. I expected him to have practically finished the search, but instead, I found him playing ball with some kids over in a clearing near the trees. They were pretty little, and there wasn't much to the game. Mostly everyone stood in a circle and tossed the ball back and forth. Roman's throws were gentle and carefully aimed so as to make it easy for the kids to catch the ball. I stood off to the side, watching them in wonder. He actually seemed pretty into it, and the oddity of a sociopathic half-angelic bastard playing with small children wasn't lost on me.

Roman caught sight of me watching them and tossed the ball over to a little girl. He left the circle to approach me, much to the dismay of the kids left behind. They entreated him to stay, but he merely waved and told them he had to go.

"Maybe we can come back later," he said jovially.

"I can't decide if that was cute or creepy," I told him. "Maybe a little of both."

"Why creepy? I only kill immortal beings. Not kids."

"The fact that you just said all that with a straight face is proof enough." I gestured around. "Did you check this place out?"

"Nope. Didn't want to steal the fun from you. Who was on the phone?"

We started walking along the beach, and I recapped what Ephraim had told me. "I almost told him what I knew about Grace," I admitted.

"No, better that you didn't," said Roman. "We still need more information."

"We're running out of time," I grumbled. "There's not much more info we can get. And there's something there . . . something weird about the day Jerome was summoned. I just can't—" I froze, staring off down the beach. "Roman. Look."

He followed my gaze. There, near a trash can, was a patch of small, rough rocks mixed in with the sand. Gray and white. I ran off down the beach, ignoring the sand filling my shoes. Holy shit. After all these fruitless searches, after relying on all these sketchy half-assed clues, we'd actually found something. We'd found Jerome, and not a moment too soon.

Ignoring the looks of some startled kids, I knelt down near the rocks and began pushing them aside, digging through the sand. I realized then I should have brought a spade or something. A few moments later, Roman arrived and stood over me.

"Well, what are you doing?" I demanded. "Help me."

"He's not here, Georgina."

"He has to be! We're near salt water. There's sand. There's white stones. For the rest of the seal's camouflage to work, he's buried here somewhere."

"I can't sense anything. He's not here."

The rocks were cutting my hands as I dug, and I felt tears stinging my eyes. Until that moment, I didn't realize just how horribly and truly afraid I'd been of Jerome not returning. My time as a succubus had been filled with upheaval. I liked the small piece of tranquility I'd carved out here in Seattle. I didn't want that to change. I couldn't let it change, not after everything else I'd been through recently.

"The whole point of the seal imprinting its magic was to mask Jerome's prison! Of course you wouldn't feel it."

"The seal hides it from anyone not actively seeking it. I am, and I'm telling you it's not here."

"Maybe it's because you're not strong enough."

With a sigh, Roman knelt down behind me. "Georgina, stop."

"Damn it! He has to be here!"

Roman reached from behind me and grabbed my arms. I struggled, but he was too strong. "Georgina, enough. Jerome isn't here. The only thing unusual about this spot is the smell from the garbage can. I'm sorry."

I struggled against him a little bit more and finally gave up. Apparently feeling certain I wouldn't fight anymore, Roman released me. I turned and looked at him, swallowing back my tears. "This was our last chance," I said softly. "We don't have any time left."

Roman studied me with his sea-green eyes. I saw no anger or threat on his face, only compassion. "I'm sorry. And you don't know for sure that it's too late."

"Ephraim will finish his assessment anytime now. And where are we going to go next? The Olympic Peninsula? Wenatchee? Hitting places at random was one thing when they were in our backyard. These others are too far away. We choose the wrong one, and that's it. Game over. We won't have time for anything else."

"I'm sorry," he repeated. From his face, I could see that he spoke the truth. "I want to find him as much as you do."

I stared beyond him out at the blue-gray water and the circling gulls. "Why? Why do you want to find someone who tried to kill you?"

Roman smiled. "Why do you cling to a romantic ideal when everything in your life has pretty much shown you that it's impossible?"

I think he'd spoken rhetorically and seemed surprised when I dragged my eyes from the water to look at him and answer. "Because of a dream."

He arched an eyebrow. "What dream?"

I took a deep breath, and like that, the images flashed

through my mind, just as vivid and real as they'd been the first time. "Awhile ago . . . Nyx was here."

He looked startled. "What, the mother of time and chaos?"

"Yeah. Long story."

"What is it about this city?"

"Beats me. Anyway, she was preying on my energy and distracting me by sending me these dreams. They were so real, Roman. You can't even imagine." My voice was small as I spoke. "I was washing dishes in a kitchen, and 'Sweet Home Alabama' was playing. In the other room, there was this little girl sitting on a blanket. She hurt herself, and I came in there to comfort her. She was maybe two or three, and she was *mine*. My daughter. Not someone else's. Not adopted. The daughter of my body. Aubrey was there too and this tortie and—"

"A what?"

"A tortie. A tortoiseshell cat." I waited, but his expression was still blank. "It's like a calico, but without any white. Just brown and orange patches. How can you be millennia old and not know that?"

"Because I don't subscribe to *Cat Fancy* magazine. And I can't believe you remember things like cat breed and background music."

"It was so real," I said quietly. "More real than my own life. I remember everything."

Whatever snarky retort was on his lips disappeared, and he turned serious again. "I'm sorry I interrupted. So, what happened then? With you, the girl, and the cattery?"

"We were just all there together, warm and happy. Then a car pulled up outside, and I carried the girl out to look. A man was getting out, and he was *the one*. My lover, my husband, her father. The one my life centered around."

"Who was he?" Roman asked, face intent.

I shook my head. "I don't know. I couldn't see his face. It was dark out, and it was snowing. I just know that I loved him, and that he and the girl completed my life."

Roman didn't answer right away as he turned my words over. "But it was a dream."

"I don't know. Nyx can show the future . . . she showed others theirs. She claimed this was mine, but it's impossible. I can't have any of that. And yet . . ."

". . . and yet, you secretly hope it might be true."

"Yeah. And when this whole stasis thing happened, I thought maybe . . ."

Again, Roman completed my words. ". . . maybe it could be true. After all, you could suddenly touch Seth. Maybe you could have a kid too?"

He'd guessed my secret hope. "I didn't know. I still don't. Maybe I can get pregnant. I mean, my body is kinda sorta human, right?"

"Yes. But not enough. I don't know every detail of this whole demonic hierarchy and the way they channel their powers, but I know you can't have kids. Even if you seem human, you're still immortal. You still belong to Hell. I'm sorry."

I held his eyes for a moment and then looked down. "Well. I guess I can't really be surprised by that, huh? And I have no reason to trust Nyx anyway. Not after what she did."

There it was. No kids. Another piece of the dream had slipped away from me. All I had left was the faceless man, the man I wanted to be Seth, and even that seemed unlikely now.

Roman tugged me up. "Come on. Let's head back before the rain comes. We'll get some ice cream. Maybe that'll cheer you up."

"I'm not really sure ice cream can fix my failed hopes and dreams or an impending demonic takeover."

"Probably not. But it'll help."

Chapter 23

Dante wasn't around when I got home, nor was he reachable by phone. That relieved me of any guilt I had about going out with Seth, meaning my only other obstacle was the accusatory look Roman gave me when we parted. I had no idea how he would spend his evening, and honestly, I didn't really want to know.

The problem Seth and I had with going out was that we pretty much had to avoid the city. We knew people in the suburbs too, but the odds of running into anyone were a lot smaller. The rainy weather Roman and I had experienced in the afternoon had blown over, and we suddenly found ourselves in semi-warm conditions that made it almost possible to go without a coat. I would have read the fortuitous weather as a divine blessing, if not for the fact that I'd given up on such beliefs long ago.

To my astonishment, though, Seth said he wanted to go downtown and felt pretty confident we wouldn't be spotted. He drove us over to Belltown, parking underneath one of the many high-rise apartment buildings that seemed to be sprouting up there every day. A mysterious key let him inside, and the elevator took us all the way to the top floor.

"What is this?" I asked when we entered a sprawling penthouse suite. It kind of made me wonder if I should have been setting my real estate aspirations in a different direction. I gave him a startled look. "You don't own this, do you?" Seth having a secret vacation home wasn't entirely improbable.

"Belongs to someone I know who's out of town. I called in a favor."

"You have friends I don't know?"

He gave me A Look, and I let the matter go. Besides, the place was so beautiful that I had plenty of distraction. The colors were all done in shades of navy and gray, and the furniture was plush and expensive. I especially liked the fact that the walls were decorated with huge reproductions of pre-Raphaelite work. Nowadays, abstract art was the trendy way to go, and it was nice to see something a little different.

"Wait'll you see the rest," said Seth, beckoning me out to the balcony.

Or, well, "balcony" was the closest word I could come up with. It was practically half the size of my apartment and faced west, showing part of downtown's glittering array of lights and all of Puget Sound. I stared in wonder, watching a ferry move across the dark expanse of water.

"Wow." That about summed it up.

We stood there for a few moments, and Seth's arm slipped around me. This high up, the unseasonable warmth had turned to seasonal gusts and coldness. I shivered, and Seth draped me in a blanket that had been neatly folded on a wrought-iron chair.

"Have a seat," he said. "I'll be back with dinner."

I grinned at the gallantry and sat at an ornate, candlelit glass table that still allowed me to take in the view. Waiting for Seth, I felt all sorts of strange feelings stir to life within me. This was it, I realized. I didn't know how I knew, but this was the end of whatever it was that we had right now. Maybe something new would take its place. Maybe we'd never have anything again. Regardless, this moment was crystallized in time for me. Nothing like it would ever come again.

Dinner turned out to be an array of tapenade and bread, as well as—to my shock—a bottle of wine. "Is that whole thing for me?" I asked.

He shook his head. "I'll have a glass."

"What? Starbucks, now this?" I peered at the bottle to

make sure it wasn't some kind of weird alcohol-free kind. Nope.

"It's a special occasion," he said with a smile, and I knew he'd gotten the same vibe that I had, that this was the end of something. "Besides, how can I live out the *Rubaiyat* if I don't have all the accoutrements?"

"Of course. Your uber-romantic date would be based on a poem." I could already see him getting into quotation mode. He cleared his throat to speak.

> "Here with a Loaf of Bread beneath the Bough
> A Flask of Wine, a Book of Verse—and Thou
> Beside me singing in the Wilderness—
> And Wilderness is paradise enow."

I tsked. "You've got the bread, wine, and me . . . but no bough. And hardly the wilderness."

"It's the urban jungle," he argued.

"And no book of verse," I continued, liking my contrary role. Then I reconsidered. "Although, I did finish *All Fools Night*."

Seth's expression immediately grew serious. "And?"

"You already know. It was beautiful."

"No, I don't. It's a mystery every time—no pun intended. The words come out, but in the end . . ." He shrugged. "You never know how they'll be received, what people will think. I'm always kind of surprised."

"What did the opening quote mean? The Kate Bush lyrics about making a deal with God?"

"You should hear the cover of that song that Placebo did. It'll blow you away." Seth gave me a knowing look. "You think there's some hidden meaning?"

"There's always a hidden meaning. You added it in after you met me, didn't you?"

"Yeah . . . I mean, it relates to the book obviously . . . to O'Neill's revelation at the end. But I guess it relates to us too." His eyes drifted away, lost in the vista around us. "I don't know. We've had to deal with so many complications. We're still dealing with them. And what can we do? Nothing—well, unless we take your side's point of view and make deals with the devil. But why? Why can't we make deals with God?"

"People do all the time. 'God, if you do this for me, I promise to be good.' Stuff like that."

"Yeah, but I don't see any contracts like you guys have. No hard evidence that it works." If I wasn't mistaken, there was a little bitterness in his voice. "How come we can only get the things we want by being bad? Why can't we get them by being good?"

"I'll ask Carter the next time I see him," I said dryly. "But I have a feeling he'd say goodness is its own reward."

We'd picked over the tapenade by now but hardly touched the wine. His claims aside, I wasn't sure Seth had even sipped his. He turned back toward me.

"You and I aren't being very good, are we?" he asked. That was an understatement.

"You and I are the victims of unfortunate timing." I paused. "And a lot of other unfortunate things."

"Would have been a lot simpler if this stasis thing had happened when we were dating. Or if we'd just given in then."

"No," I said. "No way. I don't care if this is a mess. It's worth it that I didn't end up hurting you." *You spared him physical pain,* a nasty voice inside me taunted. *But what about Maddie? Pain isn't always physical, you of all people know that. What about the heartache you've caused her?* I ignored the voice.

"I don't care," said Seth. "I would have done it. I would have sold my soul for you. You and me . . . I told you. Something's always going to keep us near each other . . . even if we aren't together."

I rose from my chair and sat on his lap, wrapping my arms around him and wondering how it was possible that my heart was both swelling and breaking at the same time. I leaned my head against his shoulder.

"I love you," I said softly. "And I forgive you." Something weird about those words made me shiver, as though I'd never said them to anyone. "And I understand now why you did what you did." I didn't elaborate on the "what." I didn't need to.

Seth kissed my cheek. "Do you ever feel like . . . we're reliving this moment over and over?"

I thought about our troubled past. "If we are, I don't want to worry about it. Not right now."

I think he was going to say more, possibly even correct me, but I didn't give him a chance. I kissed him, and like every other time, it was sweet and powerful and the most right thing in the world. We wrapped ourselves together, and somehow, despite the cold weather, we got enough clothes off and made love with the wind whipping our hair and the stars shining down on us. And like that first time, I still had that sense that we weren't close enough. Even when our bodies joined and he moved in me, it still felt like I could never, ever be close enough to him. Maybe it was this mystical connection he kept talking about. Or maybe it was just a metaphor for our lot in life.

We sat together for a long time afterward, draped in blankets and saying little. I wanted to stay there all night. Forever, even. In this affair, it was the one thing we hadn't done: spend the night together after sex. We always had to part and go on to the rest of our lives.

He finally dropped me off at my car, and we kissed for a long time before I could finally extricate myself. Seth ran his hand along my cheek and hair, reluctant to let me go. I shared the sentiment.

"What will you do now?" he asked.

"I don't know. One more search tomorrow, I guess. If there's even time. I expect Ephraim to name somebody any minute now."

Seth nodded, eyes dark and thoughtful. "Well, if you need company again . . ."

I smiled, unsure if that was a smart idea or not, but it wasn't a decision I wanted to make tonight. I didn't know if I wanted the balcony to be our last moment together in this fling or if I wanted to cling to another few precious seconds, even on the beach.

"I'll let you know," I promised. I kissed him one last time and then left to find my own car. I had just unlocked it when a voice spoke to me out of the darkness.

"Can you give me a lift?"

I sighed. I really didn't like the way everyone could sneak up on me lately. Of course, with Carter's sick sense of humor, I wasn't entirely shocked. He'd lurked while hiding his aura plenty of times in the past because he liked the element of surprise. Still. I didn't even have a fighting chance now.

I opened my door. "Sorry. I don't pick up hitchhikers."

Undeterred, he slid into the passenger seat and put on his seat belt. "Did you have a good evening, madam?" He spoke in an old-fashioned, genteel sort of way.

"Don't take that tone with me."

"What tone? I was being polite."

"You know exactly what I've been doing, so don't act like you're making pleasant conversation."

"Why are they mutually exclusive?"

I refused to look at him. "I don't want to be judged."

"Am I judging you? Sounds more like you're judging yourself, which really, is the way it should be. The best jury of your peers that you'll ever find is . . . well, you. Only you know what you're capable of and what you want to be."

"Did you find me just to delve into the philosophy of my morals?" I grumbled.

"Nah," he said. "Whenever I find you, I just sort of go with this free-form thing and see where the mood takes me."

"Maybe the mood could take you to Jerome."

"That's your quest, not mine. Any luck?"

Again, I faced that dilemma. Who could I tell what? Grace, Roman . . . so many players on the board now and no clear opponent. "Some," I said at last.

"Oh-ho," he laughed. "You could be an angel with an answer like that."

"Well, I don't think it's going to be enough to find Jerome, not unless a miracle happens." The drive was short. I pulled up outside my building, getting a lucky front spot.

Carter turned and winked at me. "Well, you know my take on those. Thanks for the lift."

"Wait," I said, realizing he was about to teleport away. "I have a question."

He arched an eyebrow. "Oh?"

"How come when mortals want things, their only option is to make a deal with Hell and sell their soul? Why can't they make deals with God in exchange for good behavior?"

It was another of those rare moments when I'd surprised Carter. I waited for the glib answer I'd mentioned to Seth, something along the lines of goodness being its own reward. The angel considered for several seconds.

"Humans make those deals all the time," he said finally. "They just don't make them with God."

"Then who are they making them with?" I exclaimed.

"Themselves." He vanished.

"Fucking angels," I muttered.

I arrived in my apartment only minutes before Dante showed up. "Oh, I'm in luck," he said, seeing me on the couch with Aubrey. "You seem to always be busy lately."

I felt a small pang of guilt at what I'd done tonight. A lie was still a lie, no matter who you were lying to.

"I'm saving Seattle," I explained, making room for him beside me.

He sat down, clean-shaven for a change and looking good in his usual jeans, thermal shirt, watch, and boots. His insecurity was driving him to buy me gifts lately, but I realized I'd need to step it up and get him some wardrobe variety once all this madness ended.

"And how's that going exactly?"

Everyone kept asking me that. Seth. Carter. Dante. And my answer was lame each time. "Not so great, actually. I think tomorrow'll be the day it all resolves, and Jerome's going to be lost forever. Even if he's not, it'll be too late for him to get his old position back. His best-case scenario'll be someone's lieutenant in northern Michigan."

Dante put his arm around me and his feet on my coffee table. "Well, succubus, don't take this wrong way, but I'll be glad when this is over, new archdemon or no. I'm tired of you being stressed all the time, and I'm tired of not getting any face time with you." He toyed with the strands of my hair. "I'm also kind of tired of how frizzy this is. Isn't there some product you can use?"

"Hey," I said. "Not funny. What happened to internal beauty?"

He seemed undaunted. "You've got plenty of that. I just want the whole package. Besides, the look on your face was great when I said that."

His hand slipped from around my waist to trace patterns between my hip and thigh. It wasn't overtly sexual but I had a feeling that between that and his good mood—which I was happy for, don't get me wrong—there was an amorous advance in my future.

"Will you read my cards?" I asked abruptly.

He gave me a shocked look. "Tarot cards?"

"Yeah."

"You know that's all bullshit."

"It is when you bend the truth for your clients. Please? Just do a quick one."

"Fine. I'll give you a card-of-the-day one. All the mysteries of the universe in one card." I could hear the eye roll in his voice as he got up to get his cards out of his satchel. He usually kept them on him in the event of an impromptu client opportunity.

"Don't lie to me," I warned. "I know more than your clients."

"Wouldn't dream of it," he said, deftly shuffling the cards. I'd seen him scam clients plenty of times, telling them what they wanted to hear. Seeing as I didn't know what I wanted, I supposed that excluded me from that category. After the cards were thoroughly randomized, he had me cut them, and then he neatly restacked them. "Draw."

I took the first card off the top and flipped it over. "Fuck." The Five of Cups. Spilled chalices. Lost hopes and dreams. Dante affirmed as much.

"Disappointment's ahead, the loss of something you had. It can be a failure or inability to resolve a recurring problem. Pretty typical reading for you."

"What's that supposed to mean?"

"Doom and gloom always surround you. I didn't make up that palm reading for you." That had been even worse than this. "It's probably just verifying that Jerome's gone for good—if you even want to believe in this. And, hey, look." He tapped the card. "One cup stayed upright. Not all hope is lost."

I wondered about that as I thought about losing Seth and the man in the dream. I wondered also if Roman was right, if it was true that I wouldn't know what to do if I ever was actually happy.

As I suspected, Dante did make sexual moves on me, but I demurred as I had all week. I knew it didn't matter at this point. My cups had emptied, and the ride with Seth was over. Yet, our time on the balcony had been so sweet and so powerful that once again, I couldn't be with someone else after an encounter like that. Soon enough my sex life with Dante would return to normal—but not tonight. He didn't seem angry at being turned down, so much as hurt. I felt a little bad about that but realized I'd rather feel guilty about betraying him than Seth.

Dante was up and gone before me the next morning, but Roman was sitting in my living room eating cereal and generally making himself at home. He had to know I was standing there, but he kept his eyes on the morning news. When he finished the cereal, he clicked for Aubrey and set the bowl down for her.

"Hey," I said, scooping it up. "Milk's bad for cats."

"You need to let her live a little," he protested, still watching the news. "So what's the plan today?"

"I don't know. I'm still in stasis, so I guess that gives us time. Want to throw a dart at the map and go somewhere?" I gestured to the atlas of the Pacific Northwest lying on my coffee table.

"Might be the most productive method we've tried," he mused.

He had that light tone he often used, but I could hear the disappointment too. It was still a mystery to me as to why he'd be so into helping find Jerome. It was a mystery best solved with coffee, I decided, and while the pot brewed, I rummaged for my own breakfast. I unearthed Pop-Tarts and again wondered about weight gain.

"Um, Georgina . . ."

"If you're asking if you can feed her anything else, the answer is no."

"You need to come see this." His voice was deadly earnest. The hair on the back of my neck stood up, and I hurried back into the living room. Roman pointed at the TV.

"You have got to be kidding me," I groaned.

The Army of Darkness had struck again. We were watching a Seattle station, but apparently, this north-of-the-border escapade had been deemed newsworthy. The prank had actually taken place over in Victoria, a city on an island just west of Vancouver but still in British Columbia. There were some very famous and very beautiful gardens there, and the Army had apparently broken in at night and done their best to clip a pentagram into a huge expanse of bushes. They'd enhanced it with spray paint.

"Jesus Christ," I muttered. The pentagram job was bad, but the group had been savvy enough to get out of there without being caught. One shot of a courtyard there showed where they'd spray-painted: ALL HAIL THE ANGEL OF DARKNESS.

"Glad to see they haven't lost their touch," Roman said wryly.

I sank down onto the couch beside him, my mind spinning. Why? Why now? I'd toyed with the theory that the Army's activities had been an absurdly elaborate distraction to take everyone's attention away from Seattle. By that reasoning, their shenanigans should have stopped once Jerome was summoned. Yet here they were again. Had they acted on their own, just for the fun of it? Had Blake discovered a spray-paint sale? Or had Grace directed them again—and if so, why?

Most of their other activities had lined up with some other significant part of the seal's creation or Jerome's summoning. Without wasting another moment, I picked up my cell and called Cedric. I actually got through to him rather than Kristin.

"What?" he demanded when he answered.

"This is Georgina. I just saw the news."

"Look, I do *not* have the time for you. In fact, you're the last person I want to talk to right now, seeing as how none of this would have happened if you'd done your job in the first place."

"Yeah, yeah, I know, but listen . . . was anything important going on today?"

His voice was incredulous. "What, you mean aside from those idiots embarrassing me *again*?"

"No, I mean . . . any events or, I don't know . . . just anything important, um, demonically . . ."

"Well, if you consider my evaluation with Ephraim important, then yes." The sarcasm dripped through the phone.

I froze. "Thank you. That's all I needed to know."

He actually seemed surprised by that. "Really?"

"Yeah, no, wait—when I talked to Kristin the other day, she said that you came to Seattle the day Jerome was summoned, but then Ephraim said when you got here, he was already gone. Is that true?"

"Yes, of course. Do you doubt him?"

"No, no . . . just making sure I heard right. And you were in Seattle for a while?"

"Yeah, was with Grace and Mei dealing with the aftermath. Look, if you want to track my activities, wait until

Kristin's back in the office." He sighed in frustration. "Fuck. I wish she was here now."

I hesitated, then figured I couldn't make things worse. "Hey, just some friendly advice . . . but the next time you're looking at Match.com or asking out succubi, why don't you look a little closer to home?"

"What the hell are you talking about?"

"Kristin. If you're looking for someone who 'gets' you, you've already got her. See you later." I hung up before I could hear his response. Roman gave me a bemused look.

"Are you matchmaking in the middle of this crisis?"

"Just doing a good deed." I tossed my cell phone from hand to hand, thinking. "Okay, so. The Army did a prank today—while Ephraim was interviewing Cedric. Not good for Cedric."

"Which is going to ruin his candidacy for Seattle."

"Likely, even though he claims he doesn't want it. Still, it makes sense that Grace would have them do it today . . . *if* she had them do it and they didn't act randomly . . ."

He shrugged. "Makes sense, but what's it matter? You already know she's got a role in this. All this does is clear him."

I frowned. I had the same sense I had the other day while analyzing the cult's activities, like I was so close but couldn't grasp all the threads. Against my better judgment, I dialed Evan. He flipped out when he realized it was me.

"Georgina! We've been wondering what happened to you. Man, you will not believe what we did today, it was this—"

"I already know," I interrupted. "It was on the news down here."

"What? Holy shit. Hey! You guys!" I pulled the phone away as he yelled at whoever was with him. "We made the Seattle news!" A moment later he returned to me. "Wow, that's awesome. International recognition!"

"Look, Evan. I need to know something. Did the Angel actually tell you to do this? And when I say that, I mean, did she actually appear in one of those visions or did you presume she wanted this?"

"She was here. Told us to leave our mark at Butchart Gardens, so the world would know her glory. Cool too, since you know, it's a powerful place and all. No wonder it's having such far-reaching effects."

"Powerful place . . ." My fist closed around all the threads. "Evan, listen to me. Are you familiar with other places of power around you?" I'd always dismissed this group's arcane knowledge, never considering they might know a few things about the unseen world.

"Of course."

Roman's eyes were fixed on me so hard, I thought they'd shoot lasers right through me. He could tell I was on to something. I took a deep breath. "Do you know of any place up there that's by a beach—on the ocean—that has white rocks or gravel or sand or anything like that? That's infused with power?"

"White rocks?" he asked. There was a few second's silence. "Well . . . there's White Rock."

"What?"

"It's this town that has, well, a giant white rock. Some kind of glacial thing, but the Indians thought it came from the gods or something. Always been a holy place."

"White Rock," I repeated flatly.

"Yup."

No, no. It could not be that obvious. Balancing the phone with one hand, I opened the atlas with the other and flipped to the section on British Columbia. There it was, on the coast, just barely north of the American border.

White Rock.

"Son of a bitch," I said.

Chapter 24

Once I'd assured Evan I wasn't calling him a son of a bitch, I got off the phone and turned to Roman.

"The vessel's not anywhere around here. It's up in BC."

Roman's eyes had followed my finger to White Rock on the map. "Okay, you get points for the compelling name, but that doesn't necessarily mean anything."

"Yes! It means everything. The Army's been a distraction from the beginning, when the seal was created, when Ephraim talked to Cedric . . . and when Jerome was summoned. They staged their event on the Space Needle—*here*, but they didn't actually do anything until Jerome was taken. As soon as he was, they acted out to draw Cedric's attention here, away from his own territory."

Realization lit Roman's features. Sociopath or not, he'd always been smart. "Because Grace then hid the vessel in Cedric's territory."

I nodded. "That's where it's at. She needed Cedric gone, in case he noticed its presence before it was hidden. I think he's down here for the thing with Ephraim, but if I call now and tell him—"

"No," said Roman quickly. "We can't tell anyone."

"What is up with you?" I exclaimed, standing up. "The clock's ticking. We may not have time for a leisurely drive before the stasis ends."

"Chance we've gotta take, love." He rose as well. "Grab your keys. Let's go."

I started heading toward my bedroom, then hesitated. "Damn. I told Seth I'd consider taking him with me. Too late now."

Roman considered. "No, do it."

"Why?" I asked in surprise.

"I'll go invisibly. I don't know if anyone'll notice you leaving, but if they're tracking you, better they think you're on a romantic getaway. Even masked, I don't want anyone in power seeing my face yet."

That put me in a weird situation. Roman's entire reasoning throughout all of this was increasingly bizarre. There was also the debate I'd had last night, about whether I should let the balcony date shine on us as my last beautiful moment with Seth or if I should eke out a few more seconds. Letting it end at last night would have been the poetic thing to do . . . but I was made of baser stuff. I called him as soon as I was on the road and picked him up shortly thereafter.

He rode in the front with me while Roman lounged invisibly in the back, which was creepy, to say the least. Fortunately, none of my talk with Seth was sappy or romantic. He sensed the urgency crackling around me and asked questions about my reasoning for the trip. I answered as thoroughly as I could, all the while trying to drive the speed limit. I couldn't risk the delay of a ticket—or count on supernatural charms to get me off.

It took a little less than two hours to get there. We'd accidentally left the atlas at home but had all but memorized the directions anyway, which were straightforward. When we'd almost reach the park where the aforementioned rock was, I had the sense to call Peter and tell him not to go outside.

"You think I'm stupid?" he asked. "I know as well as you the stasis is about to end."

"Yeah," I agreed. "But it might not end like you're thinking." We disconnected.

"This is it, isn't it?" asked Seth. A sign directed us to the beach's parking lot, and I turned toward it.

"Yeah, I think so." I could feel myself starting to panic. "God, I'm afraid . . . I don't know what'll happen . . ." Seth reached over and patted my shoulder.

"Easy, Thetis. This'll end the way it's supposed to. Do what you have to do, and we'll manage the best we can."

I parked the car and looked over at him. So much burned between us, it was a wonder it didn't suffocate Roman. Seth was right. This was the end, and we would face it and do what needed to be done, no matter how hard. That was one of the wonderful things about Seth. He knew what the right thing was. We got out of the car.

Seth and I headed off down the beach, hand in hand. It was low tide, and the receding waters had revealed a landscape that had almost as much gravel as sand. Once you moved farther inland, though, the terrain turned green and grassy—probably the result of park maintenance crews. Semiahmoo Bay itself stretched off into a dark, choppy vastness that would have probably been blue and beautiful on a nicer day. Heavy gray clouds obscured most of the land surrounding the far sides of the bay, and I thought I heard a rumble of thunder, something that wasn't so common in the mild Pacific Northwest. I hoped we'd find what we needed soon because it looked like a storm was about to break out. Ah, metaphor.

Seth interrupted my ponderings. "That," he said, "is a white rock."

I came to a halt, turning my attention from the larger panorama to the path in front of me. There, about eighty feed ahead of us, was a white rock—a huge, white rock. And from the looks of it, Evan hadn't been exaggerating when he'd said it was about five hundred tons.

"I kind of feel stupid wasting my time with scraps of white gravel," I mused, brushing hair out of my eyes. The wind promptly whipped it back.

"It was so obvious . . . and yet not. Shall we?"

I nodded, and we approached the rock, our steps filled with

both eagerness and apprehension. After all this time and all the failed efforts, it didn't seem possible that we'd really done it. Something was going to happen. Something *had* to happen.

"Whoa," I breathed, staring up at the rock's top when we reached it. It was so massive that it covered us in shadows. "I can see why people thought this came from the gods."

Seth was looking down. "Unfortunately, we've got to direct our attention to less lofty places. How are we supposed to find this? Just dig at random?"

If Seth and I were alone, that would have been the method. Now, I was hoping Roman would reveal some insight about where the vessel was—if it was even here. A small part of me panicked that us ending up here might have been the biggest misdirection of all.

I scanned the ground around the rock, but there was nothing indicative of a recent digging. On a beach like this, all of the ground was uneven. "Something like that," I said, needing Roman to pick up on his cue.

Seth had let go of my hand when we reached the rock, but now he caught hold of it again and pulled me to him. "Georgina . . ."

I dragged my eyes from the ground and met his. My adrenaline was up, ready for the conclusion to this adventure . . . and yet, my heart was heavy, knowing what the consequences of this would be. I squeezed Seth's hands and stepped closer, resting my head against his chest. His heart beat heavy within. No doubt his emotions were tangled up as well.

"I know," I said softly. "I feel the same way."

He held me tight and kissed my forehead. "When we find Jerome . . . when you free him . . . it'll go quickly, won't it?"

"Yeah. I don't know how long it'll take, but . . . well, I think it'll be pretty fast. That's how it was when he was taken."

"And that's it."

"I guess."

We stood there, both of us hurting and confused. I didn't think anything could be worse than when Seth had forcibly ended things back in December. I understood now that he'd done it because he thought it would be for the greater good, but it still smarted. And this . . . this was a pain of a different type. When Seth and I first kissed back at my apartment, I thought this could all be a vacation for me, just as it was for the vampires. Seth would be my sunshine, something I could have a brief fling with before returning to my dreary immortality. I could take the memories with me, and that would be enough.

Only now, standing with him, I realized it wouldn't be enough. It would only hurt more now, knowing exactly what I could never have again. I would never make love with Seth again, never have these intimate moments of comfort and rapport. He wasn't mine anymore. He never could be again.

"I don't know what to do," Seth said, kissing my forehead.

"What do you mean? We don't have a choice."

"We always have a choice, Thetis. After this, even when you're a succubus again . . . I don't know. I wanted so badly to protect you from all the world's hurts. I still do. But after being with you this last week, I'm starting to wonder if—"

"You have got to be fucking kidding me."

Seth and I looked up in surprise. I would have expected Roman to come bust up our romantic interlude or maybe even Grace, in defense of her prize. What I was not expecting, however, was Dante.

I didn't know where he'd come from. He stepped around the side of the rock like he'd been lurking behind it, but I suspected he'd just walked up to us unnoticed in our moment of lovers' angst. Anger radiated off him, and his eyes were as dark and stormy as the sea beyond us. And as soon as I saw him, I needed no drawn-out questioning, no build-up to a revelation. I didn't need to ask what he was doing there because I suddenly knew.

"You're the summoner," I said.

"Of course." There was a dismissive tone to his voice as he said that, like it was an insult that anyone else could have played that role. "Who else? I wasn't kidding when I told you

I was the best in the area. I can't honestly believe you never even considered me. No, scratch that. Of course I can believe that. No matter how jaded or sorrowful you get, there's still that Pollyanna piece of you that wants to believe the best in those you care about."

"You say that like it's a bad thing," I said, feeling my own anger grow. Being played this whole time was bad enough. But being played by my own boyfriend? Unacceptable. And yet . . . he was right. It had been stupid of me not to consider him, yet I couldn't believe he would have subjected me to all this torment.

"It is a bad thing. I was hoping I could break you of it, but I guess not." His eyes flicked to Seth's face and then back to mine. "Of course, I can't really talk about naïveté since you were screwing me over this whole time. Or, well, screwing him."

There wasn't really anything I could respond with. I could hardly say, "It's not what you think," because . . . well, it was exactly what he thought. Regardless of his role in Jerome's summoning, the fact remained that I had cheated on Dante, and I'd been caught.

"I'm sorry," I said lamely, my hand still clutching Seth's tightly. He'd taken a step forward. He wasn't blocking me from Dante, but there was definitely a protective stance going on.

"Yes, yes, I know." Dante gave an exasperated sigh. "Damn it, Georgina. What does it take with you? I never gave you shit about your job. I was trying to make a good life for us. And yet . . . you still went back to *him*. As soon as you could fuck him without hurting him, you jumped right on it."

"Trying to make a good life . . . is that why you did all this?" I remembered Greg's comments about how anyone assisting a demon in this affair would be getting paid in concubines and TVs. In Dante's case, it had been much more basic. He'd simply been paid in money, enough to buy me jewelry and flowers and start talking about sharing a home with me.

"Succubus, what else was I supposed to do?" He was still

speaking to me in a mocking tone, but I could see the raw anguish on his features. It tore at my heart. "You can enslave
kings and rock stars. There was no way you were going to
stick with me forever, not where I was going. The palms barely
pay the bills, and the window for when my spells could really
pay off has passed."

"None of that mattered," I said resolutely. "I would have
stayed . . ." Yet, even as I spoke, I recognized the contradic-
tion. So did Dante, as he gestured at a thus-far silent Seth.
Seth seemed very intent on something.

Dante rolled his eyes. "Yes. Clearly."

"I never wanted this . . . never wanted you to literally make
deals with the devil."

"What did you expect from me? You know what I am.
You got involved with me because you wanted to walk on the
dark side. This deal was my biggest chance—the biggest pay-
off I was going to get for my power. She needed the best, and
she could pay for my services."

"She . . . Grace."

Dante gave me a twisted smile. "I should have known
you'd figured that part out too and had been sitting on it.
Even when you trusted me . . . you still didn't really trust me.
Maybe you aren't as oblivious as I thought. And when I got
to your place and saw the atlas—well, that's when I knew I'd
underestimated you. You're lucky Grace just sent me up here
and didn't come herself. We might get you out of here alive
after all."

Seth and I still stood close, close enough that when he
spoke into my ear, he barely had to raise his voice at all. "The
watch," he breathed. "It's in the watch."

I had no time to process that further because suddenly,
Seth broke from me and advanced on Dante. "Look, just
leave her alone, okay? You caught her. She caught you. Call it
even, and let us go." I stared. It was uncharacteristically aggressive for him.

"Even?" exclaimed Dante. "It is *not* even. I did what I did
because I love her."

Seth's voice was level yet hard. "Love her? You got her caught up in that cult mess. You nearly got her killed by a demon."

Dante glowered and took a step toward Seth. "That wasn't supposed to happen. Jerome came up with the Canada thing on the fly. She wasn't supposed to be caught in the middle of this. The plan was for her to wait out the stasis like everyone else, and then return to normal once Grace was in power. Grace messed up when she told Nanette about her meddling, but then Grace made sure Nanette wouldn't fuck with her again. I worked to keep Georgina safe." Cedric had told the truth. He really hadn't told Nanette about my theories; Grace had.

"Yeah, you did a great job."

"It's not my fault!" yelled Dante. "Say what you want about me, my reasons were noble. Whereas hers"—he pointed at me—"were in keeping with the selfish little whore she's been her entire life."

And then . . . the unexpected truly happened. Seth sprang forward and punched Dante. I didn't know what was more surprising, that Seth would be so aggressive or that he could throw such a clean punch. He'd thrown himself at a mugger once, and while it had been wonderfully brave, it hadn't been nearly as precise or coordinated. I had no idea where he'd learned that. Dante appeared as startled as me. He staggered back from the blow and took a moment to recover. Then, with a snarl, he leapt toward Seth. Seth only partially dodged the blow—on purpose, it seemed—and fell back with the impact, causing both men to collapse to the ground.

They grappled around a bit, trying to get leverage and blows in, and for a moment, I was too stunned by it all to react. Then, finally, Seth's words hit me. *The watch.* I hurried over to them, careful not to get hit by a flailing limb. Seth caught a glimpse of me and did his best to grab a hold of Dante's wrist and thrust it toward me. Dante kept squirming, however—I had a feeling he'd been in a few more fights in his life than Seth had—and increased his struggles once he realized what was happening.

The watch. It made sense, really. Grace wore her part of the seal around her neck. Dante would want to keep his safe as well, and why not hidden in the only accessory that he—by his own admission—ever wore?

At last, Seth managed to immobilize Dante's wrist just long enough for me to get my fingers under the watch's straps. I gave a hard jerk, using more strength than I thought possible, and the strap broke. The watch came away in my hand, and I scurried back as Dante yelled in rage. Seth eased up on restraining Dante, now that our goal was achieved. As soon as he was free, however, Dante came after me, and Seth shot up to catch a hold of him.

I continued backing up, the watch clutched in my hand, until I hit something—or rather, someone. I turned and found myself staring into Grace's cold, hard eyes. Whereas Dante had seemed to appear out of nowhere, I knew Grace actually had. I froze, and behind me, the sounds of fighting stopped. I think the guys were just as surprised as me to see her—or maybe not. Dante had all but said he'd told Grace we were here.

"Georgina," she said. "You are such a good employee . . . and yet, you're also a bad one." Her voice was as flat and emotionless as ever, except unlike in the past, I had a feeling she was actually planning to kill me now.

"Why?" I asked, playing for time. "You had a good job under Jerome."

"Under being the operative word. I wasn't going to spend the rest of my existence as someone's second-in-command and certainly not their co-second-in-command."

"She has the seal," I heard Dante say behind me.

"I know she does," Grace replied. "You gave it to her."

"Hey, I—"

She raised her hand, and Dante screamed. Jerking my head around, I saw him writhing in pain, like he was suspended by strings that she controlled. After enduring Nanette's wrath, I knew how truly excruciating demonic torture was, and I couldn't stand to see anyone else go through that. Seth looked from me to Dante, clearly unsure what to do. Fistfights might be out of his comfort zone, though they were something he could do. But this? Totally different.

"Let him go!" I said. As stupid as it was, I reached out and tried to shake her, but I would have had as much luck budging the huge glacial rock beside her.

"I should never have relied on someone who was close to—"

Her words were cut off when she suddenly went flying through the air, slamming into the rock. The impact seemed to surprise more than it hurt her, and mercifully, her torture of Dante stopped. She looked around, eyes wide and confused.

"What the—"

Roman materialized out of the air and strode toward her, fierce and frightening. Finally, I thought. Without my immortal senses, I couldn't feel his aura or signature, but something told me he was wielding a considerable chunk of his power as he advanced. Doing so was risky. It would make his identity known to any greater immortals nearby, though with all the drama in Seattle, there probably weren't any in the area to sense him. Cedric certainly wasn't around.

Grace gave a sharp intake of breath. "You . . . I remember your signature."

That was all the warning she gave before fire streaked from her hands toward Roman. He didn't move or bat an eyelid, but the fire hit an invisible wall. It arced around him, leaving him unscathed.

"Georgina," he said, not taking his eyes off Grace. "The vessel's over by the north side of the stone's base."

I wasted no time in hurrying over to the spot he'd indicated. I heard Grace's outrage and caught her moving toward me in my periphery. But then, her anger turned to pain. Roman had blasted her with something, and her attention returned to him. My own attention was on the rocky ground as I began digging with my bare hands. In my zeal, I'd once again forgotten a spade. Seth was by my side in an instant, clawing at the sandy surface with me. Large, fat drops of rain began falling on us, but I didn't have time to care.

"Who's stronger?" he asked as the sounds of fighting raged behind us. If Roman's appearance startled him, he was ignoring it for now.

"I don't know," I said. The ground was getting harder to dig in. It was damp and caked together from a recent rain, and I could feel it building up under my nails. "Roman can theoretically be as strong as Jerome, and I'm guessing she's less powerful than Jerome. I don't know for sure, and he might be holding back. The more power he uses, the more he alerts others that he's here."

My fingers hit something hard, and Seth and I both worked to pry it out. It was a wooden box, an old cigar case from the looks of it. I managed a good hold on it, and it began lifting out.

"Here," I said, pausing. I tossed him my purse and then immediately returned to my digging. "Get my phone. Look in the numbers, and you'll find Mei. Call her. Tell her where we're at." The cigar box came up out of the earth.

"You want me to call a demon?" he asked in shock.

"We need her. Tell her where we're at. Then get away from here. Get in my car and go."

"Georgina—"

"Go!" I shouted.

Seth hesitated for the space of a heartbeat, then got up and ran with my purse, keeping well away from the combatants. I didn't know if Mei would react to a call from a mortal. I didn't even know if she'd answer, nor did I know if she could be trusted. I was relying on instinct—and that naïve hope about everyone's good side—that she and Grace weren't collaborating.

Roman's scream caused me to look up sharply. He was on his back, Grace advancing. What looked like lightning crackled toward him, though just with the fire, it split away. Only, it got a lot closer to him than before. He was weakening.

Frantically, I scraped sand off the cigar box. It looked deceptively easy to open, but when I attempted to pry the lid up, nothing happened. It wouldn't budge, and I knew no efforts of mine would make it happen. Turning to the watch I'd taken from Dante, I peered at it. The face was a pale brown marbleized pattern—one that easily blended in with the seal. It was an ingenious hiding spot. I smashed the watch against the cigar case, and on the third try, the glass cracked. I plucked away the pieces and tried to pull up the face. It was embedded firmly. Taking a small shard of the watch's surface, I slipped it under the seal's edge, and after a few moment's pressure, everything fell apart, and . . . there was no seal.

I stared. Gears, watch hands, pieces of glass, and the face . . . but no seal. Seth had been certain. I had been certain. Dante had no other place on him that he would keep it. Carter had said it was possible that the summoner might hide the seal elsewhere, and if Dante had done that, we were screwed.

"Fuc—"

I cut my own profanity off and stared at my wrist, at the glittering watch winking up at me. No. Surely it wasn't this obvious. Dante had given me the watch before Jerome had been summoned, and then I'd lost it right around the time of the summoning. I'd blamed it on myself, but was it possible that Dante had actually briefly taken it back . . . ?

Jerking the watch off my wrist, I didn't hesitate to give it the same treatment as Dante's watch. It killed me to shatter that beautiful gold-and-glass piece of work, but when the filigree face popped out, I found a piece of smoky quartz that complemented Grace's. Dante needed more credit. He'd kept the seal close to him *and* hidden it where no one who was looking for it—i.e., me—would ever think to search.

The seal was useless, though, without the other half. Looking up, I saw that Grace had her hand around Roman's neck and was lifting him off the ground. He was completely limp. I didn't quite understand, but something told me he'd completely shut off all his power. Why? It was suicide. I wanted to scream, to run over and save him, but there was nothing I could do. Her back was to me, but I could imagine the gleam in her eyes.

"When I kill you," she hissed, "my position will be secured."

Suddenly, she jerked her head back toward me. For a moment, I thought I'd attracted her attention, but she wasn't looking at me. She was looking beside me, having sensed what I no longer could: the signature of another greater immortal. Mei stood there, hard and grim. I'd always considered her stone-faced, but the look she wore was truly terrifying, and I cringed.

She and Grace locked gazes, and then a few seconds later, Grace flung Roman away. He landed with a hard thud and lay still for a moment. Then, he lifted his head and slowly began crawling across the sand toward me, every movement seeming to cause him agony.

"You have seriously screwed things up," said Mei.

"I have improved my situation," said Grace evenly. "And I can improve yours."

"I don't need your help—especially when I reveal that you were behind all this. The others will reward me. Jerome will reward me."

"You're an idiot! Do you want to spend the rest of eternity working for someone else?"

"My time will come," Mei returned smoothly. "And I'd rather work for him than you."

And without any more banter, they lunged at each other. It was a bizarre fight. Half of it seemed very human, complete with physical blows and grappling. At the same time, there was definitely a supernatural element to it, as they wielded the same kind of elements and invisible blows Grace and Roman had. The rain was pouring down, drenching both of them. With their abilities, they could have remained impervious, but they were too distracted by each other.

Roman was still crawling toward me. Holding onto the seal and the box, I hesitantly moved to meet him half-way.

"Can you open it?" I asked, handing him the box.

His breathing was heavy and pained, but he gripped the box like I had and tried to pry the lid open. His fingers clenched the wood, and I saw exertion on his face, both of a physical and magical level. At last, he grimaced. "No. Not a greater immortal power I inherited."

I looked up at the demonesses. There was a slight shimmer around both of them. As the battle intensified, they were in danger of shifting to their true immortal forms, which would be bad for me to see. "Who's stronger?" I asked.

"They're evenly matched," said Roman, following my gaze. "Grace is a little worn down, though."

I hoped it would be enough. Hugging the box to my chest, I watched them fight, ready to look away if they totally shifted form. I'd always thought they had a hard sort of beauty, but now, it was all hardness and no beauty, and it wasn't difficult to see that under their human facades, they were truly demons of hell. I could also see what Roman meant about them being evenly matched. Each time one gained an advantage, the other took it back.

Until, just when it seemed Grace might be getting the better of Mei, Mei suddenly came on full force with an attack of unseen blasts that caught Grace off-guard and made her stumble back. With inhuman speed, Mei reached forward and ripped the choker from Grace's neck. Equally fast, she threw it toward me and then turned back to block Grace, who seemed to realize the end was near.

I grabbed hold of the necklace with trembling fingers and pulled off the crescent-shaped piece of the seal. I placed it next to Dante's half, unsure what to do, but as soon as they were close enough, they merged together into one whole disc.

"Put it on the box," said Roman. "Hurry."

I pressed the seal onto the box's top, and again, it seemed to know what to do, embedding itself in the wood's surface, almost like it melted. And with that, there seemed to be no other option. I opened the lid.

The power that blasted out of it knocked both Roman and me backward, and at the same time, I felt a different sort of power snap into my body. The strings that bound my soul to Hell reattached. My immortal essence coursed through me, and with it, I felt all the other abilities Hell had granted me return. I felt strong. Charged. Invincible. My senses tuned back in to the unseen world, and the blast of powerful immortal auras filled the air.

And there, in the rain, light and color slowly coalesced out of the box and into a man-shaped form. A few minutes later, it took on a completely human appearance. One that looked like John Cusack. Grace and Mei halted their attack, both staring.

Carefully, hesitantly, Mei then took a few steps back. Jerome paid her no attention. He was focused on Grace.

"Oh man," I said softly. "You are so fucked."

Chapter 25

To her credit, Grace didn't cower. She stood firm, regaining her composure as she matched Jerome's stare with one of her own. In fact, she regained enough of herself that she remembered to avoid the rain. The drops parted around her, much as the fire had parted around Roman. Her suit and hair were dry again, crisp and perfect.

"You would have done the same thing," she told Jerome.

I couldn't see Jerome's face when he spoke. "I wouldn't have got caught. You did. You failed."

"You should be impressed with my ingenuity." She crossed her arms, almost defiant. "I'm useful to you."

"You are meaningless. I could blight you out of existence, and no one would think twice about it."

I wasn't sure about that. Demons smote each other all the time, but that didn't mean Hell liked it. It created paperwork, and if you were caught, you got sent to Hell's equivalent of prison. Grace apparently shared my doubts about how easy it would be for Jerome to kill her.

"I don't think so. As it is, you'll be lucky if you have your job when you get back. You got yourself summoned." Her eyes flicked to me and Roman, huddled together on the sand. "Your territory's in chaos. They'll send you off to a desk job—or make you somebody else's subordinate. Quite a fall from an archdemon's position."

"Not likely," said Mei, speaking up. "Not if we spin this

right. Jerome's got powerful connections. So do I. And Cedric will advocate for him."

Her willingness to help and assurance about Cedric surprised me, but then, perhaps it was back to the know-thy-enemy philosophy. Grace glared at her former counterpart.

"You're the biggest fool of all here."

"Enough," snapped Jerome. "There's been enough villainous exposition here. The matter's done." I didn't have to see him to know he was smiling at Grace—only, I suspected it wasn't a very nice smile. "I *will* see you in Hell."

He snapped his fingers, and suddenly, what looked like black ice sprang up from the ground and crawled up Grace's body. She hardly had any time to scream because it coated her so quickly and then froze into place, leaving her immobile. She had become a thorny black statue.

"What is that?" I breathed.

"Kind of a demon stasis," Roman murmured back. "A prison of sorts. He's ten times more powerful than her—it's an easy thing for him to do."

I wondered then just how powerful Roman really was. He'd seemed matched against Grace, but I still wasn't sure if he'd been holding back or not, for fear of detection. As it was, he now had his signature turned off, appearing as a human for all intents and purposes. He'd done it just before Mei fully materialized.

"You need to get out of here," I told him.

"Wait," he responded.

Indeed, Roman seemed the least of Jerome's concerns as the archdemon studied Grace's frozen form. Her defeat had been anticlimactic, really. There had been no flashy brawl as everyone else seemed to have had today, but then, I supposed when you wielded the kind of power Jerome did, there was no need. I also had a feeling that Grace had been right about something. Even if he did have connections, Jerome probably couldn't risk doing anything rash to reestablish his control back in Seattle. He probably did want to torture her and blight her from the face of the earth, but binding her and taking her to face hellish justice—such as it was—was going to do him more good. Hell would be more kindly disposed to him if he followed their rules.

He turned and faced Mei, who stood off to the side. It was the first time I'd gotten a good glimpse of my boss since his return. His face was blank and cold, but I was pretty sure I could see the fury kindling behind his eyes. Being summoned was pretty much the worst thing that could happen to a demon.

"She was right to a certain extent," he told Mei. "It could have been advantageous to turn against me."

"And be second to her?" Mei shook her head. Like Grace, she had put herself back together. "No. I won't serve you forever, believe me, but for now, I see what my best course of action is. I'm throwing my lot in with yours."

"Your loyalty is appreciated." Mei gave a small nod of acknowledgment. Unlike Kristin and Cedric, where she served him out of love as much as duty, Mei's loyalty was all pragmatism and assessment of what could advance her. Jerome knew this and accepted it. "And it will be rewarded."

"I know it will be," she said evenly. "And I'll have no co-lieutenant when we return?"

"No. Not if I have anything to do with it."

And for the first time since I had known her, Mei smiled. Her eyes then flicked to the Grace statue. "Do you need me . . . ?"

"No," said Jerome, seeming to remember us. "You can go."

Mei wasted no time. She vanished, and Jerome turned around and stared down at Roman and me. His eyes fell on me first.

"So. You're here, Georgie. Why am I not surprised?"

"Because I'm the only one who cared about getting you back *and* wasn't too lazy to do anything about it?"

The ghost of a smile flickered across his lips. "Fair enough. And you will be rewarded too."

I wanted to tell him that I didn't need a reward, but Jerome had already shifted his attention to Roman. The smile faded. "You, however, have some balls in coming here."

"Must run in the family," said Roman. As beat up as he was, he still managed mockery.

"A suicidal nature does not, however. You know you're seconds away from being destroyed, don't you?"

"Yeah, yeah," said Roman. "And I'm sure killing me would help reinforce your badass status. But the truth is, I helped save you. You wouldn't be here if it wasn't for me."

I wasn't entirely sure if he'd done as much work as me in all this, but he had certainly made it easier for me. Nonetheless, even if he had actually single-handedly saved Jerome, it meant nothing. Demons didn't operate by a sense of fairness or feel obligations. Jerome affirmed as much.

"I owe you nothing. If you want to risk your life, that's no concern of mine. I don't care whether you live or die."

Roman struggled to his feet. "That's not true, or else you would have killed me already. Maybe you don't owe me anything . . . and yet, you're indebted to me, even if you don't believe in paying off debts—and I think you do. You can't stand knowing you owe me."

Jerome narrowed his eyes. "What is it you want?"

"Amnesty."

"What?" I squeaked. No one paid any attention to me. As far as they were concerned, they were the only two people in the world, father and son.

"I'm tired of running, tired of hiding. I want a place to stay. A place I can settle down in for a while."

"You don't need me for that."

"Don't I?" asked Roman. "Any place I live, even with my signature masked, I live in fear of being discovered by the greater immortals who control it. I'm always watching my back. I want to be somewhere where I can walk around knowing I have at least some measure of protection."

"If someone else wants to kill you, I'm not going to stand in their way."

"I know that. But at least I won't have to worry on a daily basis about you being one of them."

Jerome fell silent, and to my complete and utter astonishment, I realized he was deliberating about this. I never would have thought it possible . . . and yet, as Roman had said, if Jerome's mind had been made up, he would have smote Roman already.

Last fall, when we'd learned Jerome had his twin nephilim, we'd also learned that he'd had a wife long ago, a woman he loved so much that he'd fallen from grace to be with her. Did any of that love remain? Had it burned out over these millennia as a damned creature? Did he see any of her when he looked at Roman? When Jerome had helped hunt Roman and his twin, it seemed as though he didn't care. He'd even helped kill Helena.

Now, I wondered if Jerome was truly as indifferent as he appeared, and I wondered if Roman had long suspected that. I knew Roman hated Jerome—probably more than he hated me—but was it worth an uneasy alliance with Jerome to have some peace? Had Roman realized playing off this paternal relationship might be the only way to buy him a temporary reprieve? Of course he had. That had been Roman's plan all along. Lingering love for Roman's mother . . . and a bit of obligation thrown in. That was why Roman had helped free Jerome—and why he hadn't wanted me to let anyone else in on what I learned, I realized wryly. Secrecy might have been a true concern, but he would have undoubtedly wanted to minimize others' involvement so that he could play a major role in Jerome's rescue and use that as leverage.

"Mei knows," said Jerome. "I can't control what she'll do."

"She doesn't," said Roman. "I knew what Georgina sent Seth off to do, and I had shut down just before Mei arrived. She never saw my face last time, so she didn't recognize me now. She doesn't realize what I am."

"He's right," I realized, recalling how Grace had had him in a chokehold. Roman had been gradually letting go of his power and had had very lucky timing.

"Even if that's true," said Jerome, who seemed to be growing frustrated by the logic, "I can't control what others'll do. The angels will always be a problem."

"Well, not *that* much of a problem." The new voice was accompanied by the arrival of an all-too-familiar aura, one that felt crystalline and cool. Carter now stood beside us. "Welcome back."

Jerome glanced over at the angel, and for half a second, he almost looked pleased. The two of them appraised each other, probably communicating telepathically. Or maybe not. Maybe after so many eons of friendship, they no longer needed to.

"I suppose you're going to advocate for him too," said Jerome.

Carter shrugged and glanced over at Roman. "I don't know." Angels had as much of an instinct to hunt down nephilim as demons did. I thought of Carter as benevolent, but he too had helped destroy Helena. "He did help. Maybe he'll stay on good behavior."

It was a sign of how crazy things had become when Jerome and Carter seemed on the verge of letting a nephilim stick around—and that I was the one who protested.

"Are you guys out of your minds?" I exclaimed. "You know what he's done! He killed those people and hurt others. For all we know, this is a scam. Let him back in Seattle, and he could try to kill others. He could try to kill you. He could try to kill *me*!"

Everyone turned to me, seeming a bit startled by the outburst. "And here I thought we were partners," mused Roman.

"Bind him," said Carter. "Bind him in a deal."

Jerome and Roman sized each other up, and I held my breath. An immortal deal reached a creature's soul and could not be broken without dire consequences. I'd made a couple in my life. Everything rested on Jerome now, whether he was willing to go against every immortal taboo and knowingly let a nephilim live in his territory.

Finally, Jerome spoke. "I will allow you to live in my domain. During such time, I will not harm you—unless you're discovered by others and I am given no choice. I make no guarantees about other immortals who find you and offer no protection should that occur. You in turn vow not to implicate me in any way for doing this. You promise not to harm me or any other immortals who cross into my territory, unless it's self-defense—or unless I've given my okay. You also promise to harm none of my subordinates"—he glanced at me—"anywhere in the world."

"I accept," said Roman gravely.

"And," added Jerome, a sharp glint in his eyes, "you vow to be available should I require your services in a defensive, covert, or—in very rare conditions—offensive way."

There it was. The reason Jerome could go along with something like this. In offering Roman sanctuary, he was bargaining to have a secret nephilim agent, a powerful weapon none of his enemies knew about it. I'd never heard of anything like this.

"I accept with the condition that I won't kill on your command," Roman said at last.

Jerome considered. "Agreed. The terms of this deal end should you at any time openly renounce my amnesty. Or if I also declare the deal null and void."

"I want a time frame on that," said Roman wryly. "When does my lease expire?"

"A century. Then we'll renegotiate."

"I accept it all, then."

"And I agree to the same amnesty terms as Jerome," piped in Carter. "Except I don't need you to spy or kill for me."

"Agreed," said Roman.

It was all so terribly formal, and my presence felt complete superfluous. All three of them shook hands, and as they did, power burned in the air, binding them all to what they'd agreed.

"Well," said Jerome briskly. "Now that that's done, I'm going back to clean up the mess that's been made in my absence." He gave Roman a wry look. "Considering you aren't technically in my territory yet, I'd advise you—" Jerome suddenly stopped and scanned the beach. "What about the other summoner? The human one? Was he here?"

I looked around as well. The beach was empty. "It was Dante . . ." I said slowly.

Jerome rolled his eyes. "Typical. Where is he now?"

"I don't know," I said honestly. "Grace beat him up." I'd worried he was dead, but apparently not. Glancing over to where he'd been lying, I saw what looked like tracks in the sand where he'd been dragged off. I decided to keep that to myself.

"Wonderful," said Jerome. Turning back toward us, he scrutinized me. "You will keep this deal to yourself, Georgie. And we'll discuss your reward another day."

He disappeared and with him, the Grace statue. I didn't envy her.

Roman, Carter, and I started walking back toward the parking lot. I couldn't speak for them, but my mind was reeling with everything that had happened.

"Did you see what happened to Dante?" I asked Roman.

"Afraid I was kind of busy. What happened to Mortensen after he called Mei?"

"I told him to leave, and I think . . ." I hesitated, not entirely sure how I knew this, unless it was just my understanding of Seth's nature. "I think Seth may have carried him off in the confusion. Oh man, he actually listened to me."

The parking lot was empty. My car was gone.

"They took my car," I explained. I honestly hadn't thought Seth would, despite my pleas for him to leave.

"Wow," said Roman, clearly delighted. "Your ex-boyfriend helped save your current boyfriend and then stole your car. Or—well, wait—is Mortensen your boyfriend now? Did he technically save your ex?"

"Oh, shut up. It doesn't matter. We don't have a way to get back."

"Did you tell him to take the car?" asked Carter.

"Yeah. I told him to get far away. I wanted him safe, and I guess he listened."

"Depends on how you define it," said Roman. "Him coming back for the other guy put him in the demon line of fire. Why would he do that for someone he didn't like?"

I stared at the empty parking spot. "Because he's Seth."

Carter seemed as nonchalant about all this as Dante. "Well, it's a good thing I'm here, huh?" He rested his hands on our shoulders, and I braced myself for immortal teleportation. "Ready for a ride home?"

"It beats walking," I said.

Carter paused and gave Roman a curious glance. "What are you going to do for a home?"

Roman was thoughtful for a moment. "Well, I hear Georgina's moving to a bigger place." He glanced over at me with one of his beautiful grins. "Need a roommate?"

Chapter 26

Unfortunately, Roman wasn't entirely joking.

"What are you doing?" I exclaimed when we got back to my apartment. He'd flounced on my couch and promptly grabbed a remote. There was no sign of my car on the street, but if Seth had driven it back, Carter-transportation would have arrived much more quickly.

"I have nowhere to go," he said mildly. Aubrey strolled out from the bedroom and jumped up next to him.

"You just got amnesty from an archdemon. That's unheard of for a nephilim. I thought you wanted to put down roots? Why don't you go get a place in the suburbs? Work on your lawn?"

"No one wants to live there."

I raked my hand through my hair in exasperation and then immediately rearranged it. God, I'd missed shape-shifting. If I was going to be damned, I might as well enjoy the perks.

"You can't stay here. This place isn't big enough."

"I don't mind the couch."

I prepped myself for a rant, but then someone knocked at the door. Part of me hoped it would be Seth, even though that was pretty impossible. There was no immortal signature, which meant my visitor was a human. Yes, I'd definitely missed my abilities, even if they had strings attached. I opened the door and found Maddie.

"Hey," she said cheerily.

"Hey," I said, not sure I matched her enthusiasm. "Come in."

She stepped through, then faltered when she saw Roman. "Oh, I'm sorry. I didn't mean to interrupt—"

Roman hopped up from the couch. "No, no. I'm just an old friend. Roman." He extended his hand. She shifted some papers she was holding and shook his hand in return. Her smile returned.

"I'm Maddie. Nice to meet you." She turned to me. "You got a sec? I was on my way to work and wanted to show you something."

She handed the papers over to me. They were in-depth reports of the new condo over on Alki Beach. There were detailed price listings, as well as room-by-room photos of one unit in particular. It wasn't finished yet. The floor was only a foundation, and the drywall wasn't painted. Nonetheless, the pictures were clear and gave a good idea of the spacious layout. One picture showed a balcony that opened up to a breathtaking view of the water and the Seattle skyline beyond. It was nothing like what Seth and I had shared, but it was nice.

Roman, peering over my shoulder, let out a low whistle. "Nice."

I elbowed him out of my personal space. "Where'd you get these?"

Maddie smiled. "You said you were busy, so I went over there myself and talked to the builder. This is the only one left, and they let me go through and take pictures."

I jerked my head up. "You took all these?"

"I knew how stressed you were and wanted to help. Look, keep going, and you can see all the options you can still get. There are the floor choices: maple, bamboo, cherry . . ."

I took a deep breath to steady myself. Maddie hadn't just printed out info for me. After all that searching and fine-tuning, she'd actually gone out of her way to assemble an entire dossier on this place, a place I'd just been acknowledging at random to make her feel better.

"They've got a realtor on-site, but you can get your own

too," she continued. "Someone else was just looking at it, but the guy said if you were interested and put a bid in soon, he'd consider it along with the other person's."

"Look," piped in Roman. "Two bedrooms."

"Maddie..." I swallowed. "You shouldn't have done this."

She gave me a quizzical look. "Why not?"

"It was too much work."

"Whatever. Besides, after all the stuff you've done for me? Georgina, this is nothing. Are you going to go talk to them? I'll go with you if you want."

I sank down onto the couch, flipping through the pages without really comprehending them. I'd been angry when she and Seth hooked up. I had no right, however. She hadn't known about our past. And if I hadn't been so dead-set on keeping things secret, if she had known Seth and I had dated, I felt absolutely certain she would have never, ever gotten together with him. Because she was my friend.

I felt a burning in my eyes and willed myself not to cry. I didn't entirely know what I'd done to deserve that kind of friendship. She was a good person. She believed the best in me—just as Seth did. In this dark phase, Seth had never given up on me. Both of them were so good, so kind. And at the end of the day, there really wasn't much of that among humans.

Carter had said that if there were no other complications in the world, I would be the one Seth chose. But we did have complications. I still refused to hurt him because of sex, and that problem was now in full effect again. He'd thrown himself into danger for me on the beach. There would always be danger with the life I led—danger for him, not me. I wanted him badly, wanted to reestablish what we'd had, but if I did, I'd only be subjecting him to more of this rollercoaster existence. I'd deny him a normal life, a normal love. I couldn't do that to him, no matter what he said about trying it again.

Just because things don't work out, it doesn't mean there aren't other people you can't love. Love is too big a thing for you to go without it in life. At least for humans it was. I wanted Seth and Maddie to have that. I wanted them to have the dream I couldn't have.

Maddie's expression softened as she peered at me. "Why are you looking at me like that?"

I swallowed and gave her smile. "Just still amazed you did all this."

"Will you go take a look?" she asked excitedly.

"Yeah. I will."

This earned me a hug and a smile, and then she had to scurry off to work. I sat back down on the couch, papers still clutched in my hands. Roman sat down opposite me.

"You're going to end it, aren't you?" His voice was surprisingly gentle. "With Mortensen?"

"Yeah. I mean, I knew we would, but it didn't hit me until just now. We were deluding ourselves . . . caught up by a temporary situation. They deserve to be with each other, and I shouldn't have done what I did to her." I sighed. "Nyx tricked me with the dream. It wasn't real." Without thinking much about it, I rested my hand on my stomach. Even if there'd been any chance of getting pregnant while in stasis, it was gone now. "It might be real for them, though."

Roman looked so pained, so sympathetic that it was hard to imagine he still wanted to kill me. Though I was pretty sure he did. "I'm sorry," he said. "Sorry you can't have your man and your daughter. I'm even sorry you can't have your cats."

I glanced over at where Aubrey slept, recalling the tortoiseshell cat from the dream. "Well, I think she's happier being an only child anyway."

Seth showed up later that evening. Roman was mercifully gone, off to buy groceries. No matter my protests, he seemed intent on staying with me. I thought about complaining to Jerome but was pretty sure my boss wouldn't appreciate such a petty concern right now. *If* he was still even my boss. I was taking no news as good news for now.

Seth handed me my car keys as he walked in. "It's out behind the building."

"Thanks."

"Sorry I took off like that. I didn't want to . . . God, that was so hard."

"It was what I wanted," I told him. We stood a couple feet apart, hesitant to get much closer. "I'm glad you listened to me."

"I wasn't going to, you know. As soon as I got off the phone with that demon—and let me tell you, *that* was weird—I was going to head right back, and . . . I don't know. I don't know what I would have done. I would have stood by you."

"You could have gotten yourself killed."

He shrugged, like that was inconsequential. "I did actually head back, and then . . . then I saw Dante."

I crossed my arms, still fearful about approaching him, largely because I was afraid I'd throw myself at him. "I knew that's what you'd done. But why? You don't like him. You know what kind of person he is."

Seth nodded. "I don't like him, but . . . they would have killed him, wouldn't they?"

I thought about Jerome, that cold and barely repressed anger in his eyes. He'd been pissed off, and I knew it must have killed him to not be able to take his wrath out on Grace. There were taboos about directly harming and interfering with mortals, but well, it wasn't unheard of, and there were always loopholes. He would have gotten in less trouble for it than for smiting Grace.

"Well," I said, "let's just say, they would have at least made him suffer considerably."

"I figured. And I couldn't let that happen . . . not even to him. What he did was wrong—it seriously messed things up for you and put you at risk. But in some bizarre, crazy way, he did it because he loved you. And I'm not sure someone should be tortured for that. And . . ." Seth studied me carefully. "I had a feeling you wouldn't have wanted that."

He was right. No matter how much I'd been hurt, despite

the betrayal . . . I had cared about Dante. I still did a little. "God, I have to stop getting involved with unstable men. Where is he now?"

"I dropped him off at his place. He started coming around and was able to walk and everything."

"If he has any sense, he'll be long gone. I think Jerome'll have a long memory."

"And, so . . . things are back to normal?"

I took awhile to answer. "Yeah. I'm back in full succubus glory."

He turned away and began pacing. "I knew it would happen . . . knew this was coming, and yet . . . I kept pretending it wouldn't."

"Me too. I think somewhere in my head, I had this fantasy that I could find Jerome and still be with you."

Seth stopped and looked at me. "We still can be. I meant what I said . . . that I would try again . . ."

I met his gaze levelly. "What about Maddie?"

"I. . . I would end it with her . . ."

"Do you love her?" My words were blunt. I think I caught him by surprise.

"Yes . . . but it's different. Different from the way I love you."

"It doesn't matter," I said. "You and I can't be together. If you have a chance to be happy, then you need to take it. We can't do this to her again. It's wrong. She doesn't deserve it."

"I told you I'd end things with her first if we were getting back together. I can't cheat anymore."

"You can't break up," I said, surprised by the vehemence in my own voice. "She loves you. You love her. And after what we did to her . . ."

"You want me to stay with her as some sort of compensation?"

I balked. "Well, no . . . not exactly. But you guys deserve each other. You deserve to be happy. And you aren't ever going to be happy with me. It's going to always be up and down—just like before."

"I'm starting to think all relationships are like that," he said wearily. "I still don't want to hurt you. I can't stand that—I can't forget what Hugh said, about how that would destroy you. And yet . . . something keeps pulling us back. I told you—we're never going to be able to stay apart." I knew exactly what he meant, but I didn't say so. "I thought ending things before would fix all that, that the short-term pain would be worth the long-term stability. But I was wrong. We just found a whole new set of problems, and Maddie's in the middle. I'm willing to try again . . . no matter how hard it is."

"You were right to end it with us," I said harshly. "And I'm *not* willing to do it again."

He stared at me, shocked. My words were a lie, of course. Part of me wanted to try again, to endure anything to be with him. But I couldn't stop thinking about Maddie. Couldn't stop thinking about the hurt she would go through. It was ironic, really. Last time, he'd gone out of his way to hurt me purposely because it was for the greater good. Now I was doing the same for both of them, saving her from heartache and him from more grief with me. We were in an endless cycle.

"You can't mean that. I know you can't." His face was a mixture of incredulity and pain.

I shook my head. "I do. You and me are a disaster. What we did during this stasis . . . it was wrong. It was disgraceful. Immoral. We betrayed someone who loves both of us, who wishes nothing but the best for us. How could we do that? What kind of precedent is that? How could we expect to have a solid relationship that was built on that sort of sordid foundation? One that was built on lies and deceit?" Saying those words hurt. It was tarnishing the beauty of these precious few days we had, but I needed to make my case.

Seth was silent for several moments as he assessed me. "You're serious."

"Yes." I was a good liar, good enough that the person who loved me most couldn't tell. "Go back to her, Seth. Go back to her and make it up to her."

"Georgina . . ." I could see it, see it hitting him. The full weight of betraying Maddie was sinking in. His nature couldn't ignore the wrong he'd done. It was part of his good character, the character that had gone back to save Dante, the character that was going to make him leave me. Again. Hesitantly, he extended his hand to me. I took it, and he pulled me into an embrace. "I will always love you."

My heart was going to burst. How many times, I wondered, could I endure this kind of agony? "No, you won't," I said. "You'll move on. So will I."

Seth left not long after that. Staring at the door, I replayed my own words. *You'll move on. So will I.* In spite of how much he loved me, how much he was willing to risk, I truly felt he'd go back to Maddie, that he'd believe what I said. I'd driven home the guilt, made it trump his love for me.

You'll move on. So will I.

The unfortunate part about being a good liar, however, was that while I could get other people to believe my words, I didn't believe them myself.

Chapter 27

While I'd been pretty confident in telling Seth that Dante had likely skipped town, I nonetheless stopped by his shop the next day. It had never been very prosperous looking to begin with, but now the signs of abandonment were clear. The neon PSYCHIC sign was gone. The blinds were also gone, showing a room even barer than before. The FOR LEASE sign on the door was probably the most telling clue that Dante was gone for good.

In the wake of what had happened with Seth, it was hard to know what to think about Dante. My heart almost didn't have the energy for it. I had cared about him, absolutely. He'd suited my decadent phase, and despite his blackened soul, there were parts of him that were likeable. And above all, it appeared that he'd cared about me, misguided or not. I wasn't happy about the deal he'd made with Grace, but I was glad he hadn't been there to face Jerome and Mei's punishment. No one deserved that, not even Dante. I hoped wherever he was, he'd try to start a new life—maybe one that could lighten his soul a little. I well knew, however, that humans with damned souls rarely recovered.

Later that evening, I drove over to Capitol Hill. Peter and Cody were hosting a cocktail party to celebrate Jerome's return, though I half-suspected they simply wanted to drink away the sorrows of losing the sun.

"How can we celebrate Jerome being back when he's not even here?" Tawny wanted to know. She was back to her normal, Amazonian blond self and was holding her martini glass in a precarious way. Peter couldn't take his eyes off it.

I was nursing a gimlet out of politeness. The vampires had gone out of their way to get Grey Goose and fresh lime, but truthfully, I was a little burned out on alcohol. It seemed like I'd been perpetually drunk these last four months. I was *not* burned out on cigarettes yet, but I was trying very hard to break the habit once more.

"Jerome's got plenty to keep himself busy," I said. "We're just drinking in his honor."

"But he is staying, right?" asked Cody.

We all turned to Hugh. Like the rest of us, Hugh'd had his abilities restored, and I'd honestly expected him to be a lot happier having his imp vision back. Instead, he seemed very serious, and I could have sworn he was watching me when I wasn't looking.

"Yep. He and Mei schmoozed the corporate guy pretty good and pulled in enough favors to get backing from others. Cedric and Nanette both swore up and down that no one else was better qualified to run Seattle than him."

"Nanette finally caved, huh?" I swirled the ice around in my glass. "Of course, knowing Jerome owes her now probably makes her feel secure in her territory."

Cody shook his head. "Still. Grace went through an awful lot to try to pull this off, between the Canadians and all the wheeling and dealing. And Dante." He shot me an apologetic look that I waved off.

"I don't know," said Peter. He finally seemed convinced that Tawny wasn't going to ruin his upholstery. "She's a middle management demon with so-so power. Doing what she did—seizing the opportunity when she thought Jerome looked weak—was probably the closest she'll ever get to ruling over an area like this."

"What do you mean? Would she be stuck forever? Never have her own domain?" asked Tawny, frowning.

"She might have eventually gotten assigned control of some

nonexistent town in middle America, but I doubt much more."
Hugh still looked oddly speculative. "Clearly, she didn't want
to. Neither does Mei, from the looks of it."

"So much for it being better to reign in Hell than serve in
Heaven," I said, pleased with my own wit. "Of course, I
think we're going to see a lot more in Mei's career. She might
be so-so in power, but she's got a plan."

"Have you noticed how she's a lot less scary alone?" asked
Cody.

"It was the matching clothes," said Peter sagely. "When
they dressed alike, it was too much like those girls from *The
Shining*."

More laughter and conversation ensued, though I eventually grew quiet and simply listened. Maybe I could be the life
of the party, like Seth had said, but this group could do okay
without me. I took a certain amount of contentment by being
back with them and having our lives returned to normal—
such as they were. I could never be human again, but these
were the people I wanted to be damned with.

At one point, I got up to trade my empty glass for water
and discovered Hugh had followed me into the kitchen. He
still looked troubled. The others were laughing and talking,
providing cover for our conversation.

"What's going on?" I asked. "I thought you'd be happy."

"I am, I am," he said. "Believe me, I am. God, that was
miserable."

I couldn't help a smile. Hugh had hit his stride with being
a lesser immortal. He was past the novice stages of Cody and
Tawny and could fully reap the benefits of his position. However, he wasn't old enough to have acquired all the jaded centuries Peter and I had. Out of all of us, I didn't doubt that
Hugh had suffered the most.

"Then what's going on?"

He hesitated, and again, I was struck by how out of character he was behaving. "Georgina, has Seth done anything . . .
bad lately? Rob a bank? Cheat on taxes?"

"Of course not," I said, more confused than ever.

"Has he . . . or well . . . did he do anything, uh, bad with you?"

To my chagrin, I blushed. You'd think nothing would make a succubus self-conscious, but I still tried to maintain that line between my private and business sex lives. My silent response was enough for Hugh.

"Fuck."

"What?" I asked. "We did it when I was in stasis. I didn't take any of his energy. I didn't shorten his life. And we haven't done it since Jerome came back. It's over. He's back with Maddie."

Hugh raised an eyebrow. "Oh?"

"I realized how impossible it was for us and convinced him to go back to her. I really laid on the guilt." Just mentioning what had happened made me ache all over again.

"I'm sure you did," Hugh said dryly.

"What do you mean?"

"Georgina . . ." He sighed. "There's no easy way to explain this. When I first met Seth, his soul was like . . . a supernova. It lit up a room. That guy had such a generous spirit, it was insane."

Had.

"And now?" The answer was slowly creeping in on me.

"Now, there's a shadow on him. A stain on his soul. He cheated on Maddie with you . . . and is back with her, keeping that from her . . ."

The room started swaying, and I forced myself to focus on Hugh. "What we did, it wasn't sleazy. We are . . . were . . . in love. It was sweet—that is, it meant something."

"Maybe it did, sweetie. Maybe the planets aligned when you made love. But regardless of what happened between you, he wronged her—and he feels it now. That sin is darkening his soul."

"How dark?" I asked, my voice almost a whisper now. "If he were a hit by a car right now . . ."

Hugh's face was both hard and sad. "He'd head right to Hell."

"Oh my God." I collapsed back against the counter. "I didn't think . . . didn't realize . . ."

Since I hadn't been a succubus, I hadn't been thinking like one. I hadn't worried about shortening his life or exhausting him because there was no need. While I'd known we were both deceiving Maddie and had felt a fair amount of guilt over it, I'd never considered it in terms of damnation. I'd turned off that part of my life, the part of being a succubus that counted and tallied souls—the main part of my job.

Which was stupid of me. Humans didn't need us to sin. They did it all the time on their own and did just as good a job—if not better—than we could. I didn't have to be a succubus to make Seth sin. I could have been any woman, any woman he'd had an affair with. Sin was subjective, too, and different people would feel it differently. For someone like Seth, doing what he did would leave a harsh mark—and me making him feel guilty about it hadn't helped.

"This is worse," I said. I laughed, but it was the kind of hysterical laughter that could segue to tears at any moment. "It would have been better if we'd had sex when we were dating. I'd have taken years off his life, but his soul would have stayed pure—and that's what matters in the long run. Instead, I was so adamant about refusing to do it . . . and now look. Look what I did."

Hugh caught my hand and squeezed it. "I'm sorry."

"Is there . . . is there any way he can undo it?"

"You know the answer as well as me. Sure, he can eventually swing the pendulum the other way. But it's hard. Very hard."

"He's a good person," I said stoutly.

"Maybe, but that may not be enough anymore."

"He'd need a deal with God," I muttered.

I stared at the floor, studying the tiles absentmindedly. What had I done? How could I have been so stupid? Had I been so blinded by love and lust that I'd been oblivious to the principles that had dictated my immortal vocation these long centuries?

"Georgina," Hugh said hesitantly. I looked at him. "There's something else . . . just a heads up. You know this as well as I do. When upright people screw up like this . . . they do try to rebound in their way. The guilt's got to be eating him. People like that try to do things to make up for it. Rash things. Something tells me he'll be like that."

"Thanks for the warning," I said. "Though I can't imagine he'd do something that could make this any worse."

The imp cut me a look. "Sweetie, he's human. Don't underestimate him."

Hugh was right.

The next day, I went to the condo builder's office and talked more in-depth with the real estate agent that handled their sales. We chatted for a while and talked numbers, though I still couldn't shake the feeling that I was doing this without thinking it through. The pictures were nice, the floor plan was nice, and the options were nice. Yet, I didn't know if this was just some impulsive reaction to the ups and downs in my life.

Then, when he took me to the unit itself and showed me the balcony, I knew. It was a beautiful day, one that wasn't true summer yet but could give us enough hope that winter was just about finished. Puget Sound was deep blue, and the downtown skyline gleamed in the sun against a cloudless sky. To the west, the Olympic Mountains were visible for the first time in over a month, their peaks still heavy with snow. As often happened with this kind of weather, people turned out in droves, treating it like it was high summer. Families came out, shorts came out. This part of Alki didn't have a true beach—that was at a park a little farther down—but the water was still just a stone's throw away from my building, separated only by the small road and narrow strip of grass. I watched the waves break against the shore and realized this was where I needed to be.

"I want to make an offer," I told him.

I knew Maddie would want to know, so I made sure she was the first one I told when I ended up back in Queen Anne later that night. It was early evening, my last day before returning to a real full-time schedule, and I swung by the store to catch her and tell her. Only, she sought me out first, with news of her own.

"Georgina!"

I'd barely entered when she grabbed my arm and pulled me off into the cookbooks. "Hey," I laughed. "Glad you're in a good mood. I've got news."

"Me too!"

Her face was radiant, and after all that had happened, it made me happy to see her like this. I couldn't help a return grin. "What's up?"

She glanced around covertly, then lowered her voice. "You were right."

"About what?"

"About Seth needing time—about him being preoccupied."

Oh lord. He'd finally slept with her again, now that things had ended with us. I can't say I was happy to have this news delivered to me, but for her sake, I was at least glad she could stop worrying.

"Wow, that's great, Mad—"

"He was waiting to propose!"

She shot her hand up to my face so quickly that for half a moment, I thought she was going to punch me. But, no, there was no impact—unless you counted the brilliant glitter of the engagement ring dazzling my eyes.

"Oh my God. But it . . . it's so soon . . ."

"I know," she said, breathless from her excitement. "I can't believe it. And I mean, yeah, we've only been going out for about four months, but Seth says we can have a long engagement, that he just wanted to commit things between us."

Of course he did. *When upright people screw up like this . . . they do try to rebound in their way. The guilt's got to be eating him. People like that try to do things to make up for it. Rash things.* How could I be surprised? I'd become a succubus because I'd cheated on my husband and been caught. I'd sold my soul in an effort to blot that act out, to make him and everyone else I knew forget me. Why was this any different?

"You don't think . . ." Maddie turned uneasy, once more seeking my approval and advice. "You don't think it's too fast, do you? Have I made a mistake? I mean, even if we wait awhile for the wedding . . ."

I kept smiling. "It's fine, Maddie. There's no time frame that's set for everyone. If it's what feels right to you, then you've got to do it."

Her grin lit back up. "Oh, thank you. I'm so glad to hear you say that. I mean, I said yes, and I've been excited . . . I just didn't want it to seem like I was rushing in." She glanced back down, admiring the ring. I realized something.

"It's a diamond."

She gave me a curious look. "Of course. Why wouldn't it be? Most engagement rings are."

Last year, I'd teased Seth about getting married, and he'd said that if he ever did, he'd give his bride-to-be a ruby because he thought diamonds were ordinary, and getting married was extraordinary.

I stared into the stone's glittering facets, puzzled. "Did you pick it out? Had you told him you wanted a diamond?"

"Nope. It had never come up. He just got it for me. Why?"

I shook my head and tried to look happy for her. "No reason. It's beautiful. Congratulations." I turned to leave. "I'll see you tomorrow."

"Georgina, wait."

I paused and looked back.

"What was your news?"

"Wh—oh. Yeah. I'm buying the place in Alki."

"Seriously?" I swear, she almost seemed more excited about that than the engagement. "When will it be done?"

"July."

"Oh, wow. That's great. You could have such great summer parties."

"Yep. Let's hope it gets finished on time."

She sighed happily and gave me a quick hug. "Isn't this a great day? Good news for both of us."

"Yeah," I agreed. "Great."

I walked home, too stunned over the engagement news to process it much. Considering Hugh's prediction, there wasn't much to process. I'd convinced Seth that he and I were a fantasy, that he needed to settle into reality and take what good he had with Maddie. Seth had believed me and tried to make it up to her—make it up to himself, even—with this hasty engagement. He was not a rash person usually, but the extreme circumstances had turned him into one.

My phone rang about half a block from the store. I could recognize Vancouver's area code by now, but I didn't know the number. For all I knew, Evan wanted me to smuggle them some spray paint across the border. To my relief, it was Kristin.

"Hey," I said. "How's it going?"

"Fine. Well, better than fine. Great actually." There were a few awkward seconds of silence. "Me and Cedric . . . we're . . ."

The first spark of enthusiasm I'd felt in a while leapt up in me. "Really? You guys are a . . . thing?"

"Yeah." There was wonder in her voice, like she could hardly believe it. "He told me that you were the one who said that he should go out with me."

"Oh, well. I . . . just suggested he was looking in the wrong places."

"Georgina, there is no way I can thank you enough for this." Her voice was brimming with emotion, something I wouldn't have thought possible of the businesslike imp. "This is . . . I've wanted this for so long. Loved him for so long.

And he never noticed me until you made him just pause and look. That's exactly how he said it too. That he'd been so busy chasing everything else that he'd never seen what was in front of him."

I thought I might get choked up too. "I'm glad for you, Kristin. Really. You deserve it."

She laughed. "Most would say us damned souls don't deserve anything."

"We're like anyone else, deserving both good and bad. I'm not sure being damned has anything to do with it."

She was quiet for a moment, and when she spoke again, her voice was low, almost hard to hear. I actually stopped walking and stepped off down a side street to get away from the din of traffic.

"It's funny you mention that," she said slowly. "Because . . . well, I did something for you." I suddenly had an image of Tim Horton's donuts showing up on my doorstep.

"Er, that's really not necessary. I didn't do that much."

"You did, though. To me, at least. And so . . . I wanted to do something just as big for you. I, uh, went and looked at your contract."

I caught my breath. "What?"

"We've had a lot of paperwork to file, and I managed to work in a corporate trip."

"Corporate trip" was a nice way of saying she'd visited the inner offices of Hell.

"Kristin . . . if you'd been caught . . ."

"I wasn't," she said proudly. "And I found your contract and read it."

I'd come to a complete stop now. The world around me didn't exist. "And?"

"And . . . nothing."

"What do you mean nothing?"

"I mean, there's nothing wrong with the contract. I went over and over it. Everything's in order."

"It can't be! Niphon was trying so hard to mess with me . . .

to get me recalled. Hugh was certain it meant he was trying to shift attention from the contract."

"I don't know about any of that," said Kristin, sounding truly sympathetic. "All I know is what I read. You sold your soul and took on standard succubus servitude in exchange for every mortal you knew forgetting who you were. That sound right?"

"Yeah . . ."

"That's what it said. All the language was exactly as it should be."

I didn't really have any response, so I gave none.

"Georgina, are you still there?"

"Yeah . . . I'm sorry. I just thought . . . I'd been so certain . . ." It had been a foolish hope, that maybe somewhere there was a loophole for me. But then, I seemed to fall for those things all the time, just like I had with Nyx's dream and the impossible chance of getting pregnant while in stasis. I was as naïve as Dante had said. "Thanks. I really appreciate you looking."

"I'm sorry you didn't get what you wanted. If there's anything else I can do for you—that doesn't involve breaking into records—let me know."

"Thanks. I will."

We disconnected, and I stared bleakly at my surroundings, at the quiet residential block I'd stepped off onto. "There is no way," I said out loud, "that this day can get any worse."

A rustle behind me made me jump, and I spun around. I had thought I was alone and now felt like an idiot getting caught talking to myself. I saw no one, though. Then, a bush by the sidewalk twitched a little. I took a few steps toward it and knelt down. Yellow eyes peered out at me, followed by a piteous meow. I made the clicking sound that's universal to cat owners, and after a few moments, my observer emerged.

It was a cat, a very scraggly one—and a cat I was pretty sure I'd seen before. It was smaller than Aubrey, maybe younger, and I could see its ribs poking out underneath the fur, which was matted and dirty. When I petted the cat's head, I noticed a dry texture to the fur that often indicated fleas. The cat seemed unsure of me—but not enough that it ran away. It mostly seemed curious for now, like it was trying to figure me out—and maybe score some food.

Which was fine, because I was trying to figure it out too. Clearly, this cat had no owner, or if it did, that ownership needed to be revoked. I studied its yellow eyes and every frail line of its body. The cat looked so different and yet . . . I was certain it was the one. And in a musing that was worthy of Carter, I suddenly wondered if the universe might not be done with me after all.

I let the cat sniff my hand a bit longer, and then I reached out and picked it up. It was a she. She didn't fight me as I held her to my chest and walked home. In fact, she started purring. Maybe she knew me. Maybe she was just weary of fighting all the time too.

When I shouldered open my door, Aubrey's head immediately jerked up from where she'd been napping. She made no noise, but all the fur on her back stood on end as she studied our new visitor with narrowed eyes. Roman, lying on the couch as usual, also studied us. He looked at the cat, taking in her orange and brown patched coat. Then, he looked up and met my eyes. I'm not sure what he saw, but it made him smile.

"Let me guess. That's a tortie."

"Yes," I agreed. "This is a tortie."

Please turn the page for an exciting sneak peek of
Richelle Mead's next Georgina Kincaid novel,
coming in April 2010!

Chapter 1

I was drunk.

I wasn't entirely sure when it had happened, but I suspected it had occurred around the time my friend Doug had bet me I couldn't take down three vodka gimlets faster than he could. He'd promised to take my weekend shift at work if I won, and I was going to do his stock duty for a week if he won.

When we'd finished, it looked like I wasn't going to be working next weekend.

"How did you out-drink him?" my friend Hugh wanted to know. "He's twice your size."

Through the crowd of people crammed into my condo, I peered at the closed bathroom door, behind which Doug had disappeared. "He had stomach flu this week. I'm guessing that doesn't go so well with vodka."

Hugh raised an eyebrow. "Why the fuck would anyone take a bet like that after having the flu?"

I shrugged. "Because he's Doug."

Hoping Doug would be okay, I scanned the rest of my party with the pleased air of a queen sizing up her kingdom. I'd moved into this place back in July and had been long overdue for a housewarming party. When Halloween had finally rolled around, combining the two events had seemed like a pretty reasonable solution. Consequently, my guests tonight were clad in an array of costumes, everything from elaborate Renaissance faire–quality garb to the slackers who'd simply thrown on a witch hat.

Me, I was dressed as Little Bo Peep—well, that is, I was dressed the way Little Bo Peep would be dressed if she were a stripper and/or a shameless strumpet. My frilly blue skirt stopped just above the half-way point on my thighs, and my puff-sleeved white blouse was so low-cut that I had to be careful when leaning over. The crowning achievement—literally— was my curly mane of flaxen-blond hair, perfectly arranged into two pigtails tied with little blue bows. It looked perfect, absolutely indistinguishable from the real thing because . . . well, it *was* real.

Shape-shifting always came in handy as a succubus, but for Halloween, it was golden. I always had the best costumes because I really could turn in to anything I wanted. Of course, I had to keep it within reason. Too much of a change would raise the suspicions of the humans around me. But for a hair change? Shape-shifting came in pretty handy.

Someone touched my elbow. I turned, and my smug enthusiasm dimmed a little when I saw who it was: Roman, my sociopathic roommate.

"I think someone's getting sick in the bathroom," he told me. Roman was a nephilim, half-angel and half-human, with soft black hair and sea-green eyes. If not for the fact that he occasionally went on immortal killing sprees and had me on his hit list, he would have been a pretty good catch.

"Yeah," I said. "It's Doug. He lost a vodka challenge."

Roman grimaced. "I'm not cleaning that up."

"What, you don't do housework, either?" asked Hugh. He'd recently learned Roman wasn't paying me rent because he was "between jobs." "Seems like you should pull your weight around here somehow."

Roman gave Hugh a warning look. "Stay out of this, Spiro Agnew."

"I'm Calvin Coolidge!" exclaimed Hugh, highly offended. "This is the same suit he wore at his inauguration."

I sighed. "Hugh, nobody here remembers that." That was one of the downsides of being immortal. Our memories became obsolete as more time passed. Hugh, an imp who bought souls for Hell, was much younger than Roman and me, but he had a lot more years than any human here.

Slipping away from Roman and Hugh, I headed across the room to mingle with my guests. Some of my co-workers from the bookstore Doug and I worked at were huddled around the punch bowl, and I stopped to chat. Immediately, I was bombarded with compliments.

"Your hair is amazing!"

"Did you dye it?"

"It doesn't even look like a wig!"

I assured them it was a very good wig and I dealt out praise for them in return. One person, however, earned a rueful headshake from me.

"You have more creativity than all of us put together, and that's the best you could do?" I asked.

Bestselling author Seth Mortensen turned to look at me with one of his trademark, slightly scattered smiles. Even when I was dizzy with vodka, that smile never failed to make my heart speed up. Seth and I had dated for a while, plunging me into the depths of a love I'd never imagined possible. Part of being a succubus was seducing men for eternity and stealing the energy of their souls; a real relationship had seemed out of the question. And in the end, it had been. Seth and I had broken up—twice—and while I had accepted that he had moved on, I knew that I would love him forever. For me, forever was a serious matter.

"I can't waste it on a costume," he said. His amber-brown eyes regarded me fondly. I no longer knew if he loved me, too; I only knew for sure that he still cared about me as a friend. "Gotta save it for the next book."

"Lame excuse," I said.

He shook his head. "Nobody cares what guys wear at Halloween, anyway. It's all about the women. Look around." I did, and saw that he was right. All the elaborate, sexy costumes were on women. With a few exceptions, the men's dulled by comparison.

"Peter's dressed up," I pointed out. Seth followed my gaze

to another of my immortal friends. Peter was a vampire, a very fastidious and obsessive-compulsive one. He was dressed in pre–Revolutionary French garb, complete with brocade coat and powdered hair.

"Peter doesn't count," said Seth.

Recalling how Peter had painstakingly stenciled swans around his bathroom's baseboards last week, I couldn't help but agree. "Fair point."

"What's Hugh supposed to be? Jimmy Carter?"

"Calvin Coolidge."

"How can you tell?"

I was saved from answering when Seth's fiancée—and one of my best friends—Maddie Sato appeared. She was dressed as a fairy, complete with wings and a gauzy dress nowhere near as slutty as mine. Her being with Seth was something else I'd come to accept, though I suspected the sting of it would never leave. Maddie didn't know Seth and I had dated and she had no clue about the discomfiture I felt over their whole relationship.

I expected her to slip her arm around Seth, but it was me she grabbed a hold of and jerked away. I stumbled a bit. Five-inch heels weren't normally a problem for me, but the vodka complicated things a bit.

"Georgina," she exclaimed, once we were far enough away from Seth, "I need your help." Reaching into her purse, she pulled out two pages torn from magazines.

"With wha—oh." My stomach twisted uncomfortably, and I hoped I wouldn't be joining Doug in the bathroom. The pages were of wedding dresses.

"I've almost narrowed it down," she explained. "What do you think?"

Grudgingly accepting that the man I loved was going to marry one of my best friends was one thing. Helping them plan their wedding was an entirely different matter. I swallowed.

"Oh, gee, Maddie. I'm not very good at this stuff."

Her dark eyes widened. "Are you kidding? You're the one who taught me how to dress right in the first place."

She apparently hadn't taken the lessons to heart. The dresses, while beautiful on the anorexic models wearing them, would look terrible on Maddie. "I don't know," I said lamely, dragging my eyes away. The dresses were making me conjure mental images of Maddie and Seth walking down the aisle together.

"Come *on*," she entreated. "I know you have an opinion."

I did. A bad one. And honestly, if I were a good servant of Hell, I would have told her they both looked great. Or I would have endorsed the worst one. What she wore was no concern of mine, and maybe if she showed up at her wedding looking sub-par, Seth would realize what he'd lost when we broke up.

And yet . . . I couldn't. Even after everything that had happened, I just couldn't let Maddie do it. She'd been a good friend, never suspecting what had happened between Seth and me before *and* during their relationship. And as much as that petty, selfish part of me wanted it, I couldn't let her go forward in a bad dress.

"Neither are good," I said at last. "The full skirt on that one will make you look short. The flowers on top of that one will make you look fat."

She was taken aback. "Really? I never . . ." She studied the pictures, face falling. "Damn. I thought I had this stuff down now."

I can only assume my next words came from the liquor. "If you want, I'll go with you to some places this week. You can try some stuff on, and I'll tell you what works."

Maddie lit up. She wasn't gorgeous in the popular, magazine sort of way, but when she smiled, she was beautiful. "Really? Oh, thank you. And you can look for your dress, too."

"My what?"

"Well . . ." Her smile turned sly. "You're going to be a bridesmaid, aren't you?"

At that moment, I reconsidered my earlier thoughts about nothing being more painful than helping plan her wedding. Being her bridesmaid pretty much blew that out of the water.

Those who believed we made our own hells on earth must have had something like this in mind.

"Oh, well, I don't know . . ."

"You have to! There's no one else I'd rather have."

"I'm not really the bridesmaid type."

"Of course, you are!" Maddie's eyes suddenly looked at something beyond me. "Oh, hey. Doug's back. I'm going to go check on him. We'll talk about this later. You'll give in." Maddie scurried off to her brother, leaving me numb and speechless. I decided then it was worth risking illness to go get another drink. This party had taken a definite U-turn.

Yet, when I turned around, it wasn't toward the bar. It was toward my patio. One of the best features of this condo was its expansive balcony, one that looked out over Puget Sound and the Seattle skyline beyond. As I stood there, though, it wasn't the view that captivated me. It was . . . something else. Something I couldn't explain. But it was warm and wonderful and spoke to all my senses. I imagined I could see colored light on my balcony and hear a type of music that defied all human words.

The party faded into the background as I slowly moved toward the patio. The door was open to air out the hot room, and my two cats, Aubrey and Godiva, lay near it to look outside. I stepped past them, drawn toward that which had no explanation or description. Warm autumn air engulfed me as I groped for what called me. It was all around me and yet out of my reach. It was summoning me, drawing me toward something right on the balcony's edge. I almost considered climbing on the ledge in my heels and looking over. I *had* to reach that force.

"Hey, Georgina."

Peter's voice jerked me out of the trance. I stared around, startled. There was no music, no color, no beckoning embrace. Only the night and the view and the patio furniture on my balcony. I turned around, meeting his eyes.

"We have a problem," he said.

"We have a lot of problems," I said, thinking of Maddie's

wedding dress and the fact that I'd nearly walked off my own balcony. I shivered. I definitely was *not* going back for that next drink. Sick was one thing. Hallucinations were another. "What's wrong?"

Peter led me inside and pointed. "Cody's in love."

I looked over at our friend Cody, another vampire and Peter's apprentice. Cody was a young immortal, optimistic and endearing. He was dressed as an alien, with green antennae sticking out of his shaggy blond hair. The perfection of his silvery spacesuit made me think Peter had played a role. Right now, Cody was staring across the room, mouth open as he gazed at someone. He looked like I had felt just moments ago.

Her name was Gabrielle, and she'd just started at the bookstore. She was tiny, almost pixie like, and wore black fishnets and a ripped black dress. Her spiky hair was also black, as was her lipstick. Easy coordination. Cody was staring at her like she was the most beautiful creature on earth.

"Huh," I said. Hugh dated all the time, but I'd never really thought of the vampires—especially Peter—having any sort of romantic interactions.

"I think he likes that she's dressed as a vampire," said Peter.

I shook my head. "Actually, that's how she always dresses."

We walked over to Cody, and it took him several moments to notice us. He seemed excited to see me. "What's her name?" he breathed.

I tried to hide my smile. Cody being smitten was one of the cutest things I'd ever seen and a welcome distraction from the other drama tonight. "Gabrielle. She works at the store."

"Is she single?"

I looked back at her as she laughed at something Maddie had said. "I don't know. Want me to find out?"

Cody blushed—inasmuch as a vampire could. "No! I mean . . . unless you think it wouldn't be too obvious? I don't want you to go to any trouble."

"No trouble for me," I said, just as Doug walked by. "Hey."

I caught hold of his sleeve. "Do me a favor, and I'll take my shift back."

Doug, whose skin was normally golden-tan, could have also passed for an alien with his green hue. "I'd rather have my stomach back, Kincaid."

"Go investigate Gabrielle's romantic status. Cody's interested."

"Georgina!" exclaimed Cody, mortified.

Sick or not, Doug couldn't resist a little intrigue. "Sure thing."

He headed off across the room and pulled Gabrielle to him, leaning down so she could hear. At one point, he glanced over toward us, and Gabrielle looked as well. Cody nearly died.

"Oh, God."

Doug returned five minutes later and shook his head. "Sorry, kid. She's single, but she doesn't think you're her type. She's into the Goth and vampire scene. You're too mainstream for her." I was sipping a glass of water and nearly choked on it.

"That," said Peter, as soon as Doug was gone, "is what we call irony."

"How is that possible?" exclaimed Cody. "I *am* a vampire. I should be exactly what she wants."

"Yeah, but you don't look like one," I said.

"I look exactly like one! What should I dress up as? Count Chocula?"

The party continued in force for another couple of hours, and finally, people began trickling out. Roman and I, playing good hosts, smiled and bade each of them farewell. By the time everyone left, I was weary and more than happy for it all to be over. I'd refused to drink after the balcony incident and now had a headache as a pleasant reminder of my indulgences. Roman looked as exhausted as me as he scanned the messy condo.

"Funny, huh? You throw a housewarming party to show the place off, and then people trash it."

"It'll clean up fast," I said, studying all the bottles and paper plates with remnants of food. Aubrey was licking frosting off a half-eaten cupcake, and I hastily took it away from her. "But not tonight. Help me take care of the perishables, and we'll do the rest tomorrow."

"There's no 'we' in 'clean,'" Roman said.

"That doesn't even make sense," I said, covering up some salsa. "And Peter's right, you know. You really should do more around here."

"I provide good company. Besides, how can you get rid of me?"

"I'll get Jerome to," I warned, referring to his demon father, who also happened to be my boss.

"Sure. Run off and tell on me." Roman stifled a yawn, demonstrating just how worried he was about his father's wrath. The annoying part was, he had a point. I couldn't get rid of him on my own, and I doubted Jerome would really help. Still, I could hardly believe it when Roman did wander off to bed and leave me alone with the cleanup. I hadn't thought he go that far.

"Asshole!" I yelled after him, getting only a slammed door in response.

Fuming, I finished the necessary tidying and dropped into bed a half-hour later. Aubrey and Godiva followed me, lying side by side at the end of the bed. They were a contrast in colors, like some piece of modern art. Aubrey was white with black specks on her head; Godiva was a riot of orange, brown, and black patches. All three of us drifted off to sleep immediately.

Sometime later, I woke to the sound of singing . . . or, well, that was the closest I could come to describing it. It was the same thing I'd felt earlier, an alluring, haunting pull that spoke to every part of me. Warm and bright and beautiful. It was everywhere and everything, and I longed to have more of it, to walk toward the light that shone with indescribable colors. It felt so, so good, like something I could melt into, if only I could reach it. I had the impression of an entrance, a door I simply had to push open and step through and—

Rough hands gripped my shoulders and jerked me around. "Wake up!"

Like before, the sensory overload vanished. I was left alone in a quiet, empty world. No more siren song. Roman was standing in front of me, hands shaking me as his face stared down at me with worry. I looked around. We were in the kitchen. I had no memory of going there.

"How . . . what happened?" I stammered.

The face that had taunted me earlier was now filled with concern, something that troubled a small part of me. Why should someone who wanted to kill me be worried about me?

"You tell me," he said, releasing his grip.

I rubbed my eyes, willing myself to recall what had happened. "I . . . I don't know. I must have sleep-walked. . . ."

His face was still drawn and anxious. "No . . . there was something here. . . ."

I shook my head. "No, it was a dream. Or a hallucination. I had it happen earlier . . . I just drank too much."

"Didn't you just hear me?" There it was again, fear for me underneath the anger. "There was *something* here, some . . . force. I felt it. It woke me up. Don't you remember anything at all?"

I stared off, trying to summon up the light and haunting melody. I couldn't. "It was . . . it was beautiful. I wanted . . . I wanted to go to it . . . to be part of it. . . ." There was a dreamy, wistful note in my voice.

Roman's expression grew dark. As a succubus, I was a lesser immortal, one who had once been human. Nephilim were technically greater immortals—those born, not made. As such, their powers and senses were greater than mine.

"Don't," he said. "You feel it again, you pull away. Don't let it draw you in. Under no circumstances should you go to it."

I looked back at him with a frown. "Why? Do you know what it is?"

"No," he said grimly. "And that's the problem."

Eugenie Markham is a shaman for hire, paid to bind and banish creatures from the Otherworld. But after her last battle, she's also become queen of the Thorn Land. It's hardly an envious life, not with her kingdom in tatters, her love life in chaos, and Eugenie eager to avoid the prophecy about her firstborn destroying mankind. And now young girls are disappearing from the Otherworld, and no one—except Eugenie—seems willing to find out why.

Eugenie has spilled plenty of fey blood in her time, but this enemy is shrewd, subtle, and nursing a very personal grudge. And the men in her life aren't making things any easier. Her boyfriend Kiyo is preoccupied with his pregnant ex, and sexy fey king Dorian always poses a dangerous distraction. With or without their help, Eugenie must venture deep into the Otherworld and trust in an unpredictable power she can barely control. Reluctant queen or not, Eugenie has sworn to do her duty, even if it means facing the darkest—and deadliest—side of her nature. . . .

Please turn the page for an exciting sneak peek of Richelle Mead's newest Eugenie Markham novel THORN QUEEN coming in mass-market in August 2009!

Chapter 1

Sad fact: Lots of kids know how to use knives and guns. I'd been one of them, but instead of pursuing a life of crime, I'd trained to be a shamanic mercenary. This meant that while my friends were at dances and football games, I'd been out banishing spirits and wrestling down monsters. On the upside, I grew up never fearing muggers or any other assailants. On the downside, an adolescence like that really screws with your social development.

It also meant I'd never really been like other kids. I'd had some friends, but compared to theirs, my world had been terribly stark and terribly deadly. Their dramas and concerns had seemed so petty next to mine, and I could never fully relate. As an adult now, I still couldn't really connect to kids because I had no shared experiences to draw on.

Which made my job today that much more difficult.

"Go ahead, Polly," crooned the girl's mother, smiling with over-plump lips. Too much collagen, I suspected. "Tell her about the ghost."

Polly Hall was thirteen but wore enough makeup to rival a forty-year-old whore. She sat slouched against the back of a couch in her family's perfectly decorated house, chewing gum loudly, looking everywhere but at us. The more I studied her, the more I decided she probably did have problems. I suspected they had less to do with supernatural influences and more with having a mother who had named her Polly and let her wear thongs. It was an unfortunate side effect of Polly's low-cut jeans that I could see the aforementioned thong.

After a minute of silence, Mrs. Hall sighed loudly. "Polly, dear, we've been over this. If you aren't going to help us, we can't help you."

Smiling, I knelt down in front of the couch so I could look the girl in the eyes. "It's all right," I told her, hoping I sounded sincere and not like an after-school special. "I'll believe whatever you tell me. We'll get it taken care of."

Polly sighed just as loudly as her mother had a moment ago and still refused to look at me. She reminded me of my unstable teenage half sister who was currently MIA and wanted to conquer the world. "Mom," she said, "can I go to my room now?"

"Not until you've talked to this nice lady." Glancing back at me, Mrs. Hall explained, "We hear strange noises all night: bangs, cracks, bumps. Things fall over for no reason. I've even . . ." She hesitated. "I've even seen things fly around the room. But it's always when Polly's around. Whatever this ghost is, it seems to like her . . . or be obsessed with her."

I turned my attention back to Polly, again taking in the sullen mood and thinly veiled frustration. "You got a lot on your mind, Polly?" I asked gently. "Problems at school or something? Problems around here?"

Her blue eyes flicked to me ever so briefly.

"What about any electrical issues?" This I directed to her mother. "Things shorting out? Stereos or appliances not working right?"

Mrs. Hall blinked. "How'd you know that?"

I stood up and stretched the kinks out of my body. I'd fought a wraith last night, and he hadn't been gentle.

"You don't have a ghost. You have a poltergeist."

Both of them stared at me.

"Isn't that a ghost?" asked Mrs. Hall.

"Not really. It's a manifestation of telekinetic powers, often brought on by rage and other strong emotions during teenage years." I'd evaded after-school-special mode, only to slip into infomercial mode.

"I . . . wait. Are you saying Polly's causing this?"

"Not consciously, but yeah. In cases like this, the subject—Polly—lashes out without realizing it, venting her emotions in physical ways. She probably won't stay telekinetic; it'll fade as she gets older and settles down a bit."

Her mother still looked skeptical. "It sure seems like a ghost."

I shrugged. "Trust me. I've seen this lots of times."

"So . . . isn't there anything you can do? Anything we can do?"

"Therapy," I suggested. "Maybe get a psychic to come out."

I gave Mrs. Hall the contact information for a psychic I trusted. Waiving my banishing fee, I simply charged her for the house call. Once I'd double-checked the cash she gave me, I stashed it away and made moves toward the living room door.

"Sorry I couldn't be of more help."

"No, I mean, I guess this helps. It's just so strange." She eyed her daughter with perplexity. "Are you sure it's not a ghost?"

"Positive. These are classic symp—"

An invisible force slammed into me, pushing me into the wall. I yelped, threw out a hand to keep my balance, and shot daggers at that little bitch Polly. Eyes wide, she looked just as astonished as I felt.

"Polly!" exclaimed Mrs. Hall. "You are grounded, young lady. No phone, no IM, no . . ." Her mouth dropped open as she stared at something across the room. "What's that?"

I followed her gaze to the large, pale blue shape materializing before us.

"Um, well," I said, "that's a ghost."

It swooped toward me, mouth open in a terrible screech. I yelled for the others to get down and jerked a silver-bladed athame out of my belt. A knife might seem useless against spirits, but they needed to take on a substantial form to inflict any real damage. Once solid, they were susceptible to silver.

This spirit bore a female shape—a very young female shape, actually. Long, pale hair trailed in her wake like a cloak, and her eyes were large and empty. Whether it was a lack of experience or simply some inherent trait of hers, her attack proved floundering and uncoordinated. Even as she screamed at the first bites of the athame, I had my crystal-studded wand out in my other hand.

Now that I'd regained my bearings, I could do a banishing like this in my sleep. Speaking the usual words, I drew from my internal strength and sent my own spirit beyond the boundaries of this world. Touching the gates of the Underworld, I ensnared the female spirit and sent her over. Monsters and gentry I tended to send back to the Otherworld, the limbo they lived in. A ghost like this needed to move on to the land of death. She disappeared.

Mrs. Hall and Polly stared at me. Suddenly, in her first show of emotion, the girl leaped up and glared at me.

"You just killed my best friend!"

I opened my mouth to respond and decided nothing I had to say would be adequate.

"Good heavens, what are you talking about?" exclaimed her mother.

Polly's face twisted with anger, her eyes bright with tears. "Trixie. She was my best friend. We told each other everything."

"Trixie?" I said.

"I can't believe you did that. She was so cool." Her voice turned a little wistful. "I just wish we could have gone shopping together, but she couldn't leave the house. So I just had to bring her *Vogue* and *Glamour*."

I turned to Mrs. Hall. "My original advice still stands. Therapy. Lots of it."

About an hour later, I arrived back home and was immediately assaulted by two medium-sized dogs when I cleared the door. They were mutts, one solid black and one solid white.

Their names were Yin and Yang, but I could never remember who was who.

"Back off," I warned as they sniffed me, tails wagging frantically. The white one tried to lick my hand. Pushing past them, I entered my kitchen and nearly tripped over a tabby cat sprawled on the floor in a patch of sun. Grumbling, I tossed my bag onto the kitchen table. "Tim? Are you here?"

My housemate, Tim Warkoski, stuck his head in. He wore a T-shirt with silhouettes of Native Americans that said HOME-LAND SECURITY: FIGHTING TERRORISM SINCE 1492. I appreciated the cleverness, but it lost something since Tim wasn't actually an American Indian. He merely played one on TV, or rather, he played one in local bars and tourist circles. It had gotten him into trouble with a lot of the local tribes.

With a garbage bag in one hand and a cat scoop in the other, he gave me a dark look. "Do you know how many fucking boxes of litter I've had to change today?"

I poured a glass of milk and sat down at the table. "Kiyo says we need one box for every cat and then an extra one."

"Yeah, I can count, Eugenie. That's six boxes. Six boxes in a house with fifteen hundred square feet. You think your dead-beat boyfriend's ever going to show back up and help out with this?"

I shifted uncomfortably. It was a good question. After three months of dating between Tucson and Phoenix, my boyfriend Kiyo had decided to take a job here to save the hour-and-a-half commute. We'd had a long discussion and decided we were ready to have him simply move in with me. Unfortu-nately, with Kiyo came his menagerie: five cats and two dogs. It was one of the woes of dating a veterinarian. He couldn't help but adopt every animal he found. I couldn't remember the cats' names any better than the dogs'. Four of them were named after the Horsemen of the Apocalypse, and all I could really recall was that Famine ironically weighed about thirty pounds.

Another problem was that Kiyo was a fox—both literally and figuratively. His mother was a kitsune, a sort of Japanese fox spirit. He'd inherited all of her traits, including amazing strength and speed and the ability to transform into an acutal fox. As a result, he frequently got "the call of the wild," making him yearn to run around in his animal form. Since he had downtime between jobs now, he'd left me to take a sort of wild vacation. I accepted this, but after a week of not seeing him, I was starting to get restless.

"He'll be back soon," I said vaguely, not meeting Tim's eyes.

He wasn't fooled. "Your choice in men is questionable. You know that, right?"

I abandoned him for my room, seeking the comfort of a jigsaw puzzle depicting a photograph of Zurich. It sat on my desk, as did one of the cats. I think he was Mr. Whiskers, the non-Apocalyptic one. I shooed him off the puzzle. Doing so took about half the puzzle pieces with him.

"Fucking cat," I muttered.

Love, I decided, was a hard thing. Well aware of my grumpy mood, I knew part of my anxiety over Kiyo stemmed from the fact that he was also passing part of his sabbatical in the Otherworld, spending time with his ex-girlfriend who just happened to be a devastatingly beautiful fairy queen. I sighed. Tim might have been right about my questionable taste in men.

Night wore on. I finished the puzzle while blasting Def Leppard, making me feel better. I was just shutting off the music when I heard Tim yell, "Yo, Eug. Kujo's here."

Breathless, I ran to my bedroom door and flung it open. A red fox the size of a wolf trotted down the hall toward me. Relief burned through me, and I felt my heart soar as I let him in and watched him pace around in restless circles.

"About time," I said.

He had a sleek orange-red coat and a fluffy tail tipped in white. His eyes were golden and sometimes bore a very human glint. I saw nothing like that tonight. A purely animal wariness peered out at me, and I realized it'd be a while before he changed back. He had the ability to transform to a wide range of foxes, everything from a small, normal-sized red fox to the powerful shape before me. When he spent a lot of time in this bigger form, turning human took more effort and time.

Still, hoping it would happen soon, I dumped another puzzle on my desk and worked it as I waited. Two hours later, nothing had changed. He curled up in a corner, wrapping his body in a tight ball. His eyes continued to watch me. Exhausted, I gave up on him and put on a red nightgown. Turning off the lights, I finally slipped into my bed, falling asleep instantly for a change.

As I slept, I dreamed about the Otherworld, particularly a piece of it that bore a striking resemblance to Tucson and the Sonora Desert surrounding us. Only, the Otherworldly version was better. An almost heavenly Tucson, warmed by bright sunshine and ablaze with flowering cacti. This was a common dream for me, one that often left me yearning for that land in the morning. I always tried my best to ignore the impulse.

A couple hours later, I woke up. A warm, muscled body had slid into bed with me, pressing against my back. Strong arms wrapped around my waist, and Kiyo's scent, dark and musky, washed over me. A liquid feeling burned inside of me at his touch. Roughly, he turned me toward him. His lips consumed me in a crushing kiss, blazing with intensity and need.

"Eugenie," he growled, once he'd paused long enough to remove his lips—just barely—from mine. "I've missed you. Oh God, I've missed you. I've needed you."

He kissed me again, conveying that need as his hands ravaged my body. My own hands slid along the smooth perfection of his bare skin, awakening my desire. There was no gentleness between us tonight, only a feral passion as he moved on top of me, his body pushing into mine with a need fueled as much by animal instinct as love. He had not, I realized, completely regained his human senses, no matter his shape.

When I woke up in the morning, my bed was empty. Across

the room, Kiyo pulled on jeans, meeting my eyes as though he had some sixth sense. I rolled over on my side, the sheets gliding against my naked skin. Watching him with a lazy, satisfied languor, I admired his body and the tanned and black-haired features gifted to him by Japanese and Hispanic heritage. It stood in stark contrast to the light skin and reddish hair my European ancestors had given me.

"Are you leaving?" I asked. My heart, having leaped at his presence last night, suddenly sank.

"I have to go back," he said, straightening out a dark green T-shirt. He ran an absentminded hand through his chin-length hair. "You know I do."

"Yeah," I said, my voice sharper than I'd intended. "Of course you do."

His eyes narrowed. "Please don't start that," he said quietly. "I have to do this."

"Sorry. Somehow I just can't get all that excited about another woman having your baby."

There it was. The issue that always hung over us.

He sat down beside me on the bed, dark eyes serious and level. "Well, I'm excited. I'd like to think you could support me in that and be happy for me."

Troubled, I looked away. "I am happy for you. I want you to be happy . . . it's just, you know, it's hard."

"I know." He leaned over me, sliding his hand up the back of my neck, twining his fingers in my hair.

"You've spent more time with her in the last week than with me."

"It's a necessity. It's almost time."

"I know," I repeated. I knew my jealousy was unwarranted. Petty, even. I wanted to share his happiness at having a child, but something in me prevented it.

"Eugenie, I love you. It's that simple. That's all there is to it."

"You love her, too."

"Yes, but not in the way I love you."

He kissed me with a gentleness very different from the

roughness of last night. I melted against him. The kiss grew stronger, filling with ardor. With great reluctance, he finally pulled away. I could see the longing in his eyes. He wanted to have sex again. That was something, I guessed.

His responsible inclinations winning out, he straightened and stood up. I stayed where I was.

"Will I see you there?" he asked, his voice even and neutral.

I sighed. "Yeah. I'll be there."

He smiled. "Thank you. That means a lot to me."

I nodded.

He went to the door and looked back at me. "I love you." The heat in his voice told me he truly meant it. I smiled back.

"I love you, too."

He left, and I pulled the sheets more tightly against me and made no motions to get up. I couldn't stay in bed all day, unfortunately. Other things—like my promise to Kiyo—demanded my attention today. There was a trip to the Otherworld ahead of me, one that would take me to a kingdom I'd reluctantly inherited. But that wasn't the problem. That was easy compared to what else lay in store for me.

I had to go to a fey baby shower.

Love, I decided, was a hard thing.